City of Vengeance

D. V. Bishop is an award-winning screenwriter and TV dramatist. His love for the city of Florence and the Renaissance period meant there could be only one setting for his crime fiction debut. *City of Vengeance* won the Pitch Perfect competition at Bloody Scotland 2018, and he was awarded a Robert Louis Stevenson Fellowship by the Scottish Book Trust while writing the novel. When not busy being programme leader for creative writing at Edinburgh Napier University, he plans his next research trip to Florence. You can find out more at dvbishop.com and on Twitter @davidbishop.

City of Vengeance

D. V. BISHOP

PAN BOOKS

First published 2021 by Macmillan

This paperback edition first published 2022 by Pan Books
an imprint of Pan Macmillan
The Smithson, 6 Briset Street, London EC1M 5NR
EU representative: Macmillan Publishers Ireland Ltd, 1st Floor,
The Liffey Trust Centre, 117–126 Sheriff Street Upper,
Dublin 1, D01 YC43
Associated companies throughout the world
www.panmacmillan.com

ISBN 978-1-5290-3879-8

3 5 7 9 8 6 4 2

A CIP catalogue record for this book is available from the British Library.

Map artwork by Neil Gower

Typeset in Adobe Caslon Pro by Palimpsest Book Production Limited, Falkirk, Stirlingshire
Printed and bound by CPI Group (UK) Ltd, Croydon, CR0 4YY

For Clement John Bishop,
13.12.1933–16.12.2018

Upon this a question arises:
whether it be better to be loved than feared,
or feared than loved? One should wish to be both but,
because it is difficult to unite them in one person,
it is much safer to be feared than loved.

Niccolò Machiavelli,
translated by W. K. Marriott (1908)

Author's Note

During this period, the Florentine calendar year started on March 25th. December 31st, January 1st and the days immediately after were all considered to be part of 1536.

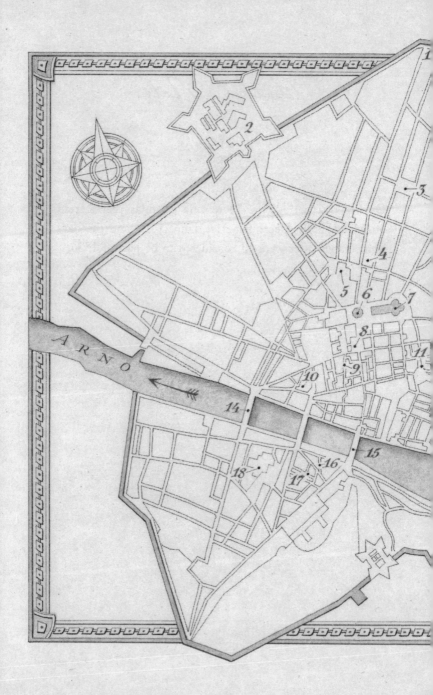

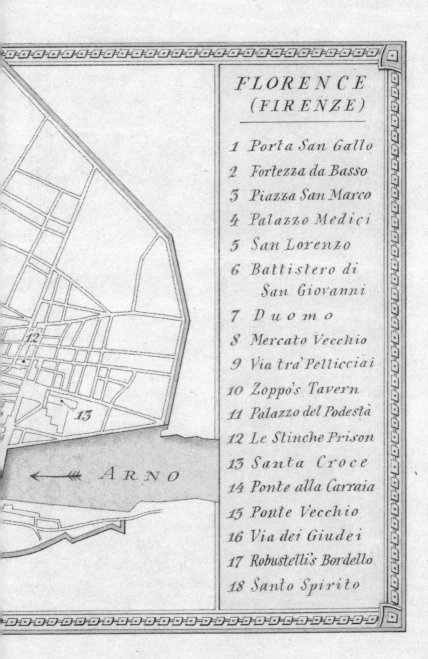

FLORENCE
(FIRENZE)

1 Porta San Gallo
2 Fortezza da Basso
3 Piazza San Marco
4 Palazzo Medici
5 San Lorenzo
6 Battistero di
   San Giovanni
7 Duomo
8 Mercato Vecchio
9 Via tra' Pellicciai
10 Zoppo's Tavern
11 Palazzo del Podestà
12 Le Stinche Prison
13 Santa Croce
14 Ponte alla Carraia
15 Ponte Vecchio
16 Via dei Giudei
17 Robustelli's Bordello
18 Santo Spirito

ARNO

To Le Casette & Venice

Bologna

Venice
Bologna

Florence

Rome

Scarperia

Castello del
Trebbio

Florence

TUSCANY &
NORTHERN ITALY

Chapter One

Cesare Aldo took no pleasure from killing, but sometimes it was necessary.

There was no honour in ending another man's life, no wisdom found in the moment when that last breath left his body. Most killings were bruising and brutal, the violence of steel and blood. Then the stench as a corpse lost control, voiding itself of dignity. Poets never mentioned that when they wrote about the nobility of the battlefield.

There was something else poets never wrote of: a tightening in the *palle* when death felt close. The blood quickened, yes, and so did the breathing, becoming fast and shallow as instinct demanded a choice: stand and fight, or flee the threat. In that moment every part of the body clenched – especially the *palle*.

Aldo felt his body tensing as the road ahead narrowed between two steep stone slopes. The birdsong that had accompanied them from Scarperia was gone, an unnerving quiet in its place. This early in the day, the road south from Bologna was more shadow than sunlight, giving potential attackers plenty of shelter. With Florence still twenty miles off, and not a *castello* or farmhouse in sight, this was the perfect place for an ambush.

Aldo twisted in the saddle to glance back at the man he was

guarding. Samuele Levi was past his prime, thick of waist and weak of chin. Doubtful he'd ever held a blade, except to open letters. If an attack came, Aldo would have to fight for both of them. He slid a hand to the stiletto tucked in his left boot. Better to be—

Something hissed through the air, and Aldo's horse flinched as if stung. A bolt was buried in the beast's neck, a mortal wound. He gripped tighter as the horse's front legs kicked at the sky. As he tumbled from the horse, another bolt cut the air where Aldo had been. His left knee hit the ground first, pain lancing through him from the sudden impact.

Levi's horse panicked, unseating its rider. The moneylender tumbled towards the stones and scrub that lined the side of the road, still clutching the two leather satchels he always carried. Levi's cry cut off abruptly as he hit the ground head first. Knocked senseless, if he was lucky. Levi's hired horse raced forwards, hooves thundering past Aldo. It sprinted away and his mount followed, hastening death with every stride.

Aldo rolled over, feigning moans of pain as loud as possible to mask slipping the stiletto from his boot. Whoever had fired those bolts would be closing in for the kill. Boots approached from the south, more than one set – two, maybe three. The last did not come close; probably the one with the crossbow, a weapon more effective at distance. Aldo moaned again, sounding as weak and vulnerable as possible. 'Please . . . please, somebody help us.' He gave a pathetic, feeble cough as a bandit loomed over him.

'Too easy.' Not Florentine, judging by the voice.

'Please,' Aldo whimpered in an effeminate tone. 'My friend, I fear he's hurt.'

'Shut up.' The bandit spat rancid phlegm at Aldo's face. It took every ounce of willpower not to strike back. Shoving a knee into

Aldo's chest, the bandit pinned him to the ground. Rough hands scoured Aldo's prone body. He offered no resistance, keeping the stiletto hidden up one sleeve, a hand closed round the hilt. 'Nothing,' the bandit announced.

'Find the other one,' a stern voice called from further away – probably the man with the crossbow. He sounded authoritative, used to giving orders.

'Over here,' a third voice called from where Levi had fallen. Aldo watched a heavyset thug with a musket examining the limp body. 'He's dead.'

'Make sure he is,' the ringleader said. 'We need to be certain.'

Aldo's attacker turned to look – and Aldo plunged his stiletto into the man's boot, stabbing through leather and flesh. The bandit screamed in pain, doubling over. Aldo twisted his blade to widen the wound before pulling it free. A swift thrust drove the stiletto up behind his attacker's chin, piercing the tongue. The bandit collapsed, fingers clawing at the blade.

The ringleader shouted a warning to the man standing over Levi. The bandit whirled round, firing in haste. A musket ball fizzed past Aldo's head, missing by a finger's width. He rolled closer to the fallen bandit, using him as a shield. While the bandit with the musket reloaded, Aldo found a blade still in its sheath on his crumpled assailant. 'A wise man draws his weapon before confronting an enemy.' The fallen bandit was too busy bleeding to reply.

Aldo pulled the dagger free, balancing it in one hand to test the weight. The bandit with the musket was still reloading, but any attempt to flee meant risking the crossbow. There was only one way to improve the odds. Aldo rose for a moment, pulling back the dagger. *Palle*, the musket-bearer was shouldering his weapon. A fresh bolt pierced Aldo's sleeve, brushing skin. He hurled the dagger, the blade flying end over end as it cut the air. A misfire born of haste spat hot gunpowder across the musket-bearer's fingers as the dagger buried itself in his throat. He stumbled over Levi and fell, one blackened hand twitching.

Aldo dropped back close beside the bandit he'd stabbed, counting himself lucky.

The ringleader cursed his men from the shadows. Cover for sliding another bolt into that crossbow, no doubt. Would he retreat, or close in to finish the job? Most bandits melted away when facing determined opposition. But the sound of approaching boots proved this was no ordinary robbery. The ringleader wanted his prize.

'You fight well. Most guards would've run for their lives.'

'I'm no guard.' Aldo searched for another weapon. Any weapon.

'A *condottiere*, then? Didn't know Florence still had any.' The ringleader was circling round, using the conversation to distract from his quest for a clearer shot.

'A *condottiere* leads men at arms. As you can see, I'm on my own.' Aldo stared at his stiletto, its blade still wedged through the fallen bandit's lower jaw and tongue. 'I'm an officer of the Otto di Guardia e Balia.'

'Ahh, a law enforcer – a professional. That explains a lot.'

Aldo rolled the bandit on his side, wrapping an arm round the man's shoulders, other hand grasping the hilt of the stiletto. 'When I get up,' Aldo hissed, 'you do too. Understand?' The bandit shook his sweat-soaked face, the stink of shit thick in the air. This one didn't wait for death to empty his bowels. Aldo twisted the stiletto. 'Understand?' This time, a nod.

The ringleader edged closer. 'I thought your jurisdiction ended at the city walls?'

Aldo rose, pulling the bandit up in front of him. 'You thought wrong.'

The ringleader stopped, crossbow ready to fire. He was shorter than Aldo expected, with a grizzled face sun-browned even in December, making the pale pink scar on one cheek all the more vivid. Beneath greying hair flint-blue eyes narrowed. 'So I can see.'

'Back off,' Aldo warned, 'or I kill both your men today.'

'Let me save you the trouble.' The crossbow fired straight and true, its bolt puncturing the wounded bandit in Aldo's arms. 'Don't come this way again,' the ringleader warned as he backed away into the shadows. 'Next time you might not be so fortunate.'

Aldo waited till the ringleader was long gone before dropping the punctured bandit. He limped across to where Levi had fallen, cursing the moneylender as each step brought a fresh stab of pain from the injured knee. The task had been simple: escort Levi from Bologna back to Florence, safe and unharmed. So much for simplicity. Now he would have to take back a body instead, and get it to the city without any horses to help.

But as Aldo approached, Levi opened one eye to peer around. 'Is it safe?' His face was streaked with blood from a deep cut to the forehead, but he looked otherwise unhurt.

'For now,' Aldo replied, shaking his head. 'You make a good corpse.'

Levi sat up, wincing. 'My kind know how to stay alive, even if it means playing dead.' He rose to one knee but sank back down again.

'Don't try moving yet.'

Levi nodded, touching two fingertips to his bloodied face.

Aldo checked the bandit who had fired the musket – he was dead. But the man who had first attacked Aldo was still alive, faint gasps audible in the narrow hillside pass. The stiletto wedged behind his jawline was trembling, as was the bolt embedded in his chest. Aldo limped back towards the dying bandit. 'Why did you attack us?'

The bandit coughed, unable to reply with a blade still pinning his tongue. Aldo pulled the stiletto free, and blood poured from the wound. 'Your *capo* murdered you. Tell me his name so I can make him pay.' The bandit gurgled, crimson bubbling from his lips. Aldo leaned over the bandit's mouth and got blood spat in his face, along with two final words.

'Get fucked.'

For most Florentines, attending church on Sunday was a chance to pray and give worship to God. For courtesans, church was a chance to be noticed. Mass offered a rare opportunity for unmarried women to meet and mingle with men of means. Whether those men were single made little difference to the courtesans, though married men were less likely to be possessive, or occupy too much of an independent woman's time. So common was the practice that some churches used a curtain of coarse cloth to divide the sexes, keeping those women without families on the left-hand side – the *sinister* side, in Latin. But a mere curtain was no match for the courtesans, women of cunning and guile.

The imposing church of Santa Croce so dominated its surroundings that the eastern quarter of Florence was named after it. Outside the church sprawled a huge, open piazza – one of the largest in the city. The piazza remained cold all morning in winter due to the long shadow cast by Santa Croce. But inside the vast church courtesans were doing their best to raise the temperatures of any man watching. They spent the precious minutes before mass competing for the pew that offered the best chance to see and be seen. Overt displays of flesh were not possible, but a sly smile and a gown that accentuated a woman's natural assets were enough to turn the head of many a wealthy merchant. If this also turned his wife's face to vinegar, well, that was simply proof of success. A sour wife usually meant her husband was liable – even eager – to reward those who offered more willing, more imaginative company.

Among the courtesans at Santa Croce, two were acknowledged as the queens of the curtain. Venus Cavalcante was a slender woman with a hawkish face whose artistry inside the bedchamber was as celebrated as the sharpness of her tongue outside it. Time's cruel passage meant she no longer drew the gaze of younger men, but Venus argued for the virtues of her mature clients. They were unlikely to rise to the occasion more than once, and their conversation afterwards was often as valuable as any payment they might leave behind.

Her chief rival was Bella Testa, a younger and more voluptuous woman with greater enthusiasm than skill, if the rumours were true. The twinkle in her eyes and the generous swell of her bosom made Bella the courtesan of choice for quite a few clients, especially the sons of wealthy families. Young Florentine men of means were happy to spend their seed in anyone willing to accept it. Make the recipient a beautiful woman – readily available, at a suitable price – and the lure was often overwhelming.

Each Sunday Venus and Bella did battle for the most prized seat in the vast church, one that provided the best position from which to be seen by men on the other side of the curtain. To achieve that, the winner had to be last into the desired pew, forcing those already seated to move along. From a distance, the courtesans' polite gestures and smiling faces were the image of courteous civility. Step closer and their hissed insults told another story.

'My dearest Venus, I wouldn't dream of making you stand a

moment longer. A woman of your many, many years shouldn't be expected to remain on her feet.'

'You're too kind, my darling Bella, but I must insist you sit first. Someone in your condition shouldn't put such a strain on herself.'

'My condition?'

'You are with child, are you not? How else to explain the spreading of your waist?'

A sharp intake of breath from those nearby brought a smile to the face of Venus. Her barb had struck a nerve with the other courtesans. But when she turned to savour their expressions, Venus found her rivals staring elsewhere.

A newcomer was approaching them, narrow of hip and dressed in a sumptuous gown. A coy face hid behind a veil, but what could be seen was exquisite – and devilishly young. The new arrival paused by Bella and Venus. 'I believe mass is beginning. Shall we sit?'

The warring women found themselves ushered into the front pew, accepting less favourable seats while the fresh face stole their prized position. Venus glanced at the newcomer during mass. This usurper was unfamiliar. The voice had been sweet and definitely Florentine, yet the features remained unrecognizable. Most galling of all, the new arrival was attracting the gaze of every likely prospect in church. Venus had been hoping to lure one man in particular, Biagio Seta, the middle-aged middle son of a family of prominent silk merchants. His childless elder brother was ill, unlikely to see another summer, putting Biagio in line for the business and all its wealth. But he had not a glance for Venus this Sunday, only for the newcomer beside her.

When mass was concluded, most families hastened home to eat together. But a few men remained in the cloister beside the church or the piazza in front of it, claiming an urgent need to discuss business. The courtesans also lingered, gossiping with their maids about who was wearing what. Once the families were gone, men with a need for company could send a message to the maid of their preferred courtesan.

Most Sundays, Venus and Bella had their pick of the offers. But today the messages were going to another courtesan. The upstart did not even have a maid, instead accepting the invitations personally. Venus watched Biagio make his approach, a coy look passing between him and the one he desired. Biagio blushed – he actually blushed! – when the narrow-hipped vixen nodded at him. The couple departed the piazza in different directions, but Venus had little doubt they would be together soon, in all the most intimate ways.

'Must be losing our touch,' Bella observed.

Venus sniffed her disdain. 'Men. They always want first taste. But the novelty soon wears off. Did you hear a name for our new friend?'

'Dolce Gallo, according to my maid.'

Venus couldn't help laughing. 'I wonder what her real name is?'

With no horses to ride, Aldo and Levi had to continue their journey south towards Florence on foot. But hours of marching did no good for Aldo's bruised, swollen left knee. It had already been unreliable before the bandit attack, weakened by an old injury from years spent as a soldier for hire, riding alongside one of the great *condottieri*. A bad fall had ruptured the joint, forcing Aldo to abandon life as a mercenary and sending him back to Florence. Falling from his horse as the bandits attacked hadn't been as bad, but the pain was all too familiar.

Levi seemed to be suffering even more, his body and spirit ill prepared for marching of any kind, so progress was slow and painful. When they stopped for the third time, Aldo pressed Levi for answers. 'You never told me why you wanted a guard for this journey.'

The moneylender dabbed a cloth to the wound on his forehead 'Isn't what happened proof your protection was necessary?'

'Yes, but it doesn't answer my question. What made you think you were in danger?'

Levi waved a dismissive hand. 'It was a sensible precaution. Bandits are common on this road – too common, from what I've heard.'

'And I've heard you make this trip three times a year, but never before have you asked the Otto for a guard. In summer, I'd understand it. But robbing people in winter is treacherous, with few rewards.' No answer. Levi might be little use against a blade, but he was a master at avoiding sharp questions. 'I'd go so far as to say today's attack was no happenstance. Those bandits were waiting for us. For you.'

That got a reaction, though Levi masked it in moments. 'They attacked you first.'

'If a target can protect himself, he doesn't need a guard. I was obviously guarding you, so it made sense to deal with me first. To eliminate the more significant threat.'

Levi shrugged. 'Speculation proves nothing.'

'Having taken me down, our attackers didn't finish me when they had the chance. "Find the other one," the ringleader said. "We need to be certain." They wanted to be sure who you were before killing us both.'

Levi avoided Aldo's gaze. 'You've a strong memory.'

'Being that close to death sharpens the mind. The ringleader was calm, he didn't panic when the first attack faltered. And he didn't hesitate to kill his own man on hearing I'm with the Otto. Few robbers are that ruthless.'

'You want to meet ruthless men, try being a moneylender.'

'Had the ringleader employed better men,' Aldo snapped, 'we'd both be dead by now. Think on that.' He peered at the sky. 'We won't reach Florence before dusk at this pace, and the horses bolted with all our provisions. We need to find shelter, and soon.'

Levi got to his feet with difficulty. 'Where do you suggest?'

'I rode with a *condottiere* who kept a home near Trebbio. We might find a welcome there. It's a few miles south. Can you get that far before sunset?'

Chapter Two

*D*usk was close when Aldo and Levi reached a modest *castello* on the outskirts of Trebbio. Their approach set dogs barking. 'Let me do the talking,' Aldo said, thumping a fist against the sturdy wooden door. The blows returned as hollow echoes from within.

'Perhaps nobody lives here any more,' Levi suggested.

Aldo pointed at a weak light spilling from a window above them. 'That's a candle.'

Footsteps grew audible from inside, coming closer.

'Who's there?' a frail voice asked.

'Cesare Aldo of the Otto di Guardia e Balia. I'm on official business for the city. My travelling companion and I require lodgings for the night.' Invoking the Otto was no guarantee of a welcome, especially this far outside the city. But the court still commanded some respect – and fear. Coin also helped smooth the way. 'You will, of course, be paid.'

Sure enough, the heavy door opened a crack. Clutching a lantern, a gimlet-eyed old man glared at the visitors. His yellow tunic was faded from years of wear and washing, while his dull green hose had been darned too many times. 'What did you say your name was?'

Aldo repeated himself, struggling to hide his frustration. The ageing retainer nodded before shutting the door. When it eventually reopened, a woman in a dark, plain dress stood behind it.

Her hair was covered by a fine shawl of light wool and her face showed no fear. In fact, she looked delighted. 'Aldo? Is that you?'

Her features were hard to discern in the flickering light of her lantern. She had seen plenty of summers, but was still a handsome woman, even in the dour mourning clothes of a widow. There was something familiar about those eyes, too. Of course!

Aldo bowed from the waist. 'Signora Salviati, I— It is many years since I last came to Trebbio. I hoped your husband's kin might still live here, I did not realize— Forgive me.'

She smiled. 'There's nothing to forgive. And who is your travelling companion?'

Aldo stood aside to let the lantern reveal the moneylender. 'This is Samuele Levi, of Florence. I'm guarding his journey south from Bologna.' Aldo gestured at the widow. 'This is Signora Maria Salviati. Her husband was the *condottiere* Giovanni de' Medici.' Levi didn't respond. 'Many called him Giovanni dalle Bande Nere, because his men wore black armour.'

Levi's eyebrows rose. 'I've heard of him. It is said he fought for those who could not defend themselves, and often refused to accept payment.' Levi gave a respectful nod.

'His deeds made him a hero to many,' Maria said, a frown creeping across her face, 'yet such heroism pays few bills. My husband's family does not favour us with its wealth so our comforts are few, but you may break your journey here for the night, if you wish.'

'We'll be grateful for any shelter you can offer.' Aldo dug an elbow into Levi's ribs.

'Indeed,' Levi agreed, reaching into his satchels for coin. 'Most grateful.'

Maria waved aside payment. 'You have no horses?' she asked, looking past them as they came inside. A strong scent of dried lavender filled the entrance hall, but couldn't mask an underlying odour of mildew and neglect. Aldo gave a brief account of the bandit attack.

'I'm not surprised,' Maria sighed. 'The road from Bologna is not so safe as it was.'

'Especially for those with determined enemies,' Aldo agreed, glaring at Levi. But the moneylender ignored the comment, focusing all his attention on their host.

'I urgently wish to be back in Florence,' he said. 'How long is the journey from here?'

Maria studied both men. 'At least another day on foot, especially if you are injured.'

'It is nothing,' Levi said, dabbing a hand to his head wound. 'I hardly notice it.'

Aldo suppressed a snort of derision.

'You must take two horses in the morning,' Maria replied. 'My son Cosimo was out hunting all day and is already asleep, but he will saddle them for you at dawn.'

'Most kind,' Aldo said.

A pretty young maid appeared beside Maria. 'Simona, prepare rooms for our guests.' The maid nodded before hurrying away. Maria smiled at both men. 'You probably haven't eaten all day. When you're ready, Simona will show you to the kitchen. Afterwards, there is something I wish to discuss with you, Aldo.'

It was the cold nights that most made Constable Carlo Strocchi miss the comforts of home. In the village where he'd grown up, a person could always find a welcome and a warm fire to banish the cold from their bones, even on the most wintery of evenings. But after his father died from a long and lingering illness, Strocchi's lack of talent and enthusiasm for working on someone else's farm had prompted him to leave the countryside. Now, after seven months in Florence, he was learning to tolerate the city. He might even like it one day, but it could never truly be home. There were certainly few comforts for those patrolling it after dark.

Strocchi stamped his boots on the trampled dirt of the street, blowing into cupped hands before rubbing his palms together. Major roads inside the city were wide and laid with stone, shallow channels running along them for waste. But away from the likes of via Largo, the narrow backstreets and connecting alleys were packed earth, which turned to mud part of the year and dust the rest. Standing still here too long in winter was asking the chill to have its frozen way. The sound of pissing nearby was not making the wait any warmer.

'Haven't you finished yet?'

'Almost!' an enthusiastic voice replied from a dark alley.

Strocchi looked up through the narrow gap between buildings at the sky. Stars, they were something else he missed from home. There a person could stand outside at night and see all the heavens above, those tiny points of light in the blue and black of evening. But in Florence buildings stood two and three rooms high, looming over you, blocking out the stars.

At last fresh-faced Benedetto emerged from the alley, wiping both hands on his hose. 'Knew I shouldn't have had another wine. Always goes straight through me.'

Strocchi stepped back from the liquid spreading across the dirt. 'So I can see.'

'Where to next?'

'Via tra' Pellicciai.' He strode away, trusting the new recruit had the sense to follow. Benedetto came hurrying after, asking a question. Another one.

'What's there?'

'It's a short street favoured by men who crave the company of other men.' Strocchi led Benedetto past the Mercato Vecchio. The stalls and shops had closed long before curfew but would be open again in the morning. 'Cerchi has a particular hatred for such men. That's why he insists on us going there.' Of course Cerchi had a hatred for many things, but the recruit would learn about the officer's angry ways soon enough.

'But only night patrols and people with ducal authority are allowed out after dark,' Benedetto said. 'That's why we have a curfew, to keep people safe during the night. Won't the street be empty?'

'If lust drives a man to break God's law,' Strocchi replied, 'then breaking the laws of Florence will be of little concern.' As he and Benedetto approached via tra' Pellicciai, Strocchi heard the sound of heavy blows and frail cries of pain. He quickened his pace.

Two heavyset men burst from a side alley and raced away, hooded cloaks hiding their faces. Strocchi sprinted after them, but the two fugitives disappeared into the night, losing themselves in the shadows cast by overhanging buildings. Realizing the pair were beyond catching, Strocchi returned to the alley from where they'd first appeared. Benedetto was staring into the darkness, one hand clamped across his mouth. Whatever he saw was draining all innocence from his cherubic features. Strocchi girded himself before looking.

A woman was sprawled in the shadows, battered and bloody. Her legs were spread apart, the hem of her *camora* up around her thighs, exposing bruised knees. The rich woollen fabric was soiled by boot marks where attackers had kicked and stamped. Her fingers splayed out at unnatural angles, bent and broken. Her face was worst of all, beaten beyond reason, blood matting her hair.

Benedetto staggered away to retch, leaving Strocchi with the victim.

He whispered a prayer before moving closer. The *camora* was a dress of quality, fine embroidery evident even in pale moonlight. The bodice flattered her slight build. It was a garment made to draw the eyes of lustful men – the dress of a courtesan. But she looked young for a courtesan, twenty summers at most.

Strocchi leaned nearer to the woman to study her bruised, swollen features, hoping he might recognize what was left of her – and she gasped in air! The shock of it rocked Strocchi back on his haunches. The victim had seemed dead, still did from any distance. But up close the faintest movement of her breathing was visible.

'Benedetto! Benedetto, get over here!'

The young constable stumbled back into the alley.

'She's alive! We need to get her to a doctor – now!' But Benedetto stayed where he was, hands flapping like a fish pulled fresh from the Arno. 'Bang on doors till you find someone to help.' Still Benedetto didn't move, his gaze on the victim. 'Go!'

Benedetto pointed at her. 'Sh-she's talking.'

He was right. The victim's lips were moving, but she made no sound. Strocchi threw his cap aside, lowering an ear to her mouth. 'What is it?'

'Al—' she breathed. Strocchi shifted his head to stare into her eyes.

'I'll find who did this,' he vowed. 'I'll make them pay.' This close, Strocchi could see just how young she was. Her eyes, there was something familiar about them—

'Aldo,' she said at last. Her head slumped sideways and she fell silent.

'Aldo?' Benedetto gasped. 'He did this?'

'Don't be a fool,' Strocchi hissed. 'Aldo's still out in the Dominion. Besides, we saw two men. Go find help. Getting this poor soul to Santa Maria Nuovo is what matters now.'

Maria Salviati did not expect to find love again, not while stuck in this crumbling *castello*, but she missed having someone in her bed. Even when her husband was alive, Giovanni had spent much of their marriage fighting for righteous causes elsewhere. He was a Medici, but from the junior branch of the family. Where his cousins revelled in political intrigue and expanding their fortunes, Giovanni had cared only for ensuring his men were well paid, well treated, and well equipped with the finest armour. That often meant spending his wife's dowry to support his battles. When he died at twenty-six, little was left behind for Maria and Cosimo.

Ten years was a long time without a husband or his coin, but she had chosen to stay a widow, devoting her time to Cosimo and preparing him for life as a Medici. She would not remarry, and certainly not to the sort of men suggested by her brothers. Maria still shuddered when remembering one of those put forward. Signor Lionelle Pio da Carpi had been at least thirty summers older than her, with a most unpleasant body and rancid breath. It had taken a letter to her uncle, the Pope, asking for his intervention to save her from marrying da Carpi. That was a favour she could only call upon once, but it had been worth using.

Once Levi went to bed, Maria dismissed Simona for the night. Aldo remained in the kitchen, warming his legs by the fire. He looked more sinew than muscle, long of limb and lean of face. Time was adding silver to his dark hair and creasing his features, especially around those ice-blue eyes. But little else about him had changed in the many years since she'd seen Aldo last. He must be closer to forty than thirty, yet he had not surrendered to indulgence. That jawline remained strong and resolute, while his shoulders were broad and his waist narrow. Aldo could still turn a mature woman's head, if he wished. Maria filled his cup with more wine, pulling a chair close.

'It gets cold here at night,' she said. 'Worse in the winter.'

Aldo nodded, his face giving nothing away.

'Giovanni favoured you of all those who rode with him.'

'He was a great leader. We would have followed him to death.'

'He believed you'd become a great *condottiere* yourself.'

'In that, he was wrong – I prefer not to lead.'

'You'd rather others showed you the way,' Maria said, resting a hand on Aldo's thigh.

'Signora Salviati—'

'We've known each other a long time, Cesare. You may call me Maria, if you wish.' Her hand slid further up the firm, muscular thigh to cup his groin – but found no response there. She gazed into his face, searching for answers. Was it her advances that failed to excite him? Or did he prefer another kind of company? He'd paid no attention to Simona earlier, and she was a comely young thing. The discomfort in his eyes confirmed the suspicion.

'Forgive me,' he said. 'An old wound means I'm unable . . .'

'Please, say nothing more of it.' Maria removed her hand, settling back in the chair. She knew his excuse was a lie, designed to preserve her dignity and shield his nature. So, no woman would turn Aldo's head. In her younger days that might have been shocking, but she had seen enough of the world to know better. Besides, such secrets could be useful.

'You had something to discuss with me, signora.'

'Yes. My son Cosimo is a young man of considerable promise. I've fought to see him schooled in letters and diplomacy. He is a true Medici, born within wedlock – unlike some others that I could name. Yet my son is denied his rightful place in Florence because he is not one of the favoured family line.' There, it was said. Years of frustration, poured out to a passing acquaintance. It was a risk, but she had the upper hand here – so to speak.

Aldo put down his wine. 'I understand your concern, but what would you have me do? I am a court functionary, nothing more.'

'You are not part of the nobility, true, but you are still an officer of the Otto. That gives your words and actions consequence – even importance, in the right circumstances.'

'My word carries no weight in Florentine society.'

'Perhaps you underestimate your influence.'

Aldo shrugged. Maria wanted to slap him, to threaten him with what she now knew. But that would achieve nothing beyond making an enemy of someone who might be useful.

'I'm waiting on a letter,' Maria continued. 'If I receive the response I hope, then my son could soon be going to Florence to prepare for his future. It would help to know he had an ally in the city, should he ever need one. Please. If my husband's memory means as much as you claim, then you must be willing to help his son.'

Aldo hesitated before nodding. 'Very well. I'll do what I can, signora.'

'Thank you.'

He rose from the chair and limped towards the door, favouring his left leg. 'One last thing,' Maria called after him. 'In the morning, Cosimo will help you with the horses. Please, talk to him about his father. Tell him . . . tell him the good stories.'

Aldo gave a wry smile. 'With Giovanni dalle Bande Nere, all the stories are good.'

Chapter Three

Monday, January 1st

*A*ldo woke early in the cold *castello*. The temptation to linger in a warm bed held little allure, even in winter – sleeping men made easy targets. Rising before dawn gave a better chance of surviving the day. He pulled yesterday's clothes back on, nose wrinkling. Both the tunic and hose stank of too long on the road, but his change of clothes had been carried away on the lost horses. He could have asked Signora Salviati for replacements, but knew borrowing further from her was not wise. Bad enough they were accepting fresh horses. She might only be a Medici by marriage, but the family expected its debts to be settled, one way or another.

After emptying his bladder, Aldo searched for the stables. The *castello* had seemed careworn at night, but dawn revealed how decayed it truly was. Broken shutters hung across openings, and everywhere plaster was crumbling. No wonder the signora wanted her son's star to rise in Florence. They would not survive much longer in a home fast becoming a ruin.

The stable housed a handful of horses. It was obvious someone cared for the animals; they were in good shape. A young man strode in, full of easy confidence, nodding to Aldo before ensuring each horse had water and fodder. Aldo watched him work, appreciating the assured movements. Cosimo Medici was certainly his father's son: he had the same piercing, intelligent eyes; that noble brow and firm jaw; and an obvious affection for animals, treating them with love and respect. Cosimo was still young, seventeen summers at most, with only a few wisps of hair on his chin and below his nose. But the taut physique showed a love of being outdoors. In that he resembled another young man Aldo had known long ago. Vincenzo lived for the countryside as much as he'd lived for pleasure. It was what had made him . . . Aldo frowned. That had been a different time, a different place. Little good ever came from digging into broken feelings, or broken promises. Let the past be the past.

'Mama says you rode with my father?' Cosimo asked while tending to the horses.

'He was my *condottiere* before you were born. I owe him much.'

'I struggle to remember what he looked like, even when I look at his portrait.' The words sounded more regretful than bitter. What did the son truly think of his father?

'He died far too soon,' Aldo said.

Cosimo fetched a saddle from a hook on the wall, nodding at another beside it. Aldo brought the second, helping to put it on a chestnut mare. 'Mama tells me stories about Papa, but I've heard them all so many times. It's hard to know what's true.'

'Ask me. I know some of the truth, what I can remember of it.'

Cosimo tightened the saddle on the mare before straightening up. 'There's a tale from not long after I was born. A nurse was holding me at an upstairs window when Papa returned from battle. He shouted at the nurse to throw me down. She—'

'She refused, but Giovanni insisted, promising he would catch you.' Aldo smiled. 'Poor girl, don't think I've ever seen someone so scared.'

Cosimo laughed. 'So it's true?'

Aldo nodded. 'Your father bellowed at her, losing patience. Finally, after praying for forgiveness, the nurse threw you down for your father to catch. And caught you were.'

'Of all the stories, I was certain that one must be a myth. One of the servants first told it to me when I was a boy, but they claimed my mother was the one who threw me down. Mama says she would never have been so foolish. She always insists it was a nurse.'

'Myths are stories told too many times. The truth is usually still inside them.'

Cosimo smiled with the unblemished love of a son. Aldo didn't mention that it was he – not Giovanni – who had caught the baby. Let the young man enjoy his myth.

Reporting to Florence's ruler was a daily duty for *segretario* Massimo Bindi. Each morning he waddled to the ducal residence, wearing his thickest woollen cloak to ward off the early chill, hands tucked inside the long wide sleeves for warmth. Bindi preferred sober black or red for his cloak, doublet and hose, colours befitting a *segretario*. Not for him the vibrant blue worn by some preening merchants, or the lurid hues favoured by younger men these days. Some of them even sported hose with legs of different colours, as if determined to see their stupidity displayed to all and sundry. Peacocks had more sense of decorum.

Bindi passed the Duomo and continued his slow progress north along via Largo, cursing as his boots slid on cobbles left icy by overnight frost. The imposing shape of Palazzo Medici appeared ahead, a hefty monolith of sharp corners and impressive size. Its three levels were all pale sandstone, but the stonework became finer and more elegant on each successive floor. The street level had coarse, rusticated stones with small windows set high enough in the wall to prevent anyone seeing inside. The middle level had smaller stones and numerous arched windows, while the upper level bore the finest stones of all beneath a jutting roof. Merchants sat on the cold benches outside the palazzo, each man hoping for an audience with the Duke, their horses tied to thick metal rings bolted to the palazzo wall. Bindi savoured their envy as he marched straight inside.

The Duke's administrative *segretario* was waiting within, as he did most mornings. Francesco Campana ushered Bindi up to the palazzo's middle level, few words passing between them. Campana was dressed in the traditional black gown of an administrator, the simplicity of his clothes giving little indication of his closeness to the Duke. Bindi knew better than to share idle comments with Campana, whose plain face and reserved manner belied his significance. He was known to have the Duke's ear when it came to appointments. Should Bindi wish to leave the Otto for another post as *segretario*, the approval of Campana would be needed to secure a more prestigious and more lucrative position.

Campana escorted Bindi to the private *officio* of Alessandro de' Medici but did not follow him inside. Most mornings Bindi's report was mundane: a brisk summary of cases due before the magistrates of the Otto di Guardia e Balia, if they were sitting that day; a tally of prisoners in the cells at Le Stinche; and an accounting of the court's current finances. Rare was the day when there were more dramatic matters to report; incidents of violence, sexual depravity or significant civic disorder. There was no need for Campana to be present.

Bindi was master of all he surveyed within Palazzo del Podestà, but he could never relax in Alessandro's company. The Duke was the most powerful man in Florence and could ask a question about anything at any moment. If the answer dissatisfied him, he could dismiss Bindi from the hard-won position of *segretario* on a whim. It was terrifying.

Alessandro ignored him at first, too busy laughing with someone else. Bindi did not permit himself to look up until addressed – that would not be proper – but sometimes risked a peek to discover who else was present. Today Alessandro was holding court from an ornate gold chair behind an imposing desk, an armoured breastplate worn over his lavish doublet of black satin. Rumour had it that the Duke owed his thick, curly hair and dark skin to his mother being an African slave. Some even dared call him Alessandro the Moor, but not to his face – not unless they wished to end their days in Le Stinche.

To the Duke's right lurked his insipid cousin, Lorenzino. The younger Medici was a brooding presence, clammy and pale. Two years ago Lorenzino had achieved notoriety after beheading four statues in Rome, leading to his expulsion from the city by the Pope. Only Lorenzino's youth – he was twenty at the time – and family connections spared him a harsher punishment. Now he clung to Alessandro, basking in the Duke's reflected glory, even after his cousin sided against Lorenzino's branch of the family in a costly legal dispute. The matter hadn't come before the Otto, but Bindi knew the relevant court officials. Most men would have broken ties after such a costly betrayal, yet Lorenzino had become even closer to the Duke.

'Ahh, there you are,' Alessandro said. 'We're looking forward to your report, Bindi.'

'Indeed, Your Grace?'

'Of course. It's a highlight of our day.' The Duke smirked, and his cousin laughed.

Bindi smiled, accepting this derision with apparent equanimity. Little *merda*.

'What delights do you have for us this Monday?' Alessandro continued. 'Perhaps a fascinating new case involving pickpockets on Ponte Vecchio?'

'An amendment to the number of recent arrests?' Lorenzino chimed in.

'Or is it an awe-inspiring account of the Otto's revenues and expenses?'

Bindi bowed his head a moment, masking the anger in his eyes. 'My apologies if these daily reports are too dry, Your Grace. I could submit them on paper, if you prefer?'

The Duke made a grand gesture with both hands. 'Bindi, we wouldn't dream of denying you the opportunity to thrill us. Please, we pray you – report.'

The *segretario* did as he was bid, outlining the status of the Otto and its current cases. Alessandro and Lorenzino whispered to one another throughout the recitation, the younger Medici sniggering and sneering in deference to his cousin. Very well. Be like that. Bindi included far more detail than he did most days. It seemed the least he could do in the circumstances for such distinguished nobility. When his report was finally at an end, both men had fallen silent, bored into submission. Never belittle a civil servant.

'Thank you for that,' Alessandro scowled. 'Most thorough.' Bindi feigned a smile, turning to leave. 'However, you omitted something. An important matter, in fact.'

'Your Grace?'

'An attempted murder, last night, within the walls of Florence. We learned about it via a doctor who came from Santa Maria Nuovo to deliver a tonic for Lorenzino. Why did you not include that in your most fulsome report?'

Bindi froze. If there had been such an incident, he should know about it, he should have been told about it. Could this claim from the Duke be a ruse of some sort? But the mocking tone in Alessandro's voice and the curl of Lorenzino's lip left little room for doubt. Bindi willed the grand marble floor to swallow him whole – without success.

'Well?' Alessandro said. 'You had plenty to report before, have you no reply now?'

'I . . .' The *segretario* opened and closed his mouth, helpless. He shook his head.

'Then we suggest you find out,' Alessandro said. 'Include it in tomorrow's report.'

Bindi bowed as low as his ample belly would allow before scuttling away. Someone would pay for making him suffer this humiliation. Someone would pay dearly for it.

When Aldo went to rouse Levi, the moneylender was awake, washed and ready to leave. 'Should I expect any more bandits between here and Florence?' he asked.

'It's possible,' Aldo conceded, 'but unlikely. The ringleader from yesterday lost both his men; he won't have had time to hire any more. And most attacks happen up on the high, narrow passes. It's why the Bologna road is less dangerous in winter.'

'Good. I need to get home to my daughter.'

Aldo led the way to the stables. 'How old is she?'

'Twenty. Rebecca has looked after me since her mother died.'

'Then she's no doubt capable of looking after herself for another few hours.'

'You don't have children, do you?' Levi grabbed Aldo by the arm, stopping him. 'I promised my wife before she died that no one would hurt our daughter. A young, unmarried Jewish woman in Florence is easy prey for those who would exploit the vulnerable.'

Aldo glared at Levi until he let go. 'I know what the city can do to the vulnerable.'

Cosimo was waiting with two horses, Signora Salviati by his side. Aldo introduced her son to the moneylender, but Levi was more interested in leaving. Had he not insisted on staying in Scarperia for *Shabbat*, they'd have been in Florence days ago. But Aldo chose not to raise that again. Changing the minds of those with faith was almost always a lost cause.

Aldo suppressed a smirk as Levi struggled to climb atop one of the borrowed horses. 'He's not a natural rider,' Cosimo observed, joining Aldo by the second horse.

'Not exactly,' Aldo agreed. He paused, sensing the young Medici had a question to ask. Cosimo moved closer, his voice hushed so his mother wouldn't hear.

'That story you told me about the nurse throwing me down as a baby for my father to catch – was it true?'

'Every word.'

Cosimo studied Aldo's face. 'I've been thinking about the way you phrased it. "The nurse threw you down for your father to catch. And caught you were."' He smiled. 'My father didn't catch me, did he? That was somebody else.'

Aldo hesitated before nodding. Giovanni's son was no fool. He had all his father's perceptiveness, and something else too – the cunning of a Medici.

'If I asked who it was that caught me,' Cosimo continued, 'would you tell?'

'I promised I would not say. Your father is gone, but my loyalty to him remains.'

'Can we leave?' Levi called out, at last safely in the saddle. Aldo mounted his own horse, wincing at the pain from his stiff and swollen left knee. Cosimo gave a small nod.

'Your loyalty to my family is appreciated.'

Aldo rode away from the *castello* at a slow trot, Levi bouncing along beside. All being well, they should reach Florence well before curfew.

In the *ospedale* at Santa Maria Nuovo, Strocchi willed himself to stay silent. Never contradict an officer of the Otto, not even a *bastardo* like Cerchi. But staying silent wasn't easy, having spent an entire night praying by a bedside for a miracle, only to watch the victim die as dawn approached. It was even harder to keep quiet while Cerchi was stalking back and forth in front of Strocchi and Benedetto, thumbs shoved into his belt either side of an ornate silver belt buckle. It featured a lily, the emblem of Florence. Cerchi had been given the buckle as a reward for helping a prominent merchant avoid prosecution, and had worn it ever since.

'You've made me look a fool!' Cerchi's narrow face was crimson with rage, spittle flecking his thin brown beard and drooping moustache. 'The *segretario* was waiting for me when I arrived at the Podestà this morning, demanding a full report and wanting to know why I'd let him go before the Duke without knowing about this!' Cerchi stopped in front of Strocchi. 'All you had to do was send –' he glared at the trembling Benedetto – 'this idiot, whatever his name is, to tell me what had happened. Then I could have forewarned Bindi.'

'Benedetto's a new recruit, he doesn't know where you live. And I couldn't come,' Strocchi added, before Cerchi could hurl another accusation, 'in case the victim recovered enough to describe the attackers.'

Cerchi couldn't deny the truth of Strocchi's words. Instead, he snorted like an angry bull stuck behind a locked gate before asking a question. 'Do you know how shit travels?' Strocchi fought to urge to reply with the first words that came into his head. 'Down, it travels down,' Cerchi snarled. 'The Duke shit all over Bindi because of this mess. The *segretario* then shit all over me. So, from now on, I'll be shitting all over you two. Understand?'

Strocchi nodded, his gaze fixed on the floor.

Cerchi shoved him aside to see the body. 'Who is she exactly?' The constables exchanged a wary glance. Cerchi pulled down the sheet, exposing the beautiful, bloodied gown still clinging to the victim. 'She's obviously some merchant's wife. Either that, or a courtesan. If she is somebody's wife, her husband will come looking for her. If she's just a courtesan, another *puttano* should recognize this dress.'

Strocchi hesitated before replying. 'In most cases you'd be right, but—'

'What do you mean?'

'—but this victim isn't female.'

'Don't be ridiculous,' Cerchi insisted. 'She's wearing a dress!' He pulled the fabric up to expose the groin, and lurched back in surprise at the proud maleness there.

'The doctor examined the victim to see if she had been . . . forced,' Benedetto said, blushing with embarrassment. 'That's when we discovered she is – was – a he.'

'Yes, I have eyes,' Cerchi snapped. He gestured at the victim's groin. 'Cover that up!'

Benedetto blundered forwards to help, kicking a bowl of bloody water over Cerchi's legs in the process. Strocchi had to bite his tongue to keep from laughing as Benedetto bent to dry Cerchi's brown hose.

'Get away from me,' Cerchi hissed. 'What idiot left that bowl there?'

'It's my fault,' Strocchi volunteered. Benedetto was in enough trouble already. 'I was washing the victim's face to see if I could recognize who it was. The face looked familiar last night, but now the features have swollen—' He stopped, staring at the exposed legs lying on the bed. There was an angry red birthmark on the right calf.

'Well? What is it?' Cerchi demanded.

Ignoring him, Strocchi moved closer to study the victim's face. The eyes were still open. Yes, it was him. 'This man was in the cells last week. We arrested him after you ordered us to arrest anyone visiting via tra' Pellicciai after curfew.'

'Quite right,' Cerchi scowled. 'The depraved men who use that street, looking for their next *cazzo* to suck – they should all rot in Le Stinche.' Benedetto nodded along, either in agreement or appeasement. Neither was a pleasing quality. 'So what's the pervert's name?'

'Corsini – Luca Corsini.'

'Well, he got what he deserved. Sodomites are a plague on the good name of this city, but dressing as a woman to trick other men – that's beneath contempt.' Cerchi's face soured further. 'His kind deserve no justice. Whoever killed him did the court a favour.'

'Murder is murder,' Strocchi insisted, 'no matter the victim.'

Cerchi jabbed a finger at the constable's chest. 'Are you questioning my judgement?'

'No sir, of course not, but—'

'But nothing. Let the good sisters bury this pervert and that can be an end to it.'

Strocchi didn't trust himself to respond wisely.

Benedetto was less hesitant. 'Won't the *segretario* want a report?'

Cerchi rounded on him but Benedetto kept talking. 'You said that Bindi was demanding more information. Won't he want your report?'

Strocchi hid a smirk. Perhaps the new recruit wasn't so shallow as he first appeared.

Unable to refute the facts, Cerchi claimed the suggestion as his own. 'Much as the city might wish an end to such perversions, there is still a murderer at large—'

'Two murderers,' Strocchi said. 'We saw two men fleeing.'

Cerchi chewed on his moustache, knuckles whitening at his sides. 'Anything else you've forgotten?' He peered at both constables, eyes narrowing. 'Any other details?'

'The victim did say one word to us,' Benedetto replied. 'It was a name: Aldo.'

That caught Cerchi's interest.

Aldo eased back on the reins as his borrowed horse crested the hill. Spread across the valley below was Florence: a jumble of grand palazzos and humble hovels, bustling marketplaces and quiet piazzas, churches and workshops, all elbowing one another for room. Above them loomed the Duomo, terracotta bricks divided into curving vertical segments by columns of pale stone, keeping a proud watch amid the plumes of smoke billowing from the city's chimneys.

A high wall guarded Florence from outside attack. To the east, the Arno shimmered before disappearing into the city. The river emerged again to the west, bound for Pisa and the Ligurian Sea. Farms and orchards lined the road down to the northern gate, producing food for the sixty thousand souls inside the city.

'Why are you grinning?' Levi asked as his horse stopped beside Aldo.

'Good to be home.'

'We're not there yet.'

Aldo leaned back, smacking Levi's horse on the rump. It cantered down the road with the moneylender bouncing in the saddle, protesting all the way. Aldo urged his own horse forwards, catching up with Levi as they neared Porta San Gallo.

'There's still time.'

'For what?'

'One last chance to tell the truth,' Aldo said. 'Who wants you dead, and why?'

The moneylender stayed silent, staring straight ahead.

'A debtor who finds it cheaper to have you slain than pay what they owe, or a rival eager to cut the competition?' No reply. Aldo snatched the reins from Levi's grasp, pulling both horses to a halt. 'My protection ends once you pass through that gate. Tell me who or what it is you fear, and maybe I can help you – or your daughter.'

Levi hesitated before giving Aldo a thin smile. 'Thank you for getting me here, but I have few doubts about my safety inside the city.' He tugged the reins free and his horse trotted towards Porta San Gallo. Aldo scowled. He'd spent five days and nights with Levi, yet was no closer to knowing the moneylender or his motives.

Chapter Four

*I*t took Strocchi hours to find a true address for Corsini. The Otto's records revealed several arrests of him in recent months: petty theft, pickpocketing and indecent acts. But the accused gave a different address each time, forcing Strocchi to eliminate them all. After narrowing the list to a single address in the city's southern quarter, Strocchi persuaded Cerchi to come with him to the dead man's last home.

'We're wasting our time,' Cerchi complained as they crossed Ponte Vecchio, picking a path through the blood and rancid offcuts spilling from the butchers' shops that lined the bridge. 'Corsini was obviously killed for soliciting someone disgusted by his sodomite ways.'

'We saw two men fleeing via tra' Pellicciai. Why would he proposition two men?'

'Probably wanted a *cazzo* at both ends,' Cerchi scowled. 'His kind like that.'

Strocchi ignored the comment, guiding him right as they left the bridge. 'There could be another reason. The way Corsini was attacked, that many blows to the face – as if they were trying to destroy who he was. It was only by chance that I recognized him.'

Cerchi shrugged, his lack of interest putting an end to any further debate. It made for an uncomfortable silence as they marched alongside the Arno, but that was better than listening to Cerchi sneering at the vices of others. As if he was without sin.

Oltrarno was the quarter of Florence that Strocchi had yet to explore fully. It had few of the grand palazzos seen elsewhere in the city, though some buildings still had an old tower, stretching up like stone sentinels above the roofs of humbler wooden houses. Oltrarno was home to many Florentine artisans and skilled craftsmen, living alongside those whose days were spent dyeing fabrics and tanning skins for merchants to sell. Corsini's last address was down a forlorn, neglected alley west of the last bridge. The sun never touched these stone walls, and the packed dirt pathway stank of stale piss and boiled brassica water. The stench would be unbearable in summer. For once Strocchi was almost grateful for the cold.

'This is the place.' He banged on a door. Most of the other buildings were neglected, but this one showed signs of care. Whoever lived there had not abandoned hope. Not yet.

Another hammering brought feet stomping to the door. It swung open, revealing a sour-faced woman dressed from head to foot in black. Her teeth were yellow and broken, but her shoulders remained proud and her back firm. 'What took so long?'

'You're expecting us?' Strocchi asked.

'I made my *denunzia* this morning. The constable at the Podestà said he'd pass it on to an officer called Cerchi.' She sighed. 'You don't know what I'm talking about, do you?'

Strocchi noted how Cerchi was avoiding her gaze, suggesting he had been given the complaint but ignored it. Any citizen could make out a *denunzia* accusing someone of a crime. The document could be signed or remain anonymous if the complainant believed they would be in danger if their name became known to the accused. Cerchi ignoring a *denunzia* was typical. He was always eager to pass judgement on others, but slow to help anyone besides himself. Strocchi pressed on.

'We're looking for where Luca Corsini was living, Signora . . . ?'

'Signorina,' she corrected. 'Signorina Mula. What's happened? Is he dead?'

This woman was quick. The Otto should employ her instead of Cerchi.

'What makes you ask that?'

Mula gestured at a narrow staircase behind her. 'I haven't seen my tenant since yesterday, but I caught two men up in his room last night, searching for something.'

'Can you describe them?'

She hesitated, before shaking her head. 'It was too dark, and they were wearing cloaks with the hoods up over their faces. I told all of this to the constable.'

Strocchi nodded. Nobody paid her any attention, even when she reported a crime. Florence could be a cruel city. 'Did they take anything?'

'Not that I saw.' Mula jerked her head at Cerchi. 'Doesn't this one say anything?'

'I speak when there's something worth saying,' Cerchi snapped.

'Then you must be silent a lot.' She stepped to one side. 'See for yourselves.'

Cerchi pushed past her. Strocchi followed, mouthing an apology on his way by.

The victim's room was an attic, tucked into the eaves. A bed took pride of place, facing the only window. The few pieces of furniture were tipped over or broken, contents strewn across the wooden floor. Male and female clothes were everywhere – dresses, blouses and expensive embroidered undergarments mingling with waistcoats, caps and discarded hose. An ornate coat splayed across the bed, its vibrant red lining torn out.

'The intruders were definitely looking for something,' Strocchi said. 'It's not chance that this happened the same night Corsini was left for dead.'

Cerchi shrugged, making as little effort as possible to help. He picked at the male garments with only a thumb and forefinger. Strocchi worked his way from one side of the room to the other. It didn't take long for Cerchi to get impatient. 'Let me know if you find anything useful,' he said, stalking from the attic. 'And don't waste all day in here.'

Strocchi heard Cerchi arguing with Mula on the way out. She didn't sound happy, but few did after encountering him. Still, it prompted an idea. If the landlady had interrupted the intruders, they probably hadn't found what they sought. That meant it was still in the attic. But an hour of effort revealed nothing more than the dead man's love of rich undergarments and shoes – gifts from admirers, no doubt. How long had Corsini been dressing as a woman to find fresh clients? None of the Otto's records mentioned him being arrested in female attire.

The attack took place after curfew on Sunday. Courtesans often used the communal mingling after mass to entice new men. Had Corsini done the same, and brought home a client with a violent streak? No, that didn't make sense. The attack was by two men, north of the river and after dark. But it might be worth questioning other courtesans in case any recalled seeing the female Corsini at mass.

Content at having a new lead, Strocchi did his best to tidy the attic before leaving. As he put a small table back on its legs, there was a creak from underneath. The floor was made up of long, wide boards but one section under the table was a short length – tricky to spot in daylight, let alone after dark. Strocchi prised at the shortened section with his nails and found a snug hiding place beneath it. Inside were a few pieces of jewellery – little more than trinkets, truth be told – and a slim, leather-bound book.

Reading was not easy for Strocchi, though it had improved from having to search the Otto's dense, closely written records. Thankfully, this volume had large, flowery writing. But the words! Graphic descriptions of copulations and penetrations and . . . Living in Florence had broadened Strocchi's knowledge of the world, but he still felt such an innocent at times. Far more innocent than Corsini, it seemed!

Each page described a different encounter, a new visitor. Corsini wrote about their urges, inventing names for them: Tickleballs, Bentprick and Horsecock. A simple code rated endowment and abilities – Horsecock scored well on length, but less for technique. Corsini had been quite an artist too, sketching a likeness of each man's face and *cazzo*.

None of the men had their true names mentioned, but Strocchi recognized one of them from the sketch and Corsini's gushing, gossipy writing: '*Bentprick loves to brag while I kneel between his thighs sucking him. How many ships he uses to bring woollen cloth from Flanders and France, how bold he is compared to his rivals. I think he counts the ships out loud to extend his pleasure – mostly it just gives me a sore jaw! But he's promising me the most gorgeous new* giornea, *so I let him brag.*'

Bentprick could only be Agnolotti Landini, an importer of foreign cloth and a much-feared force in the Arte di Calimala, the guild of cloth finishers. In one of his first tasks as a constable, Strocchi had been to Landini's workshop after a foreman stabbed a worker in a dispute. Landini was there too, but seemed more concerned about a lost day's work than the fate of either man. He had several large moles on his face, making him easy to recognize in Corsini's drawing. There were others in the diary that sounded and looked familiar. Had Corsini become a favourite among powerful men? Was he – or she, sometimes – passed from one to another? That would explain the lavish items in Corsini's humble room.

The lurid details in the diary could destroy a prominent merchant, or at least his reputation. Anyone brought before the Otto for sodomy faced punishments ranging from public humiliation and fines to floggings, imprisonment – and worse. The severity depended on the accused's age and whether he was using someone else, or being used. Strocchi had heard of men being hanged, their bodies set alight while still swinging in the air, and the ashes flung into the Arno to prevent a Christian burial. More than enough reason for murder.

A scrap of torn paper was caught in the binding. Had one of Corsini's visitors found himself there, and ripped out the evidence? Strocchi frowned. It was guesswork, but still rang true. Cerchi would have to see the diary. There were two murderers to be found, and the killing deserved a proper investigation, no matter what Corsini did with his time or his body.

The tavern lurked in a narrow road just north of the Arno, in the city's western quarter. It was little more than a hovel serving dregs, and anyone crossing its threshold craved oblivion, or the women upstairs. Aldo wanted neither. He stopped in the doorway, eyes adjusting to the dark interior. Two men slumped at the bar, while the rhythmic thudding of a bedhead on the floor above broke the dreary silence. At least the cold kept away flies.

A pox-faced cripple hunched in the far corner, nursing a mug of wine. One leg ended at the knee, while a sloppy leer twisted his features. Few of the women upstairs would part their thighs for him, even if he paid double. But Zoppo paid for nothing if he could avoid it.

'You've been staying open past curfew,' Aldo announced. 'Again.'

Zoppo shrugged. 'What the nose doesn't see, the eye can't smell,' he slurred.

Aldo glared at the drunks by the bar. 'Go. Now.' Once the men had lurched out, Aldo bolted the door shut behind them. Zoppo straightened, his apparent inebriation gone.

'Wondered when you'd be back.'

'Almost didn't make it back,' Aldo replied, joining him in the corner. A sniff of the wine in Zoppo's mug revealed its rancid stench. 'You got anything better than this?'

A new bottle appeared on the table, accompanied by a crooked smile. Broken teeth pulled the cork free, and a generous glug filled a fresh mug. 'Only the best for you.'

Aldo took the drink, swirling the liquid round before inhaling. It'd have to do. Besides, he didn't come for the quality of Zoppo's cellar. The tavern keeper was a valuable source, with friends among many of Florence's less law-abiding citizens. Zoppo could find out truths and secrets that were beyond the reach of a court officer – for a price, naturally. When Bindi had ordered Aldo to guard Levi on the way back from Bologna, Aldo wanted to know why the moneylender needed guarding. He'd had to leave for Bologna before Zoppo could report back, but the question still remained. Guarding Levi had nearly got Aldo killed, and he wanted to know why. 'So, what did you learn about Samuele Levi?'

Zoppo emptied his old wine onto the floor, startling a flea-bitten cat, before filling his own mug from the fresh bottle. 'Not much,' Zoppo admitted. 'You know the Jews, always keeping to themselves. Can't say I blame them, the *merda* gets thrown their way. But I heard a few things. Wife died three years ago, slow and painful, leaving him with a daughter—'

'Rebecca.'

'That's her. Of marrying age now, and pleasant on the eye too.' Zoppo licked his lips.

'Never mind her,' Aldo scowled. 'Tell me something I don't know about Levi.'

'He's got plenty of enemies but few friends,' the cripple said, downing his drink and pouring another. 'Too fond of undercutting his rivals, and he takes on clients most won't touch. One of the other moneylenders comes in sometimes to drown his sorrows.'

'Must have plenty of sorrows to come here.'

Zoppo ignored the jibe. 'Levi has always had enemies, but things fell apart after his wife died. From what I hear, he's been even worse lately. Shouting at neighbours, cutting off any debtors who can't make their payments. Levi won't have a business at all soon if he keeps this up.' Zoppo raised a hand to stop a question forming on Aldo's lips. 'And before you ask, no, nobody knows why the sudden change. Or if anyone does, they aren't talking.'

Aldo downed the wine, one hand digging in his coin pouch.

'Paying for a drink?' Zoppo gasped in mock surprise. 'This'll be a first.'

Aldo slapped a fistful of *giuli* on the table. 'Spread these round. Levi is hiding something. Whatever that is, it nearly got both of us killed on the road from Bologna. I want to know what he's concealing, and why.'

Zoppo swiped the coins into his eager right hand. 'Anything else?'

Aldo rolled up both sleeves. 'Where do you want it?'

The cripple frowned. 'Hit the face this time. Visible bruises are always better for the reputation. Besides, one of the girls might give me a *pugnetta* out of pity.'

Aldo cracked his knuckles. 'I wouldn't hold your breath.'

Rebecca Levi smiled. Joshua Forzoni knew she'd never let him inside without Father's permission – the unlikeliest of possibilities – but it didn't stop Joshua asking. His warm brown eyes got a playful glint as she chatted with him on via dei Giudei, his lips curving into a mischievous smile. She enjoyed spending time with him, despite what Father thought.

'Why do you ask the question when you already know the answer?'

Joshua beamed. 'Because I like seeing you smile before you say no. It makes me think that one day you might say yes.'

His eyes, she could get lost in those eyes. Rebecca punched his arm instead. When he winced, she laughed at him. It was safer.

'You're stronger than you look,' Joshua complained, though with no hurt in his voice.

'And you're not as handsome as you think.' The words slipped out, spoken too fast.

'So you agree that I'm handsome?'

'I agree that you think you are.'

Joshua moved closer, his fingers intertwining with hers on the doorframe. The touch of his skin created a warm shiver of excitement. She knew this was wrong, but it felt—

'What are you doing?' a voice shouted.

Rebecca pulled her hand free, willing herself not to blush as she turned to face her father. He stomped towards them, a leather satchel tucked under each arm. He'd been away for days. Why did he have to come back now? 'Please, Father—'

'You bring shame on our family by flaunting your lust out here in the street. Worse still, to do so with this non-believer—'

'You've no right to say that,' Joshua insisted. 'My father may not have been born a Jew but my mother was, and so was I.'

Samuele's nostrils flared as he quoted the teachings. '"You shall not give your daughter to his son and you shall not take his daughter for your son; for he will cause your child to turn away from Me and they will worship the gods of others."'

But Joshua persisted. 'We were only talking . . .'

Rebecca stepped in between them. 'Go home, Joshua. This is between Father and I.'

'But he said—'

'Go!'

She stared into his eyes, those beautiful eyes, willing him to understand. Instead he looked wounded, betrayed. Still, he maintained respect, bowing to them both as he left. As soon as he was out of sight, Rebecca stalked inside. Her father followed, closing the door. People might hear raised voices, but only a fool shouts at their family in front of the world.

'Is this how you behave when I am away?'

'We were talking,' Rebecca insisted, 'nothing more.'

'Has he been inside my house? Has he been in your bed?'

How could Father think such a thing? 'You know I would never do that. I'm still your daughter, whatever you think of me.'

He shook his head, dumping the satchels on a table. 'If your mother were alive to see this, her only child, tempting on our doorstep—'

'We were talking, Father. Talking!' Rebecca stopped herself, willing the anger inside to settle. Be like a stone in the river, Mother always said, let the water pass over you. It shall get lost in the sea, but all you will be is smoother. Put aside anger and it cannot control you.

Samuele was leaning on the table, his shoulders hunched. The long trip from Bologna always left him exhausted. But this was worse, as if the whole world was pressing down on him. Pride would not let him give way, but what price must he be paying for that?

She went to his side, resting a hand on his gnarled knuckles. 'Are you hungry? Thirsty, perhaps? I could fetch—'

'No.' He pulled his hand away to grapple with the binding on his satchels. 'You will not see this Joshua again. Put him from your mind. He is not worthy of you, of this family.'

'He says he loves me.'

'That means nothing.'

'And I think I might love him.'

The hands wrestled with the bindings, but the knots wouldn't undo.

'Did you hear me, Father?'

Fingers twisted and tugged, but still the taut ties did not yield. 'I said—'

'I heard you!' Samuele hurled both satchels across the room. 'Whatever you think you feel, it shall not be,' he spat. 'You are never to see him again. Never!'

Rebecca could take no more. 'Why are you being like this? I know something is worrying at you, I hear you pacing every night.'

'Do not talk to me of things you cannot understand.'

'If Mother was here, she would make you see sense.'

'If your mother was here, she'd be ashamed of you.'

That was too much. Grabbing her shawl, Rebecca strode to the front door.

'Where are you going?' Samuele demanded.

'Wherever I want,' she snapped, pulling open the door. 'When Mother was dying, she made me promise to look after you. That's the only reason I've stayed. But no more.'

'Rebecca, come back here!'

'I wish you were the one who had died!'

Palazzo del Podestà always put a chill through Strocchi. The tall brick fortress loomed over the surrounding streets, its sparse windows far too high for anyone to see in. Few Florentines went inside by choice. But it was home to the Otto, so Strocchi had no option. Pulling his coat close, he marched through the gated entrance, Corsini's diary in hand.

The interior of the Podestà was even colder than the narrow streets outside. Sunshine might brighten the bricks and stones in the high walls, but it never made them any warmer. Ahead of Strocchi was a courtyard with a well at its centre. Cloisters with vaulted stone ceilings stretched round three sides of the courtyard, metal brackets secured to each column for burning torches at night. Beyond the cloisters were heavy wooden doors leading to ground-level rooms. Most were storage areas or cells, but several led to interrogation chambers. Strocchi could hear no screams today.

On his right a wide stone staircase rose to the middle level, where a *loggia* led to the court's administrative area. Aside from the chapel in the north-east corner, it was all Bindi's domain. Ugh, that man. Fat and bloated as a well-fed spider – and just as poisonous. He was present whenever the Otto sat, advising the magistrates. All eight men were replaced several times a year, as was customary, but the *segretario* remained a constant presence within the Otto. To cross Cerchi was dangerous; to anger Bindi was far worse. A third level at the top of the Podestà was accessible only by passing through Bindi's domain, so Strocchi had yet to see it – constables had no reason to go there.

Strocchi's gaze scoured the courtyard for Cerchi, but he saw only other constables and a few guards. He glanced up to the second level. Cerchi was there, glaring out from the *loggia*. *Santo Spirito*, he was with Bindi. Strocchi considered withdrawing, but Cerchi spied him, and summoned the constable with a gesture. Strocchi muttered a prayer on his way up the stairs, asking the Madonna to watch over him. Miracle of miracles, it worked. The *segretario* was waddling away when Strocchi reached the *loggia*. But the scowl on Cerchi's face was a swift reminder of his early morning promise: shit always travels downwards.

'Let me guess,' Cerchi snapped. 'You didn't find anything in the *buggerone*'s room.'

'Not in the room.' Strocchi held out the diary. 'But this was under the floorboards.'

Cerchi took the slim book, skimming the pages without bothering to read a word. 'Doesn't look much to me.' He thrust it back at the constable.

'If you look at what Corsini put here,' Strocchi said, opening the book again, 'and here – and here – you can see how it might be important.'

Cerchi sighed, his impatience all too obvious. 'I'm a busy man, I don't have time to read every sick word that pervert wrote.'

'It's an account of all his lovers. Older men, mostly.' Cerchi's expression soured, but Strocchi pressed on. 'Corsini didn't name anyone, but his descriptions and these drawings are enough to identify several of his visitors. There are some very important men in here.'

'An example, give me an example.'

Strocchi turned to the page that had first caught his eye. 'This one, Corsini calls him Bentprick. But the description of a business importing wool from Flanders, and this sketch of the man's face – that has to be the cloth merchant Agnolotti Landini.'

Cerchi grimaced. 'Landini was a magistrate here when I was a constable. Treated us like something to scrape off a boot.' He peered at the drawing. 'That does look like him, though – I remember those moles on his face.'

'There are a few others I recognized. Rich merchants, most of them.'

Cerchi's eyes narrowed. 'You think the pervert was blackmailing them?'

'There's nothing in the diary to suggest that,' Strocchi replied. 'It reads more like a foolish boy in love with older men and dressing up. I think this book was where he kept his secrets, things he dared not tell anyone else.'

'If he was extorting money from these sodomites, they would have reason to kill him.' Cerchi looked down at the courtyard, tapping a finger against his mouth. 'Well done, Strocchi. Maybe you're not as useless as I thought.'

Never had praise tasted so sour. 'Thank you, sir.'

'I need you to go through that diary, noting all the men inside it. Each one is a potential suspect for the murder of this *buggerone*. What was his name again?'

'Luca Corsini.'

'Yes, him. He's the victim here, remember.'

Strocchi swallowed a bitter laugh. 'Sir, I would never question your judgement—'

'I should hope not,' Cerchi interjected.

'—but these men are merchants, not trained killers. I doubt any of them has held a weapon, let alone kicked or beaten anyone to death.'

Cerchi shrugged. 'So Landini or whoever paid someone else to do it. They're still guilty of murder, even if they never got blood on their hands.'

That morning Cerchi couldn't be bothered to search the victim's things, now he was eager to find potential suspects. Why?

'Get to work. I need those names today, and the diary too.'

'Yes, sir.' Strocchi headed for the steps, but a last command stopped him.

'Oh, and don't tell anyone else.' Cerchi gestured at their surroundings. 'You know what the Podestà is like. Wouldn't want any of the suspects hearing about this, would we?'

*A*ldo strode into the Podestà courtyard, struggling not to favour his left knee. Most of those working for the Otto were limited by their laziness or lack of learning. Being guards was the best they could hope for between wars. But amid the indigent and the idiots nestled a few vipers, men whose ambition helped overcome other flaws. Revealing a weakness to them was asking to be bullied, or worse. Aldo gritted his teeth and kept walking.

He nodded to Strocchi in passing. An upbringing in the Tuscan countryside had given Strocchi strength of body and spirit. The constable was one of the few working for the Otto to show promise, so Aldo had been teaching him the ways of the city, how to cultivate the likes of Zoppo as sources. Normally Strocchi's tall back stayed as straight as his morals, but today the constable appeared borne down, a slim, leather-bound book in his grasp. Before Aldo could ask what was troubling him, a sneering voice echoed round the courtyard. 'You must be upset, Aldo. Your little whore got beaten to death last night.'

That had to be Cerchi. The man was little more than a bully, but a shrewd, ruthless streak made him dangerous. Aldo spied his fellow officer smirking down from the *loggia*. If something was amusing Cerchi, that meant trouble. It likely explained what was worrying Strocchi too. 'What are you babbling about?'

'Corsini. Two men attacked him last night.' Cerchi swaggered down the staircase. 'Of course, we didn't realize the victim was male, at first. The little *buggerone* was dressed as a courtesan, probably trying to trick good, decent men into filling his bony behind. It was only after the body was examined we found out what the pervert had been doing.'

Aldo didn't react, letting Cerchi glory in his own voice. Corsini was a mischief-maker and too fond of a strange *cazzo*, but otherwise harmless. Why would anyone beat him to death? It was understood – if not accepted – that young, unmarried men needed to sate their lust. Older men did too, married or not, but that was another matter.

'Poor little Corsini didn't survive the night,' Cerchi said, reaching the bottom of the steps, 'but he did whisper one word before the end: your name. Now, why would a dying pervert waste his last breath naming you?'

Still Aldo didn't speak, certain there was more. Cerchi was being far too smug. Let him say what he wanted to, get the bile out of his system.

'Then young Strocchi remembered seeing Corsini here, in the cells. He was arrested twice in the last month for luring other men into satisfying his sick cravings.'

Cerchi seemed fascinated by this. Perhaps it excited him more than he cared to admit? He wouldn't be the first to turn self-hatred into a crusade against others. Or else he truly was repulsed by the way some men sought their pleasure. Probably the latter, Aldo decided. Cerchi lacked the imagination for anything more adventurous.

'I talked to our guards,' Cerchi continued, 'and found those in charge of the cells when Corsini was last brought in. He was due before the Otto but you had him released. No reason given, no penalty paid. You just let the *buggerone* walk free. That got me thinking.'

It must have been a new experience.

'Why would an officer of the Otto have a pervert freed? And why would this pervert say that same officer's name as his final word?' Cerchi stepped so close Aldo almost gagged on the stench of rancid body odour. 'Well? What was Corsini to you?'

Aldo stared at Cerchi's face, the fervour and avarice behind that drooping moustache and beady eyes. Cerchi had become an officer after throttling a man inconvenient to Bindi. To the *segretario*, promoting Cerchi was a small price to pay for ending a problematic case. But for Cerchi, becoming an officer of the Otto was the gateway to countless bribes and rewards. Worst of all, it gave Cerchi power. That made him dangerous, if nothing else.

'Isn't it obvious?' Aldo asked. 'Corsini was a useful source. He could get people to tell him things they'd never say to anyone else. That's why I had him released. He was no help in the cells. But I warned him it wouldn't – couldn't – happen again.'

Cerchi's eyes narrowed. 'What about him saying your name before he died?'

Aldo shrugged. 'I'm not the only person with that name in the city.'

A snort of dissatisfaction.

'Is that all? Or do you need more help to solve your case?'

Cerchi glared, his face souring by the second. Finally he spat on the stones in front of Aldo before stalking off. Angering Cerchi was satisfying, if not very wise. Aldo knew why his name had been the last word Corsini said, but didn't feel like sharing the reason with a *bastardo* like Cerchi. The last time Aldo freed his informant from the cells, he had been blunt with Corsini. There would be no more interventions, no more reprieves from the Otto. If Corsini got himself arrested again, he would have to face the consequences.

Corsini had fluttered his eyelashes, but without success. Aldo had no interest in young men, nor those who dressed as women to attract a lover. Instead he offered a warning: sooner or later, that fondness for strange *cazzo* would get Corsini a beating – or far worse. But the young man had been unrepentant. If something like that did happen, he had trusted Aldo would make sure justice was done. That was why his last word had been Aldo's name. But justice was not so easily found in Florence, not for the likes of Luca Corsini.

Rebecca hesitated, knuckles clenched in front of the door. She'd been walking and walking, the shawl round her shoulders not enough to keep out the cold. The sun was already hidden behind buildings. A young, unmarried Jewish woman alone outside after dark: it was wrong.

But what Father had accused her of . . . He was to blame for this.

Did she really love Joshua? Or had she said that to shock Father, to make him listen? The truth of it would have to wait for another time. For now, she needed a place to get warm, a place to be safe. She knocked four times, her heart pounding. If anyone other than Joshua came to the door, she'd go home. But the door opened and it was him.

'Rebecca? Is something wrong?'

'Father, he . . . He said terrible things to me. We both did, but I . . .' Words failed her. She wouldn't cry. Not here, not like this – not in front of him.

Joshua took hold of her hands. 'You're shivering. Come inside.'

'No, I shouldn't.'

Joshua put his coat round her shoulders. The scent of him filled her nostrils, woodsmoke and hard work. He stepped out, shutting the door. 'What did Samuele say to you?'

Rebecca shook her head, not wanting to repeat those hurtful words.

'Please. Tell me.'

Shame reddened her cheeks as she repeated Father's accusations.

Joshua's grip on her tightened, his lips becoming a thin line. 'He had no right.'

'Samuele is my father, he has every right—'

'No. He should treat you with respect, the way that you always respect him.' Rebecca had never seen Joshua like this. 'I'm going to talk to him.'

'You mustn't,' she insisted. 'Father didn't mean what he said. Long days and nights of travelling would make anyone tired and angry. Besides, this wasn't about me. Something else is worrying him. He snaps at me because he can't face whatever's wrong.'

'That's no reason to hurt you,' Joshua insisted, shaking his head. He opened the door to call inside. 'Rebecca Levi's out here, she needs somewhere warm to wait.'

'Father will calm down,' Rebecca said. 'He'll be sorry by morning.'

Joshua shook his head. 'It's time someone told your father he cannot always do as he pleases. Go inside. I won't be long.'

Signora Tessa Robustelli was humming a lullaby to Piccolo when Clodia ran into the *officio*, her painted breasts bouncing. 'Come quick, there's a man who won't leave,' the wide-eyed young woman wailed. Typical. Ten minutes until curfew and some fool had chosen their *bordello* by Piazza della Passera as the place to spill his seed. No doubt he'd come south of the Arno to get drunk and was now too far gone to stagger home.

Robustelli scooped up her tiny dog and strode out to confront this fool, Clodia close behind. The *bordello* was humble, a plain wooden building with two levels, pressed between grander stone houses. Given the chance, the families living either side would happily have driven Robustelli and her women out. But there'd been a *bordello* at Piazza della Passera for decades, and she'd no intention of that changing. It was three minutes' walk south-west from Ponte Vecchio, a most convenient location. It gave a safe place for everyone who lived here. What happened inside these walls was legal, so long as they observed the laws enforced by the Office of Decency. Besides, it was home. 'What does this man look like?'

'Tall. Unshaven. Tired. He looks old. Even older than you, signora.'

Robustelli rolled her eyes. To Clodia, anyone over twenty-five was grave fodder.

'Did he ask for anyone in particular?' Robustelli asked. Most regulars had favourites. Some favoured Elena, who always appeared innocent, even as she straddled a *cazzo*. Matilde from the Low Countries was popular because she had a wicked way with her hands. Clodia was new and that always excited men, even if her painted breasts took some getting used to.

'No, signora. I think he might be asleep. Or dead.'

That was the last thing they needed. Explaining a dead body to the Office of Decency was always a nightmare. The court's officials turned a blind eye to most things, if their vision was clouded with enough coin. But a corpse was too much, even for the greediest of them.

Robustelli paused outside the doorway. A sound like someone dragging stone answered one question: the visitor lived, though his snoring could wake the dead. Piccolo whimpered at the cacophony. Robustelli handed the dog to Clodia before marching inside.

'Cesare Aldo, I should have known it was you – wake up!'

The man slumped across the cushions continued snoring.

'Wake up!' Robustelli kicked the tall, rangy figure. Aldo's piercing eyes snapped open, a hand reached for the stiletto in his boot. 'No need for that,' she said. Piccolo jumped from Clodia's hands and scampered across to lick Aldo's face. 'You're home.'

He waved the dog away, struggling to a sitting position. 'Must've fallen asleep.'

Robustelli ushered Clodia forwards. 'This is Cesare Aldo, an officer for the most powerful criminal court in Florence. Aldo, this is Clodia. She's new, down from Milan.'

Clodia covered herself with both hands. 'He enforces the law?'

'In his way,' Robustelli replied. 'But don't worry, Aldo won't arrest you – he lives here. His room is upstairs, the one at the back.' She smiled. 'Aldo is a rarity – a man with no interest in women. He doesn't give us any trouble. In fact, having him here helps keep most trouble away.'

'I see,' Clodia said, her voice suggesting otherwise.

'Don't worry your pretty head about it,' Robustelli insisted. 'Off you go – and take Piccolo with you.' Clodia collected the dog on her way out.

'Not troubled too much by thinking, that one,' Aldo observed.

'We could charge more if she could think.'

Robustelli studied Aldo. Five days on the road had aged his face five months, but she kept that to herself. Enough years on her back had taught Robustelli that most men valued compliments over truth. 'Drink?'

'Not tonight. Sleeping in my own bed is all I need.' He shuffled to the doorway, a hand rubbing the side of his left knee. 'But you can do something for me.'

'Anything,' she said, and meant it.

'Nobody wakes me before dawn. Not unless it's a matter of life and death.'

Agnolotti Landini was celebrating. After days of worry, three ships laden with wool from Flanders were now safely in port. Better a delay than the loss of such precious cargo, or the ships carrying it. Crews could be replaced if need be, but the wool was essential to keep his dyers busy through the winter, and losing the vessels would have broken Landini at the bank. Few in the Arte di Calimala risked shipments this late in the year, but among all the cloth merchants in the guild, fortune had favoured him once more.

Landini smiled at those round the dining table in his palazzo: his three strong sons, all blessed with comely wives, and at the far end of the table was his Pasqua, still beautiful after all these years. She was the iron in their marriage, an implacable resolve whenever disaster seemed certain. To Pasqua, success was not enough – they had to be seen to be successful. Landini had built this sumptuous palazzo for her, at considerable cost. The dining room was decorated with brocades of many colours, damasks and velvets, while bright geometric carpets adorned the chairs and window seats. Only the finest ceramics from Montelupo were allowed to be used. Appearances mattered above all else to Pasqua, above even money.

Landini tapped his goblet and a servant refilled it with wine. After a delicate sip, the merchant rose to his feet. 'Let us drink! To risking the wrath of the high seas and emerging triumphant!

To doing what others dare not and proving them wrong! To our family –' his sons and their wives all lifted drinks in response – 'and to my wonderful Pasqua, without whom I would be but a shadow of the man I am. *Cento di questi giorni!'*

Everyone drained their wine and banged on the table, echoing his call to have a hundred such days. Servants came with wooden platters of spiced veal and roast kid, while those following brought spiced pies and sweetmeats. The rich aromas of saffron and nutmeg filled the air as the feast was laid out. Landini noticed his *maggiordomo* approaching. Careful not to draw the attention of others, Piero stepped close enough to whisper in his master's ear.

'Excuse me, sir, but an officer of the Otto is here to see you.'

Typical. For every moment of triumph, there was always an official ready to interfere. Florence had dozens of different courts overseeing every aspect of city life. Didn't the guilds do enough to bring prosperity to the people? Well, not all the people, but certainly to those who deserved it. Anyone who couldn't – or, more likely, wouldn't – work could always go to church for alms. It was the way of things, and some things never changed.

Landini sighed, pushing back his chair. 'Forgive me, everyone, but a small matter needs my attention. Please, stay seated. I will return as soon as I can.'

He followed Piero, pausing to whisper in Pasqua's ear. 'Someone from the Otto, probably soliciting for a bribe.'

She nodded, the smile never leaving her face.

Landini sauntered down the marble steps to his palazzo's ground level. The visitor was lurking by the outer doors, admiring the building's rich interior. No, not admiring – coveting. At Landini's approach the visitor bowed, a sneer visible beneath his drooping moustache. There was something unsettling about his features:

beady eyes, a sharp nose and a thin chin. Yes, that was it: he resembled a rat. Repulsive.

'Signor Landini, I'm sorry to interrupt your meal. It sounds like a happy occasion.'

'It is. My family is here, so if we can make this quick?'

'Of course. My name is Meo Cerchi. I represent the Otto di Guardia e Balia.' The visitor held out a hand, Landini took it. The grip was clammy and grasping. Cerchi leaned closer. 'A pleasure to meet you . . . Bentprick.'

'I beg your pardon?'

'That's what Corsini calls you. Sorry, called you. He's dead now. Beaten to death last night. But you knew that.'

Landini pulled his hand free, a shiver of dread twisting inside him. 'I don't know what you're talking about.'

'Your little friend, Luca Corsini.' Cerchi smiled. 'You remember him, don't you?'

Landini was suddenly aware of his *maggiordomo* close by. 'Thank you, Piero, that will be all for now. Please return upstairs and look after the guests.'

'Yes, signor.' The servant moved away. Landini waited until he was out of hearing before speaking again.

'Now, what was that name you mentioned?'

'Luca Corsini,' Cerchi replied. 'I doubt anyone will weep for that *buggerone*. But, as an officer of the Otto, I'm obliged to find whoever killed him.'

Keep calm. This man was a parasite. Given nothing, he would soon go away.

'The violent death of any citizen is regrettable and, of course, deserves investigation – regardless of who the victim might be. But what has this to do with me?'

'I'm glad you asked.' Cerchi pulled a slim, leather-bound book from his tunic. 'Corsini wrote about all the men who visited him in here, describing the sordid little details of their meetings, the things they would have him do.'

'Sorry, I still don't—'

'You're in here,' Cerchi said, his smile twisting into a leer.

No, no, no. 'That's impossible.'

'Really? Well, let's see if any of this sounds familiar.' Cerchi flicked through the diary. 'Corsini called you Bentprick because your manhood curves in quite a distinctive manner. Normally, I doubt the magistrates of the Otto would require you to disprove such a sordid accusation, but when it comes to murder – and a brutal one, at that . . .'

This couldn't be happening. How had . . . ?

'There's more,' Cerchi volunteered, brandishing the book. 'It seems you liked to brag about how many ships you send to France and Flanders for woollen cloth.'

'That's common knowledge. I'm a leading importer within the Arte di Calimala.'

'It might be common knowledge among merchants, but not to perverts like Corsini. And how many of your guild members boast about business while being sucked by someone young enough to be their son? Corsini is quite explicit in his descriptions.'

Landini's stomach was churning, the rich food and wine threatening to come back up. He steadied himself. These accusations were nothing without proof of fact. He would have been arrested by now if someone had made a *denunzia* against him. 'I'm sorry, but I can't speak to the idle fantasies of this young man, whoever he was.'

'He sometimes dressed as a courtesan, if that helps? I suppose it meant clients could overcome their shyness about fucking another man.'

'Have you anything to confirm these accusations?'

'I'm glad you asked.'

Oh God. He did have proof.

Cerchi opened the diary so Landini could see a particular page. There it was: a likeness of him in ink. Ridiculous boy, how could he have been so stupid? But nowhere was the name Landini, just Bentprick. Perhaps there was still hope. Perhaps. Perhaps.

'I suppose that bears a passing similarity to me, but other than that . . . The words could be describing any merchant who imports woollen cloth.'

'Yes,' Cerchi agreed. 'That's why you'll come to the Podestà tomorrow.'

'I'm sorry?'

'I need to question you about this. It's important we clear you from any suspicion as soon as possible.' Cerchi's eyes flicked sideways, towards the marble staircase. 'I notice you haven't asked where or when he was killed. Not that it matters – dead is dead, after all. But if rumours were to circulate that you had some involvement with these . . . this . . .'

'I had nothing to do with any of it,' Landini insisted. 'You, you said he was beaten to death last night. I was here the whole time with my wife Pasqua, she will vouch for me.'

'Good. Then we can ask her now.' Cerchi turned to the stairs. Landini saw Pasqua descending to join them.

'What's taking so long?' she asked, pausing halfway down. 'Our guests are wondering where you are.'

'I'll be right back,' Landini replied, forcing a smile.

'Very well, see that you are.' Lifting the hem of her gown, she swept back upstairs. Her questions would have to be answered later.

'No wonder you went to little Corsini,' Cerchi sneered. 'I doubt that witch would offer any man pleasure without claiming his *palle* as payment. Or did she watch?'

'That's disgusting! My wife would never involve herself in anything so—'

'So you visited Corsini alone. How often did you see him?'

'You will not put words into my mouth—'

'We both know you prefer putting things into other people's mouths.'

Don't lash out. 'I've had quite enough of this. You will leave. Now.'

'Of course, whatever you wish. But I commend your bravery, signor.'

'My bravery?'

'Yes. Most men say anything to avoid having their good name destroyed.' Cerchi's face was stricken with apparent regret. 'But if this is how you wish things, be at the Podestà first thing tomorrow to face these accusations.' Cerchi turned away.

'Wait, no, please.' There had to be a way out of this. There had to be. 'Perhaps I was hasty before. I apologize if my words offended you.'

Cerchi stopped, but did not look back.

'You said it was important to clear my name. Is there another way to achieve that?'

Still Cerchi did not show his face. 'There might be.'

'How might that be done? A generous donation to the court, perhaps?'

Cerchi turned, eyes full of greed. 'I'd be happy to accept a gift on the Otto's behalf.'

So that was it. He wanted payment for his silence. Landini felt on surer footing at last. Driving a bargain was his greatest talent, after all. 'And how much should this gift be?'

Cerchi smiled. 'I'm sure a wealthy merchant like yourself can set his own terms. Bring your purse to the Podestà tomorrow and we'll settle this matter.'

Landini bolted the door once Cerchi was gone. But a pinprick of doubt still scratched at him. They had not agreed a price. They had not agreed a price.

Aldo knew it was a dream when Vincenzo lifted the red mask, but that didn't matter. They hurried away from the procession, finding a dark alley. Urgent hands pulled at each other's clothing, lifting tunics and tugging down hose, while their mouths met – kissing, tasting, wanting. But Aldo felt another hand at his shoulder, pulling him from this precious—

He snapped awake. 'What? What do you want?'

Robustelli was clutching a lantern. 'There's a constable downstairs. He says it's—'

'A matter of life and death.' Aldo dragged himself upright, shifting the bedclothes to cover his erect *cazzo*. 'What time is it?'

'Early. Or late, depending on how you see it. Still dark, either way.' Robustelli grimaced. 'You want me to send him away?'

It was tempting to say yes. But sleep was gone now, taking Vincenzo with it. 'No, I'll deal with this. The constable, what does he look like?'

'Young. Eager. Wide-eyed. Haven't seen him in here before.'

Probably a recruit. Cerchi was fond of giving night patrols to newcomers, seeing how long they'd last. Aldo pulled on fresh clothes, his boots and the heaviest cloak he owned.

The constable waited by the front door, his hands worrying a cap clutched over his crotch. 'First time inside a *bordello*?' The young man nodded, blushing to the roots of his tousled hair. 'You'll get over it. Tell me what's happened.'

'A body's been found in via dei Giudei. Stabbed.'

That was the Jewish commune, not far from Ponte Vecchio. 'Male or female?'

'It's a man. Apparently he's a moneylender. His name is—'

'Samuele Levi.'

The constable frowned. 'How did you know that?'

Aldo ignored the question. So much for Levi being safe here in the city. Had the bandit ringleader stalked them back to Florence? Unlikely. Whoever the killer was, they couldn't leave the city until the gates were unlocked at dawn. 'What's your name, constable?'

'Benedetto.'

'Open the door, Benedetto,' Aldo urged. 'We haven't got all night.'

Chapter Six

Tuesday, January 2nd

Jews had been part of Florence as long as Aldo could remember, though less than a hundred lived in the city. They kept to their own kind, living and working south of the Arno, in and around via dei Giudei. Unlike Christians, Jews were free to operate as moneylenders. That marked them out as different, but also gave their community a minor importance. The Medici respected that and let the Jews observe their own laws. Most days it was not a problem.

Today was different.

'You can't keep denying me,' Aldo warned the line of bearded men in his way, stopping him getting any closer to Samuele Levi's house. 'I'm an officer of the Otto with authority to investigate crimes involving the loss of a life.'

Still they remained steadfast, arms locked together, staring past him. Aldo gestured at the first hints of dawn colouring the sky. 'Once the sun rises, the city gates will be unlocked and Samuele Levi's killer will be able to escape. Is that what you want?'

'It does not matter what they want,' a stern voice replied. A familiar figure with an impressive long white beard was approaching, dressed in full-length robes and skullcap. 'It only matters that they do what is right and proper.'

'Yedaiah.' Aldo bowed, showing the new arrival proper respect. This man was a leader to the Jews of Florence; his word was beyond question among them. 'Your people have their own beliefs and traditions, I understand that. But this city has laws that must be obeyed. Murder is murder, it cannot go ignored.'

Yedaiah stopped within touching distance, his eyes a warm hazel. 'We do not plan to ignore this senseless act. We take care of our own, as we always have. It is how we have survived so long. We will see that justice is done.'

'When it comes to an unlawful killing, the will of the Otto overrules your laws. And the longer your men delay me, the more likely it is that justice goes undone.'

Yedaiah shrugged. 'Be that as it may, we cannot let you pass. I'm sorry. Our beliefs, our culture, must come first.' He rested a gentle hand on Aldo's shoulder. 'You look tired, Cesare. Go home, get some sleep. Come back later.'

'I sent my constable away to rest, I can't leave until his replacement gets here.'

Yedaiah nodded before strolling by. The line of men parted to allow him through before closing ranks again. A second set of footsteps approached, demanding attention. But this Jew was unfamiliar to Aldo. He was short and stout, his eyes only just level with Aldo's chest. The newcomer's hands rubbed together, like a greedy child eager to snatch fresh food from a table. The agitation of his dark, bushy brows and gleaming eyes betrayed a hunger for news. 'Is he dead?' the man asked, craning to see past.

'Who?'

'Samuele Levi, of course – rumour is he's been murdered.'

'Never mind that,' Aldo said, a firm hand against the man's chest to stop him getting any closer. 'What's your name, and what has this to do with you?'

The newcomer grabbed at the hand, intent on pushing it away. Instead Aldo shoved him face-first against a wall, one wrist pinned against his back.

'Let me go!'

'Your name. Don't make me ask again.'

'Sciarra. Aaron Sciarra.'

'And what is this to do with you?'

'You can't—'

A shove upwards brought a satisfying cry of submission.

'He's one of my rivals. Levi and I, we're both moneylenders.'

Aldo stepped back, releasing Sciarra's arm. The man cowered like a beaten dog, wincing as he nursed his wrist. 'You've no right to do that.'

'Don't tell me what I can't do,' Aldo replied, studying the new arrival's face before gesturing at Levi's home. 'You don't seem upset about this.'

'Why should I?' Sciarra replied. 'Levi's a cheat and a liar, making promises he never keeps. Go ask his partner – sorry, former partner. Ask Malachi Dante if you don't believe me. I'll be glad if Levi is dead. All the more business for me.'

'Keep this up and you'll talk your way into an interrogation cell.'

'I didn't kill him, if that's what you're suggesting. But good luck finding who did. Levi has plenty of enemies. That's what comes of doing deals with those you shouldn't.'

'Such as?'

Sciarra scowled. 'That's your job, not mine. But you'd best start with the outsiders.' He made one last effort to see past Aldo before skulking away, muttering under his breath.

* * *

Strocchi was waiting in the Podestà courtyard when Cerchi sauntered in, a smug smile creasing his narrow features. Strocchi had
spent a sleepless night fretting about the list he'd made of Corsini's
visitors. Two names were beyond dispute thanks to the descriptions
and their likenesses in the diary, but the others were little more
than guesses. To accuse innocent men was wrong, Cerchi had to
agree with that.

'Sir, I need to talk to you about the Corsini case.'

'What?'

'Luca Corsini – the young man who was murdered.'

The puzzled expression on Cerchi's face cleared. 'And?'

'That list I gave you, I'm not sure about all the names on it. I'd
like to help with the investigation.' Strocchi held his breath, waiting
for a response. But instead of berating him, Cerchi began laughing.
'What's so funny?'

'You, Strocchi! Maybe you haven't heard, but someone killed a
Jewish moneylender last night. *Segretario* Bindi is far more
concerned with that than he is the death of some little pervert
with no family and no connections.'

'Corsini was beaten and kicked to death,' Strocchi protested.
'His killers are walking around free. They could strike again at any
time.'

Cerchi sneered. 'One less pervert is one less pervert. If it were
up to me, I'd give the men who attacked him a reward.' He strolled
away but Strocchi followed.

'You don't mean that, do you, sir? Everyone deserves justice,
don't they?'

Cerchi stopped, shaking his head at the constable. 'You want
to find who killed that pervert? Fine. Go ahead. Waste your time.
But I'm keeping the diary and that list.' Before Strocchi could
reply, Cerchi's gaze was drawn to a man lurking by the gates. The

officer dismissed Strocchi and stalked across the courtyard to confront the visitor.

Strocchi followed him part of the way, wanting to argue for the list's return. But then he saw who was waiting to meet Cerchi – Agnolotti Landini. The wool importer was wearing a dark blue cap, the shadow covering much of his face, but several moles were still visible. Strocchi moved to the shadows at the edge of the courtyard, watching the two men.

Landini held out a purse that looked heavy with coin. Cerchi ignored it, reaching into his tunic for Corsini's diary. Cerchi hissed at the merchant, but Strocchi could hear only a few words – interrogation, cells, the Otto. Landini paled, pulling out another, larger purse. Cerchi took that one, weighing it in his hand. The merchant's fearful expression faded as Cerchi nodded his acceptance – he even smiled. Before the two men parted, Cerchi leaned close to whisper in Landini's ear. 'You can't mean that,' the merchant gasped, his shock making the words loud enough for Strocchi to hear.

'Every month,' Cerchi announced, strutting back into the courtyard. Strocchi sank back behind one of the thick stone cloister columns to avoid the officer's gaze. Whatever had passed between the two men, it was not something Cerchi wanted others to know.

Once Cerchi had crossed the courtyard and gone into the officers' room, Strocchi watched Landini. The merchant looked a broken man: shoulders slumped, head down, hands clasping at each other. Landini stumbled away, bumping into a peasant girl with a basket of frost-burnt brassica. He apologized to her before continuing his listless journey.

Either Cerchi was using the diary to extort money, or a suspect was paying Cerchi to look the other way. Guilt twisted Strocchi. Whatever the truth, it was his fault. He'd brought Cerchi the diary. There was only one way to stop this – find whoever killed Corsini.

Waking in a strange bed confused Rebecca at first. But the Forzoni family home was warm and full of life, so different from the house she shared with Father. Even the bed was more comfortable, the sheets perfumed with the delicate scent of quince apples. Rebecca heard Joshua's sisters laughing as they prepared food in the kitchen, and she could smell bread baking. Even the light was different, beaming in through the window when she woke. Father expected her to be up before dawn, no matter how early that might be.

There was a distant knocking, followed by murmured, urgent voices. The words were hard to make out, but Rebecca heard her name mentioned. She splashed water on her face, tying back unruly brown curls before hurrying to the kitchen. Everyone fell silent as she went in, none of them able to meet her gaze. None but Joshua, and his face looked ashen.

'Rebecca, I'm so sorry. It's your father . . .'

Then she was running, sprinting along narrow dirt streets, as fast as her feet would allow. Round a corner and she would be home. Everything would be fine. Father would be . . .

An outsider was arguing with a line of Jewish men outside her home. No, please don't let it be true. Every instinct told her to turn away but she had to know. She had to. Mournful faces watched from windows and doors on either side of the street. She could hear whispers, see fingers pointing. Something was wrong. Something was very wrong.

* * *

Aldo saw the young woman hesitate. She was twenty at most, wearing a simple dress with flowers embroidered across its front and sleeves. She was slender and pretty, yet there was a resemblance to Samuele. Must be the daughter, what was her name? Rebecca, that was it.

She stopped in front of Aldo, her lips moving but making no sound.

'It's your father. I'm sorry – he's dead.'

Rebecca crumpled, one hand clawing at a sleeve, fingers tightening round the material until her knuckles were white. She tore the sleeve open, her howl of anguish echoing in the narrow street. '*Barukh atah Adonai Eloheinu melekh ha'olam, dayan ha-emet!*'

Aldo had heard the words before, a blessing Jews cried out in response to death and tragedy. Her words would get Yedaiah's attention. Aldo gave her a few moments to recover before introducing himself. 'I guarded your father on his way home. I was with Samuele.'

That got her attention. 'You were with Father when he died?'

'No, before that – on the road from Bologna.' Voices were arguing in Hebrew behind Aldo. He kept talking to Rebecca. 'I saved his life. I offered to protect him here in Florence too, but Samuele insisted he was safe.'

She nodded. 'He's stubborn. Always has been. Always will—' Grief stopped her words. Aldo risked a glance over his shoulder. Yedaiah was coming.

'I couldn't save your father, but I can find out who did this to him.'

'Leave her be,' Yedaiah called. 'She needs to be with her grief, not with outsiders.'

'Rebecca, help me find the truth about what happened to Samuele.'

'I said, leave her be.' Yedaiah stepped between Aldo and Rebecca, his face stern.

'Rebecca, please.'

'No.' Yedaiah bristled. 'We will deal with this. Please go, before—'

'Let him stay,' a quiet voice said.

Yedaiah swung round to face Rebecca. 'My child, you cannot—'

'I'm not your child,' she said, her voice growing stronger. 'I am no man's child, not now Father is dead. This man says he can find whoever killed Father. Let him try.' Rebecca's expression hardened. 'Or would you deny the wishes of a grieving daughter?'

Yedaiah inhaled, his back straightening. 'Very well.' He narrowed his eyes at Aldo. 'But you will not touch anything inside, and you will do nothing to desecrate the body.'

'I understand.' Aldo glanced at Rebecca. She was firm and implacable as Samuele had been. Like father, like daughter. 'Did Samuele work here, or elsewhere?'

'Here. He hated the other moneylenders at Mercato Nuovo.' She grimaced. 'His clients were always coming into our home, pleading for money or more time to repay him.'

Aldo went to the door. It stood ajar but there was no splintering to the wood, and no damage to the bolt. That suggested Levi had let his attacker in – a debtor, maybe, or a rival? Or had it been someone closer to home? Killings in Florence were not infrequent and were usually personal, fuelled by family, love, hate or greed.

Aldo pushed the door further open and inhaled a faint smell of metal – blood had been spilled here. It was dark inside, a single lamp offering little light or warmth. However Levi spent his money, it wasn't here. There were a few pieces of simple furniture, but no ornaments and no art on the walls. The sole visible extravagance was a rug on the floor. Samuele's body was sprawled across it, fully clothed and face up.

Aldo went inside, making a slow circle of the chamber. A black cloth was covering a mirror near the front door – put there by Yedaiah, no doubt, as was Jewish tradition. Nothing was tipped over, nothing looked out of place. No ransacking or obvious signs of robbery. The rug under Levi was flat to the floor, its edges undisturbed. The room was unremarkable – aside from the dead body. Dried blood stained his robes below the left breast. Aldo resisted the urge to close Levi's staring eyes, all too aware of Yedaiah watching from the doorway.

'A single stab wound between the ribs,' Aldo observed. 'That takes skill. Angry attackers with a knife are never content with one strike. They want to be sure. They want the victim to suffer.' Aldo crouched for a closer look, his bad knee protesting at the strain.

'You believe this was planned,' Yedaiah said.

'The killer took the blade away, and left no trace of themselves behind.' Or had they? Samuele's blood had seeped into the rug, spreading outwards. A crescent shape was visible in the pooled blood. Someone wearing a boot or shoe had come too close to the body – a clumsy mistake. Aldo peered at the floor. Yes, there were more crimson crescents, moving away from the body, heading outside, each one fainter than the last. Should have seen those earlier, but the murky interior had hidden them at first.

Aldo touched a finger to the nearest crescent – it was dry, so several hours old. The clumsy footstep was at the edge of the blood. That meant it happened some time after Levi was stabbed, when he was already dead, or close to it. Had the killer returned to be sure of their handiwork, perhaps to retrieve their knife? Or had a late-night visitor stumbled on the murder and fled in panic? And where was Rebecca while her father was bleeding to death?

* * *

Strocchi went to via tra' Pellicciai, revisiting the alley where Corsini had been attacked. It looked different in daylight, a narrow passage of packed dirt with nothing to show a man had been brutally kicked, beaten and left for dead there. No windows overlooked the alley, but the constable knocked on all the nearby doors, hoping someone might have seen or heard what happened there on Sunday night. Nothing. Nobody remembered anything or, if they did, none of them wanted to admit it, let alone make a *denunzia*.

Frustrated by his failure, Strocchi crossed the Arno to revisit the dead man's home. The door was open; the landlady must have stepped out. But when Strocchi went upstairs he found only furniture. Someone had stripped the attic room bare.

Footsteps clumped up the stairs. Signorina Mula appeared in the doorway, her face souring when she recognized the constable. 'I was hoping for a new tenant.'

'What happened to Corsini's things?'

'Sold what I could, burnt the rest. What was I supposed to do?'

'His killers might have left something behind.'

'You didn't tell me that. Besides, he owed rent.' She stomped away, leaving Strocchi to continue his search. But all it proved was how thorough she'd been in emptying the attic. Despairing, Strocchi went downstairs and found Mula sweeping the dust from her home onto the dirt path outside the front door. She paused to let him by.

'Don't suppose you've remembered anything about those intruders you disturbed?' Strocchi asked. Mula stopped sweeping long enough to offer a shrug. Of course she hadn't. Did nobody care that a young man had been murdered? What kind of city was this?

* * *

Rebecca Levi was lying. She kept evading Aldo's gaze, one hand picking at the torn fabric of her sleeve. Yedaiah still hadn't let Rebecca inside the house, so Aldo was questioning her out on via dei Giudei. The death of a parent was all too often life-changing, he knew that from bitter experience. The shock of what had happened could explain some of her behaviour, but not all of it. Not the lie she was struggling to conceal.

'I was with my cousin Ruth last night,' she repeated, watching Yedaiah's men come and go from her home. 'Father and I argued after he returned from Bologna. I spent the night at Ruth's house, hoping that would make him see sense.' She stopped, tears near brimming over in her eyes. 'I said such terrible things to him, things I can never take back.'

Aldo watched her weep for a while, offering no kind words, no show of sympathy. Patience was a powerful tool when talking with a witness – or a potential suspect.

'I said Mother made me promise to look after him, and that was the only reason I'd stayed,' Rebecca continued, getting control over her grief for a moment. 'I said I wished he had died instead of her.' She broke down. 'N-now they're both gone!'

Her grief was compelling. Somewhere within it was a lie, but asking a direct question would not uncover the truth. Instead Aldo pointed at her plain shoes.

'Were you wearing those yesterday? Could I see underneath them?'

'I . . . yes, of course.' Rebecca lifted her feet in turn. Neither sole bore any blood. She did not ask for an explanation, but her gaze slid towards the front door of her home. A sign of guilt, or was she realizing why he had asked?

'Another moneylender was here,' Aldo said, 'a quarrelsome man called Sciarra.'

Anger flushed Rebecca's face. 'Father hates him. They hate each other.' Realization stilled her voice for a moment. 'You don't think he . . . ?'

'It's too early to make a *denunzia* like that, not without proof. But business rivalries can drive men to desperation. Sciarra mentioned another man, called Dante?'

'Malachi Dante – he was Father's partner for years.' She shook her head. 'But Dante could never wish us harm. Yes, their partnership ended on bad terms, but Malachi was like an uncle to me when Mother died. He's the gentlest man you'll meet.' Yedaiah emerged from the house, gesturing for Rebecca to come inside. But one last question had to be asked.

'Samuele paid to have me guard him on his journey home from Bologna.' Aldo watched Rebecca closely. 'Do you know why your father thought he was in danger?'

She did not hesitate. 'No, but it was one of the things we argued about. I knew he was afraid of something, but he wouldn't say who or what it was.' Rebecca was telling the truth – about that, at least. 'I'm sorry. I wish I knew more.' The young woman went to the front door of her home, Yedaiah moving aside. She took a deep breath before going in.

Aldo could hear her howls of grief as he strode away.

Chapter Seven

'We cared for Luca Corsini while he was breathing,' the abbess at Santa Maria Nuovo said, a careworn scratch in her voice. 'If a patient dies, their family or friends choose what happens next. Should no one come forward, the body is given a pauper's burial. This *ospedale* only looks after the living – God takes care of the soul.'

Strocchi frowned. In his home village, how you were treated in death mattered as much as how you were treated in life. If you had nobody to see you to your rest, people came forward to do it for you, without having to be asked. The village nestled in a bend on the Arno, downriver from Florence. Spring and autumn floods often left debris behind, and more than once a body had washed up nearby, unfortunate souls who had drowned in the Arno. The villagers considered it their duty to give those remains a proper burial. But here in the city, you could die in the street and most Florentines would step over your corpse.

His dismay must have been obvious. The abbess's manner softened.

'I have the dead man's clothes, if you care to see them.' She led Strocchi through the *ospedale* corridors and cloisters to a small chamber. He recognized the courtesan dress Corsini had been wearing, folded on a wooden bench beside a delicate pair of shoes.

'There was nothing else?'

The abbess shook her head. 'No purse, no coins, and nothing worn beneath the dress.' The chiming of distant bells caught her attention. 'Excuse me, I have patients to tend.'

'Of course,' Strocchi said. 'And a thousand graces for helping.'

Once she was gone, he unfolded Corsini's dress. Muddy boot prints remained where the victim had been kicked, and blood flecked the bodice, mute evidence of the attackers' brutality. Strocchi closed his eyes, picturing the hooded men as they fled that night, willing himself to recall some telling detail that might help find them. But nothing came.

Turning to leave, Strocchi saw a small fresco painted on the wall facing the abbess's desk. It showed the Holy Madonna, her hands clasped in prayer, eyes looking up to Heaven. There was a golden halo round her beatific face, and her dress was a vibrant blue. The abbess was fortunate to have such a beautiful fresco opposite her desk, to enjoy and inspire.

Staring at the Madonna's dress, a fresh notion occurred to the constable. There could not be many gowns with such a distinctive pattern to the fabric or with such exquisite stitching. Strocchi was no expert in women's clothing, but this dress was almost certainly unique. That meant someone must be able to recognize it.

He went back to the bench and tore out a piece of fabric the size of his hand, slipping it inside his tunic. After folding the dress and putting it back, Strocchi paused at the fresco to offer thanks to the Madonna, and make a prayer of supplication. 'Let me find the men who did this,' he whispered, 'so they may face justice.'

Another door closed in Aldo's face. He'd spent much of the day visiting homes on and near via dei Giudei, without success. Had they seen anyone outside Levi's home the previous night? Had strangers been coming to the moneylender more often? But the responses were the same: a slammed door, or an earful of rapid Hebrew followed by a slammed door. Little surprise after what had happened, but that didn't make it any less frustrating.

Bells announced mid-afternoon mass, a sign of the fervour that gripped Florence between Christmas and Epiphany. But people living on via dei Giudei ignored it – they answered to a different faith. The chimes made Aldo realize he hadn't eaten since the previous night. No wonder his temper was fraying.

'Sir! Sir!' Benedetto ran towards him, waving a piece of paper.

'No need to shout.'

The constable slid to a halt, proffering the sealed document, too breathless to explain.

'This is for me?'

A nod.

Aldo took it, breaking a red wax seal bearing the Otto's emblem. Inside, *Segretario* Bindi had spattered black ink across the page. The more ragged his writing, the worse his mood. This was near illegible.

Benedetto recovered enough to gasp a question. 'What does it say?'

'It seems Duke Alessandro himself has taken an interest in Samuele Levi's murder. The *segretario* is ordering me to give the Duke a progress report before curfew.' Bindi would never volunteer that, the Duke must have demanded it. Getting caught between them was dangerous ground. Bindi could make life a misery for any man under his command, while the Duke could have almost anyone in the city summarily executed if he so chose.

Benedetto frowned. 'The Duke cares about Jews?'

'Probably not, but moneylending is important for banks and all the guilds. There were two attacks on Jews last summer at the

Mercato Nuovo, where many of the moneylenders do business. Nothing serious, idle threats from drunken debtors, but Alessandro gave orders that the Jewish community be protected. Now one of them is dead, murdered in his own home. The Duke will want to know why.' That was going to be a problem. Men of privilege and power did not grasp the potential complexities of a murder. They expected results, delivered at their whim. But killers were not always easy to catch.

Aldo noticed an older Jewish man with a silver-flecked beard lurking not far behind Benedetto, watching them. The man's robes were cut from rich cloth but had become ragged at the hem through wear. He had known wealth and plenty, but not of late. Dark smudges beneath his eyes were evidence of worry or lack of sleep, or perhaps both. The man gave Aldo a subtle nod. Word had spread about the outsider asking questions.

The constable was still waiting, doubtless told not to return without a response. 'Did you get some rest?' Aldo asked him. Benedetto nodded. 'Good. Go back to the Podestà, and tell the *segretario* I've read and understood his orders.' The Jewish man waited until Benedetto was well away before introducing himself with an ingratiating smile that didn't stop him looking haggard.

'My name is Malachi Dante, I am—'

'Samuele Levi's former partner,' Aldo said. 'Why did your business fall apart?'

That slapped the welcome from Dante's face. But after hours of being ignored or abused, it was time Aldo got some answers. The Duke would expect progress, evidence, even suspects by curfew – no, he would demand them.

'I-I wouldn't agree that our business fell apart . . .'

'Levi forced you out. It was acrimonious, everyone says so – Sciarra, Rebecca . . .'

Her name brought a show of concern from Dante. 'Rebecca? How is she?'

'Her father is dead, slain in his own home, and not one person seems willing to help me find who did this. So, are you here to ask questions or to answer them?'

'I . . .' Dante faltered at the accusation. 'I'll do anything I can to help.'

'Good. Then tell me why your partnership ended.'

Dante glanced round before answering, his voice lowered to a husky, tired whisper. 'Samuele is . . . was . . . a difficult man. Short on temper, long on recriminations. He had no sympathy for those who couldn't meet their debts.' Dante paused, fingers rubbing at his tired eyes. 'Samuele started loaning coin to strangers, people I didn't know. It was asking for trouble, and I told him so. He said I'd no right to question his judgement.'

A scowling Jewish woman stalked by, glaring at Dante. He waited until she was gone before leaning closer to Aldo. 'I was like a brother to Samuele after his wife died. And Rebecca, she's the daughter I would have wished for. But her father forced me out. He bought my half of the partnership, and then blackened my name so I couldn't start a new business.'

'That must have made you angry.'

'I was furious,' Dante admitted, 'at first. But mostly I was worried. Samuele had been taking on powerful, dangerous clients. I never knew their names, but I could tell by the way Samuele acted that he was out of his depth. Now this . . .' Dante succumbed to tears, burying his face in both hands. The grief seemed real, but was it born of loss or guilt?

Aldo waited for the moneylender to recover a little before asking another question. 'When was the last time you saw Samuele?'

'Last night,' Dante said, regaining control. 'I had heard he was back. I went to his door, hoping to plead with him, to make him see sense. He let me in, but we didn't speak for long. Samuele seemed . . . defeated. Like a man expecting the worst. And now this . . .'

Levi had been anxious on the road back from Bologna, but not defeated. If what Dante said was true, something must have happened after Levi's return to Florence.

'Did you see anyone else near Samuele's house last night? Someone out of place?'

Dante shook his head. 'Only Rebecca, and she was leaving as I arrived. The poor girl was so upset, I don't think she even saw me. They must have been arguing again.'

Aldo confirmed Dante's address and warned him against leaving the city.

'Is there anything else I can do to help?' Dante asked. The offer appeared genuine, his face full of apparent concern.

'Perhaps. People round here are suspicious of anyone asking questions. Levi wasn't well liked – but murder is murder. Unless people talk to me, I have little chance of finding who did this – or stopping them from killing again.'

Dante nodded. 'Leave it with me. Samuele's funeral will take place before curfew. I'll talk to Yedaiah and my neighbours then, make them understand. Maybe I can open some doors for you. Samuele and I were partners a long time; let me do this last kindness for him. Come back tomorrow and people will talk, if I can persuade them.'

At first, Renato Patricio was amused by the visitor to his sewing room near Santa Croce. The eastern quarter of the city was a respectable area, for the most part, but he still had to pay bribes to ensure it stayed open. Indeed, paying greedy men to smooth the path of transactions was so common, Renato included the cost of such bribes in the price of his exquisite gowns.

It was the same with the young men Renato invited to his bed. Petty thefts and demands for money were now often the price for such encounters. It was a sad truth that getting older meant his young lovers only pretended their passion in exchange for favours or gifts. But most at least had the courtesy to smile while they were fucking him.

This Cerchi seemed to expect money for his silence and was offering nothing in return. Not that Renato would have wanted anything from the unwelcome visitor. Cerchi had all the charm of an unwashed, pox-ridden *cazzo*. He had blundered into the sewing room, ordering Renato to send everyone outside so he and Cerchi could talk in private.

Once the workers were gone, this ugly little-minded man strutted about as if he owned the sewing room, grasping at delicate cloth with grubby fingers and making veiled remarks about the different ways people sought their pleasures. Plainly Cerchi had spent no time – or money, for that matter – in the world of fine clothes, otherwise he would know his heavy-handed hints were wasted. Renato's love life – such as it was these days – was an open secret among his customers, but they were all wives of rich merchants. That had protected him from arrest, so long as he was discreet and pursued his private passions behind closed doors.

'You've no shame about being a *buggerone*,' Cerchi sneered.

Renato shrugged. 'I wouldn't use that word, but I am what God made me.'

This seemed to infuriate Cerchi further. 'God had nothing to do with you, or your sickness. You will suffer eternal torments for your perversions.'

'Well, I'll be in good company. All the greatest artists prefer the company of men.'

It was an exaggeration, of course, but put a stop to his ugly tirade. Instead, Cerchi pulled out a slim book and pointed to a page inside. On it was a rather flattering drawing of Renato, alongside some flowery handwriting.

'This belonged to Luca Corsini, a pervert who satisfied men like yourself.'

'Ahh, what a lovely boy. I haven't seen him in ages, how is he?'

'Dead,' Cerchi snapped. 'Murdered on Sunday night.'

'But that's terrible! He's such a sweet thing. So pretty, too.'

'Not any more. He was beaten to death in an alley, his face smashed in.' Cerchi seemed to rejoice in saying that. 'I've been ordered to find out who's responsible.'

'Well, I hope you catch them – and soon.' Renato's hands were shaking. It was horrible to picture anyone suffering such a death. The pain didn't bear thinking about.

Cerchi smirked. 'The *buggerone* got what he deserved. If I'd my way, perverts like him – like you – wouldn't be allowed to live in a city where people worship God.'

'Then I consider myself fortunate you are not in charge of Florence. Now, if you don't mind, I have gowns to complete and workers waiting to come back in.'

Cerchi brandished the book again, a greedy gleam in his eyes. 'All of the men inside this are potential suspects. That gives me the right to interrogate or torture them until I get the truth, no matter how long it takes.'

Renato was finding it hard to swallow, his mouth too dry. He'd been quite wrong. There was nothing amusing about this man. Cerchi was dangerous, quite dangerous. 'But you've no proof any of them are involved in this.'

'Not yet. But people are eager to talk once you suspend them from the *strappato*. That device can loosen the most silent of tongues. Have you seen it being used?'

Renato couldn't speak at all now, so shook his head.

'The suspect is bound by the wrists, arms behind them. The arms are then raised so they are lifted on to their toes, all their weight going through their shoulders.' Cerchi leered with satisfaction. 'The *strappato* isn't usually fatal, but those suspended from it for too long – well, their hands and arms are never the same again.' He gestured at the exquisite cloth strewn around the room. 'For someone who does such fine work – it'd be a shame.'

Cerchi came closer, until his foul breath was all Renato could inhale. 'But you know all about shame, don't you?'

'Surely there must be another way? Some other means of finding the truth?'

Cerchi frowned. 'Who said anything about the truth? The purpose of the *strappato* is to obtain confessions. A suspect tells us anything we wish once they've been subjected to it. That could be admitting their guilt – or naming others. Friends. Colleagues. Former lovers.'

He was like a cat toying with a mouse before the kill. 'Who knows which poor men of Florence will be revealed as visitors to this little pervert?'

Renato sank onto a wooden stool, the world he'd built crumbling around him. Even if he eluded torture at the hands of this vile creature, others might name him to save themselves. This was a nightmare – one without hope of waking. Or was it?

Cerchi was watching him, waiting for something. Who knows which poor men of Florence, he had said. Of course! Only the poorest of Florentines had to face the full weight of justice. Those with the means could buy their freedom by paying fines – or bribes. Few public officials could not be purchased for the right price, if it was draped in enough flattery. But what would satisfy this grasping intruder?

'I'm not sure I have shown you the proper respect,' Renato said.

Cerchi did not reply, his narrow face impassive.

'As an officer of the Otto, your time must be of great value. Perhaps I could offer something for your trouble in investigating this matter.'

Cerchi gave the smallest of nods, as if acknowledging the truth in Renato's words. Good. The sneering *merda* was open to bribery. But what amount? Too little would be taken as an insult. Too much had the potential to be ruinous. 'I was thinking twenty *scudi* might be sufficient,' Renato ventured. That was half a year's wages for the skilled workers who finished his gowns – generous by any measure.

Cerchi smiled. 'That would be acceptable,' he said. 'As a first payment.'

'A first payment?'

'You did not expect to buy your way out of this with a handful of coins?' He loomed over Renato, waving that damned book. 'Keeping your behaviour away from the Otto will mean regular payments. But taking money from someone like you turns my stomach, so it must be worth my while. I want twenty a month from now on.'

'A month?' Renato spluttered.

'Should I make it twenty a week?'

'No, please, I didn't . . . please, no.' Renato held out both hands, showing his empty palms, making himself subservient to this bully. This *bastardo*. To his surprise, the display seemed to satisfy Cerchi.

'Twenty a month it is. Bring your first payment to the Podestà early tomorrow. Meet me outside the gates. And don't make me wait.'

Aldo knocked at the door to Yedaiah's home on Borgo San Jacopo, round the corner from via dei Giudei. It was one of the older buildings south of the river, and still had its original stone tower. That a Jew owned such a home showed how successful Yedaiah was as a cloth merchant, one of the few professions men of his faith were allowed. But Yedaiah was respected both within and beyond the Jewish community, as much for his wisdom as his wealth. Aldo couldn't depend on Dante's promise alone; he needed the approval of Yedaiah if anyone was going to discuss the murdered man.

There was no answer at first, so Aldo kept knocking. Eventually the sound of hurried footsteps approached, and the door swung open. Yedaiah frowned at seeing Aldo again. 'This can wait, whatever it is,' the elder said, closing his door behind him. 'I've a funeral to lead, and tomorrow I must journey to Lucca to visit my sister. She's gravely ill.'

'I'm sorry to hear that,' Aldo said, 'and I wouldn't ask if it wasn't important.' He followed Yedaiah along Borgo San Jacopo, turning right into via dei Giudei, away from the river. Aldo explained the lack of progress in finding who attacked Samuele Levi, and Dante's promise to persuade neighbours to talk. If Yedaiah urged others to do the same, it would greatly increase the chances of finding the killer. 'Jews were abused at Mercato Nuovo last summer, now one of your kind has been murdered. Help me stop this happening again.'

Yedaiah paused his progress along the narrow, muddy road to

peer at Aldo. 'You think those past attacks and what happened to Samuele are related?'

'In all honesty? No,' Aldo admitted. Ahead he could see Rebecca emerging from her home, supported by a handsome young man, with Dante close behind. 'But I can't be certain of that, not until I find and catch the man who killed her father. Don't you want that too?'

The Jewish elder scowled. 'I only let you into this because Rebecca pleaded with me, and now you want my help to do what I could be doing myself.'

'Would you rather go to Lucca and see your sister, maybe for the last time? Or stay here and spend a day asking members of your community what they saw last night?' Aldo didn't enjoy using Yedaiah's own troubles against him, but it was a necessary evil.

Yedaiah shook his head. 'You'll say anything to get what you want, won't you?'

Aldo shrugged. 'If I have to.' He watched six Jewish men bringing a simple wooden coffin out of the Levi house before hoisting it up onto their shoulders, accompanied by the sound of Rebecca's weeping. 'Well?'

'I'll talk to our neighbours, for her sake,' Yedaiah agreed. 'But on one condition. Stay away from the funeral. Leave that young woman to mourn in peace. Can you promise that?'

'I'll do my best,' Aldo replied.

Chapter Eight

$\mathcal{M}$aria heard the horse approaching the *castello* long before the messenger came knocking at the door. Living in the countryside all year round was irksome, but it meant there were few arrivals that came as a surprise. Cosimo was out hunting with one of the servants, but they had gone on foot. The sound of hooves coming up the stony path this late in the day could mean only one thing: the letter she'd been expecting from Florence had finally arrived.

A few minutes later the maid Simona brought the letter, red wax sealing it shut. Maria waited until the servant had gone before examining the correspondence. The hand that had addressed it was firm and confident, no hesitation visible in the ink, while the seal pressed into the wax confirmed her suspicion about the sender: Francesco Guicciardini. His was a strong voice among the Palleschi, the pro-Medici faction in Florence's senate. Alessandro was the Duke, certainly, but men like Guicciardini helped smooth the path for him in matters affecting the city state. In return, the Palleschi had profited greatly from Medici patronage.

Maria broke open the seal and unfolded the letter. It was brief, almost never a good sign. The opening paragraph was full of thanks for Maria's own correspondence, the usual pleasantries expected in such a letter. The closing paragraph would be just as bland, ending with platitudes and well wishes that had all the worth and value of horse *merda*. The middle was where the knife was wielded, where the favour would be given or withheld.

It is with regret . . .

Maria bit back a curse, fighting the urge to hurl Guicciardini's words into the fire burning close by. Her request had been simple: that Cosimo be allowed to accompany the senator on his next journey outside the city. Maria sought no charity, she'd offered to pay her son's way, but Cosimo needed more experience of diplomacy and statecraft. He had been to Venice and other cities with his tutor, but to travel alongside the great Francesco Guicciardini and witness such a man at work . . . Perhaps her flattery had been too blunt, her true intention too obvious. Spending time with Guicciardini would enable Cosimo to build his own loyalties among the Palleschi. Stuck out here in the country, a young man could create few alliances for his future. A few months beside Guicciardini could have changed things.

But that wasn't to be.

It had been a gambit with limited prospects of success, but Maria did not regret trying. Guicciardini was a man of discretion. He would not tell others of her letter, or the desperation that no doubt seeped from every line. To be a woman in this world was hard enough; to be a mother and a widow was worse still. All the responsibility and none of the power.

Shouted voices and laughter in the courtyard outside the *castello* announced Cosimo's return. Maria looked out through the shutters at her son. He had the proud stance of his father, the same strength of body and spirit. But he possessed other qualities Giovanni had never displayed. Cosimo was patient when patience was needed, and steadfast in his devotion to her. He could see past easy deception too, and understood the value of letting others win a battle when a longer war was being fought. Cosimo might not yet have seen eighteen summers, but he had a maturity his father had lacked. If only her boy could have a chance to use those qualities.

He would show them all, one day.

After an unanswered visit to Sciarra's home, Aldo headed north. He paused to buy scraps of cured ham and the end of a stale loaf from a peasant girl on her way back from the market. Fresh food cost more during the winter, and the best always sold early. He stopped on Ponte alla Carraia, leaning against the side of the bridge. Sitting down to eat was a luxury when working for the Otto, as was cooked food.

Aldo gnawed on his meagre meal while watching workers on the riverbanks busy washing wool in the discoloured water, making the most of the few daylight hours at this time of year. The low winter sun was already arcing towards the hills west of the city. All too soon the bell inside Palazzo della Signoria would ring out over the city, heralding the end of another day. Curfew helped prevent plenty of trouble, but it also made bringing the truth to light that much harder. Suspects could hide behind closed doors at night, and so could secrets.

Aldo threw the last of his food into the Arno, not bothering to watch it join the other detritus in the river. Butchers on Ponte Vecchio threw their most rancid offcuts into the water, whatever couldn't be sold or made into *lardo*. There it joined all manner of refuse, soap, tannin, shit and dyes from the workshops along the riverbank. You never knew what you might see if you looked over the side of Florence's bridges.

He crossed the river before cutting a ragged path east along narrow backstreets towards Zoppo's tavern. A familiar figure was waiting outside.

'Closed,' Strocchi said, pointing at a sign on the door. 'Seems Zoppo is ill.'

'Might teach him not to drink his own poison – assuming it's true.' Aldo had met the constable here before, when they needed to talk away from the Podestà. 'Must be important if you've waited for me.'

Strocchi nodded. 'It's Cerchi.'

'That *coglione*. What's he done now?'

'How long have you got?'

'The Duke is expecting me at his palazzo to report on Samuele Levi's murder. You'd best talk to me on the way.' Aldo strode off, doing his best to ignore the pain in his left knee. The constable followed, matching pace. Strocchi told Aldo about the diary, and the list of potential suspects. 'Sounds reasonable enough,' Aldo agreed when they reached the wider expanse of via Calimala. He turned left, heading north. 'So what's troubling you?'

Strocchi described Cerchi's meeting with Agnolotti Landini. 'At first it seemed he was paying a bribe but, the more I think about it, the more this looks like—'

'Blackmail,' Aldo agreed. 'Cerchi must be using the diary to extort money. And if it succeeded with someone as powerful as Landini, the greedy *bastardo* won't stop there. Cerchi will work his way through that list, tricking each man into paying.'

'What do you mean, tricking them?'

'Knowing Cerchi, he'll wave the diary in their faces, telling them about the terrible secrets inside without quoting any words. You see, Cerchi has his own secret – he can't read.'

Strocchi stopped, amazement filling his face. 'What?'

Aldo paused to appreciate the constable's reaction. 'He hides it well, but he always makes others read out documents and papers for him.' Strocchi shook his head. 'Who's next on the list?'

'The dressmaker, Renato Patricio.'

Aldo nodded, keeping his alarm hidden. Landini he had never met, but Renato – that was a different matter. Before becoming a mercenary, back when Aldo was still learning how to survive on the streets, Renato had befriended him. Their different tastes meant they never became lovers, but Renato knew well enough the kind of man Aldo was. The dressmaker was fond of gossip but could be trusted to keep a confidence. Indeed, it was one of the reasons why he'd become so beloved by wives of rich merchants – they could tell Renato anything, safe in the knowledge it would go no further, and in return they kept his secret too. But there was a world between the idle nonsense of bored wives, and the threats an officer of the Otto could wield. If Cerchi went to Renato demanding money or answers, there was no telling how the dressmaker might react.

'Patricio is a rich target,' Aldo said. 'But threatening him is dangerous, too. His clients have important, influential husbands, and that means powerful allies.'

Aldo squinted between the buildings to spy the Duomo. Late afternoon sun was hitting the orange bricks. No way he could make his report to the Duke and warn Renato before dusk, but visiting the dressmaker after dark was far too incriminating. Better to wait for morning when a passing encounter could be explained away.

'I'll talk to Cerchi, see if I can't make him listen to reason.'

As if that had ever worked before. Aldo resumed his journey, Strocchi falling in step beside him.

'What's happening about the Corsini murder?'

The constable confessed to taking on the investigation himself. But nobody near via tra' Pellicciai remembered the victim, even when Strocchi showed them the distinctive dress fabric. Corsini's possessions were gone, and his body would soon be rotting in a pauper's grave. The only apparent clues were in the diary – and Cerchi had that.

'Stop blaming yourself,' Aldo said, careful to keep recrimination out of his voice. 'You couldn't guess what Cerchi would do with that book. Focus on what happened to Corsini, and why it happened. Ask yourself, who benefits from his murder?'

'He didn't have family. There was little of value in his room, aside from a few gowns given to him, so that probably rules out robbery.'

'Was the killing quick, or did they take their time?'

Strocchi's expression hardened as he described how Corsini had been kicked and beaten, the brutal injuries to his face. 'They made him suffer. They wanted to destroy him. But why kill Corsini on a Sunday night? Why take such a risk by doing it then?'

'Good questions. Something must've happened on Sunday, forcing the killers to attack when they did.'

Aldo led the constable round the Battistero di San Giovanni, avoiding all those hurrying home after mass. 'You said Corsini was wearing a courtesan's dress?'

Strocchi dug into his tunic and pulled out a fistful of fabric. 'Looked like it was custom-made for him, and high-quality cloth, too.'

Aldo recognized the intricate pattern – that had to be Renato's work. The dressmaker must have created it as a present for Corsini, or for someone else who gave it to the young man. Either way, Renato was linked to the victim. Aldo and Strocchi headed north again, away from the Duomo.

'Was there anything strange about his room?'

Strocchi shook his head. 'It was a mess, the place had been ransacked.'

'When?'

'Not long after Corsini was attacked. His landlady disturbed two men, and they fled.'

'They were looking for the diary,' Aldo surmised. 'Where did you find it?'

'Hidden, under a floorboard.' Strocchi paused. 'When I first opened it, there was a scrap of paper caught in the binding – as if someone had torn out a page.'

Aldo nodded. 'Whatever was on that page could well lead you to the killers – or whoever paid them to attack Corsini.'

'But Cerchi has the diary, and he's refusing to give it back.'

'There's more than one way to the truth. Constable, it's time you went to church.'

Strocchi frowned. 'What do you mean? I go as often as I can.'

'No doubt. But tomorrow, you're searching for the last man to visit Corsini's bed.'

It was part of the Jewish faith to bury the deceased as soon as possible. Rebecca had sent word to her uncle Shimon and cousin Ruth in Bologna, but she knew that would take a day to reach them. It would be another day if not more for them to travel to Florence, assuming they were able to make the journey immediately. Better to bury Father now, Yedaiah had said, so she could begin to mourn properly. Rebecca had raised no objection.

At the funeral it seemed as if all feeling had left her body. She stumbled through what needed to be done, saying the words when it was expected of her, but she remained empty and numb. It was a simple service, because all were equal in death. The plain wooden coffin was lowered into the ground at the only graveyard in Florence that permitted Jewish burials.

When the time came Rebecca put earth on Father's coffin, the dirt hitting it with a dull sound. She stepped aside to let others do the same, watching them come forward one by one – Dante, Yedaiah, Dr Orvieto and others. During it all Joshua was at her side. He wept, but Rebecca could not. She willed tears to come but her face remained dry. She had cried for days and days when Mother died. Why did burying Father bring her no sorrow? Was she that bad a person, that bad a daughter? Was some tiny part of her glad Father was dead?

She staggered on her way out of the graveyard, the ground muddy and uneven. Joshua was there to stop her from falling. She smiled at him in gratitude, and he reacted as if stung. Why? Could he see there was no grief in her eyes, her heart? Joshua took his hand from her arm and the moment passed. He opened the gate for the mourners, and Rebecca noticed a dark crimson stain at the front of his boot, discolouring the leather.

The officer from the Otto, he had asked to see beneath her shoe. When Yedaiah had finally let her into the house, she had realized why: there was a puddle of blood under Father's body, with a shape where someone had stood in it. Joshua had gone to see Father that night. A terrible thought struck Rebecca. Could Joshua have been the one who killed Father?

No. No, she did not believe that for a single breath. She had seen the pain in his eyes the next morning, there was nothing to suggest Joshua was a killer. But he did have a crimson stain on his boot. Had he found Father dead on the floor, and kept that discovery to himself? By doing so, he had let her have one last precious night without sorrow. For that, she was grateful. Yet she could not help envying Joshua. He cried for her father in a way she seemed unable to do.

* * *

After Strocchi went home for the night, Aldo strode on to Palazzo Medici. The ducal residence was imposing, its ground floor made of formidable, rough-hewn stone. The level above was all elegant brickwork, while the top floor was even more refined. The palazzo windows became smaller on each level, so the building appeared taller and lighter as the eye moved upwards. The result was impressive, even to someone who had spent his childhood living and playing in a rich merchant's palazzo. The death of Aldo's father had put an end to that.

Aldo presented himself at the entrance and was ushered to a courtyard surrounded by interior colonnades. Through stone arches he could see polished marble and exquisite sculptures, fine tapestries and golden ornamentations. Tall windows overlooked the courtyard, the Medici shield of six round *palle* adorning stonework above each central archway. There could be no doubting who lived here, or their wealth.

Dusk was gathering overhead. Aldo blew into his hands, rubbing them together and stamping both feet to keep warm. Men of power might require attendance at a particular time and place, but it was no guarantee they'd be ready then. Such was the nature of privilege.

Aldo heard a familiar voice approaching. Cardinal Cibo emerged from an archway, a red cape over his cream cassock, scarlet *zucchetto* atop his dark hair. The representative of the Holy Roman Emperor Charles V in the city, Cibo was a man of importance. It was the Emperor's forces that had besieged Florence, ending the republic and returning the Medici to power. Alessandro was the Duke of Florence, but Cibo's reports and recommendations held a significance far greater than his quiet, watchful demeanour might suggest. The cardinal was busy muttering instructions to an attendant, but waved them aside after spying Aldo in the courtyard. 'I didn't expect to see you here,' Cibo said.

'His Grace summoned me.' Aldo could have elaborated, but said no more. Never volunteering more than necessary was safer and wiser in most circumstances, especially when encountering men of power and significance.

The cardinal came closer, his piercing gaze fixed on Aldo. 'So you're investigating the murder of this moneylender? Good. Then we may yet find out what happened.'

'We?'

Cibo stroked his greying beard. 'Those I represent are eager to see Florence flourish, and this city relies on men like Levi to keep its business flowing.'

'Indeed.' Aldo noted the cardinal's evasion, and that Cibo knew the dead man's name. 'I haven't seen your cousin much lately. How is he?'

Cibo's eyes narrowed. A distant relative had disgraced himself the previous summer, and only a timely intervention by Aldo prevented the matter becoming a far greater scandal. 'Much happier now that he's living with his sister in Massa Carrara, thank you.'

A courtier appeared from the archway where Cibo had been, beckoning for Aldo. 'It seems His Grace is ready for me now.'

But the cardinal raised a hand to stop Aldo leaving. 'I wonder, might you be able to provide me with news of this matter? A brief report in writing will suffice.'

'My first duty is to the Duke, and to the Otto.'

'Yes, of course,' Cibo agreed. 'Nonetheless, a daily summary would be appreciated.'

Aldo nodded his acquiescence. Better to placate an ally than needlessly make a foe. But why was the Emperor's representative so interested? Did Cibo simply crave knowledge, or was there another motive? 'If you'll excuse me, I must share what I know with His Grace.'

Aldo was ushered up stone stairs to the palazzo's middle level, where the corridors were adorned with ever more ornate tapestries and statues. The courtier introduced himself as Francesco Campana, administrative *segretario* to the Duke. Aldo had heard of Campana, but never encountered him before. He was said to have the Duke's ear, guiding Alessandro and helping to mitigate rumoured excesses. Campana knocked on a pair of richly decorated doors.

'Come!' a male voice called.

Aldo entered alone, Campana closing the doors behind him. Two guards stood within on either side of the entrance. Too many Medici had been targets for enemy blades in the past. Even here, inside his own palazzo, Alessandro liked to have guards close at hand. Aldo crossed the marble floor to stand before an imposing desk, his gaze lowered.

'Ahh, you must be the officer Bindi has looking into the murder of this Jew.'

'Cesare Aldo, at your service.'

Having been spoken to, Aldo could raise his eyes. Duke Alessandro was as dark skinned as people said, with thick curly hair and a prominent nose. It appeared the rumours about his parentage were true. The Duke wore a metal breastplate for protection, but his black satin sleeves displayed the finest of embroidery. He lounged in an ornate chair behind the desk, one leg draped over an armrest, his confident eyes studying Aldo. Everything about the Duke confirmed his authority. Aldo had at least ten summers in age and experience more than Alessandro, but there could be no doubting who was in charge here.

The Duke waved a hand. 'Your report.'

Aldo offered a brisk summary – where and when the murder had taken place, along with the apparent means. 'Most likely it was a trained killer, or a hired blade. The person who did this may have already escaped the city, but I believe whoever paid them lives here in Florence. Discovering who, that is, their identity, is my next task.'

'You have suspicions?'

Aldo kept his face expressionless. 'Levi's main rivals both had reason, as did his daughter. His debtors may have cause – but whether they possess the means is unknown.'

The Duke nodded his understanding. 'Could this killing be linked in some way to the attacks on moneylenders at the Mercato Nuovo last summer?'

'It's possible,' Aldo replied, 'but I do not believe it likely. Those incidents were the work of surly debtors, too drunk to know better, and too stupid to avoid arrest. This murder required skill and cunning. And of the two men we arrested last year, one has since drowned after falling into the Arno while drunk, and the other hung himself to escape his debts.'

The doors opened behind him, but Aldo stayed facing forwards. Turning away from the Duke would be a sign of disrespect. The doors closed again and a thin, pale figure strolled past to stand beside Alessandro. There was a familiarity between the two men, yet something subservient – even craven – about the new arrival.

'Lorenzino, where have you been?' the Duke said. 'Now our visitor will have to repeat everything he's just told us. You don't mind, do you?'

'Of course not,' Aldo lied. His second summary was even brisker than the first, and Lorenzino showed little interest until it ended.

'How long?' he asked. 'How long until you know who killed this Jew?'

'I can't be certain,' Aldo admitted. A fire in the hearth kept the room warm. Yes, that must be why beads of sweat were soaking into the collar of his tunic.

'That isn't good enough.' Alessandro stood, his mood darkening. '*Segretario* Bindi assured us you were the best officer for the job. We want this killer found. If you cannot do it, we will hold both you and the Otto responsible. You'll report to us every evening before curfew until this matter is concluded to our satisfaction.'

Aldo nodded. Levi's murder was fast becoming a curse for those touched by it. Lorenzino leaned close to the Duke, whispering in his ear.

Alessandro's smile returned. 'Well said, cousin – please, share your suggestion.'

A thin smile twisted Lorenzino's lips. 'The commander of the Duke's guard is out of the city at present, but Captain Vitelli is due back from his country estate after the feast of Epiphany. If the Otto and its officers are unable to bring the killer to justice by then, Vitelli and his men shall take over.' He paused. 'So, you have until Saturday to solve this murder.'

Biting back an unwise reply, Aldo bowed to the Duke. 'It will be my pleasure.'

'Very well,' Alessandro said, settling back into his chair. 'You'd best get started.'

Aldo marched to the doors and let himself out. Four days. Four days to find an unknown killer who was likely long gone from the city. It was impossible.

Chapter Nine

Wednesday, January 3rd

*M*assimo Bindi believed in Florence. The city was home, and he was its humble servant. At times Florence stumbled beneath the influence of those who did not have its best interests at heart. Mad monks that held sway over the people and their fearful souls. Wilful men clouding minds with talk of a republic where all might be equal. Guilds and merchants battling for financial supremacy. Armies fighting for territory. Kings and cardinals grappling for control.

But Florence endured, thriving when times were good and surviving when life was not. Some said it was a beacon of beauty and artistry in a world full of conflict and doubt. Bindi cared little for such notions. All the sculptures and frescos would crumble to dust in time. It was the city's system of justice that made Florence great.

The *segretario* waddled into the Podestà not long after curfew lifted. Days were short in winter, leaving little time to achieve all that must be done. Even when the Otto was not sitting, swift and purposeful justice did not remain idle. Legal papers still had to be prepared, and a vigilant eye maintained on any outstanding matters. The rule requiring new magistrates be installed thrice a year – intended to stop anyone abusing the power of the Otto –

made preparedness even more important. How else could the court's functionaries guide the Otto towards a correct decision in matters that might otherwise be ill-judged?

Duke Alessandro's morning briefing was another reason to start early. Recalling what had happened on Monday still brought Bindi a blush of shame and anger. That was bad enough, but now a mere officer was reporting to the Duke about matters arising from the moneylender's murder – a flagrant breach of established protocols! It had been pointed out to His Grace that granting a daily audience to the likes of Aldo was highly irregular, but Alessandro was not to be gainsaid in the matter. His wishes must come first, as the Duke had pointed out. No matter how vexing they might be, nor what further humiliation they might cause. So be it.

Bindi stalked into his *officio*, slamming the door behind him. A pox on all those who achieved power not through a lifetime of hard work and endeavour, but by the mere accident of whoever happened to be their father. That a half-Moorish *bastardo* like Alessandro could command such a glorious city by whim and caprice – it rankled. It rankled.

But so be it.

Someone was knocking at the door. Bindi lowered himself into the sturdy, high-backed chair behind his desk before replying: 'Come!'

Aldo entered, closing the door after himself. 'You needed to see me, *segretario*?'

'Indeed.' Bindi beckoned him closer. Aldo was different from most who served the Otto. The majority were brutes, all too eager to enjoy whatever petty power the role offered, thieves ready to snatch up rewards and bribes at any opportunity. Aldo took his due, but no more. He bent the law, but never broke it – or hid such things well, if he did.

Aldo had something of a hunting dog about him – lean, sinewy, ready for action. Most of the men under Bindi's control had wives, and some kept a mistress. But not Aldo: he slept in a *bordello*. Despite that, he was literate, had proven himself a shrewd judge of character and was certainly no man's fool. In short, Aldo was one of the best officers serving the Otto.

Bindi would have deemed Aldo a threat had he displayed the slightest hint of ambition. The fact Aldo showed none made him all the more suspect.

Most men became uncomfortable when made to wait. They would volunteer answers for unasked questions, eager to babble out secrets or confess their guilt. But Aldo remained quite still, revealing nothing and watching everything. It was beyond insolence.

'Tell me what you shared with the Duke last night,' Bindi snapped.

Aldo's response was unsatisfying: much had been done, but few answers found.

'And what didn't you tell His Grace?'

Aldo rubbed a hand across his greying stubble. 'Sir?'

'You gave him the facts you could prove. Now tell me what you suspect.'

Aldo frowned for several moments before replying. 'If the killer's still in Florence, we'll need some luck to find him. But it seems likely that whoever hired the killer lives here. Guilt or pressure should force them into the open.'

That could take days. Bindi sighed. 'You'll continue giving His Grace a report each evening, but I expect your full report first thing the next morning – what you can prove, and what you can't. Should anything significant arise, you will tell me first. Understand?'

Aldo nodded. 'The Duke has given the Otto until Epiphany to find the killer. If we fail, the matter will be handed over to Captain Vitelli and the Duke's guard.'

The *segretario* struggled to keep hold of his temper. Taking a murder investigation away from the Otto was an outrage, an affront to the court's authority. Worse still, it would create a dangerous precedent. That could not be allowed to happen. 'What do you need?'

'Another officer would help. Cerchi, perhaps?'

Bindi snorted with disbelief. Cerchi and Aldo's mutual loathing was notorious. This must be a *stratagemma* of some sort. 'Take a constable.'

'What about Strocchi? He shows promise.'

'You can have Benedetto.'

The sour response on Aldo's face was quite exquisite.

Aldo marched down the Podestà staircase, still fuming. Asking for Cerchi directly had been a mistake. The *segretario* might enjoy forcing the two officers to work together, knowing how much they disliked each other, but only if it was his idea. Aldo cursed himself for not being more artful. Spending a day with Cerchi would have been worth it to prevent that *bastardo* extorting coin from Corsini's visitors. For all his flaws, Cerchi was no fool. Soon enough he would realize those men could name others like themselves. Eventually, inevitably, one of them would mention knowing an officer of the Otto. Cerchi's hunger for having coin in his hand would delay that day, but not forever. Aldo had to get Corsini's diary and the list Strocchi had made away from Cerchi first.

The prospect of having to work with a raw recruit like Benedetto wasn't helping Aldo's mood. The young constable was likely to be a hindrance more than anything else, but the *segretario* did love his petty victories. Aldo spied Cerchi lurking inside the front gates. Waiting for another blackmail target, perhaps. 'Made any progress with the Corsini killing?' Aldo asked as he reached the bottom step.

'What's it to you?' Cerchi snapped, face full of disdain.

Aldo feigned a smile. 'Nothing. I just don't like losing a decent informer.'

'There was nothing decent about that pervert.'

A prudent man would walk away, instead of rising to the bait. 'A poor choice of words on my part,' Aldo agreed. 'I was thinking about what you asked yesterday. Corsini once said some of his clients could get violent. If you think one of them is the killer . . .'

'Keep your thoughts to yourself,' Cerchi replied. 'The last thing I need is your help.' He stalked away, crossing the courtyard and going into the small chamber off the cloisters where officers stored their cloaks and weapons. As the heavy wooden door slammed shut behind Cerchi, Benedetto strolled in through the Podestà gates, rubbing sleep from his eyes.

'You're helping me today,' Aldo told the weary constable, striding past him and out through the gates. 'Try to keep up.'

Aldo headed south from the Podestà, Benedetto scampering along beside him. 'I've been with the Otto since the end of November,' the constable volunteered. 'Mamma thought it'd be good for me. She says I ask too many questions.'

'Anyone can ask questions. Listening to the answers is what matters.'

'Of course.'

'Not just what people say, but what they don't. Their sins of omission.' Aldo jagged left along a dark, narrow street. Buildings rose on either side, the upper levels jutting out so only a sliver of grey sky was visible overhead. The weather was turning. No snow yet, but the air had a crisp bite. Aldo avoided the dung outside a stable, but Benedetto was not so quick. 'How people stand tells you a lot. Folded arms often show they've something to hide.'

'I see,' Benedetto said, hopping on one foot and shaking dung from the other.

'When we get to via dei Giudei, watch and listen. Understand?' Aldo turned right.

'Yes,' the constable replied, just about keeping pace. 'Can I ask a question?'

Aldo nodded.

'We're heading towards Santa Croce. Aren't most Jews south of the river?'

Perhaps this constable wasn't so empty-headed as he looked. 'I need to meet an informant first. They won't talk near strangers. Stay here, I'll be back soon.'

Leaving the constable to scrape his boot on a doorstep, Aldo went on another three streets to Renato's workroom. He deserved to be warned about Cerchi, what the *bastardo* was capable of doing. But when Aldo reached the workroom all the staff were gossiping outside. A fabric cutter said Renato had set everyone to work before going out earlier. Nobody knew when he'd be back, but they weren't expecting him soon. The warning would have to wait.

Strocchi found his third church visit of the morning as frustrating as the first two. Nobody recalled anyone like Corsini. Didn't the constable realize how many masses there were between Christmas and Epiphany? No, the cloth from the courtesan's dress did not look familiar. And the church certainly did not allow courtesans within its walls. The idea was repugnant.

Strocchi didn't bother with polite questions at Santa Croce. Instead he cornered a young priest in a side chapel, demanding answers. It was well known that courtesans used church services to attract men – why else make women without families sit on one side of a curtain? The priest kept glancing at a sour-faced, grey-haired woman praying nearby. 'Please, you shouldn't speak of such things here.'

Strocchi refused to match the hushed whisper. 'Did you notice any new faces among the courtesans at mass on Sunday?'

'I don't pay them any attention.'

'So you admit they were here.'

'Please, I have duties to attend to.'

'And I'm trying to find out who beat a young man to death.' Strocchi brandished the handful of fabric. 'Have you seen anyone wearing a dress made of this?'

The priest peered at it, shook his head. 'I'm sorry, truly I am.'

Strocchi let him go, despairing at the unwillingness to help. Where was the sympathy for those struggling with sinful lives? When did conviction usurp compassion or forgiveness?

The constable caught sight of his angry reflection in a window. Holy Madonna, what was this city doing to him? Bullying a young priest, that was worthy of Cerchi. No matter the righteousness of the questions, there had to be a better way of finding the answers. Strocchi knelt down to pray for guidance. A reply came sooner than he expected.

'You wanting a courtesan?' a hoarse voice whispered. Strocchi looked round. The only person nearby was the woman in the pew, her head still bowed. 'I said, you wanting a courtesan?' Her face lifted to meet Strocchi's gaze.

'No,' he replied. 'Not the way you mean.'

'All men think that, until they spend a few hours with my mistress.'

Strocchi went to the pew, leaning over it to correct her. 'I'm investigating a murder. A courtesan was beaten to death. Finding the killers is all I care about.'

The maid shrugged. 'Whatever you say.' She rose to leave, crossing herself.

'Wait. Were you here on Sunday with your . . . mistress?'

'We're here most Sundays. Why?'

Strocchi showed the fabric. 'Have you seen this before?' Her eyes widened. Strocchi moved round the pew to question the maid further, but two priests were stalking towards them – the young one from earlier, and an older, more senior figure.

'What's your name?' the older priest demanded of Strocchi.

'Find me outside,' the maid whispered before scurrying away.

After several minutes of being berated by the older priest, Strocchi was surprised to find the maid still waiting outside. 'The cloth I showed you, where'd you seen it before?'

The maid tilted her head at the church. 'Here, on Sunday. There was a new courtesan wearing a dress like that. Caused quite a stir.'

'What did this newcomer look like?'

'Only saw her from behind. Maids stay at the back.'

'Could your mistress describe the new courtesan?'

A shrug.

'Where is she?'

'Courtesans don't appear before noon, except on Sundays. She'll be gossiping with the others at Piazza San Lorenzo this afternoon, if the weather holds.'

Strocchi nodded his thanks. The maid held out an empty palm. Informants expected payment, even from constables. He dug in his tunic and found two silver *giuli*. The maid glared at the coins, but took them anyway.

Chapter Ten

*A*ldo hesitated outside the first doorway on via dei Giudei, Benedetto at his side. It'd be another frustrating day if Dante hadn't made good on that promise. Aldo banged on the door. Eventually it opened to reveal a hunched old man, his long beard thick with silver and grey.

'I'm Cesare Aldo, an officer of the Otto di Guardia e Balia, investigating the murder of Samuele Levi.' No reply. 'He was killed the night before last, just along this street.' The old man peered at the Levi house, the effort creasing his face. 'Did you see anything strange on Monday? Anyone you didn't recognize?'

Still no reply; did he even understand what was being said?

'We need help,' Aldo persisted. 'Unless you and your neighbours tell us what you saw, whoever murdered Levi will escape justice. Is that what you want?'

The old man glanced at Benedetto before reaching for the door.

'This is important,' Aldo said, but the door was already swinging shut. He shoved a boot against it, betting his resolve was stronger than the old man's push. 'Malachi Dante, he talked to you, yes? Dante promised you would help us.'

The old man stopped pushing the door. 'Dante?'

'That's right.'

'He's a good man.'

'So I hear,' Aldo agreed. 'What can you tell us about Samuele Levi?'

The old man – Moise Bassano – didn't have much to say. Levi was ruthless, even by Florentine standards. Dante had been a moderating influence; after he was forced out, Levi doubled rates to squeeze every last *giulio* from his debtors.

Bassano had more sympathy for Rebecca – a beautiful young woman with a kind heart, the image of her poor mother. How that child ever sprang from the loins of such a grasping, unhappy man was a mystery. Perhaps she was put on this earth to temper her father; but if so, it hadn't worked. The world would be a better place without Samuele Levi, and few Jews on the street would disagree with that.

Aldo nodded, encouraging the old man to keep talking. 'What about his debtors? We've heard Levi was lending to outsiders, strangers.'

A shrug. Bassano paid little attention to such comings and goings, due to his failing eyesight. Everything was becoming a blur, fading away from him. To have lived this long in such a world was a curse. But it was the way of things.

Aldo thanked the old man. 'Does anyone else live in your building?'

'No, my Marietta is long gone, and we were never blessed with children. Try Doctor Orvieto next door. He looked after me all of Monday night. That poor man has no rest from his patients, no rest at all.' Bassano retreated inside, closing his door – gently, this time.

'Levi's neighbours are talking,' Aldo said, allowing himself a smile. 'Now we have a chance.' He led Benedetto to the next house. A Hebrew inscription was carved into the wood, the name Orvieto below it. The door swung open before they could knock, a keen-eyed man with a stained apron and crimson hands emerging from the dark, a bloody knife in his grasp.

'You must be from the Otto,' he said, switching the knife to his left hand before offering his right to Aldo. 'I'm Doctor Orvieto.' Realizing the hand was still wet with blood, he wiped it on his apron. 'Malachi told us you'd be visiting. Please, come in, come in.' Aldo introduced himself and Benedetto as the doctor ushered them to a large room at the back of the building. It should have been the kitchen; instead it resembled a butcher's shop.

A dead goat lay atop a table in the middle of the room, its torso split open, exposing the internal organs. Orvieto waved his knife at the animal. 'Fascinating to see the insides of different beasts, don't you think? To bear witness to our maker's handiwork.'

Aldo nodded. 'You're examining it?'

'Yes. I have a student with me most days. Taking apart an animal helps teach him the ways of the body before he treats a living patient.'

'I've seen doctors practise their skills on dead swine. They say a pig carcass is close to that of a person in many ways.'

Orvieto smiled, swiping the air with his knife. 'Alas, the teachings of my faith forbid me from touching that animal in particular. Is your colleague unwell?'

Benedetto was swaying at Aldo's side, colour draining from the constable's face. 'So it would seem,' Aldo replied. 'Is there somewhere he can . . .?' The doctor pointed to the back door. Benedetto lurched past the dead animal, one hand clasped across his face. The sound of retching was audible from outside moments later.

Orvieto draped a bloodstained cloth over the goat before washing his hands in a bowl of water. 'You don't seem so bothered.'

'Fight on enough battlefields, you see worse.' Aldo watched the doctor, his brisk movements. Orvieto was tall, with wide shoulders and sinewy arms. His hair was brown with flecks of silver, but his long beard had autumn red in it too. Those strong hands were deft and precise, while his warm hazel eyes held a gleam inside them, a familiarity . . . Aldo pushed the thought aside. He was here for information. 'Was Samuele Levi one of your patients?'

'Everyone on via dei Giudei is my patient. I help families through illness and infirmity, bring their children into the world. And I see many of my neighbours to their rest – including Samuele, and his poor, dear wife.' Orvieto wiped his hands on a clean cloth.

Aldo noticed the doctor looking at him. Was the physician simply appreciating a fellow professional, or was it something else – something more? 'I know your faith has particular traditions when it comes to the end of life. Did you see Samuele's body?' The doctor nodded. 'What did you make of it?'

'Death would have been quick. A single wound from a blade. No hesitation.'

Aldo smiled, despite himself. Orvieto's eyebrows rose in response. 'I don't often get the chance to talk with someone who sees death with such clarity,' Aldo explained. The sound of retching continued outside. 'Most people are more like Benedetto.'

The doctor nodded. 'My student is the same. A strong young man, but ruled by his feelings. I had to send him home; he knows the Levis. To succeed as a physician, you must focus on the body, as much as the person.' Orvieto washed and dried his knife, returning it to a drawer full of blades. Any of them could have been used to slay the moneylender.

Aldo frowned. The doctor had an appealing way about him, but it was worth remembering that everyone was a potential suspect. 'Did you ever borrow from Levi?'

'No,' Orvieto replied, without hesitation. 'That man would squeeze a *giulio* from marble if there was profit in it. You won't find many with a good word for him.'

'So I'm learning. What about his rivals – Dante, and Sciarra?'

'Do I think they could have killed Samuele?' Orvieto stroked his beard. 'Dante is the gentlest of men. I doubt he could harm a spider, let alone a person. As for Sciarra . . .' The doctor paused. 'He's a grasping little man, but I've never seen him wield a weapon of any kind. The way Samuele was slain, that required genuine skill.' Orvieto picked up a short knife, balancing it in his palm. 'May I show you?'

Aldo spread out both arms, inviting an attack. 'Please.'

The doctor approached, blade in hand, until they were close enough to embrace. Looking Aldo in the eyes, Orvieto thrust the knife at his chest. It stopped a hair's breadth from Aldo, the tip sharp and steady. 'This was a close killing. Almost . . . intimate.'

'So I see.'

For a moment there was nothing but the two of them, looking in each other's eyes. Then Benedetto stumbled through the doorway, wiping the back of a hand across his mouth. Orvieto stepped aside, lowering the blade.

'What did I miss?' the constable asked.

'The doctor's been most helpful,' Aldo replied. 'Better?'

Benedetto nodded, though his greenish pallor suggested otherwise.

'Then we should move on.' Aldo ushered the constable towards the hallway, pausing to look back at Orvieto. 'Two last questions. Where were you on Monday night?'

'With Moise Bassano until dawn – he's not a well man.' That confirmed what the old man next door had said. Despite his ease around a blade, there was no obvious way Orvieto could have killed Levi, not while tending to Bassano all Monday night. The doctor arched an eyebrow. 'And what was your other question?'

Aldo smiled. 'Your first name.'

'It's Saul.'

'Pleased to meet you.'

Orvieto nodded, the corners of his mouth curving upwards. 'If you need anything . . .'

'I'll know where to find you.' Aldo urged Benedetto back out to the street. They had dozens more people to question. Everything else had to wait – for now, at least.

Strocchi was doing his best not to be awed. Having been in Florence close to a year, standing inside Palazzo Landini was far from his first time inside a rich merchant's home. But the grandeur still impressed him. Back home, only the church had a staircase. Palazzo Landini had three levels, with servants bustling between them. This grand residence might not be far from the glowering presence of the city's prison, but inside the palazzo was a world away from the squalid degradations of Le Stinche.

A haughty woman swept towards Strocchi, her face full of steely resolve. 'I'm Pasqua Landini,' she announced. 'I hear you wish to speak with Agnolotti.'

'Yes, signora. It's about the murder of a young man—'

'How much?' Pasqua demanded.

'I'm sorry?'

'How much for you to go away?' She snapped her fingers twice and a servant appeared, clutching a pouch heavy with coin. 'Well?'

Strocchi stepped backwards. 'I didn't come for money, signora. I'm a constable with the Otto. I simply wish to ask your husband some questions.'

Her eyes narrowed. 'You're not here on behalf of that repulsive officer?'

So Cerchi was using Corsini's murder to extort money. Strocchi fought back the urge to curse. 'No, signora. I'm not like him.'

'I see.' Pursing her lips, Pasqua dismissed the servant. 'Sorry, but my husband cannot answer your questions. He's at church, seeking forgiveness for his sins. His many sins.' She stalked away, pausing to glance back at Strocchi. 'And before you ask, no, I do not know which church Agnolotti has gone to. Frankly, it would be better if he never returned.'

Aldo let Benedetto talk to the family in the next house. The recruit was nervous, but effective enough. Aldo directed Benedetto to talk to those on the side of the street opposite the Levi house, while he took the other side. 'If you find someone who saw any strangers on Monday, come and fetch me. If you discover any witnesses to Levi's murder, bring them to me.'

Benedetto went away with his chest puffed out, full of pride. That wouldn't take long to wear down, but for now it made him useful.

The homes on Aldo's half of the street brought few surprises. Yes, everyone knew Levi – or knew of him, at least. An embarrassed couple admitted borrowing money from the dead man, but could prove where they were observing the curfew the night he was slain. Most professed sympathy for Rebecca, but none had a good word for her father.

A goldsmith called Volterra lived next to the Levis. He recalled seeing outsiders come and go. There had never been more than two at a time. Were they always the same men? That was hard to tell. They hid their faces behind hoods. But one of them was rich, judging by the quality of his cloak. Volterra recalled hearing the men argue with Levi. It sounded as if the moneylender was trying to back out of a loan. The goldsmith thought he might recognize the rich man's cloak, if he saw it again – but couldn't be sure.

Aldo moved on to Levi's rival Sciarra, hammering at the door until the moneylender came to an upstairs window. 'We're asking if anyone saw strangers the day of Levi's killing.'

'I told you all I know,' Sciarra spat.

Curse this man and his obstinacy. 'You said nothing but riddles. Come down here.'

'Not for the likes of you.' Sciarra held up an arm, swathed in bandages. 'Yedaiah will hear about your methods.'

'Yedaiah only has authority to deal with Jewish disputes. Besides, he's away visiting his ailing sister.'

'Then I'll report your brutality to the Otto, tell the magistrates how you treat people!'

Sciarra obviously knew nothing of the court's interrogation methods. It was useless arguing with this fool. Sciarra was full of piss and bluster, but lacked the *palle* to kill another man. That didn't mean he was beyond hiring someone to do it, but—

'Captain Aldo!' Benedetto waved from a house opposite the Levis' front door. He had a stout old woman beside him, her sour features framed by a headscarf.

Aldo strolled towards them. 'I'm an officer, Benedetto. The Otto only has one captain, Duro. He commands the guards at Le Stinche – and is a lot less forgiving than me.'

The constable gestured at the old woman. 'This signora found the body. She's the one who summoned the night patrol.'

At last – a witness who might actually have seen something. Aldo quickened his pace, eager to question the woman. But a male figure lurking at the northern end of the street caught Aldo's eye.

The man resembled the ringleader of the bandits who had tried to kill Levi. Aldo gave Benedetto brisk instructions as he passed the constable – take the witness inside and stay with her, no matter what happened. Do it now.

The man was still at the end of the street, looking at his surroundings as if lost. Florence was a labyrinth for those who didn't know it well. The Duomo and the Arno were helpful landmarks, but often hidden from view among the narrow streets and close buildings.

Aldo continued towards the lithe figure, careful not to catch his eye. The man turned to face via dei Giudei, revealing a scar down one cheek. It was him! Aldo pushed by a girl carrying salted fish from the stalls near Ponte Vecchio. She spat a curse, drawing the bandit's attention. He saw Aldo, their eyes locking for a moment.

Then the bandit bolted.

Chapter Eleven

*A*ldo raced after the bandit, ignoring the pain in his knee. By the time he reached Borgo San Jacopo, the bandit was running hard for Ponte Vecchio. But the approach to the bridge was choked with sellers hawking poultry, fish and produce to potential buyers, all of them arguing about prices. The aroma of fresh bread filled Aldo's nostrils as he passed a baker. In the next doorway three youths were playing dice, pushing and shoving at each other, shouting to be heard over the babble of voices. Ahead the bandit had to swerve round a trader holding live chickens high in the air, one in each fist, proclaiming their price a bargain. The birds clucked and protested, flapping their wings, feathers fluttering down.

Aldo got within eight paces of the bandit before the throng closed in around him too. A leering hawker lurched in front of him, proudly displaying a length of brocade. 'Something for your wife, sir? Take this cloth to a dressmaker and once your wife sees the results, you will be making babies together that same night?' Aldo pushed him aside with a stiff arm and a curse so harsh it made the hawker's eyes widen in shock.

The bandit glanced back, and Aldo could see panic in his quarry's eyes. Good, now the *bastardo* knew how it felt to be stalked. The bandit shoved his way through a circle of young men watching two of them compete at *civettino*, the game known as little owl. The two contestants were in the middle of the ring, deflecting each other's playful kicks and punches. The bandit charged between them, his shoulder colliding with one of the contestants, sending the youth sprawling on the muddy, *merda*-strewn street. Those watching cried out in protest but the bandit kept going. An old man leaning on a wooden crutch stopped to look and a shove from the bandit sent the cripple tumbling into a display of wizened lemons, collapsing the stall. A cascade of people moved to help the cripple, while others helped themselves to the fruit. The crowd parted and the bandit was free again, running for the bridge.

Aldo snarled at those in his way to step aside. The bandit had to be stopped before he crossed Ponte Vecchio. Once north of the river, it would be much easier for him to disappear. Aldo hurdled the fallen cripple, narrowly avoiding the head of an eager woman stooping over to gather the rolling lemons into her apron. She hurled abuse and a rock-hard lemon at Aldo, the fruit striking him in the back. He hurried on, ignoring the stream of insults.

Up ahead the bandit looked over his shoulder again – and ran straight into a heavy carcass balancing atop a butcher's shoulder. The bandit staggered back before lurching on, but the impact had stolen his momentum. Aldo was only a few steps behind him as the bandit recovered, lurching towards the southern end of Ponte Vecchio. The bandit lashed out with a boot as he passed a stall hugging the corner. His well-aimed kick upset the display of fish so they went spilling across the cobbles marking the start of the bridge, a slither of silver scales and crimson guts spreading in front of Aldo. One leap to clear the mess and—

Aldo came thudding down on the road, his shoulder crashing into the stones, legs and arms flailing. People were laughing and pointing, some of them close to tears of glee. He must look an utter fool, sprawling in fish guts. Aldo tried to get back up, sharp pain stabbing through his good knee. The fish seller was yelling at him, demanding to know who'd pay for these losses? Aldo dug in his pouch and threw two coins on the cobbles before stumbling onwards, up the rising slope of the bridge.

But by the time Aldo had staggered to the highest point on Ponte Vecchio, the bandit was gone, vanished into the restless sea of faces that filled the bridge during daylight. *Palle!*

Aldo limped back the way he'd come. Why was the bandit in Florence? His actions in the hills proved the man was no fool. If he had held the blade that killed Levi, the bandit would have left the city as soon as its gates opened the next morning. Coming to via dei Giudei two days later made no sense. Yes, the skill of the murder did suggest the work of a professional. But Levi was killed after dark, in a close-knit part of the city. Levi knew whoever stabbed him, or else he wouldn't have let them into his home. The bandit preyed on easy targets along high mountain roads – not wary Jews in an unfamiliar city.

Aldo stopped at the end of via dei Giudei, recalling the ambush in the hills. The bandit with the musket had told the other two that Levi was dead. Aldo only discovered Levi was still alive after the ringleader had retreated. Of course! The bandit had come to the city for his payment, believing he and his men had killed their target. That meant whoever hired them to murder Levi lived close by. Catch the bandit and his client's name would soon follow.

The stench of raw fish invaded Aldo's nostrils. His hose was stained with blood, guts and scales. It was enough to turn the stomach if he'd eaten anything since dawn, but there wasn't time to solve either problem now. The bandit was still in Florence, unfamiliar territory, it seemed. Quick action could ensure he stayed in the city.

Benedetto was in the doorway opposite the Levi home. 'Why did you run off?'

Aldo ignored the question. 'Is the witness inside?'

'Yes.'

'Good, I'll talk to her. Do you know your way to the north gate?'

'Of course.'

'Get there, fast as you can. There's a killer in the city, a fugitive. I need you to check everyone leaving through Porta San Gallo.' Aldo described the scar-faced bandit, making Benedetto repeat the words twice. 'Tell the guards to warn other gates in case he doesn't head north. He mustn't get out of Florence.'

The constable nodded. 'What if he comes to Porta San Gallo?'

'Have the guards hold him, and then find me. No, you stay there – send a messenger to find me. Now, go. Go!'

Benedetto dashed away. Aldo leaned against the door, his good knee throbbing with pain. Another visit to Dr Orvieto might be needed, perhaps some strapping round the knee or a massage. Tempting, but talking to the witness was more urgent.

The stout old woman was in the warm kitchen at the back of her home, feeding a black cat. She scowled when Aldo introduced himself.

'Rebecca Levi asked me to find who killed her father, Signora . . . ?'

'Galletti – Elena Galletti.' She reached down to stroke the cat's back, but her piercing gaze never left Aldo.

'How well do you know the Levis?'

'The wife, she was a beauty, but Samuele is – was – an ugly man. In spirit, at least.'

'It seems likely he was killed after curfew. Did you see anyone enter or leave after dark?'

A shake of the head; she wasn't going to make this easy.

'What about earlier?'

'I heard them arguing.'

'Who?'

'Rebecca and her father – they've been arguing a lot lately. I saw her leave, but didn't hear her return. I sleep back here.' She nodded to a narrow bed in a corner.

'Did you see anyone else?'

'Malachi Dante arrived just after Rebecca left. He didn't stay long.' The cat crossed the stone floor to sniff at Aldo's ankles. 'She likes you.'

'She likes the fish on my hose,' he admitted. 'I slipped by a stall on Ponte Vecchio.' That brought a smile to the old woman's face. 'How was it you saw the body after dark?'

Galletti called to the cat, summoning it back. 'I was putting her out. She likes to roam after dark. I saw the Levis' door open, a lantern lit inside. I went across, looked in . . .' Her eyes widened. 'He was lying on the rug. I could tell he was dead. The night patrol was passing the end of the street, so I called to them.'

'Did you see a knife?'

She shook her head. 'But I didn't go inside.'

It'd been too much to hope she had seen more than the night patrol had reported, but still worth asking. Aldo thanked her as she showed him out. He paused on the step. 'Did you go to Samuele's funeral?'

Galletti frowned. 'I had no tears to shed for that man. But we are all taking turns to sit *shiva* with Rebecca. She needs her people around her now.'

'Is Rebecca's cousin with her – Ruth?'

'No. It's a long way from Bologna.' Galletti shut the door, but her words lingered. Aldo cursed himself for not realizing the truth sooner. He had first met Levi in Bologna, at the home of his brother Shimon. Rebecca's cousin Ruth must be Shimon's daughter. So Rebecca had lied about where she spent the night Levi was killed. What else was she hiding?

Venus waited until well after noon before venturing out to Piazza San Lorenzo. It was important to see and be seen, but few women looked their best in the harsh light of January, and a courtesan must always look her best to attract the right kind of men. She was not a common *puttano*, available to be used and cast aside. She was a woman of refinement, able to excite and sustain a conversation as skilfully as she did any *cazzo*. A selection of regular visitors was her goal. Catching their eye required care and attention to every moment, every possibility.

Most women seen on the streets of Florence were maids, servants or those who worked in the *mercato*. The wives and daughters of wealthier men were expected to stay at home, or in a convent. Courtesans need pay no heed to such expectations.

Yes, they did have to dress as if married or widowed, but that was a necessary ruse to cheat laws enforced by the Office of Decency. Common *puttane* had to register with that court, stating where they lived and where they worked. But its officers were no match for the cunning and guile of true courtesans. An outward show of respectability – not to mention the occasional bribe – was enough to avoid such strictures. And when it came to bindings and constraints, Venus always preferred to be the one tying the knots.

She glided into the piazza, her maid a few paces behind. Other courtesans went in pairs while parading beside the Basilica di San

Lorenzo, but Venus hunted alone – after all, why risk the competition? Besides, the idle gossip of other women bored her. The conversation of men was far more enlightening, and rewarding.

Venus was on her second slow circuit when she noticed the young man watching her. His interest seemed intense, though he was far younger than her usual – it was doubtful he'd seen twenty-five summers. His face was new to her, bearing no likeness to any of the prominent merchant families. His robes did not promise much either, but he was tall and held himself with a quiet strength of character and purpose. If this newcomer was seeking a courtesan, the woman who took him home could be in for quite a time.

Venus gave him a warm smile, testing the water. He strode towards her, making no attempt to hide his interest. But as he approached, so did that plump-hipped *fica* Bella! She possessed all the subtlety of marble – before a sculptor had worked on it. Before Venus could tell her rival to fornicate away, the young man addressed them both.

'Excuse me, ladies, my name is Carlo Strocchi.'

'A pleasure to meet you,' Bella replied quickly, offering a hand for him to kiss. He ignored it, instead clasping his own hands behind his back. A man of taste, it seemed.

'I'm a constable with the Otto di Guardia e Balia,' he continued.

Oh, a minor court official. How disappointing. Venus didn't bother keeping the disdain from her face. At least he wasn't a troublemaker from the Office of Decency, hoping for a bribe. But the longer he occupied her time, the less chance she had of attracting a suitable male. 'And?'

Venus gave the briefest of answers when the constable asked stumbling questions about another courtesan. Never admit, never apologize, and never explain was always wisest. But she couldn't hold her tongue when he pulled a handful of familiar dress fabric from his tunic. 'That cunning little vixen! She stole my seat on Sunday, and my best prospect.'

'Your prospect?' Bella laughed, loud enough to send pigeons flying. 'Biagio Seta was never yours, my dear. You had your eye on him and she got there first.'

Venus rolled her eyes. 'Don't pretend you had no plans for him.'

'What if I did? Some of us can still attract men with all their own hair.'

Annoyingly, the constable stepped between them before Venus could use her nails on Bella. 'Ladies, please! Whatever your disagreements, they must wait.' Venus refused to respond before her rival. Eventually Bella shrugged her assent, and Venus gave a nod of agreement. 'Now, could you describe this new courtesan?'

'Young,' Bella said, always too eager to please.

'Very young,' Venus clarified.

'Even younger than me,' Bella added. The *cagna*.

The constable nodded his understanding. 'What about . . . the face?'

'It was hard to see,' Venus replied, noting the way he was carefully choosing his words.

'Hidden behind a veil,' Bella added, motioning with her hands.

'She was delicate, and quite pretty – in an unusual way. Called herself Dolce Gallo.'

The constable's face reddened. 'It seems that "she" was actually a "he". Your rival on Sunday was actually a young man called Luca Corsini.'

Bella gasped at this, but it was little surprise to anyone who'd been paying attention. 'No wonder,' Venus said. 'I've been after Seta for a while, but he didn't seem interested.'

'Worried about losing your appeal?' Bella asked, with a smirk. 'Bit late for that.'

'Biagio preferring the taste of *cazzo* to a real woman explains a lot,' Venus continued, ignoring the remark. 'It's hard enough attracting the right kind of men without boys dressing up as girls to steal away the best men.'

'What happened to this Corsini?' Bella asked, the first sensible thing she'd said.

'He was beaten to death,' Strocchi replied. Venus crossed herself, muttering a prayer. But the constable wasn't finished yet. 'You say Corsini caught the eye of a man called Seta?'

Venus sighed. 'Biagio Seta – his family are silk merchants. They have a palazzo near Santa Croce. But you can't think that he beat anyone to death? Biagio is a big baby, afraid of his shadow. The older brother Alessio was the real power in that family, before he fell ill.'

Bella nodded. 'There's as much chance of Biagio killing a man as there is of Venus welcoming Duke Alessandro to her bedchamber.'

Venus feigned a smile. 'My darling, you really must learn to hold that tongue.'

'At least my tongue is still capable of arousing a man.'

'Not from what I hear.' The constable slipped away while Bella protested. Let him go. With no men around worth catching, there was still fun to be had vexing her.

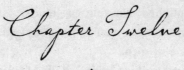

Chapter Twelve

$\mathcal{A}$ ldo went to the *bordello* for a change of hose before returning to via dei Giudei, hoping it would lessen the aroma around him. Bad enough to call on Rebecca Levi while she was sitting *shiva* for her father – to do so stinking of fish would only add further insult. The handsome young Jewish man who had been taking Rebecca to her father's funeral answered the door.

'I'm Cesare Aldo, an officer of the Otto, investigating Samuele Levi's murder.'

The young man glanced over his shoulder. Rebecca was sitting cross-legged on the floor inside, rocking back and forth. Comforting her were several young women, all bearing a strong resemblance to the young man. 'Please,' he said. 'She buried her father yesterday.'

The floor had been scrubbed clean, Aldo noted. 'I must speak with her.'

The young man pulled on a pair of boots before stepping outside, closing the door behind him. 'She is sitting *shiva*. This is private. You've no right to come here.'

'I have every right. Rebecca was the person that asked me to find whoever murdered her father.' Not strictly true, but close enough. 'I have an official duty, too. The Duke of Florence has ordered me to see justice is done here.'

'I understand, but Rebecca – she blames herself for Samuele's death.'

Had the daughter murdered her father? Was she ready to confess?

The young man leaned closer. 'Rebecca wasn't at home the night Samuele died. She seems to believe he might still be alive, if she'd stayed with him.'

'Or she might be dead too.'

'That's what I keep telling her, but she won't listen.'

Aldo nodded. 'Sorry, I don't know your name.'

'Joshua Forzoni. I'm learning to be a physician with Dr Orvieto.'

So this was the doctor's student – strong as well as handsome. Perhaps Joshua was more than Orvieto's student? No, there was nothing about the young man to suggest that – and his concern for Rebecca seemed far more than brotherly.

'I met Orvieto, he told me you were most upset about what's happened.'

'We all are,' Joshua said, his eyes cast down. 'My sisters have been friends with Rebecca since they were girls. They're inside with her now.'

But there was more to it than that for Joshua, wasn't there? The nervous look over his shoulder, the way he spoke about Rebecca. He loved her.

'It's good she has friends to comfort her,' Aldo agreed. 'Samuele wasn't the kindest of fathers, from what I've heard.' The young man hesitated before nodding. 'I wish this wasn't necessary, but I must speak with Rebecca.'

Joshua finally gave way. 'I'll fetch her. But please, be gentle.'

Aldo watched Joshua return inside, slipping off his boots. There was a dark stain on the leather at the toe end of one, and a larger, crescent-shaped stain under the sole. But before Aldo could go closer to examine it, Rebecca was coming to the door. 'You needed to see me?'

Aldo nodded. 'You mentioned arguing with your father the

night he died. You told me that you stayed with your cousin Ruth afterwards.'

'Did I?' She hesitated, eyes darting to one side. No doubt realizing her lie had been discovered. 'Sorry, I-I was confused. It must have been the shock. My cousin Ruth lives in Bologna, with my uncle. Father often visits them.' She corrected herself. 'Visited them.'

'So where were you the night Samuele was killed?'

A glance back at Joshua, that same nervous look he'd given her earlier. Rebecca stepped outside, pulling the door closed behind her. 'I was with Joshua. I-I spent the night with him.' She couldn't meet Aldo's gaze. 'I'm sorry for lying to you yesterday. I didn't want anyone to know. Father doesn't – didn't – approve.'

Understandable, but she was still hiding something. 'Where does Joshua live? With his sisters, the rest of his family?' She nodded. 'And they're happy for you to spend the night in his bed, even though you're not married?' Rebecca was shivering now, though that could be from standing outside in bare feet. Aldo heard a noise at the door. Someone was listening.

'Who scrubbed the floor inside your home?'

The question made Rebecca blink. 'I-I did.'

'Can't have been easy, getting that clean.'

'No, it wasn't.'

'Especially the marks left by whoever stepped in Samuele's blood.' Rebecca began to reply, but stopped herself. 'If I looked at all the boots inside, what would I find?'

'Enough!' Joshua ripped open the door. Rebecca burst into tears, and Joshua hugged her to his chest. They certainly cared for each other. Had that been reason enough to kill?

'Tell me what happened,' Aldo said, keeping his voice low, unthreatening.

'After I argued with Father, I walked round till it got dark,' Rebecca replied between sobs. 'I realized it was late, but I couldn't face going home.'

'She came to our house,' Joshua said. 'Rebecca told me what happened, the terrible things Samuele had said to her. I came here to confront Samuele.' He paused, swallowing hard. 'The door was open when I arrived, which was unusual. I went inside, and—' Joshua stopped, taking Rebecca's face in his hands. 'Your father was on the floor. I could see his blood. I went over to help him – but he was already dead.' Joshua looked close to tears. 'I'm sorry I didn't tell you when I arrived home that night. I meant to, but you were already asleep when I got there. I couldn't bear the thought of waking you to say what I knew. I wanted you to have one last good night's sleep before—' He stopped, overcome by emotion.

Aldo watched Rebecca. Her shoulders relaxed, as if a weight was leaving her. She had seen the blood on Joshua's boot and feared the worst. That was why she had lied, to protect him. She must care for Joshua to do that, or hate her father more than she realized.

'What about the knife?' Aldo asked. 'Was there a blade in Samuele's chest?'

Joshua paused before answering. 'No, there wasn't.'

So the killer took it with them. 'Did you see anyone else outside, near the house?'

'I don't . . .' Joshua's eyes widened. 'Yes, I did. It was dark, but I saw a man hurrying away along the street.' He pointed north, towards the Arno.

'What did this man look like? Was he tall, short? Fat, thin?'

'I can't be sure. But he was carrying something with square corners – a book, maybe.'

Had robbery been the reason for Levi's murder? 'Rebecca, have you noticed anything missing from inside the house? Something that matches what Joshua describes?'

She shook her head, shivering more now. Joshua pulled her closer, his face full of concern. 'Please, can I take her in? She's freezing out here.'

A messenger boy came into the street, shouting Aldo's name. Aldo nodded at Joshua and Rebecca to go in before gesturing to the boy. 'I've a message from Constable Benedetto,' the boy said. 'A man with a scar on his cheek is being held at Porta San Gallo.'

Aldo put a coin in the boy's expectant hand. 'Anything else?'

'Benedetto says you should hurry. The man hurt two guards when they first stopped him. Benedetto says he isn't sure how long they can keep the man there.'

Aldo added another coin. 'Run back to the north gate. Tell Benedetto I'll be there soon, and it's vital they hold that prisoner – understand?' A nod, and the boy sprinted off.

Maria gave herself a night and a day to overcome the disappointment of Guicciardini's letter, but time had not removed all her frustration. She paced the floor of her bedroom for an hour, turning over the possibilities, the significance behind his words. Finally, she set that aside and chose to focus on the path ahead. It was easy for a prominent Palleschi senator to dismiss her request by letter. Such men would find ignoring her more difficult if she secured an invitation to visit their residences. To do that she needed to be in Florence, moving among the wives of the Palleschi, winning their favour. A Medici could not be so easily ignored in person.

Maria sent Simona to fetch Cosimo from the stables, knowing he would be tending to the horses. He was dismayed when she announced her plans. 'Am I not to accompany you?'

'Not this time,' she said, touching a palm to his face. 'Better if you remain here, and keep watch over the *castello*. My efforts to secure a better future for you will require me to call on other wives and widows. I find women are more willing to help each other when talking among themselves. We may not have the brute force of men, but that does not mean we lack anything in the way of guile and cunning.'

In the past Maria might have expected her son to pout and protest at being left behind. Instead he nodded, accepting the simple wisdom of her words and experience. He had grown into a man able to perceive when someone spoke the truth. That was an ability which should serve him well amid the courtly intrigues of Florence, should her plans succeed.

'Where will you stay?' Cosimo asked.

It was a good question. In years past Maria had been a guest of her sister Francesca, whose husband Ottaviano had a residence not far from Palazzo Medici with the most beautiful gardens. But to the chagrin of Ottaviano, many rooms at his home had been given over to Duke Alessandro's young bride Margaret and her ladies. The Duke and Margaret were still living apart, supposedly because of her youth, so she needed a respectable home. Judging by letters from Francesca, Ottaviano had been given little say in that decision. Whatever the truth of it, another lodging was needed when Maria reached the city.

'I shall find a bedchamber at Casa Vecchia,' she said. The thought of sharing a residence with Alessandro's craven cousin Lorenzino gave her little joy, but necessity made for unlikely neighbours. At least she would be near Palazzo Medici, and that put her close to the true power within Florence. The challenge was turning that to an advantage for her and Cosimo.

Palazzo Seta lacked the splendour of the Landini family home, but Biagio Seta's smiling sister Madelena gave Strocchi a warm welcome when he was ushered up to a plush chamber on the middle level. She was much the same age as Strocchi, but her clothes were evidence of a life more pampered than his. A flowing dress of golden silk brocade caressed her womanly form, while the tight bodice drew his eye to the swell of her bosom. Madelena caught the direction of his gaze as she sat on a chair draped in vibrant patterned cloth, picking up a half-finished embroidery and needle. But instead of being offended by him, she seemed amused.

Aware that a blush was starting to colour his cheeks, Strocchi willed himself to focus on her face. Was that a twinkle of mischief in her eyes? Was she enjoying his unease? He knew it was unusual for an unmarried, unaccompanied young woman to receive an unknown male visitor in a merchant family's home, but Madelena had sent the servant away before Strocchi could ask his questions. He pressed on, determined to find Biagio Seta.

Madelena was full of apologies that her brother was not there to meet the constable. 'He's in Pisa visiting the weavers. Our elder brother Alessio hasn't been well, and his business partner couldn't make the trip, so Biagio offered to go instead.'

'When did he leave?'

Madelena pondered a moment, setting aside her embroidery to answer. 'Late on Sunday afternoon, I believe. It was all decided in great haste.' She shook her head. 'Why he couldn't wait until Monday, I don't know.'

But Strocchi did. Leaving then meant Seta couldn't be accused of killing Corsini. Had he paid for the murder? That would be impossible to prove without a confession. There was another potential explanation for his hasty departure: Seta had known the murder was imminent. Even if he hadn't paid for the killing of Corsini, he might know who had.

'When are you expecting your brother back?'

'Tomorrow,' Madelena replied, the hint of a smirk playing around the curves of her cupid's-bow lips. She rose from the chair, holding the embroidery just below the line of her bodice, drawing Strocchi's gaze downwards as she approached him. 'What a strange profession you have. Everything you say ends in a question. Isn't that frustrating?'

'Only when I don't get any answers,' Strocchi replied. He backed away from the advancing Madelena, bowing on his way out. She couldn't be more than a summer or two older than him, but he had never felt more out of his depth in the company of a woman.

Renato smelled the visitor before seeing him. 'Did somebody bring fish in here?' he demanded, looking up from his needle and thread. There was a figure in the workroom doorway, its face hidden by shadow. Renato squinted, his eyes taking a moment to adjust after long hours of fine stitching. 'Cesare? Is that you?'

The visitor nodded before stepping outside.

Renato set his work down. He'd been thinking about Cesare since one of the cutters described a man asking questions that morning. It was years since Renato had spent time with Cesare. He could still picture Cesare as a young man – how striking he had been despite the cuts and bruises suffered while fighting to stay alive on the city streets. They had been kindred spirits for one glorious summer, though never lovers – much to Renato's regret. On the rare occasions their paths crossed now – which wasn't often, even in a city as small as Florence – a nod was all that passed between them. Their lives couldn't be more different, Renato supposed. But he had no illusions as to why Cesare was visiting now. This was about that silly diary. Bracing himself, Renato went outside.

Cesare was not looking his best. The years had added to his rugged charm, and the wrinkles at the corners of those piercing eyes only enhanced that. But he hadn't shaved for at least a day, and those greying bristles made him look jowly. Then there were his crumpled clothes, a distinct aroma of fish about them – never Renato's favourite scent.

Aldo cleared his throat. 'I haven't got long. I need to ask you about a young man—'

Renato held up a hand. 'I hope you're not planning to demand money. I've already handed over plenty to that vile colleague of yours.'

Aldo frowned. 'Cerchi's come to you already?'

Renato wrinkled his nose. 'What a repulsive creature, how do you work with him?'

'Tell me what happened.'

Seeing the urgency in Aldo's eyes, Renato did his best to recall both encounters with Cerchi – the grasping visit to the sewing room, and then handing coin to the ungrateful *cazzo* outside the Podestà that morning. 'The cheek of him! First he threatens to have me tortured, and then he expects me to be grateful when I pay what he demands.'

A boy passed them, pushing a barrow laden with cloth for another sewing room. Renato lowered his voice so as not to be overheard. 'I'm not the only one who was friends with that poor young man, you know. I've been warning others to expect a visit. Not all of them can afford to pay what the Otto is demanding.'

'Cerchi fills his own purse,' Aldo said, scowling. 'The Otto works to protect citizens.'

'Well, it's not doing a very good job. There are several important men in this city who are rather worried. Some of them might start naming others to save themselves.' Renato edged closer, despite the fishy smell. 'What would happen if Cerchi found out what kind of man you are, Cesare? He doesn't seem to respond well to people like us.'

'And I don't respond well to threats,' Aldo replied, anger flashing in his eyes.

'I wasn't threatening you,' Renato said, shocked anyone could suggest such a thing. 'But you have to stop him, before someone gets hurt. For your own sake, if not for others.'

Aldo rubbed a hand across his stubble before giving a curt nod.

'Thank you,' Renato gushed, reaching for Aldo's arm. A cold look made Renato withdrew his hand. 'Of course, you're right. Forgive me.'

Aldo shook his head. 'No, you've done nothing for me to forgive. Take care.' With that he was gone, striding away into the afternoon, headed north. Renato couldn't help notice his old friend limping a little. Perhaps Cesare was the one who needed to take care.

Chapter Thirteen

Strocchi hammered at the doors of Palazzo Landini. The homes of most merchants stood open during the day, encouraging those with business to enter and be known. The Landinis had closed their doors to visitors, but Strocchi refused to leave. Not this time. After what seemed an age, a timid servant unlocked one of the doors. 'Signora Landini warns you to leave,' he said, 'otherwise she'll summon a constable.'

'I am a constable,' Strocchi snapped, pushing his way inside. He marched to the courtyard at the heart of the building. 'Has your master returned from church?'

'Ch-church?' the servant stammered, peering up to the palazzo's middle level. Pasqua Landini was watching them from a window. She stepped back out of sight.

Strocchi went up the main staircase two steps at a time, making no effort to be quiet. Signora Landini emerged as he reached the top, her face sour as turned milk. 'You've no right coming here. How did you get in?'

'I came to question your husband, signora. It's obvious he is here, otherwise you wouldn't have shut the doors.'

'My husband isn't well,' she maintained. 'Come back tomorrow, he may be better.'

'This morning he was busy at church, now he's too ill to see me. Which is it?' She gave no reply. 'I'll find him if I have to

138

search every room.' Strocchi strode along a wide corridor, calling for Agnolotti Landini, the signora scurrying after him.

'Please, you must understand,' she said, panic rising in her voice. 'My husband has been under a terrible strain—'

Strocchi stopped so sharp they almost collided. 'A young man was beaten to death, and I want to know why. I doubt your husband had anything to do with it, but he can help me find those responsible. Where is he?'

Signora Landini wrung her hands before pointing past Strocchi to ornate doors at the end of the corridor. Strocchi stalked towards them, calling ahead of himself. 'Signor Landini, I'm Constable Strocchi, from the Otto. I need to ask you some questions. Can I come in?'

Silence.

'Signor Landini, may I enter?'

Still no reply.

Strocchi turned the handle, expecting it to be locked. Instead the door opened on a grand bedroom full of rich fabrics and furniture. Late afternoon sun poured in through tall, elegant windows. One of them was wide open, with Agnolotti Landini sitting naked on the window ledge, staring out at the city. From there it would be all too easy for Landini to throw himself over the side and tumble to the stone street below.

Now Strocchi understood why the palazzo doors had been closed.

Aldo quickened pace as Porto San Gallo loomed ahead, bare orchards on either side of the road, the city wall sprawling beyond them. Two days ago he and Levi had come through the gate together. Now the moneylender was dead and Duke Alessandro was expecting – no, demanding – a progress report soon. With so few people using the gate this late in the day, there was no need to be subtle. Aldo cracked his knuckles. Good.

Benedetto crossed himself as Aldo approached. 'Madonna, I feared you wouldn't get here before dark.'

'The bandit, is he still here?'

'In the guard house,' Benedetto replied. 'Says his name is Marsilio Carafa. The guards are convinced he only came through the gate early this morning. I sent a messenger to the other gates, telling them to watch out for him, like you said. All of them reported back while I was waiting for you to arrive. None of them have seen anyone matching Carafa in the last week.'

'Bring him out,' Aldo said.

Benedetto fetched the prisoner. Carafa's wrists were bound together, the ropes so tight his wrists were raw and bloody. 'Finally,' the bandit complained as he emerged. 'Now cut these and let me go. I don't want to spend another minute in your pox-ridden city.'

'Sorry,' Aldo said, 'but you'll be staying a while longer.'

Carafa's scarred face fell. 'You again.' He sniffed the air. 'Enjoy the fish?'

Aldo stepped so close their noses were almost touching. 'You tell me.' He snapped a knee up into Carafa's groin. The bandit crumpled, breath whistling out between his teeth. He mouthed curses from the ground, but no sound came out. 'Sorry,' Aldo said, 'I can't quite hear you.' Carafa made an obscene gesture in reply. 'Benedetto, get him up.'

The constable helped Carafa to his feet, the bandit still wincing.

Aldo punched Carafa in the stomach, doubling him over. Benedetto looked at Aldo with obvious concern. 'This man led a gang of murderous bandits who attacked and almost killed me,'

Aldo said, loud enough for anyone watching to hear. 'We can take him back to the Podestà and use the Otto's interrogation tools to loosen his tongue – or he can talk here.'

Carafa straightened up, pain still contorting his face. 'Get fucked.'

'Maybe later.' Aldo clamped a hand round the bandit's *palle*. 'Right now, I have to stay here and question you.' The hand tightened into a fist, bringing a gasp of anguish. 'Who hired you to kill Samuele Levi?' The bandit shook his head. Aldo squeezed harder.

A whimper escaped Carafa's mouth. 'It was one of his rivals.'

The grip loosened, but didn't let go. Not yet.

'One of the other Jews. Cheap *bastardo* hasn't paid me yet, so I came to collect.'

Aldo nodded, suspicions confirmed. 'That's why you risked coming to Florence. When did you arrive?' Another squeeze. 'When?'

'This morning, I got here this morning!'

The grip loosened again.

'So this man didn't kill Levi?' Benedetto asked.

Carafa frowned, confusion evident. 'What do you mean? My men and I killed Levi on Sunday, twenty miles north of here.'

'Not quite,' Aldo replied, letting go. 'Levi only pretended to be dead. I got him safely back here the next day. Somebody else murdered Levi in his own home a few hours later. It's likely your employer took matters into his own hands – or got someone else to finish the job. Either way, you've had a wasted trip.'

The bandit spat at the ground. 'Can I go?'

'Not yet. I've still got one question,' Aldo replied. 'Who hired you to kill Levi?' The answer was obvious, but having him named would put it beyond doubt.

Carafa sneered before replying. 'Dante. His name was Malachi Dante.'

That cast a new light on the last two days. Aldo stepped away from the bandit. 'Very well. We're done here.' He strode away from the gate, heading south, back into the city.

'What do you want us to do with the prisoner?' Benedetto called.

'Take him to Le Stinche!'

'What? No!' Carafa protested. 'You said you'd release me!'

'I said I still had one more question,' Aldo replied. 'Don't worry, you won't be there long. You're a hired killer who tried to murder an officer of the Otto and a citizen of Florence. The Otto doesn't look kindly on the likes of you. Justice will be swift.'

Strocchi wasn't sure his words were reaching Landini. Yes, the merchant had stepped away from the open window and put a robe over his nakedness, but Landini's mood kept lurching between grief-stricken guilt and self-loathing anger. He would never hurt that boy, Landini muttered to himself, would never even dream of it. They were friends, good friends yes, but nothing more. No, that wasn't true, he loved that young man, loved him like no other. It was . . . Landini broke down weeping.

Strocchi spared a glance round the bedroom, having never been in such a lavish room dedicated solely to sleeping. A carved wooden chest stood against one wall, while a wash basin occupied the far corner. But much of the chamber was occupied by an elaborately carved bed. The sheer size of it was twice anything Strocchi had seen before. He shuddered to think how much it must have cost. The constable could see mulberry twigs lying beneath the bed, put there to draw fleas away from the mattress.

Landini was back up, pacing again, his agitation worrying the constable. Keeping his voice low, Strocchi made sure his words were soothing: the murder was senseless, a tragedy. Those who killed Corsini deserved to be punished, to suffer for what they had done. Landini could help make that happen. His name need never be known . . .

Landini shook his head. He'd handed over a ransom to preserve his good name, with no assurances in return – only the promise of further payments, further humiliation. His family would be shamed if the truth was known, their business destroyed. Landini stared into Strocchi's eyes. 'I did love him, truly I did.'

'I know.'

'Thank you.' The merchant smiled, his back straightening. 'Let me get dressed, then you can ask all the questions you wish.'

Strocchi nodded, happy to see the merchant's burden lifting. As Landini opened one of the drawers in a chest the delicate scent of violet and rose filled the room, no doubt from bags filled with petals to cleanse the air. Reassured, Strocchi went to the bedchamber doors, aware Landini's wife must still be waiting outside, stricken with worry. No wonder she'd been so dismissive earlier. She'd been wearing a brittle mask to hide what was happening in her home.

As Strocchi reached the doors, heavy footsteps pounded across the room. He spun round to see Landini hurtling towards the open window. Strocchi shouted at him to stop—

But it was too late.

Aldo couldn't hide his limp by the time he reached the Arno, dusk already approaching. It'd been tempting to report to the Duke while passing Palazzo Medici. But Carafa's claim had to be investigated first. Better to be certain before naming a suspect. Orvieto's door was open as Aldo struggled along via dei Giudei. A slip on the icy stones sent a fresh stab of pain through one leg. That settled it. Aldo found Orvieto was in his back room, grinding herbs in a pestle. 'I'm not seeing anyone else today,' the doctor said without turning round.

'Then you should shut your front door,' Aldo replied, leaning on the wall for support. Orvieto took one glance at him and brought Aldo a chair. 'I look that bad?'

'Where does it hurt?' the doctor asked as Aldo sank onto the seat.

'My knees. One's an old wound, the other got injured today.'

Orvieto knelt by the chair. 'Can you push down your hose?' Aldo rolled them to his calves with difficulty. Orvieto's hands were warm and firm, massaging and flexing both knees. It would have been even more pleasurable had the pain not made Aldo wince.

The doctor sat back on his haunches. 'Nothing torn, but you'll have quite a bruise. Mostly you're suffering from exhaustion. You need to rest.' He inhaled, nose wrinkling a little. 'And stay away from fish stalls.'

'Don't remind me,' Aldo said. 'I have to report to the Duke before I can get some sleep.' He reached to pull his hose back up.

'Wait,' Orvieto said, a hand on Aldo's thigh. 'I've something that will help.' He went to a shelf of heavy glass jars, a thick stopper on each. The doctor selected one and opened it, slapping a thick cream out onto his palms. He returned and rubbed the lotion into each knee. Aldo expected a heavy, acrid stench of the kind that seeped from apothecary shops. Instead the scent was pleasant and its effect was swift, warmth seeping into both joints.

'That's remarkable. How much do I . . . ?'

Orvieto waved away payment. 'Come back when we can talk. I appreciate a man with experience and a strong stomach.' Before

Aldo could reply, Orvieto was handing him a cloak. 'Now, put this on. It'll help keep you warm and hide that smell. You could do with both.'

Aldo was approaching Dante's home as Levi's former partner was emerging. 'Going somewhere?'

Dante reacted with dismay before composing himself. The dark smudges beneath his eyes were even blacker now, while his cheeks looked hollow and empty.

'I'm sitting *shiva* with Rebecca tonight,' Dante replied, walking on.

Aldo fell in step beside him. 'You look like something's troubling you.'

Dante hesitated before nodding. 'I'm worried what Samuele may have put in his *zava'ah*. It's a letter some Jews write when they sense that death is near, passing on the wisdom they have learned. It can be used to give thanks or to forgive, others use it to chastise and rebuke. It can be a lasting message of love – or a way to punish those you leave behind. Samuele was not an easy man. If he wrote a *zava'ah*, it could be devastating for Rebecca.'

Aldo studied Dante as they walked. 'I met an acquaintance of yours – Carafa.'

Dante stumbled a little. 'Who?'

'You might not know his name, but I'm sure you'd recognize his face,' Aldo said, 'especially since you commissioned him for a murder. He's named you as the person who hired him to kill Samuele Levi on the road from Bologna.'

Dante stopped, his shoulders slumping. 'How did you find him?'

'He came looking for you – looking for his payment.'

'I tried to call him and his men back, I honestly did – but it was too late.' Dante rubbed a hand across his temples. 'One mistake, undoing a lifetime of good work.'

No wonder Dante had rushed to see his former partner when Samuele returned from Bologna. That guilt also explained why he'd been so helpful to the investigation. 'Why did you do it?' Aldo asked. 'Why hire someone to kill Levi?'

'Samuele betrayed me, tricked me out of the business I'd spent years building up alongside him. He cast me aside like I was nothing, and then blackened my name to everyone he met. I took to drinking, hoping it would take the pain away . . .'

There had to be more than that, something to push Dante past all his beliefs. Aldo didn't speak, trusting that guilt would prompt an answer. It didn't take long.

'I could have borne all that,' Dante said in a trembling whisper, 'but Samuele forbade me from speaking to Rebecca again. She was like a daughter, and he . . .' Words failed him for a moment. 'I had nothing to live for, nobody left. I decided Samuele had to pay for that.'

'Why pay to have Levi killed away from Florence?' Aldo asked. 'Why not here?'

'To spare Rebecca,' Dante said. 'I didn't want her seeing Samuele's body.'

'Your mistake nearly got me murdered on the road from Bologna.'

'I know. I'm sorry.' Dante paused. 'Was Carafa the one who killed Samuele?'

'No, Carafa only entered the city this morning.' Aldo smirked. 'Squeeze a man's weak spot hard enough, and he'll always tell you the truth.' He studied Dante. 'Could Samuele have known that you had hired bandits to kill him?'

'I don't see how. Nobody knew, except Carafa and the man who introduced us. He's a cripple, runs the tavern north of the river where I went to drink sometimes. I didn't want anyone from our community seeing me like that.'

Zoppo. Aldo would give that *merda* far worse than a black eye the next time they met, but that could wait. More important was the fact that Levi had believed someone other than Dante wanted him dead, otherwise Levi wouldn't have paid for a guard on the road home from Bologna. The attack by Carafa and his men, which Dante had commissioned, was simply an unhappy coincidence. Aldo put that to one side. Levi had far more debtors than he did competitors. That made it just as likely the person behind Levi's murder was someone who owed him money, and decided to repay him with a blade to the chest.

'When you worked together, how did Samuele keep track of loans?'

The question seemed to surprise Dante. 'We had a ledger,' he replied, 'a book, bound in leather. Our names were inscribed on it in Hebrew. Samuele scratched mine off when he forced me out.' Aldo recognized the book Dante was describing. Levi had carried the ledger in one of his satchels on the journey from Bologna, checking it was secure several times.

Dante paused as they neared the Levis' home. 'What will happen to me now?'

Aldo knew he should arrest Dante for conspiring to have Levi killed, throw him in a cell alongside Carafa, let the two of them rot together in Le Stinche. But curfew was close, and Aldo believed Dante was no threat to anyone but himself now. 'That depends on the judgement of the Otto when this matter comes before the court. I will be making a *denunzia* against you, and you are prohibited from leaving the city. All gates will be barred to you till the court makes a decision. Is that understood?'

Dante nodded, meek and weighed down by his guilt.

Aldo knocked on the door. A young woman – one of Joshua's sisters, judging by the resemblance – opened it. 'I need a moment with Rebecca.'

The young woman refused, but Dante intervened to persuade her. When Rebecca came to the door, her face was blotchy with grief. Aldo asked to see Levi's ledger. She searched for several minutes before returning empty-handed. 'I don't understand why anyone would take Father's ledger. All the entries are written in Hebrew – only a Jew would be able to read what's inside it. Father spent years building up the business, every detail was in that . . .' Her eyes widened. 'The man Joshua saw, he must have taken it.'

Aldo nodded. Samuele Levi was almost certainly killed for what was inside that ledger.

Aldo made a breathless dash north to Palazzo Medici, grateful his knee was pain-free. He reached the ducal residence just as the bell high in the tower of Palazzo della Signoria rang out over the city, announcing the start of curfew. As an officer of the Otto, Aldo had the authority to be out after nightfall. But arriving late to see the Duke would not go unnoticed, nor unpunished. He kept the details of his report brisk, all too aware how soon the patience of powerful men could wear thin, but did mention the missing ledger and its potential significance. 'Well done,' Alessandro said. 'You've learned much in a day.'

'Levi's former partner is preparing a list of the clients he can recall from the stolen ledger,' Aldo replied. 'That won't include any new debtors added to the book since their partnership ended, but it's a start.'

Lorenzino lurked at his cousin's side, a sneer twisting his face.

'That could take days, and the feast of Epiphany is only getting closer. Captain Vitelli has mentioned in the past that he believes the ducal guard could be more efficient at enforcing the city's most serious laws. It would give his men a suitable task to occupy them during times of peace.'

Aldo bowed his head, seeming to acknowledge the wisdom of such a suggestion. As if any reminder was needed of how few days were left to bring Levi's killer to justice. Having been a mercenary, Aldo knew how blunt and brutal men at arms could be. Putting Vitelli's guards in charge of enforcing the law would soon lead to bloodshed, with tyranny not far behind. That had to be avoided, for the city's sake as well as for the future of the Otto.

Lorenzino raised an eyebrow at Aldo. 'You said the dead man knew that someone planned him harm – how can you be so certain?'

'Levi paid the Otto to supply a guard – myself – for his trip from Bologna. He believed his life was in danger, but refused to tell me who wanted him dead.'

'Yet he only paid for you to guard him on the return trip,' Lorenzino said. 'If he believed himself to be under threat, surely he would want guarding in both directions?'

It was an astute question, and one for which Aldo didn't have a swift answer.

'That's enough for now,' Alessandro said, dismissing Aldo with a gesture. 'We're expecting company this evening and we wouldn't wish to keep them waiting.'

Aldo bowed deep to the Duke – and less so to Lorenzino – before withdrawing. If the rumours were true, Alessandro was unlikely to be meeting his wife Margaret. She was half the Duke's age and lived at another Medici residence nearby with her ladies-in-waiting. Alessandro was known to visit his mistress Taddea

Malaspina and their two illegitimate children. Taddea and her older sister Ricciarda resided with Cardinal Cibo at Palazzo Pazzi because Ricciarda was married to Cibo's wayward and often absent brother, Lorenzo. But if Alessandro was expecting company at his own home, that suggested someone else was coming. Those less favoured by the Duke muttered that he was too fond of preying on the daughters and wives of noble families, the pale Lorenzino often at his side. But rumours and mutterings were not proof, least of all for the fornications of those in power.

As he left the palazzo, Aldo glanced across the courtyard. A heavyset man was arguing with a servant. Shadows hid much of the man's face, but he had a prominent hooked nose. Aldo paused to adjust his borrowed cloak, Orvieto's scent enveloping him. As he did, the hook-nosed man strode away. There was no mistaking the book he was carrying, nor the Hebrew on the binding.

It was Samuele Levi's stolen ledger.

Chapter Fourteen

Thursday, January 4th

*A*ldo was exhausted, his limbs aching with weariness. He'd spent the night willing sleep to come, but couldn't stop thinking. It was almost a relief when the sky outside his shutters became a mottled bruise of dark blue, and the struggle to fall asleep could be abandoned. The cream Orvieto had rubbed into Aldo's knees was still helping, for which he was grateful.

Aldo shaved in cold water, scraping away bristles by touch in the inky pre-dawn light. Dressing fast, the warmth of Orvieto's borrowed cloak was a welcome addition. Then out into the cold morning air, careful not to disturb Robustelli or the others still asleep inside the *bordello*. The streets would still be empty, with the city's night patrols already bound for their beds, making it a good time to walk and think, to ponder the questions that had defeated sleep. Heading north-east towards Ponte Vecchio, Aldo sidestepped a patch of ice left behind by overnight rain and early morning frost.

It seemed certain now that Samuele Levi's killer had taken the ledger. The book's presence at Palazzo Medici suggested a link to the ducal household. Was it possible that Alessandro was behind the murder? That made no sense, not when the Duke and Lorenzino were so keen to see the case solved. So why was the ledger inside Palazzo Medici, and how had it come to be there?

Ponte Vecchio stood empty as Aldo crossed the bridge, butcher shops on each side still shut. Their doorways were stained crimson from the previous day, and countless days before. Most of the blood got sluiced into the Arno but the rest froze overnight, tainting the cobbles. Above the shops were the shuttered windows of those who lived on Ponte Vecchio, their homes perched above the shops and other businesses. In winter the smells of rotting meat and offal were masked by the cold, but in summer the stench must infest every part of those homes, as would the flies drawn by the rancid offcuts and spilled blood.

Aldo continued north-east through slumbering streets. The sky was getting lighter, day replacing night. Something else about Levi's ledger nagged at Aldo – why hadn't it been destroyed? The book was a direct link to the murder. Most killers would discard it, or tear out any pages concerning them and throw the rest into a fire or the Arno.

Traders began opening shops as Aldo passed, putting their goods out on hinged shelves, making best use of the limited space in the narrow thoroughfares. A few hawkers were already looking for trade, though their meagre winter produce would not be easily sold. A servant knocked in vain at a *buchette del vino*, getting no reply from the small wooden window set in a palazzo wall. Wealthy families with vineyards on their countryside estates sold the excess wine through such windows, but it was too early for that, even in Florence.

Aldo pressed on. For the murderer to keep hold of the ledger was madness, unless . . . Of course! Dante had said the entries were all written in Hebrew. Few outside via dei Giudei would be able to read that. Finding a non-Jew to translate the ledger would not be easy. It would need a man of education, someone from the church . . . Was that why Cibo had been visiting the Duke so late on Tuesday? Aldo realized he had stopped outside Le Stinche.

The prison was a glowering stone stronghold. Most inmates were debtors, making it a place of suffering and despair for anyone unable to buy their way out. But Aldo had put more than a few prisoners inside it over the years for other crimes besides debt. Carafa was being held inside it now, but his case could wait. Solving Levi's murder came first.

Turning west, Aldo headed towards the Podestà. Cibo's interest in the case raised another question: why was the Holy Roman Emperor's representative so intrigued by the Levi murder? Was Cibo involved with it somehow? Or did the cardinal simply crave information, which was currency to men like him? Answering that meant paying a visit to Cibo, and the sooner the better. The feast of Epiphany was only two days away.

Strocchi stumbled from Santa Maria Nuovo after another night spent at the bedside of a dying man. This time he'd been praying that Agnolotti Landini might survive his fall. The nuns offered little hope, and their pessimism proved wise. Landini's shallow breathing caught one last time before stopping as dawn broke over the city. All the prayers in the world would not have been enough, Strocchi knew that, but he had been the only one on his knees. None of the Landini family visited during the night. Were they too overcome by shock, or too ashamed? To be so forsaken by those meant to love . . .

Forget them, Strocchi decided. They didn't matter. Landini was dead, another victim of Corsini's diary. But it was men of flesh and blood who had murdered Corsini. They kicked and beat the young man until he was all but unrecognizable, ending his short life. The killers deserved to be found and punished for their crime – for their sin.

But the silly gossip of a young man had now become a weapon in the hands of Cerchi. How many others would it destroy? Strocchi strode away from the hospital. No more. No more extortion, no more lies. No more threats and bullying. No more would Cerchi use that diary to fill his pouch. Finding the men who murdered Corsini – that would be justice.

Aldo kept his report to Bindi brief, omitting any mention of the stolen ledger until he had a better understanding of why it was at Palazzo Medici.

'You've heard what happened to Agnolotti Landini?' the *segretario* asked.

Aldo shook his head, careful to show no reaction. Had the merchant reported Cerchi for extortion? Unlikely. Perhaps Cerchi had subjected Landini to the *strappato* to make the other men in Corsini's diary loosen their coin pouches? Maybe, but – like most bullies – Cerchi preferred making threats to taking action.

'Jumped from a window at his palazzo last night,' Bindi continued. 'Seems he was involved with the dead *buggerone*. Strocchi was there when Landini fell.'

That would weigh heavy on the constable. Aldo shrugged for Bindi's benefit. 'Unfortunate, but I can't see any connection to Levi's murder.'

Bindi nodded his agreement. 'Do you still need Benedetto?'

'No.' The recruit had proven more useful than expected, but things would move faster without him following along like an over-curious dog. Raised voices seeped into the *officio*. It sounded like Strocchi shouting, and someone sneering back at him – was that Cerchi?

'Deal with that,' Bindi snapped. 'Tell those men to take their dispute elsewhere, or else they'll suffer the consequences.'

Aldo bowed on his way out. Hurrying down the wide stone staircase, he could see Strocchi raging at Cerchi in the Podestà courtyard, two guards holding the constable back. 'You did this,' Strocchi shouted, red with rage. 'You drove that poor man to kill himself!'

'Landini was anything but poor,' Cerchi sneered, 'his family won't suffer. In fact, they're probably happy that he's dead. His kind don't deserve to live.'

Aldo put himself in front of Cerchi, in case Strocchi got free. 'Enough. Bindi is threatening to discipline both of you unless this shouting ends now.'

'He started it,' Cerchi said. 'Make him apologize.'

'For telling the truth?' Strocchi spat. 'Should I tell them what you made Landini do?'

'Enough!' Aldo glared at the constable, willing him to see sense. 'Strocchi, I want you to wait outside in the street. Go. Now.'

Strocchi's mouth twisted but eventually he gave in. Shaking off the others, he stalked out of the Podestà. Once Strocchi was gone, Aldo feigned ignorance rather than acknowledge the smugness on Cerchi's face. 'What's got him so angry?'

'Just another dead pervert,' Cerchi replied. 'A visitor to your friend Corsini.'

'I've told you already, Corsini was my informer,' Aldo said, making sure his words were loud enough for everyone watching to hear. 'Are you any closer to catching the men who killed him?'

Cerchi smirked. 'Are you any closer to arresting whoever murdered that Jew? From what I hear, the Duke's demanding answers by Epiphany.'

Resisting the urge to kick Cerchi in the *palle*, Aldo went outside.

Strocchi was pacing back and forth in front of the Podestà gates. 'This is your fault,' the constable snarled on seeing Aldo. 'You said you'd talk to Cerchi.'

Aldo nodded, accepted his mistake. Visiting Cibo would have to wait a while longer. 'Getting the diary yesterday might have saved Landini,' Aldo said, 'but he'd been on that path a long time before Cerchi got to him. I'll need your help to stop anyone else getting hurt.'

Strocchi's hands kept clenching and unclenching. 'What do you want me to do?'

'Apologize to Cerchi. And make it convincing.'

Rebecca craved solitude: to be alone, to have the chance of going for a walk, to have nobody helping, or watching, or worrying about her. But sitting *shiva* was a duty she must complete, seven days of mourning to be endured, whether or not she'd loved Father. It meant the house was full of neighbours and friends of the family. Her friends, of course – Father didn't have any. Not since he drove Malachi away. Not since Mother died.

At first, the presence of others had been a comfort. People bringing food, though she had no hunger. People talking to her – or talking at her, since she had little to say. No matter where she turned, someone was close by. It was meant as kindness, no doubt, but the constant, suffocating presence denied her any chance to know how she felt, what she felt. Maybe that was the point of sitting *shiva*, but it made her want to scream.

Joshua did his best to help. Rebecca could see her pain reflected in his eyes. Others came and went – his sisters, Malachi, Dr Orvieto – but Joshua was the most frequent presence. She'd seen more of him in the past two days than they had managed in two months of stolen moments. He was here again with his sisters, ready to do anything she asked. It was strange. What had seemed exciting and forbidden about him – about them, about what they might do or be one day – was different now. At first she had worried that her reason to be with Joshua had died a little with Father. It had, but what replaced that was something more meaningful, something deeper. She was seeing Joshua for himself, for all the qualities that he had, not simply as the temptation of the forbidden.

By far the worst part of sitting *shiva* was being unable to stop her thoughts racing, to stop dwelling on things. She hadn't felt like this when Mother died. Then, it had been as if her heart was missing, replaced by a gaping hole of loss and longing. Now all she felt was angry.

How many more days before she could go back to being herself?

She paid no heed to the knock at the door. Yet another person coming to share their grief, to say how sorry they were. But this voice at the door was different. 'I'm her cousin, and these are my brothers. We've come a long way to be here, so you will let us in.'

Rebecca got to her feet without even noticing, lifted by that voice. The darkness fell away, clouds parting on a bitter day to reveal the warmth of the sun. Then Ruth was hugging her. This was what she'd been missing: a loving family.

Tears streamed down Rebecca's face.

Aldo marched Strocchi back into the Podestà, pushing the constable ahead of him. 'Where's Cerchi?' Guards gathered to watch, no doubt hoping for another fight. Cerchi swaggered out of the small storage chamber reserved for use by officers. Aldo shoved Strocchi at him. 'You know what to do,' Aldo commanded the constable.

Strocchi glared over his shoulder at Aldo. Good. That anger would make this all the more satisfying for Cerchi. Strocchi mumbled something. 'Louder,' Aldo urged as he strolled by, heading for the officers' chamber.

'I'm sorry,' Strocchi repeated, raising his voice a little.

'Still can't hear you,' Cerchi replied, smirking.

Aldo didn't bother listening to the rest, certain Cerchi would do everything possible to make the apology long and painful for Strocchi. The more drawn out, the better – it meant there would be more time to search through Cerchi's things for the diary.

Once inside the officers' chamber, Aldo pushed the door to so nobody could see him. The air inside was rank, and the light of a single lantern made it hard to see. Cerchi's things were strewn round the small room, forcing Aldo to search through them one by one. The clothes reeked of body odour and stale piss, while Cerchi's boots were caked in mud and *merda*.

No sign of Corsini's diary. But there was something lying in the shadows beneath a low wooden bench fixed to a stone wall. It must have fallen from Cerchi's tunic while he was changing. Aldo dropped to the stone floor, stretching out an arm.

A long silence stopped him. There were no raised voices out in the courtyard. Had Strocchi finished? Aldo listened for a sound. Then Cerchi shouted a comment and everyone in the courtyard laughed, enjoying the joke. Strocchi must have the forbearance of a monk.

Aldo pulled the object from beneath the bench. It wasn't the diary, but Strocchi's humiliation had still served a purpose: it was the list of potential suspects he'd made from the descriptions and sketches in Corsini's diary. Better than nothing, and it might help—

'Looking for something?' Cerchi asked from the doorway.

Aldo slid the list inside his tunic before facing Cerchi. He was standing in the door, hands tucked either side of his gleaming silver buckle, the Florentine lily standing proud in the metal. 'My good knife,' Aldo replied, getting to his feet. 'Thought I left it here yesterday, but can't find it anywhere.' He approached the door, but Cerchi didn't move aside.

'My best boots were stolen from in here not long ago,' Cerchi said. 'Half the guards are worse thieves than the ones we throw in Le Stinche. We should get a lock on this door.'

'Good idea,' Aldo agreed. 'Did you get an apology out of Strocchi?'

'Eventually. Be careful of that one. Shit's getting ideas above his rank.'

Aldo nodded. 'Nothing worse than a constable who thinks he knows better than us.' Cerchi stood aside, letting Aldo leave. Sweat was sticking the list to Aldo's chest as he strolled across the courtyard, grateful to breathe in the cold air outside.

Strocchi was waiting outside the Podestà. Aldo handed him the list. 'Cerchi must be keeping Corsini's diary with him at all times, but you can destroy this, at least.'

'How do we get the diary back?'

'I'll find a way. But if you're nearby when it disappears, Cerchi will have you in Le Stinche. Last time a constable got imprisoned there, he was dead within a day.' Strocchi paled, his hands crumpling the retrieved list. 'Don't worry, I'll get that diary,' Aldo promised. 'You keep looking for whoever killed Corsini.'

Strocchi revealed that he had found the dead youth's last visitor. 'But Biagio Seta was out of the city when the attack took place.

From what I've heard, he doesn't sound like a man capable of ordering a murder – although he might know who did.'

'Be careful how you approach him,' Aldo said. 'Asking for help can be more effective than making accusations – it appeals to men's vanity.' The word chimed as soon as it was spoken. Vanity. Yes, that could be the solution. 'What day is it?'

'Thursday,' Strocchi replied. 'Why are you smiling?'

'Because I know how I'll have that diary away from Cerchi before night falls.'

'Thank you for coming,' Rebecca said, drying her eyes.

'We didn't want you to be alone,' Ruth replied, her brothers talking with Joshua and his sisters across the room. 'But it seems you've plenty of friends here.'

Rebecca leaned closer, lowering her voice. 'They mean well, but . . .'

'They're not family.'

Ruth always understood. Being with her was picking up an unbroken thread, as if no time had passed since they last talked. This must be what having a sister was like, though the bickering of Joshua's siblings suggested otherwise.

'Have you slept?' Rebecca shook her head. 'You will, when you're ready.'

She hesitated before whispering. 'I-I'm almost glad that Father's gone.'

Ruth nodded. 'Your father was a difficult man.'

'And angry,' Rebecca said. 'So angry, especially since Mother died.'

Ruth clasped Rebecca's hands. 'Did Samuele say why he came to see us last week?'

'No.'

Ruth's father Shimon and Samuele shared the risk whenever one of them was making a large loan. That much Rebecca knew. But her cousin revealed Samuele had sent word about needing a sum far beyond anything that had passed between the brothers before.

'How can you be sure of this?'

'My father's eyesight is failing,' Ruth replied. 'He'll never admit it, but he struggles to see much. I help: reading letters, counting coin. He still makes all the decisions. For now.'

Rebecca envied that. Father had made sure she knew little of the business, though his debtors came to the house for loans and to make their payments. Father had always sent her out of the room. How was she meant to live now, without any way to provide for herself? 'I know Father came back from Bologna with little in his satchels.'

Ruth nodded. 'Samuele didn't take the coin, I still don't know why. Instead, he left a letter with us. He said we should burn it after a week, unless something happened to him.' She opened a satchel, pulling out a tightly rolled document, sealed with red wax.

Father's hand was easy to recognize in the single word written by the seal: *Rebecca*. She took the document. It coiled in her palm like a serpent. Inside were the last words Father had written. Did it hold parting words of love for her, or something more venomous?

Rebecca took a deep breath, broke the wax and started to read.

7th of Tevet, 5297

To my daughter,

I write this in the house of my brother, and have asked him to have it delivered should the worst happen. I entered into an agreement with a man of importance who flattered me, and

*that blinded me to his purpose. But when I learned the truth,
I sought to withdraw from our pact – to no avail. If I have
been killed, the man of whom I wrote will be the one behind
it. I dare not name him here, but you will find him in my
ledger, if you look long enough.*

Rebecca shook her head. So that was why Father had been so
anxious, so angry the last few weeks. He had been protecting her
from the truth, carrying the weight of his mistake on those tired
shoulders. The memory of her final words to him stung even more
now.

But with the ledger gone, what hope was there of finding those
responsible for his death? Rebecca pushed that away – it was
somebody else's concern. She continued reading.

*I fear I have not been enough of a father to deserve your
tears. Losing your mother hardened my heart more than it
should, so I worked hard to ensure you would not know need.
Every man has doubts, but my belief in our faith will never
be shaken, even now.*

*I pray you will abide by my wishes in this letter, though
they may break your heart. Nonetheless, I forbid you from ever
being with Joshua Forzoni.*

You know our teachings. I beg you, forget him.

Your father,

S. Levi.

Rebecca stared at the letter, its close Hebrew text filling the
page. She couldn't seem to breathe. Ruth was talking, but the words
sounded distant, as if spoken by someone far away. The room was
swirling, lurching. No, not the room, it was her. She was . . .

Chapter Fifteen

Knowing the opportunity to take Corsini's diary from Cerchi would not arise until later, Aldo had a choice to make. He could visit Cibo now to discover why the Holy Roman Emperor's representative in Florence was so interested in the murder of a Jewish moneylender. Or he could go to Zoppo's tavern and confront the cripple. A man of faith or a man of filth – which was it to be? Trading words with the cardinal could wait. Vengeance was more urgent.

Aldo made his way west from the Podestà, cutting a jagged path across the major roads where cobbles lined the street. He preferred the narrower side roads of packed dirt, staying away from the channels where human waste and passing feet turned the earth to mud. A prickling at the back of his neck made Aldo stop, and glance over a shoulder – but there was nobody watching him. The rumble of a cart rolling along a nearby street echoed between the tall buildings, competing with shouts from hawkers busy selling their wares. In the cramped heart of Florence, there were always other people around.

Aldo stopped again in the narrow alleyway outside Zoppo's tavern, but this time he was listening. Only when he heard the cripple muttering inside did Aldo kick open the door, storming into the fly-blown tavern. The guilt in Zoppo's face confirmed Aldo's suspicions.

'Dante told you, didn't he?' Zoppo asked, retreating so fast he had to hop. 'He said I introduced him to Carafa.' Zoppo slipped and fell to the packed dirt floor but kept scrambling away, until his back was trapped against the bar. 'That *bastardo* Carafa is in Florence, if you're looking for him. Came here yesterday, demanding directions to Dante's home.'

'Carafa's in Le Stinche now,' Aldo sneered, grabbed Zoppo's sweat-stained tunic to haul him up off the floor. 'Give me one reason why you shouldn't be sharing a cell.'

'It wasn't my fault,' Zoppo insisted, his voice pitiful. 'I didn't know why Dante wanted to meet someone like Carafa. Honest, I didn't!'

'*Palle*. I'd wager good coin it was you that suggested Dante should pay a bandit to kill Levi.' Aldo pulled back a fist. 'Your matchmaking nearly got me murdered.'

'But I didn't know that Levi had hired a guard from the Otto. How could I?' Zoppo squeezed his eyes shut, bracing for the pain. 'Helping men like Carafa, that's what I do. It's how I hear what you want to know. If I wasn't so useful to men like him, I'd be no use to you.'

The duplicitous *merda* had a point, but Aldo wasn't going to admit that. 'You want to stay out of Le Stinche, you have to earn that privilege.'

Zoppo opened one eye, wary. 'I'll do whatever it takes. Just name it.'

Aldo unclenched his first. 'A man was in Palazzo Medici close to curfew yesterday – heavyset, with a prominent hooked nose. He was carrying a ledger with Hebrew writing on it. I want to know who that man is, who he answers to, and anything else you can find out about him.' Aldo could have returned to Palazzo Medici in search of the answers, but that would only draw attention. Using Zoppo and his contacts was safer. 'And I want to know where that ledger is now.'

'Don't want much, do you?' Zoppo said, the usual leer returning to his face.

'And you have to get me the answers before curfew.'

That wiped the smile away. 'Curfew today? But . . . How am I supposed to—?'

'Use your imagination.' Aldo let go of the clammy tunic and wiped both hands on his hose. 'Otherwise I'll have you thrown in Le Stinche before the bell in Palazzo della Signoria stops chiming tonight.' He strolled towards the splintered door. 'And I'll spread word you've been my informant for years. Every thief in that prison will think you put them inside.'

'But they'll crucify me,' Zoppo protested.

'I know.'

The stone floor was cold beneath Rebecca's face. Someone with kind hands lifted her cheek, slipped a soft cloth underneath. Ruth kneeled in front of her. 'You had me worried.' Rebecca pulled herself up with Ruth's help, wincing as pain stabbed her head. There was a lump on one side, sore and tender to the touch. 'You fainted.' Rebecca looked round; they were alone. 'I sent the others away. Thought you could do with the peace.'

'Thank you.' The letter was still clenched in her fist.

Ruth sighed. 'I should have waited before giving that to you.'

'No, I needed to see it.' She offered Ruth the letter.

'Samuele addressed that to you.'

'You need to see for yourself.'

Ruth took the letter, eyes widening as she read it. 'Where is your father's ledger?'

'Stolen. Taken by his murderer.'

Ruth read on, closing the letter before returning it. 'Joshua Forzoni, is that . . . ?'

Rebecca nodded.

'But why would Samuele forbid you from seeing Joshua?'

'His father was not born a Jew.' Rebecca grimaced. 'What should I do?'

'Show the letter to whoever is pursuing Samuele's killer.'

'Yes, I will – but what about Joshua? He loves me. He'd do anything for me.'

'But do you love him?'

Rebecca hesitated. The truth was she didn't know her own heart any more. 'I used to tease him, knowing that would anger Father. It was nothing serious. But now – now I'm not so sure.' She peered at her cousin. 'Could I have been in love with Joshua all along?'

'It's obvious Joshua has strong feelings for you,' Ruth replied. 'But only you can know what is in your heart. You are the one who must decide what happens next. Do you care enough for Joshua to break with your father's wishes?'

Rebecca didn't have an answer for that.

'Have you thought about what you might do after sitting *shiva*?' Ruth asked. 'Did your father have coin put aside for you, or for a dowry?'

Rebecca shook her head, ashamed at how little attention she had paid to her own future. She had supposed she would marry one day, though Father did his best to dissuade any potential suitors. None of them was good enough for his only daughter, he'd said. Now he was gone and she was left behind, alone, with no way to support herself.

Ruth put an arm round Rebecca's shoulders, pulling her into an embrace. 'I'm sorry, I shouldn't be asking you questions like that. Not while you're still in shock. But you need to think about these things, while you still have the support of friends and neighbours. Once you finish sitting *shiva*, you will be alone. But it doesn't have to be like that.'

Rebecca didn't understand. 'What do you mean?'

'We have a home for you, in Bologna, if you want it. There is no haste needed for this, you can decide in your own time. But should you choose, you could come and live with us. Soon I will be running the business. My brothers are strong and honest, but they haven't the wit or will to become moneylenders. I will need help with that. You could be that help.'

Rebecca wasn't sure what to say; it was a lot to take in. 'Can I think about it?'

Ruth smiled at her. 'Of course. I will always love you, cousin, whatever you decide – whether that is staying here in Florence or joining us in Bologna. I simply wanted to give you a choice, another path to consider. It is difficult enough for the likes of us, when nobody will listen to what we think or say. But there is another life waiting for you, if you wish it.'

After giving Zoppo reason to fear for his life, Aldo took a ragged path back to the eastern quarter of the city. Approaching the Podestà, he turned north, and moments later reached Palazzo Pazzi. No Pazzi had lived in this grand building for decades, not after all of them were driven out following a failed plot against the Medici. But the family name remained, as did the Pazzi crest of twin dolphins on the stone shield by the main entrance.

Aldo went inside to seek an audience with Cibo, who resided at the palazzo. It was also home to the cardinal's sister-in-law Ricciarda Malaspina, and her sister Taddea. The Duke had two illegitimate children by Taddea, with the boy Giulio a potential heir until the Duke's own young wife Margaret gave birth to a son. Little wonder Cibo welcomed Alessandro's visits to the palazzo. It was the Emperor who had installed Alessandro as hereditary ruler of Florence despite the Duke having been born out of wedlock. It made sense to have his heir and mistress under the same roof as the Emperor's representative in the city.

A servant escorted Aldo to the cardinal's *officio*. Cibo was hunched in a grand chair, sifting papers by a blazing fire. He dismissed the servant before beckoning Aldo closer. 'You have news about the murder of that moneylender?' Aldo reported his findings, mentioning the stolen ledger but not where he'd seen it. The cardinal pursed his lips. 'Fascinating, I'm sure, but nothing you couldn't have told me by letter. Why are you really here?'

When dealing with men of power and influence, it was frequently safer to answer one question with another. 'Why are you so interested in the murder of Samuele Levi?'

Cibo got up, moving nearer the fire as if to warm his hands. Aldo followed him. 'The Holy Roman Emperor had no financial transactions, nor any direct involvement with Levi,' the cardinal said. 'My interest in this incident is prompted by other matters.'

Aldo gave no reply. Silence often extracted answers from the most reluctant of men.

'Whispers have reached me of a plot,' the cardinal continued after a moment. 'A plot to create unrest among the people of Florence so that they demand a different leadership.'

'Such rumours are always being whispered,' Aldo said. 'By exiles outside the city, intent on usurping the Medici, or by those within Florence who hope to see it become a republic again. Nothing ever comes of such drunken boasts and wistful dreams.'

'Not in most cases,' Cibo agreed. 'Drunks and the wistful

overthrow few tyrants, that needs men at arms. But this particular plot may have found a way to fund its insurrection.'

The implication was clear: the plotters planned to borrow coin to pay for mercenaries. No wonder Levi was heard arguing with his visitors. To have become involved with such a scheme was asking for trouble, not to mention offering little chance of a return.

'I understand,' Aldo said.

Cibo smiled. 'Good. Then you can share with me what you've kept from the Duke, and that self-important fool Bindi. I've said more than I had to. Now it's your turn.'

Refusing would end the grudging trust Aldo shared with Cibo, whereas revealing a little knowledge now might help to unlock another secret from the cardinal. It was worth the risk. 'I believe Levi's ledger was stolen by his killer. Last night I saw a man carrying that ledger.'

Cibo stared into the flames. 'Where?'

'Inside Palazzo Medici.'

The cardinal stayed where he was a moment before returning to his chair. 'That does explain why the Duke wasn't surprised by what I told him.'

Aldo recalled meeting Cibo as the cardinal left Palazzo Medici not long before curfew on Tuesday. 'You went to warn him about the conspiracy, but he already knew.'

Cibo nodded.

That suggested a new motive for the murder. If Alessandro knew about the plot, it was possible he had sent someone to confront Levi at home on Monday night. Aldo pictured how the stubborn moneylender would react when someone demanded the names of his debtors. 'If what you say is true, it's possible Levi was stabbed by accident, or to silence him. Whoever did that then stole the ledger, believing the plotters must be named in it. They hadn't realized all the ledger entries are written in Hebrew.' That explained why the ledger hadn't been destroyed; whoever took it still needed to know what was inside.

But there were pieces of the puzzle that didn't fit together. Why was the Duke so eager for the Otto to investigate Levi's murder? Didn't that risk the involvement of his own men being discovered? Another possibility troubled Aldo. His investigation into the killing might be a ruse, a feint serving another purpose – to draw out or identify the plotters so the Duke's guards could strike against them first. Alessandro's apparent concern for the murder of a Jewish moneylender had always seemed out of proportion. Despite himself, Aldo grimaced.

Cibo was watching him. 'You have a different theory?'

'Nothing I can prove. Not yet.'

'Then keep looking, and keep me informed. There may be more to this than either of us realize. This city has suffered enough in recent years. What it needs now is stability.'

It was a good speech, Aldo decided on the way out, but the cardinal had omitted another reason for his interest. If the Duke fell, the city would be left vulnerable to forces from inside and outside its walls – and that could lessen the Emperor's hold over Florence.

Madelena Seta smiled as a servant ushered Strocchi into the richly decorated room. 'Back again, constable? If we keep meeting like this, people will talk.'

Strocchi bit back a sharp reply. He'd come to Palazzo Seta for answers, not to indulge this woman's taste for intrigue. In his home village there was no need for such games. But in Florence the daughters and wives of merchant families were kept cloistered.

Any young man visiting a palazzo could become a prime target for mischief. 'You're too kind, signorina,' he said, bowing low. 'I'm here to see your brother Biagio. Has he returned from Pisa?'

Madelena sighed. 'Yes, though you will find him poor company.' She gestured at a waiting servant, who hastened from the room. Madelena set aside her embroidery to approach the constable, playful dimples appearing in her cheeks. 'Tell me, do you have someone special in your life? Someone who lifts the burden of your manliness?'

Strocchi's brow furrowed. What exactly was she asking?

Madelena stopped in front of him, close enough that he could inhale the scent she wore. Its exotic aroma curled into his nostrils, intoxicating the constable's senses. 'You seem like a man full of . . . spirit,' she whispered, reaching out a hand to cup his groin, making Strocchi gasp. 'Is there someone that helps to relieve your . . . pent-up feelings?'

Not trusting himself to speak, Strocchi shook his head. Holy Madonna, the hand was moving up and down now. It was like having the sun there, warmth spreading through him. She stared into his eyes, clearly enjoying the power she had.

The sound of approaching footsteps saved him. Strocchi stepped back, arranging his own hands to hide any evidence of what had happened. Madelena retreated to her embroidery as a flustered, cherub-faced man of thirty summers bustled in.

'I'm Biagio Seta. You wanted to see me?'

'Yes.' Strocchi was all too aware of Madelena, her playful eyes still full of forbidden promises. 'Perhaps it might be best if we talked in private.'

'Of course.' Seta turned to his sister. 'Madelena, would you mind leaving us?'

She pouted her way from the room, pausing only to blow the

constable a kiss when her brother wasn't watching. Strocchi waited till he could no longer hear her footsteps before speaking, giving himself time to focus and Seta time to worry.

'A young man called Luca Corsini was attacked on Sunday night. He was kicked, beaten and left for dead by two men. Corsini may have looked weak and delicate to his attackers, but he lived for several hours before dying.'

Seta shook his head. 'You can't think I had anything to—'

'You were outside the city when this happened,' Strocchi cut in, 'so you can't have been part of it.' Seta nodded, relief evident on his chubby face. 'Not directly, at least.'

Seta's hopeful expression faded.

'On Sunday morning, Luca attended a mass at Santa Croce. He was dressed as a courtesan, quite a striking one, I'm told, and using the name Dolce Gallo. This newcomer caught the eye of several men at the church. Including you.'

Seta stared at the floor, offering no attempt at a denial this time.

'Two witnesses saw you contacting this new young courtesan after mass. I believe you arranged to meet Corsini that afternoon. If so, you were one of the last people to see him alive.' Still no reply. 'I've spoken to Corsini's landlady. She remembers the men who visited his room on Sunday.' Signora Mula had only talked about the intruders who came later, but Seta wasn't to know that. 'If I brought her here, she would have little trouble recognizing you.' That was a lie, but Strocchi could confess his own sins later. 'Well?'

Seta dabbed at his face with a cloth before slumping into his sister's empty chair. 'I didn't mean any of this to happen. I swear, I didn't know what they'd do.'

After days of lies and evasions, the last thing Strocchi had expected was a confession. It was so long since anyone had given him a direct answer, he wasn't sure what to say next.

'I certainly didn't mean the young man any harm,' Seta continued, squirming in his seat. 'He was so beautiful and so . . . But when I saw that drawing, I had to do something . . . It wasn't my fault, I swear it wasn't . . .'

Strocchi held up a hand to stop the words tumbling from Seta. 'You admit you were with Corsini on Sunday?' Seta nodded, biting his bottom lip. 'What time did you leave?'

'Four. I know because I heard a clock chiming somewhere nearby. I was late, terribly late, scrambling around for my clothes, and that's when I found it.'

'His diary.'

Seta nodded, hands twisting the sweat-soaked cloth he was clutching. 'It was . . . I'd never read anything like it. That silly boy, he wrote about the men who visited him. He even drew sketches of them. I recognized one.'

'So you tore that page out.'

'Yes.'

'What did you do next?'

'Stuffed the page inside my boot and got away from there, fast as I could.'

'And who was on that page? Who had you recognized in Corsini's diary?'

Seta shook his head. 'I can't tell you. He'd destroy me.'

Strocchi moved closer till he was looming over Seta. 'You've admitted being with Corsini not long before he was beaten to death. What do you think the Otto will do, if you're brought before it, charged with sodomy and conspiracy to kill a man?'

'I didn't conspire with anyone,' Seta protested, close to tears. 'I never wanted anyone to get hurt. I thought they would warn him, that was all.'

'Who?'

No reply.

'Who was it?' Strocchi demanded, grabbing Seta by the robes, pulling him up off the chair. 'Who sent the men that beat and kicked and murdered Corsini?'

But Seta didn't reply, fear all too evident in his face. Strocchi stared into the stricken man's eyes and saw himself reflected, anger and hatred twisting his features until he looked like Cerchi. Strocchi let go and Seta slumped into the chair, a blubbering mess.

Was this justice? Was this what it took to uncover the truth?

Strocchi turned away, giving himself a moment to think. The page Seta had torn from Corsini's diary was the key. Someone's likeness had been on it, someone who Seta knew – his older brother? No, the courtesans had said Alessio was sick. The sister had confirmed Alessio was too ill to go to Pisa. Strocchi studied Seta. He was squirming in the chair, as if at war with his own body. Or his own conscience. Seta wanted to tell the truth, it just needed the right questions to draw him out.

'I was sorry to hear of your brother's illness.'

'Thank you,' Seta replied.

'Has he been sick for some time?'

'Since last summer.'

Not a likely visitor to Corsini's bed, then. If Alessio was not in the diary, there was no reason for him to have Corsini slain. So who, then? When Strocchi first came to the palazzo, Madelena had mentioned a business partner. 'Your family are silk merchants?'

'Yes.'

'You must be grateful Alessio has someone to manage the business while he's ill.'

Seta flinched, so much that the chair moved under him. Strocchi stared, but Seta wouldn't meet his eye. 'Your family's partner lives in Florence, yes? What's his name?'

Seta waved a trembling hand, refusing to answer.

Strocchi gestured to the doorway. 'Shall I call a servant, and ask them? Or should I question your sister? Madelena seemed eager to please me a few minutes ago. I'm sure she would tell me anything I wanted to know.' A long silence. 'Well?'

Seta mumbled a reply, too quiet to be heard.

'Who?' Strocchi demanded.

'Ruggerio. His name is Girolamo Ruggerio. But you can't – you mustn't . . .'

'The man you saw sketched inside Corsini's diary – it was Ruggerio, wasn't it?' Seta gave a tiny, timid nod. 'Was it Ruggerio who ordered Corsini's murder?'

Seta curled himself up on the chair, knees tucked into his bulging belly.

'If you can't speak it aloud, just nod,' Strocchi said, lowering his voice. He didn't want to frighten Seta out of admitting the truth, not now. 'Was it Ruggerio?'

A nod.

'Did he tell you what was going to happen?'

A shake of the head.

'But you knew.'

Another nod.

'That's why you fled to Pisa on Sunday. You heard him arranging the attack.'

Seta hesitated, then gave a third nod.

There, the truth at last. It still wasn't proof, but far more than Strocchi had hoped. Now, for the hardest part. 'Biagio, you need to make a *denunzia* against Girolamo Ruggerio.'

Seta stared at Strocchi, wide-eyed. 'You don't know him, what he's capable of . . .'

'The *denunzia* wouldn't have to name you as his accuser.'

'He would still know it was me. Who else could it be?'

'One of the men who carried out the attack,' Strocchi suggested.

'The twins are completely loyal, they would never—' Seta clamped a hand over his mouth, horrified by what had slipped out. He shook his head, rising from the chair.

'Corsini was attacked by twins? Do they work for Ruggerio?'

Seta bolted from the room, flapping a hand as if to deflect any more questions. 'He'll destroy us,' Seta insisted on the way out. 'All of us.'

'What about Corsini?' Strocchi called. 'Doesn't he deserve justice?'

But Seta was gone.

Chapter Sixteen

*A*ldo resisted the temptation of going back to the tavern for quick answers from Zoppo. Give him time and the results were always better. Besides, getting that damned diary away from Cerchi had to take priority, before it caused any more damage. Aldo returned to the Podestà and found Benedetto laughing with a guard outside the gates. 'The *segretario* needs someone to fetch Cerchi,' Aldo said to the young constable. 'Can I trust you to do that?'

'Yes sir,' Benedetto replied, looking as eager to please as ever. That wouldn't last long if he stayed working for the Otto, but it was useful enough now. 'Where will I find him?'

'Cerchi is a creature of habit,' Aldo said. 'Every Thursday he visits a particular house near the Mercato Vecchio, run by an old friend of his, Signora Nardi. You know it?'

'The *bordello*?' Benedetto asked, blushing.

'That's the one. Cerchi won't appreciate being interrupted, but Bindi said this was important. Still think you can do it?'

'I won't let you down.'

'Good. You'd best hurry.' Aldo watched the constable scurry away before following, careful to stay well behind him. Coming round a corner, Aldo almost collided with a stooped young man who was begging for alms. Waving the sandy-haired youth away, Aldo continued stalking his quarry. Benedetto was soon knocking on the door to Signorina Nardi's *bordello*, no doubt bemusing those inside – regulars never waited for an answer. Aldo used a side entrance to enter while the constable was occupied talking to a black-haired woman out front.

Erotic frescos adorned the walls inside, while golden statues of nubile women pouted and posed in corners. The air was thick with musk and sandalwood, along with the sound of men grunting and women crying out in apparent ecstasy. This place might attract a richer standard of visitors than those south of the Arno, but a *bordello* was still a *bordello*.

'You lost?' Signorina Nardi asked when he slipped into her *officio*. She was a buxom woman of thirty summers, filling her robes. 'Or did Robustelli see sense and throw you out?'

'Neither. Is Cerchi in his usual room?'

Nardi arched a well-plucked eyebrow. 'What are you up to, Aldo?'

A knock at the door interrupted them. The black-haired woman who'd been teasing Benedetto at the *bordello* entrance stuck her head inside. 'There's a constable asking to see Cerchi.' She smirked. 'He's very polite.'

'Is the entire Otto planning to relocate itself here?' Nardi asked.

'Thought you'd appreciate the extra business,' Aldo said.

'Our visitors don't appreciate meeting officers of the court inside these walls. It tends to wilt their enthusiasm – and their *cazzi*.' She gestured at the woman in the doorway. 'Isabetta, go tell Cerchi he's wanted.'

'That'll be a first,' Aldo said as the door closed again.

'You still haven't answered my question,' Nardi persisted. But Aldo ignored her, listening as heavy footsteps stomped past, Cerchi complaining as he went by.

'I'll be gone before you know it,' Aldo promised, winking at Nardi on his way out.

The best room in the *bordello* was equipped with a bed on a raised dais, draped in the finest silks. A young, naked woman kneeled on the floor in front of the bed, eyes covered by a thick cloth secured behind her long red hair.

'I'm ready,' she giggled in a girlish tone. Ignoring her, Aldo searched Cerchi's clothes, which were strewn across the floor. 'Master,' the young woman asked, 'is that you?'

'Shhh,' Aldo replied while listening for footsteps outside. Cerchi's tunic and hose were missing – he must have pulled them back on to go to the front door. Luckily, his boots were still on the floor. Aldo found Corsini's diary tucked inside one of them, the pages featuring a selection of lurid sketches, and the dead youth's flowery hand. Such a slender volume, yet it had cost two men their lives. Aldo slid the diary inside his tunic.

'What you're saying makes no sense.' Cerchi's anger echoed through the *bordello*. 'Why would the *segretario* need me now? Did Bindi say this to your face?'

'No, it was Aldo—'

A string of obscenities heralded stomping feet, getting louder by the moment. *Palle*, he was coming back! Aldo pressed himself against the wall in the shadows behind the door. Cerchi stalked in, snatching up his belt, boots and discarded clothes.

'Master, is that you?' the young woman asked again, her voice trembling now.

'Who else would it be?' Cerchi demanded, pulling on his boots. He stopped with his left leg halfway inside its boot. 'Why'd you ask that? Has someone else been in here?'

'I don't know,' she said, lifting her blindfold. 'I couldn't see anything.'

Cerchi searched both boots, muttering under his breath. 'Where is it?' He spun round, gaze scouring the floor. Aldo held his breath in the shadows.

'Are you looking for something?' the young woman asked. 'Can I help?'

Cerchi slapped her across the face. 'If I wanted anything but your mouth, I'd take it.'

She put a hand to her reddened cheek, eyes blazing with anger. Turning to confront Cerchi, she caught sight of Aldo. He put a finger to his lips. Don't say anything. Please.

Cerchi pulled on the rest of his clothes, still cursing as he stomped out of the room. Aldo stayed by the wall, listening to Cerchi arguing with Nardi and swearing at Benedetto before finally leaving. 'Sorry,' Aldo said. 'He'd no right to hit you.'

The young woman shrugged. 'He takes what he wants. *Bastardo* doesn't even pay. But he usually only hits me when he can't get it up. That's why I have those.' She pointed to a table laden with concealing powders and rouge. 'What was he searching for?'

'Better you don't know,' Aldo replied on his way out.

Maria Salviati had set off at first light from the *castello* at Trebbio, leaving Cosimo with strict instructions to watch for any messages. In truth, Maria held out little hope of achieving great success during this trip to the city. But she had to try if her son was ever to attain his rightful place within Florentine society. Perhaps she could shame Alessandro into action? No, that was too fanciful a notion. She had considered appealing to his young wife Margaret for help, but the Duchess was little more than a child and still recovering from a miscarriage. It was doubtful Margaret had much influence over Alessandro at present.

The journey south was tiresome and exhausting, hours of bouncing along rough roads before entering the city through Porta San Gallo. Once inside Florence the progress was slower, but the streets far smoother. Maria watched from the carriage window as it passed the front of Palazzo Medici, guards standing sentry outside the ducal residence. When Giovanni was alive she had dreamed of becoming mistress of this grand palazzo. But her husband had no ambitions to become ruler of Florence, preferring battles and the company of his soldiers to the more subtle warfare of courtly intrigues. Then one such battle had taken his leg and, after the rot spread from the amputation wound, his life.

The carriage turned east before stopping outside Casa Vecchia. It was a far less impressive residence than that of the Duke, but would have to do for this brief visit. Most insultingly of all, she would have to sleep on the top floor, while the Duke's cousin had the more desirable middle level. Giving way to Lorenzino was vexing, but she had little choice.

Maria left the servants to unload her trunk while she swept inside. It was too late to call on anyone important or useful today – that must wait until tomorrow. If no satisfaction could be gained, she might despatch a message to the Podestà, summoning Cesare Aldo. Given the choice, Maria preferred to hold all the favours owed her in reserve, calling on them only in times of great need. But Aldo's position with the Otto made him a particularly useful ally. He would doubtless have knowledge her usual acquaintances could never supply. And what she knew about his nature meant Aldo was vulnerable. Maria had no wish to reveal his secret, but others might not be so scrupulous. One day it would be his undoing.

Better to make use of him while she could.

Bindi was preparing for the next Otto sitting when Cerchi barged in, not bothering to knock. The *segretario* could forgive Cerchi being a creature of brute force and no conscience; those qualities made him an effective – if blunt – enforcer. But insolence was not to be borne.

'Benedetto said you wanted to see me?'

'I'm a busy man, with considerable calls upon my time.'

'Is it true?' Cerchi spat, hands twisting into fists at his sides.

Bindi sat back in his chair. Impatience deserved only silence. He counted to ten in his head, watching Cerchi seethe before deigning to reply. 'You've been an officer for some months now, haven't you?'

Cerchi nodded.

'And you understand the procedure for those who wish an audience with me, yes?'

Cerchi hesitated before nodding again.

'Then you know what to do.' Bindi returned to the large stack of papers. After a long silence Cerchi stalked from the *officio*, shutting the door behind him before knocking on it. Bindi let the upstart wait before replying. 'Come in!'

Cerchi returned, eager to resume his rant. '*Segretario*—'

Bindi held up a finger for silence, reading two documents before looking at the new arrival. 'Ahh, Cerchi – you wished to see me?'

'Yes, *segretario*. Benedetto said you needed me.'

'I made no such request.' Cerchi's eyes narrowed. 'Was there something else?'

'Aldo stole an important piece of evidence.'

'What evidence?'

'A diary, written by the *buggerone* murdered several days ago.'

'Why would Aldo steal that? Was he mentioned in the diary?'

'No. At least, I don't think so.'

'Do you have any proof that Aldo took it?'

'He searched my things in the officers' cell this morning, and then he sent Benedetto to distract me when I was . . . busy.'

Bindi sighed. Cerchi was not telling the whole truth, but it mattered little. This was yet another skirmish between the two officers, which was of little interest. 'Are you any closer to knowing who murdered that young man?'

'No, *segretario*.'

'Then I suggest you concentrate on that, instead of wasting time with petty squabbles and accusations. Bring me proof Aldo is impeding justice and he'll stand accused before the Otto. Until then, I have better things to do. Close the door on your way out.'

Cerchi departed, pouting like a sulky youth. Bindi enjoyed the spectacle.

Renato was grateful to see Aldo return to the sewing room, especially after recognizing what was in Aldo's hands. Renato gave his workers the rest of the day off, announcing it was as thanks for all their hard work finishing gowns for the feast of Epiphany. He ushered them out of the sewing room, closing the door tight behind them before approaching Aldo.

'Is that what I think it is?' Renato asked, struggling to keep the joy from his voice.

Aldo nodded, opening the diary on a bolt of azure brocade. Renato recognized the sketch of himself inside it, a pleasing likeness – lovely Luca was always a flatterer. 'How did you get it?' Renato asked, before waving his own question away. 'It doesn't matter.'

'Do you want to burn it, or should I?' Aldo went to the sewing room hearth where the flames were burning orange. Renato took the diary from him, but stopped short of dropping it into the fire. Of course the book had to be destroyed, it was far too dangerous in the wrong hands, the last few days had proven that. But burning the last remnant of the beautiful young man who had filled each page with silly words and drawings felt wrong.

'Why are you hesitating?'

'Luca was such a pretty thing,' Renato said. 'In another time, another place, he would have been beloved.' Aldo snatched the diary, tearing pages out and throwing them on the fire.

'Corsini's dead, and so is Agnolotti Landini. This puts an end to it.'

Renato saw the flames reflected in Aldo's eyes. 'You never used to be this angry.'

'And you never used to be this sentimental.'

'It comes of getting older.' Renato couldn't help noticing the cloak Aldo wore. The material was superior to his other, much simpler clothes, and so was the cut. 'Where did you get that?' Renato asked, reaching to touch the fabric. 'A gift from an admirer?'

Aldo stepped back, out of reach. 'Tell Corsini's other friends that the diary has been destroyed,' Aldo said. 'Cerchi should leave you all in peace now. If he doesn't, let me know.'

Shadows filled the narrow street as Aldo emerged from the sewing room. A few hours still remained before curfew, but tall buildings either side of the dirt road were already masking the sun's light. He pulled the borrowed cloak closer to himself, savouring how Orvieto's scent suffused the fabric. The troublesome knee had been better thanks to the doctor's treatment. That was a relief but took away a reason to visit Orvieto again. Aldo rolled his eyes. Was it necessary to have a reason? No, but it was better than admitting how much he missed the doctor's smile, the warmth of that gaze. It was too soon to know what those feelings meant, or where they might lead. Not when everything else was so uncertain.

'You took it, didn't you?' an accusing voice demanded. Cerchi stepped from the shadows, his narrow face twisted by anger. 'Where is it?'

'What are you talking about?' Always better to feign ignorance when standing accused, it gave more time to craft a better answer.

'The diary written by your little pervert.'

'If you mean Corsini, I told you already, he was my informant.' Aldo moved to go by the other officer, but Cerchi blocked his path.

'Admit the truth – you sent Benedetto to Signorina Nardi's earlier to distract me, knowing it would give you a chance to steal the diary from me.'

'I sent Benedetto to fetch you back to the Podestà. From what I hear, you're doing nothing to find the men who murdered my informant.'

'I've been to Bindi about what you did,' Cerchi sneered, stepping even closer.

Aldo retreated a pace to escape the stale garlic on Cerchi's breath. 'I'm sure the *segretario* was fascinated by that. Is he planning to punish me for reminding you to do your job? Or did he tell you to do some work instead of wetting your wick in a *bordello*.'

Cerchi didn't reply, his fists clenching and unclenching at his sides. 'Those perverts that Corsini was meeting – they paid you to steal his diary, didn't they?'

Aldo laughed. 'Not everyone serving the Otto is so easily bought as you.'

'Then why were you just in there visiting Patricio? He was in that diary too.'

'Was he? Please, show me the page with his name on it.' Aldo couldn't resist smirking at Cerchi. 'Oh, that's right. You said somebody stole the diary. That's a shame. Not that you could even read what was inside it.'

'You arrogant *merda*,' Cerchi snarled, taking a wild swing with his right fist.

Aldo leaned back so the flailing arm missed him. Cerchi stumbled forwards and Aldo stepped to one side, leaving a leg behind. Cerchi tripped over it and tumbled into a pile of horse dung on the muddy street. He was still shouting abuse as Aldo strolled away.

Strocchi went to Zoppo's tavern hoping Aldo might be there. The constable needed counsel, and he didn't want to be asking his questions inside the Podestà. The tavern's front door had been kicked in and was now leaning against a wall by the entrance – no doubt left there by some unhappy customer. Zoppo was all charm at first until he learned Strocchi had come looking for Aldo, not a place to drink.

Yes, the cripple was expecting a visit from Aldo but no, he didn't know when. Zoppo invited Strocchi to have a drink until Aldo arrived. The rank aromas inside the tavern were too much for Strocchi to stomach any longer. He declined the offer and waited outside.

It was a relief when Aldo came striding along the alley, a cloak swirling behind him. 'What are you doing here?' he asked, glancing back over one shoulder.

'I need your advice,' Strocchi said. He repeated what Biagio Seta had revealed.

'Ruggerio's a dangerous man to cross,' Aldo said. 'Not only is he a significant figure in the silk merchants' guild, Ruggerio is also active in the Company of Santa Maria, one of the most powerful confraternities in Florence. That means he has alliances in business and the Church. I wouldn't have picked him for one of Corsini's visitors, but it takes all kinds. You think Ruggerio paid for the attack on Corsini?'

'He seems the most likely from what I've discovered, but I need to be certain before making a *denunzia* against him. Can I ask your informant? I wasn't sure if I could trust him.'

'Zoppo is a self-serving *merda*, but his information is usually right.'

Strocchi followed Aldo inside. Zoppo was still lurking behind the bar, spitting phlegm into a cup before rubbing it with a greasy rag. 'Who wants a drink?' he asked.

'Nobody with sense,' Aldo replied. 'What do you know about Girolamo Ruggerio?'

'The silk merchant? Enough not to cross him – why?'

Aldo nodded to Strocchi, who took over the questions. 'What about his guards? There are two in particular, they could be related.'

Zoppo's lopsided smile faded. 'You mean the Basso brothers. From up north, both have got yellow hair. Fists like anvils, and faces like sides of meat. Best avoided, I hear.'

'Handy men to have on your side,' Aldo said.

'Word is they've been spending plenty in bars and *bordelli*. Men like them coming into money usually only means one thing. They did someone else's dirty work and got well paid for it. Why are you asking? This got something to do with that dead *buggerone*?'

Strocchi was sick of hearing the victim dismissed that way, but still nodded.

Zoppo gave a low whistle. 'Whatever you're hoping to prove, those two aren't going to help. From what I've been told, the brothers are loyal. To the death.'

Strocchi kept his face impassive, but his heart sank. The closer he got to the men who murdered Corsini, the further away justice seemed to be.

Aldo beckoned him aside. 'Got what you needed?'

'Yes, but there's someone else I need to see.'

'Tell me you're not going to Palazzo Ruggerio.'

'Not now, but I will in the morning, if you'll go with me. Men like Ruggerio can ignore a constable, but I'm hoping he will pay attention to an officer of the Otto.'

Aldo scowled. 'I wouldn't depend on that, but I will go with you tomorrow.'

After bidding farewell to Strocchi, Aldo returned to the fetid gloom of the tavern. He'd noticed a new smell earlier, an acrid scent amid the spoiled wine and despair. Zoppo was still lurking behind the bar, but he seemed more furtive than usual. Aldo dug in his pouch and threw two coins on the bar. 'That's for helping Strocchi.' Zoppo nodded, sweeping the coins into his hand. 'So, what have you heard about the man with the hooked nose?'

The cripple scowled. 'I didn't have much time. And Palazzo Medici isn't exactly where my eyes and ears spend their days. But I do have something for you.' Zoppo reached under the bar and pulled out a bundle wrapped in rough cloth. The acrid smell grew worse. Much worse.

'What is it?'

Zoppo tilted his head to one side. 'I need a promise first. Your word that you'll never threaten to tell anyone else about our arrangement.'

Aldo couldn't keep his gaze from what was clutched in those grasping hands. If it was what he thought . . . 'Yes, of course.' He reached for the wrappings but Zoppo pulled back.

'Your word, Aldo. Say it. Or else we never do business again.'

He meant it, every word. Aldo looked Zoppo in the eyes. 'I, Cesare Aldo, do vow and promise never to tell – or threaten to tell – anyone about what you do for me.'

'And don't you forget that,' the cripple said. Still scowling, he pushed the object across the bar to Aldo. 'Here, take the damned thing. It's been stinking my place out.'

Aldo pulled the object closer before carefully unwrapping the clothes folded round it to reveal what was inside: a leather-bound book. The outside was burnt and charred, as if it had been thrown atop a roaring fire, but a few Hebrew symbols were still legible on one side. It was Levi's stolen ledger. Aldo stared at the book. 'Where did you get this?'

'Better you don't ask,' Zoppo said. 'Pulled from a fire is all you need to know.'

Aldo opened the book. More than half the pages had been torn out, judging by the threads left hanging from the binding. The pages that remained were all blackened round the edges, but close Hebrew text was still legible on most of them. It was fortunate whoever had wanted to destroy the ledger had thrown it on the fire closed, otherwise nothing would have remained inside it. Aldo closed the covers, swaddling the ledger in cloth again. 'Well done.'

Zoppo accepted the appreciation with a nod. 'The hook-nosed man you were asking about? Used to be a page, carrying a shield in parades and tournaments, according to some people, before discovering his true talent. He's had a few different names too, depending on who you ask. The name my people have heard used the most is Scoronconcolo. People say he's good with a blade, and not afraid to use it. Bloodthirsty was the word.'

Aldo leaned closer. 'And?'

'From what I've heard, this Scoronconcolo has been in Palazzo

Medici a lot lately. Got ideas above his rank, apparently, which was why people were happy to talk. Some admit to being afraid of him. Got a sharp tongue as well as a sharp blade. He's a dangerous one to cross, especially since his master has the ear of the Duke.'

There were two men at Palazzo Medici who had that distinction. Aldo dug three more coins from his pouch and slid them across the bar to Zoppo. 'Who's his master?'

The cripple swiped the coins into his hand. 'Your hook-nosed man works for the Duke's own cousin. Scoronconcolo is the faithful servant of Lorenzino de' Medici.'

Chapter Seventeen

For the third time in four days, Strocchi found himself at the last place Corsini had called home. Knocking on the front door got no response, so he hammered it with a fist, setting off a chorus of barking dogs nearby. Signorina Mula opened the door, scowling at him. 'Haven't you anything better to do?'

'The intruders who ransacked your attic on Sunday night – can you describe them?'

'I told you already. They wore cloaks with hoods hiding their faces.' Mula reached for the door to shut him out but Strocchi blocked it with his right boot.

'I've another witness who described what the two men looked like.' A lie told in the hope of catching a truth. Strocchi lamented the need to use falsehoods so often, but if this succeeded it would be worth the penance his sin required.

'If you've another witness, you don't need me.'

'Please,' Strocchi insisted. 'Hear me out.'

Mula folded her arms, scowling. 'Say what you must, then go.'

'The two men, could they have been brothers?'

'Brothers?'

'Twins. Two big men, heavy – with blond hair.'

Mula's eyes widened at the mention of hair colour. She did what she could to hide the reaction, but not fast enough.

'You did see them,' Strocchi said. 'I knew it.'

The widow shook her head. 'It was too dark.' She kicked Strocchi hard in the calf, making him withdraw his leg. 'Don't come back here. I've nothing more to say.' The door slammed shut, setting the dogs off again while Strocchi nursed his leg.

Blond hair was not common in the city, certainly not for men – any glimpse of it would have stuck in her mind. So why deny the truth? Because she was scared. Strocchi had one faint hope left: that he and Aldo could get a confession from Ruggerio. They would probably need the Holy Madonna herself on their side for that.

Keen to avoid Ponte Vecchio, Aldo used Ponte alla Carraia to cross the river while musing over what Zoppo had revealed. Scoronconcolo being Lorenzino's servant seemed to confirm what Cibo had implied – that Levi died after getting involved with a plot to overthrow the Duke. Lorenzino was a Medici, after all; it was in his interests to protect Alessandro. What better way to do that than Lorenzino sending his faithful servant to confront Levi.

It was the Duke's cousin who had insisted the murder investigation be completed by Epiphany. Lorenzino must have evidence that the plot to overthrow the Duke was planned for the feast day. It certainly made sense for the conspirators to strike while Captain Vitelli and most of the ducal guard were outside the city. But what other secrets were Alessandro and Lorenzino withholding about Levi's murder? Were they using the Otto's investigation as a way to uncover the conspirators, or was some other motive behind all of this?

After reaching Oltrarno Aldo turned east, moving parallel to the river, the remains of the ledger tucked under one arm, still wrapped in rough cloth. That the ledger was burnt suggested two outcomes. The contents had proven to be of no use, or those who took it were unable to find someone trustworthy to read the Hebrew entries. They certainly couldn't take the ledger to ask one of Levi's neighbours for a translation, not without it being recognized.

Turning south into via dei Giudei, Aldo was still debating whom he should ask to examine the ledger. Rebecca would be able to read her father's writing, but that didn't mean she would understand what the entries denoted. Besides, she was still sitting *shiva*. Better to leave her in peace, if possible. Aldo paused outside Sciarra's front door, but dismissed asking him for help. It would be impossible to trust a word coming out of that man's mouth. Instead Aldo went to the far end of the narrow road, stopping outside Dante's home.

He knocked at the door, pushing his way inside as soon it opened. Dante objected to the intrusion until reminded of the *denunzia* against him still to be put before the Otto. And Aldo had another reason to want to talk behind a closed door. Uneasiness had nagged at him much of the day, the prickling skin sensation of being watched or followed. Each time he glanced round, there was nobody there and nobody looking at him. But the instinct still clawed at his senses, and trusting his instincts was usually what kept him alive.

Inside Dante's house was dark, shutters drawn on what daylight remained outside, a few flickering candles not enough to lift the gloom. Dante seemed to have shrunk in the few days since the murder. His frayed robes were hanging off him, while his face was gaunt and hollow-cheeked with dark smudges of exhaustion under the eyes. 'Can you not let me grieve in peace?' he asked. 'Is it not enough I have admitted my guilt?'

Aldo unwrapped the burnt ledger on a small dining table, the pungent aroma of burnt leather and paper billowing outward. 'Do you recognize this?'

Dante's eyes widened. 'That belonged to Samuele and me. What happened to it?'

'That doesn't matter,' Aldo said, opening the charred cover. 'I need you to look inside, see if you can read what is left.'

Dante brought a lit candle closer to illuminate the blackened pages. He turned to the back of the ledger, fingers tracing the torn binding threads. 'We spent years building our business together. That somebody could tear it apart like this . . .'

'Can you read the entries?'

Dante peered at the ledger. He pointed to where the missing pages should be. 'Someone has ripped out the oldest entries. Only the pages for the past few months are here.'

Aldo nodded. That matched his own suspicion. Someone had torn out the back pages, hoping to erase the most recent entries. But Hebrew was written right to left across the page, and from the back of a book towards the front. 'So you should able to tell me who Levi was lending money to in the last few weeks and months?'

'Maybe. Samuele was more interested in coin than bookkeeping. Before he forced me out, I used to write all the debtors and loans in here. His entries were erratic, at best.'

'How long will it take?' Curfew was not far away; the Duke would be waiting.

Dante shrugged. 'A few hours. Maybe more.'

'Start with the most recent entries. Look for new debtors, and large loans – anything beyond what Levi would normally make. I'll be back soon,' Aldo said, already leaving.

* * *

Aldo stopped outside the door to Orvieto's home. It was open, inviting him to enter. There were far more urgent things that had to be done, but still Aldo knocked. 'Come in,' the doctor called. 'I'm at the back.' Aldo went inside, shrugged off the borrowed cloak. It would have to be his reason for returning, though he had no wish to give it back.

In the room at the rear of the house Orvieto stood at the far end of the table, its surface awash with glass-stoppered bottles of powders and unguents, each of them bearing Hebrew and Latin inscriptions. The handsome young man besotted with Rebecca Levi – Joshua, that was his name – sat to one side, staring at the bottles.

Aldo held out the cloak. 'I'm returning this.'

Orvieto beamed, coming round the table to take the garment. 'I was testing my student on his knowledge of remedies.' Joshua gave Aldo a polite nod. 'How's the knee?'

'Better.' Aldo smiled. It hadn't hurt all day. 'Much better, thanks to you.'

'My pleasure,' the doctor replied, resting a hand on Aldo's shoulder. The touch sent a small thrill through him, reviving memories of strong hands massaging the salve into . . .

'I'll leave you to your lessons,' Aldo said, retreating towards the doorway. Better to go before he made himself any more of a fool. One of Orvieto's eyebrows – hidden from Joshua – was raised, a silent promise or perhaps an invitation.

'Cesare,' the doctor said.

Aldo paused in the doorway. 'Yes?'

'Why don't you keep the cloak for now. I have others, and most of my day is spent here in the warmth.' Orvieto came closer, pressing the garment into Aldo's hands. 'You can always bring it back later.' That was an invitation, said without doubt or hesitation.

'Thank you,' Aldo replied, gazing deep into the doctor's eyes before giving a final nod to his student. Aldo strode back to the front door, but Joshua followed him out.

'Are you still hunting for Samuele's killer?'

Aldo didn't have time to reassure Rebecca's would-be suitor. 'Yes, but you must excuse me. I have to report my progress to the Duke before curfew.'

Joshua stepped in Aldo's way to stop him going. 'Have you talked to Rebecca today?'

'No. I promised Yedaiah I would leave her in peace, as much as I could.'

'You misunderstand,' Joshua said. 'I think you should talk to Rebecca, or at least to her cousin. Ruth came from Bologna to sit *shiva*. She brought a letter that Samuele wrote. The way she and Rebecca were talking – it sounded important.'

Aldo thanked Joshua, and went directly to the Levi home. The young woman who opened the door had some of the family traits in her stern face. Aldo introduced himself, expecting to have to argue his way in. But Ruth Levi was willing to talk, so long as they spoke outside. 'Rebecca is sleeping, I don't want her disturbed.' She fetched a shawl and came back out, closing the door behind her. 'I saw you at our house in Bologna,' Ruth said. 'You were the one who guarded Samuele on his journey home.'

'For all the good it did.'

'You did your duty. He died in his own home, not on the road.'

Aldo told her what Joshua had said about the letter. Ruth pulled it from inside her shawl. 'I thought you might want to see this.' It was in Hebrew, but Ruth translated part of the text for him, fingers moving from right to left across the page. 'Rebecca's father feared for his life. He had decided to withhold a loan to a man of importance.'

'Did your uncle name this man of importance?'

Ruth shook her head. 'These are Samuele's exact words: *You will find him in my ledger, if you look long enough.*' She stopped, frowning. 'Is that why the ledger was stolen?'

'Probably,' Aldo replied. He kept news of the ledger's recovery to himself; the fewer people who knew about that, the better. With any luck, the incriminating page would still be inside it, and legible enough for Dante to read. 'Is there anything else in the letter that might help?' Ruth shook her head. 'Do you know why your uncle was in Bologna?'

'He needed coin for a new client, a sum far beyond anything he'd ever loaned before. A small fortune, my father called it. In the past, the two of them shared the risk when making a large loan. This would have been many times greater than any loan they'd made before. Yet when Samuele left Bologna, he chose not to take the coin my father had ready.'

So there was no robbery. Aldo had suspected as much. Certainly the satchels Levi clung to all the way back from Bologna had shown no sign or sound of being filled with coin. But that absence, the fact Levi had chosen not to make the loan, could well be the reason why he was stabbed and left to die. 'This man of importance – does Rebecca know who it is?'

'No, I don't believe so. My uncle refused to let her be any part of his business, even though he insisted on debtors coming here to the house.' Ruth leaned closer. 'Something else in her father's letter is troubling Rebecca. He forbade her from being with Joshua Forzoni. I'm not sure my cousin knows her own heart yet, whether or not she truly loves this Joshua. He certainly seems to love her. But your father's last wish is a hard thing to break.'

* * *

Aldo was still pondering what to report when Campana ushered him into Alessandro's *officio* at Palazzo Medici. Accusing the Duke of any involvement with Levi's murder was madness, but there had to be a way of proving what happened. Aldo was surprised to find Alessandro alone behind his desk. There were guards flanking the room's entrance as usual, but the absence of Lorenzino offered an opening, a chance to discover at least some of the truth. 'Your Grace,' Aldo began, 'my investigation has uncovered something important. I believe the moneylender was killed not for being Jewish, but because he'd been drawn into a plot against you. It seems someone arranged to borrow a large amount from Levi for that purpose.'

Alessandro sighed, showing no surprise at this revelation. 'Conspiracies are all too common in this city. They seem to follow the name Medici wherever we go. Our dear cousin has been talking about little else for several days now.'

'I was also sceptical at first,' Aldo agreed, moving nearer the desk. 'But it is possible the plotters planned to use the loan to pay for men at arms, mercenaries who would lead this attempt to overthrow you. It seems Levi discovered the true purpose of the loan he'd agreed to make, and refused to go ahead with the arrangement.'

'So the plotters killed him?'

'That is one possibility. But my investigation leads me to suspect another hand in this matter. One rather closer to you than Your Grace might realize.' Aldo took a breath before commencing his *denunzia* – and heard the doors swing open behind him. Lorenzino strolled past a moment later as another person entered the *officio*, closing the doors after them. The new arrival strode by Aldo to join the Duke's cousin by the desk: Scoroncocolo.

Aldo studied Lorenzino's servant, assessing the man he'd

only seen once before, across the courtyard of the palazzo. Scoronconcolo was heavyset, but that bulk was solid, nothing weak or flabby about him. Two piercing eyes glared at Aldo from either side of that hooked nose, above a cruel mouth. He stood like a soldier, ready to fight, to kill if needed. Aldo had met such men before. They knew how to wield a blade, and never hesitated to do so when necessary. This was the man who had stabbed Samuele Levi.

'Ahh, cousin,' Alessandro said, smiling at Lorenzino. 'You've arrived at a most vital moment. This officer from the Otto –' the Duke stopped to look across the desk – 'Sorry, what was your name again?'

'Cesare Aldo, Your Grace.'

'That's it! Yes, Aldo here was about to tell us the names of those responsible for the murder of the unfortunate moneylender.'

Lorenzino narrowed his eyes at Aldo. 'Were you? How interesting.'

'So, who is it then?' Alessandro asked, his face beaming. 'Anyone I know?'

Aldo opened his mouth to reply but all he could hear was roaring in his ears. It was obvious the Duke had no knowledge of Scoronconcolo's involvement, nor it seemed that his own cousin had sent the servant to confront Levi. To accuse either man now would be asking for a knife in the back. 'Sorry, Your Grace, but I'm still waiting on one last piece of evidence before I make a *denunzia* against those responsible.'

'How disappointing,' Lorenzino said, a sneer twisting his pallid features.

'Indeed,' the Duke agreed. 'We had rather hoped for an end to this matter. You may go.'

Aldo nodded, withdrawing to the double doors. He should

leave now without saying anything further. That was the safe choice, the wiser choice. But the chance to witness how Lorenzino and his servant responded could not be resisted. 'Forgive me, Your Grace.'

'Yes?' the Duke said.

'I told you yesterday about a ledger taken from the money-lender's home by his killer. I'm happy to say that ledger has been found.'

Lorenzino's expression remained the same, but Scoronconcolo lacked his master's experience of courtly intrigues. His eyes widened before darting sideways to Lorenzino.

'It seems the killer attempted to destroy the evidence by burning it,' Aldo continued. 'Happily, another hand removed the ledger from the flames before the damage was too great. The surviving pages are being translated from Hebrew to see what they reveal. I should have more answers for you tomorrow.' Aldo bowed to the Duke and left the *officio*.

Before, he'd been all but sure; now he was certain: Scoronconcolo murdered Levi, acting on orders from Lorenzino. What were they willing to do to conceal their crime?

The bells announcing curfew had long fallen silent when Aldo returned to via dei Giudei. He took an erratic route south from Palazzo Medici, stopping and listening in case anyone was following him, but saw and heard nobody. This investigation was playing tricks on him but it didn't hurt to be cautious. Having goaded Lorenzino and his murderous servant, it was wise not to bring that trouble on someone else.

Aldo knocked at Dante's house. He slipped inside as soon as the door opened, closing it behind him. He followed Dante through the house, the acrid aroma of the charred ledger leaving no doubt where it was. The blackened book lay open on a table, candles and lanterns clustered round it to light the smudged pages. 'Have you found anything yet?'

Dante slumped into a chair by the table, exhaustion etched in his sad face. 'Perhaps,' he replied, looking through the remnants. 'The flames did more damage than I first thought.'

Aldo stepped closer. 'Show me what you've found.'

Dante pointed to a particular line of Hebrew. 'This entry here stood out. The amount is twenty times larger than any sum Samuele and I ever lent out as partners.'

That sounded like the loan for which Levi had sought to share the risk with his brother in Bologna. A small fortune, Ruth said. 'Are there any other entries with loans close to that amount? Had any debtors recently been borrowing more and more?'

'No. I've checked before and after. This was a single loan, sought by a new debtor.'

Aldo's blood was quickened, and so was his breathing. Every part of him clenched. 'Who's the debtor?'

'There's no name here, just three letters.'

'Is it a code? Did Levi usually disguise the names of his debtors?'

'No, this is exceptional. I think he was trying to protect himself or the debtor, in case somebody else should see inside the ledger.'

That made sense if the debtor was this man of importance Levi had mentioned in his last letter to Rebecca. 'What are the three letters?'

Dante frowned. 'I think they're initials – they would likely translate as L, D and M.'

Aldo swallowed hard, his mouth and throat gone dry. Only one person involved with the investigation had a name to match those initials. If that person had tried to borrow a small fortune from Levi, it could mean only one thing.

Lorenzino de' Medici was plotting to overthrow his cousin, the Duke of Florence.

And Lorenzino knew Aldo had the evidence that could prove it.

Chapter Eighteen

❦

Friday, January 5th

*A*ldo knew what happened to those who went too long without sleep. He had seen it in men broken by battle, cursed to live the same bloody moments over and over again in dreams. Such men would do anything, take any apothecary's concoction to avoid sleep. They became ever more erratic, their actions without reason. It was much the same with suspects deprived of rest to encourage a confession: they did talk, but made little sense. Finally – mercifully in some cases – those who went long enough without sleep succumbed to madness or death.

Aldo had no wish to do the same, but the tangle of questions in his head refused to be silent. After a second night of staring into the darkness, he abandoned sleep and sat up to think things through. What could he prove, and what did he suspect?

What at first had seemed a simple stabbing was now far more complicated. It began when Lorenzino de' Medici arranged to borrow a small fortune from Levi to pay mercenaries to overthrow the Duke. Levi even hired a guard from the Otto to protect him on the road back from Bologna because he expected to be carrying that same fortune. But the moneylender changed his mind while away from Florence, and brought no coin back in his satchels.

Lorenzino sent his servant Scoronconcolo to Levi's home after curfew on Monday night to collect. When Levi refused to make the loan, Scoronconcolo stabbed him. Then the servant took the ledger, fearful that his master's name might be inside, and left Levi to die.

But if all that was true, why was Lorenzino so eager to see the killing investigated? Why insist the murder be solved by the feast of Epiphany? He was part of – perhaps even the leader of – a conspiracy to overthrow the Duke, but the plotters had been left without the coin to execute their plan. Did Lorenzino warn his cousin about the plot to try and conceal his own involvement? But he must know this *stratagemma* could only hide the truth for so long.

Another question nagged Aldo. Did the younger Medici have the *palle* to lead an uprising against his cousin? He acted the fawning sycophant well, yet appeared restless in the Duke's company – like a horse tugging at the bridle, waiting for a chance to throw its rider. Lorenzino had been swallowing his ambition for years, playing a dutiful cousin even when the Duke ruled against him. Was it the dispute where Alessandro had ruled against Lorenzino's family that had planted the seed of hatred in the younger Medici's heart? For now, the motivations behind the plot didn't matter. If Lorenzino truly believed himself capable of toppling the Duke, he would seek a way to do so.

But how, and when?

Aldo opened the shutters at his window. Dawn was close. Vitelli and the ducal guard would be back in the city within a day or two of Epiphany. Whatever Lorenzino planned, it would happen before then. But the conspirators had no coin or mercenaries, and a direct strike against Alessandro would not be simple. The Duke kept two guards alongside him wherever he went. That was one lesson Alessandro had learned well from past Medici.

Enough. The task was to find who had killed Levi. This conspiracy was something much larger, far beyond an officer of the Otto. He should take what he knew to Bindi, or to the Duke. But there was precious little evidence to support such a *denunzia*. Until he could prove beyond doubt that there was a conspiracy to overthrow Alessandro, making such an accusation against Lorenzino was asking to end up like Levi.

Aldo emptied his bladder and washed in icy water, dressing in haste to stay warm. He could ignore what he'd found. Let the Medici have their intrigues, let the conspiracy run its course. Alessandro would survive or fall, Lorenzino would succeed or fail. Did any of that matter? One duke was little different from the next. But Cibo had been right to mention the city's suffering in recent years – a siege, so many needless deaths, so much instability. If Alessandro fell, all of Florence would suffer.

No, Aldo would not allow that to happen. He loved Florence, though that love had often gone unrequited thanks to the city's laws, and sometimes its people. Florence was a cruel home at times, but it was where he had become a man, and the place he had come back to when injury ended his time as a soldier. He had been born in this city and had little doubt he would die here as well, one day. If he could save Florence from the plotters, he would. He had to try.

Besides, he had the ledger and Lorenzino knew it. There was no ignoring that.

Bindi had no sooner sat behind his desk at the Podestà when somebody was knocking at the door to his *officio*. Could these people not think for themselves? He had a report to prepare for the Duke. 'Come in,' Bindi called, not bothering to hide his irritation. Better they know his mood, and keep their interruption short.

Aldo entered, with something wrapped in cloth under one arm. He looked haggard, heavy bags under both eyes, greying stubble on his jaw. Bindi beckoned the officer forward and the harsh, burnt aroma came with him. What had he been doing? But when Bindi asked that question aloud, he didn't like the answer Aldo gave.

'Absolutely not,' the *segretario* said. 'His Grace trusts me to offer wise counsel, to act as his strong right hand in guiding the deliberations of the Otto. What would he think of me if I repeated your wild claims about a plot against him? I would be judged a madman or a fool, and the credibility of this court would be damaged.'

Bindi glared at Aldo, wondering what had put such folly into his mind. Those who served the Otto could be hot-blooded, even foolhardy, but Aldo had always been reliable – until today. Was the man drunk? He gave no sign of that, no slurring of his words and no unsteadiness in his stance. Had he gone without sleep so long his reason had suffered? Aldo certainly looked tired enough for that to be the case, but it was no excuse for this display. Whatever the reason, Bindi would not let himself be dragged into it.

Nevertheless, Aldo persisted. He pulled the bundle from beneath his arm, shoving it on the desk, demanding the *segretario* unwrap it. Reluctantly, Bindi did so and the source of that stench was revealed. Aromas of burnt leather assaulted his nostrils as the rough cloth fell away to reveal a charred book, a few Hebrew symbols still visible on the cover.

'This ledger belonged to the murdered moneylender,' Aldo said. 'Levi was murdered for reneging on a loan after he realized the coin was meant to fund an armed uprising against Duke Alessandro. The killer stole the ledger to conceal his master's name, and later tried to burn the book. One of my informants obtained the ledger, and gave it to me.' He leaned over the desk, opening the book to jab a finger at a blackened page of smudged text. 'This entry shows a client with the initials L D M wanted to borrow a small fortune from Levi.'

The *segretario* peered at the Hebrew notations. 'That could mean anything.'

'I believe Lorenzino and the other conspirators plan to over-throw the Duke tomorrow, during the feast of Epiphany. Vitelli and his men are due back any day, the conspirators have to strike before then. You have to warn the Duke,' Aldo said. 'He wouldn't listen to me.'

Bindi recoiled. 'You've mentioned this madness to His Grace?'

'Not his cousin's part in it, but I told him about the plot.'

The *segretario* rose, struggling to control his anger. 'You had no right to do that! I gave you a simple task, reporting your findings about the murder investigation to the Duke before curfew each day, nothing more than that. But you went to His Grace, and told him this nonsense about conspiracies and threats against him? Where is your proof for any of it? A burnt book and some whis-pers you've heard somewhere?'

'Cardinal Cibo was the one who—'

'Enough!' Bindi slammed the ledger shut on his desk. 'You have brought the Otto into disrepute with your high-handed belief that you knew better than anyone else. Get out of my sight, before I have you dismissed from the court's service.'

Aldo opened his mouth to reply, but nothing emerged. At last the depth of his error seemed to be dawning on the officer. He reached for the ledger but Bindi snatched it away.

'Go!'

Aldo hesitated a moment before retreating to the door, pausing to bow on the way out. Bindi wrapped the rough cloth round the foul-smelling ledger and locked it in a drawer under his desk. He sank back into his chair, both hands clenched into tight fists. He shuddered to think what was waiting at Palazzo Medici when he made his morning report.

Strocchi was shivering in the Podestà courtyard when Aldo stalked down the stone staircase. The early morning chill was not nearly so bitter as Aldo's face. Strocchi hesitated before speaking, but a promise was a promise. 'Sir?'

'What?' Aldo snapped at him.

Strocchi swallowed hard. 'I'm going to talk to Ruggerio about the murder of Corsini. You agreed to help me question him.'

'I don't have time for that now.'

'Please, I can't do this alone.'

Aldo looked like a man at war with himself, ready to lash out at anyone who got in his way. But whatever was eating at him, he swallowed it down and gave a curt nod. 'Where?'

'Ruggerio works from his palazzo near Santa Maria Novella most mornings,' Strocchi said, leading him out through the gates. They strode without talking for several streets, Strocchi struggling to keep pace with Aldo. But as they passed the Mercato Vecchio, the constable dared to make a comment. 'I asked people about Ruggerio – not mentioning why I wanted to know, of course. They say he's a powerful man, with important friends.'

'You don't lead the silk merchants' guild without accumulating power.'

'So how do we question him about Corsini? I did what you suggested with Biagio Seta; that worked well. But he was a weak, frightened man. Ruggerio is different.'

'Ruggerio is dangerous, and no fool. If he ordered Corsini's murder—'

'He did,' Strocchi insisted. 'I'm certain of it.'

'If he ordered the murder,' Aldo continued, 'he'll never admit that. Men like Ruggerio don't bloody their own hands. That's why he has the Basso brothers, to do what he won't.'

'But how do we get justice for Corsini?'

Aldo grimaced. 'Forget justice. The most we can hope for is that Ruggerio makes a mistake, or stumbles on his own self-importance. Threats will not trouble him. The only person who can undo Ruggerio is Ruggerio.'

Strocchi suspected Aldo was probably right, but that didn't make it easier to hear. 'Sir, can I ask – what has made you so angry?'

'If you wish to remain with the Otto, it's better you don't know.'

'I'm not sure I do wish to stay,' Strocchi said. The thought of leaving the court's service – of leaving Florence – had been on his mind all night, but it was the first time he'd given it voice. 'Not if men like Ruggerio can order a murder without any consequences.'

'Give it time,' Aldo replied. 'You've potential, Strocchi, but you also have an unbending way about you. We work for the Otto, hunting those who break laws and and – where possible – stopping others before they can. But it's the magistrates who sit in judgement on those who trespass against the law, not us. If you believe in the teachings of the Church—'

'I do.'

'—then you must trust that everyone faces their true judgement, sooner or later.'

Strocchi nodded. It made sense, but the injustice of life in Florence still rankled. 'Are you any closer to knowing who killed the moneylender?'

'That's why I was arguing with Bindi,' Aldo said, his tone a warning not to ask more. A grand residence loomed ahead of them – Palazzo Ruggeri. Its three levels were built of the richest materials, every aspect of the design intended to show off its splendour and beauty. The wealth required to maintain such a palazzo was beyond imagining for most citizens.

'This must have cost a small fortune,' Strocchi observed.

'Yes, it's—' Aldo stopped. 'What did you just say?'

'That this must have cost a small fortune.'

'Of course . . .'

For the first time that morning, the constable saw a smile on Aldo's weary face. 'Sir?'

'Let's see what Ruggerio has to say,' Aldo said, resuming his brisk pace. 'Whatever happens, don't let him make you angry. Trust me, losing control with men who hold more power than you never makes things any better.'

Renato had been having a lovely morning. Free from the worries of recent days, he'd enjoyed a night of drinking and delicious flirting. Better still, he'd woken with a clear head and a most beautiful companion at his side. Second helpings were always more enjoyable, especially as they gave a chance to savour the most succulent of treats.

He strolled to the sewing room, expecting to find his staff assembling a beautiful gown he'd designed for that old *strega* Lucrezia Fioravanti. Instead the benches were clear and the room empty, except for one glowering face he'd hoped never to see again: Cerchi.

'Where are my workers?'

'I gave them the morning off.'

'You'd no right,' Renato spluttered. Cerchi gave an insolent shrug.

'I thought you wouldn't want them listening to our conversation.' He pointed to the door. 'I can have a constable fetch them back, if you wish.'

'I've nothing to say to you,' Renato snapped, struggling to keep his temper. 'Poor Corsini is dead. You should be finding those who killed him, not harassing innocent citizens.'

Cerchi's smile faded. 'There's nothing innocent about *buggeroni* like you,' he said, coming so close his stale breath assaulted Renato's senses. 'But this isn't about that pervert.'

'Then what . . .?'

'Aldo. You're good friends with him, aren't you?'

'What makes you say that?'

'I've been talking to your workers, to people in the houses round here. He's visited you twice in the last few days. You were seen with him outside, talking like old friends.'

One of his neighbours must have been watching them. Renato thought back to what he and Aldo had discussed. 'Why are you spying on me?'

'Not on you.' Cerchi rubbed a hand across his greasy, drooping moustache. 'I wanted to know why Aldo came here.' Renato stepped back to escape this vile *bastardo*, but was trapped against a bench. 'You warned Aldo to be careful,' Cerchi said. '"What would happen if Cerchi found out what kind of man you are, Cesare?" That's what you said.'

No, not that. Anything but that. Renato shook his head.

'Do you deny saying those words?' Cerchi hissed. Renato looked away, unable to hold the officer's gaze. Cerchi grabbed him by the jaw, rough hands digging into Renato's delicate skin. 'Look at me when I'm talking to you, *buggerone*. Do you deny saying those words?'

Renato willed himself not to cry but couldn't stop the tears. He'd always been a coward, had known that long before he knew his own talent and tastes. 'No,' he whispered.

Cerchi stared deep into Renato's eyes. 'Now, I want you to think carefully before you answer my next question. I'll take you to the Podestà and have you tortured if you don't give me the truth. Do you understand?'

Renato nodded, ashamed of the tears running down his cheeks.

'So, tell me – what kind of man is Cesare Aldo?'

Chapter Nineteen

*A*ldo and Strocchi were kept waiting in the courtyard of Palazzo Ruggerio while a pinch-faced servant went to ask if his master was free to receive unexpected visitors. Aldo knew the strategy well, but the constable was soon pacing the stones.

'Patience,' Aldo said. 'The more agitated you look, the longer they'll have us wait.' Strocchi did as he was told, and the servant returned soon after.

'These men will take you to Signor Ruggerio.' He gestured to a marble staircase. Two mountains of muscle were waiting, their impassive faces framed by short blond hair. These must be the Basso brothers. They were even more formidable than Zoppo's description.

Aldo noted bruises and cuts across their thick, meaty knuckles. The wounds were healing, but neither man had a single mark on his face. Anyone beaten by these brutes would struggle to survive the experience. 'Those look painful,' Aldo said, pointing to their hands.

Neither man spoke. The one on the left gestured at Aldo and Strocchi to go up. The brothers fell in step behind them. When they reached the top, the other Basso pointed through a doorway to a richly decorated room. Aldo and Strocchi went inside to wait, while the brothers marched away in unison, heavy feet pounding the marble.

Aldo noticed Strocchi's hands trembling. 'Put them behind your back, then they can't betray you.' Someone was approaching, the footfalls lighter than those of the brothers.

A close-eyed man in his later years appeared from a side door, a smile fixed on a much-lined face. His scalp was smooth and gleaming without a trace of hair, while thin, pursed lips gave him the look of a reptile. Aldo almost expected a long tongue to slither out.

'I'm Girolamo Ruggerio,' the silk merchant said in a smooth voice. He wore an exquisite robe, his family crest woven into the silk. 'How can I help two officers of the Otto?'

Either the servant had made a mistake, or Ruggerio was inviting the visitors to correct him. Aldo smiled, ignoring the error. 'Signor Ruggerio, we are investigating a death.'

'A death? How regrettable. Who was it?'

'A young man called Luca Corsini.'

'The death of the young is worst of all,' Ruggerio said. 'So much lost potential.'

Strocchi was bristling at the platitudes, but Aldo bowed his head as if in grateful acknowledgement of such wisdom. 'Even more regrettable is the way it happened.'

'Really?' Ruggerio replied, showing no more than polite interest. Most merchants would have asked why such matters concerned them by now – but not Ruggerio.

'Yes, he was beaten to death on Sunday night.' Aldo affected a look of polite confusion. 'I'm surprised a man of your influence and importance had not already heard about it. Murders are few in this city, thankfully, unlike some.'

'Indeed,' the merchant agreed. 'These are dangerous times for those who venture beyond the places where they belong.' A warning, hidden inside another platitude. Clever.

'Did you know him?' Strocchi asked, restraint failing him.

Ruggerio's smiled widened. 'Know who?'

'Corsini.' The constable's hands clenched into fists at his side. 'The victim.'

'Not that I recall.' The merchant lowered himself into a grand golden chair with decoration so ornate it would be suitable as a throne. Ruggerio crossed his legs, delicate fingers adjusting his robe to cover thin, naked legs, but he did not invite them to sit. Another show of power. 'Why do you ask? Should I know this . . . Cortini?'

'Corsini,' Strocchi corrected him.

Another mistake. The constable was so capable, it was easy to forgot how little grasp Strocchi had of the city's intrigues. Time to see if Ruggerio could be unsettled.

'The dead man was wearing a dress made of silk from your workshop,' Aldo said. 'Beautiful, and far beyond his means. It seems likely it was a gift – from an admirer.'

'Perhaps one of my partner's family gave this gift. I've heard his brother Biagio can be quite generous, though I never listen to such gossip.'

A sly comment, stepping aside from any suspicion while pointing towards Biagio as a suspect. Aldo returned the merchant's smile. 'And then there's the matter of your guards.'

'Yes?' Ruggerio's smile faded, eyes flickering to one side – a tiny hesitation.

'Constable Strocchi here saw the attackers fleeing. He says they both bore a strong resemblance to your guards – the Basso brothers, I believe they're called.' Strocchi stiffened at this stretching of the truth. Ruggerio must have noticed too, his gaze shifting to the constable.

'Is that correct?'

Strocchi nodded.

'You saw the Bassos fleeing this attack? In the dark?'

Say yes. Say yes!

'The brothers look a lot like the men I saw,' Strocchi replied.

Ruggerio's smile returned. 'Did you see their faces, perhaps their hair?'

The constable swallowed. 'The attackers wore cloaks, with hoods over their heads.'

Aldo watched the merchant settle back into his throne. The moment was lost.

'So you can't be certain it was them.' Ruggerio spread his hands wide. 'In which case, I'm sorry but I can't help further. And I have urgent business that needs my attention.'

'We've another witness,' Strocchi blurted. Aldo willed the constable to fall silent, but he blundered on. 'Two men broke into the victim's room that same night to search his possessions. They were seen running from the building.'

Ruggerio arched a dismissive eyebrow. 'And can this witness be any more certain of what they saw than you, constable?' He drew out the last word with utter disdain.

'Who's this witness?' Aldo demanded as he and Strocchi left Palazzo Ruggerio.

'Corsini's landlady. I went to see her again after what Zoppo told us.'

'And she's made a *denunzia* against the Bassos?'

'I think she will. In time.'

'You think she will?' Aldo stopped. 'She refused, didn't she? Do you realize how much danger you've just put her in?'

'I didn't name her.'

'You didn't have to. The Bassos know where Corsini lived, and who saw them that night. Sooner or later, Ruggerio will send his men to make sure she doesn't talk.'

Dismay consumed the constable's face. '*Santo Spirito*. I didn't . . . It was Ruggerio, he was so . . . He knew we couldn't prove . . . Sir, I'm sorry—'

'Don't waste my time with *apologia*,' Aldo said. 'Take that landlady to somewhere that's safe. Drag her into the Podestà if you have to, but get her away from that house.'

'And if she refuses? Signorina Mula's a stubborn woman.'

'Then you'll have to stay there with her.'

Aldo left word with the Podestà he would be at via dei Giudei, before marching south. Strocchi's mention of a small fortune before their meeting with Ruggerio had brought a realization. Levi was not the only moneylender in Florence. The plotters had almost certainly approached others, and Aldo was willing to wager that Sciarra would be near the top of their list. If Sciarra could identify Lorenzino or Scoronconcolo as one of the men seeking the loan, it would be proof that the conspiracy was rooted deep inside Palazzo Medici.

Aldo crossed Ponte Vecchio, pushing through the butchers and their customers, careful to avoid the fish sellers at the southern end. From there it was a brisk stride to Sciarra's house. Many moneylenders ran their business from the Mercato Nuovo, but it was still early so it was likely he would be home. When Aldo reached Sciarra's door he could hear movement inside. He demanded Sciarra come out, battering at the sturdy wood. Soon neighbours were looking out of their windows and doors to see who was making so much noise.

'I'm here from the Otto di Guardia e Balia,' Aldo shouted, nodding to those watching. 'Sooner or later you'll answer my questions. We can do it here, or at the Podestà.'

'This is a Jewish commune,' Sciarra hissed through the door, 'you have no authority here.'

'Before he left to visit his sister, Avraham Yedaiah told everyone to help the Otto find who killed Samuele Levi. Only those with something to hide have refused.' That brought whispers from those watching. They all knew Sciarra and Levi were rivals.

'I didn't kill anyone,' the moneylender protested. 'I've nothing to do with this.'

'The longer you refuse to help,' Aldo replied, 'the more suspicion falls on you. That can't be good for business.' No reply. 'An innocent man has no fear of the truth. A guilty man hides behind locks and doors. Which one are you?'

After a long silence the bolts were drawn back, and the door cracked open, Sciarra peering up at Aldo like a caged animal.

'Can I come in, or do you want to be questioned out here?' Aldo gestured at those watching. Sciarra opened the door for him, slamming it shut once Aldo was inside.

The house was fetid, the stench of rotting food and cat's piss clouding the air. How long had it been since Sciarra last opened a window? Aldo followed him to a dark room, a single lantern providing the only light or heat. The moneylender retreated to a chair, covering himself with a heavy cloak. A cat whined in a nearby basket. 'Ask your questions.'

Aldo moved the lantern closer to Sciarra, its light revealing a fresh bruise under one eye. 'Who are you hiding from? An angry client, or somebody else?'

Sciarra shook his head, scowling. 'I'm not afraid of anyone.'

'They've been here, haven't they? Was it the Medici cousin?' No reaction. 'Or did he send his servant, the one with the hooked nose and the eager blade?' Sciarra flinched. So, he'd had a visit from Scoronconcolo. 'Before or after Levi's murder?' Sciarra shook his head. Aldo loomed over the moneylender. 'Was it before or after they killed him?' Sciarra's face twisted with guilt or pity or shame – it didn't matter which.

'Both,' he whispered.

That was why Sciarra had come running when rumours spread of Levi's murder. He knew he could have been the one stabbed, and feared those responsible would return. 'When did they come back?' Sciarra shook his head, refusing to answer. In the last day or two, judging by the bruise under his eye. He probably had others, hidden beneath his clothes. Another possibility occurred to Aldo. 'The last time the Medici servant came, it wasn't about a loan, was it? He wanted you to translate the Hebrew entries in Levi's ledger.'

Sciarra shifted in his chair, wincing. 'I tried to read it,' he admitted, 'but I couldn't make sense of what the fool had written.'

'And that's why the servant beat you.' Sciarra sniffed, and nodded. Aldo stepped away from Sciarra, giving him room. This snivelling little *merda* could help provide the proof needed to show there was a plot against Alessandro, but convincing him to come forward was going to be difficult. 'You need to make a *denunzia* against them.'

Sciarra laughed – a bitter, fearful sound. 'And end up like Levi?'

'The Otto can protect you.'

'From the Duke's own cousin? You must think me a fool.'

'So you admit Lorenzino de' Medici threatened you?'

'If you say I admitted that,' Sciarra said, 'I'll swear a *denunzia* against you. I'll say you were the one who beat me. People will believe that after you forced your way in.'

'I'm not the person you should fear.'

Sciarra spat at Aldo, but his aim was weaker than his courage. 'Get out of my house.'

Strocchi was doing his best but Signorina Mula would not listen. Not to him, not to reason, and not to any suggestion of leaving her home. She was even more stubborn than he'd feared, refusing to open the door. 'You've been here again and again,' she said from behind it. 'Why can't you leave me in peace?'

'Because your life may be in danger.' Strocchi explained why, keeping his voice low so people in the nearby homes wouldn't hear.

'I didn't see anyone and I can't describe those intruders,' Mula insisted. 'Send anyone you like, I'll tell them the same thing.'

'The Bassos won't be asking questions. We believe they beat and kicked your tenant to death. They'll do the same to you.'

'And whose fault is that? Go away. Leave me in peace.'

Strocchi sat down against the door. If the brothers came, he'd be no match for one of them, let alone both. Maybe being a constable of the Otto might deter them. But Mula was right: this was his fault. He had to face the consequences.

She opened the door a few minutes later. 'You're still here.' Mula scowled, pulling her black robes together beneath her chin. Strocchi got to his feet.

'I've orders to protect you,' he said. 'Whether you want that or not.'

The signorina was younger than Strocchi remembered, but her sour attitude added years to what must once have been a pretty face. Mula emptied a bowl of dirty water into the ditch outside. 'Can't have you out here all day, people will think I've broken your heart.' She opened the door for him. 'But keep your hands to yourself. I'm a respectable woman.'

Frustrated by Sciarra's cowardice, Aldo strode along via dei Giudei to question Dante. It was doubtful Lorenzino or Scoronconcolo had gone to Levi's former partner for coin. But the bruise under Sciarra's eye was fresh, so the plotters might still be trying to secure their loan.

As Aldo approached Dante's home, a young man with a stooped back stepped out of the doorway. There was something familiar about his fresh face, that sandy hair. Aldo had seen the youth before, but where? That was it, he'd been begging for alms the previous day. They'd almost collided when Aldo was following Benedetto to Nardi's *bordello*.

The youth smirked. 'Spare a *giulio*?'

'What are you doing here?'

'Delivering a message,' the youth replied. 'I've a message for you too, Cesare Aldo.'

Aldo stopped. How did this upstart know his name? He shouldn't, unless . . . 'You were the one following me yesterday.' The youth nodded, still smirking. 'What's the message?'

'A new power is rising in Florence, one that needs capable men. Men who understand the way the world works.' The youth pulled from his tunic a pouch that sounded heavy with coin. 'Step aside, let history find its path, and you'll be well rewarded.'

Aldo had no intention of taking the money but was curious to know the price of his silence. 'How much? How much is Lorenzino willing to pay?'

'More than enough.'

'And if I refuse to step aside?'

'Then you'll suffer for it, as others have. Well, what's your answer?'

'Tell me your name, and I'll tell you my answer.' The youth laughed. 'What are you afraid of?' Aldo asked. 'We both know whatever is happening will take place tomorrow. You said it yourself, if your master succeeds, you will be part of the new power ruling this city. But if he fails, my knowing your name will be the least of your problems. So, what is it?'

The youth hesitated, but only for a moment, arrogance getting the better of him. 'They call me Il Freccia.' Nicknaming someone with a stooped back The Arrow was a cruel jibe, but Il Freccia had embraced it. 'Now tell me, what's your answer?'

Aldo bent forwards, rubbing both hands against his left knee. 'It's a tempting offer, especially for an old soldier whose joints aren't what they used to be.' As he talked, Aldo slid one hand to the stiletto in his left boot. But before he could pull it free, Il Freccia had his own blade pressed against Aldo's neck, sharp metal scraping across the stubble.

'Touch that stiletto and I cut your throat,' the youth hissed. Aldo lifted both hands out sideways in the air, palms open. 'I'll tell my master that you said no.'

'Tell him what you like, he won't succeed.'

Il Freccia slammed the hilt of his blade up into Aldo's jaw, making him tumble over. As Aldo tried to regain his feet, the youth kicked him in the left knee. Aldo cried out in pain, and the youth strolled away, still smirking. By the time Aldo could stand, Il Freccia was gone.

A wet trickle ran down Aldo's neck. He touched two fingers to it and they came away red. The blade hadn't cut him, so the blood had already been on its edge. Il Freccia had come from Dante's home. Delivering a message, the youth had said.

Aldo called ahead as he staggered to the door.

No answer.

Dante was sprawled on the floor inside, a crimson stain on his chest, blood pooling out beneath him. Aldo rushed to Dante's side. His eyes were open. 'Can you hear me?'

Dante opened his lips, but instead of words he coughed crimson. The dark smudges beneath his eyes had gone grey, the skin around them ashen. Aldo snatched a discarded cloth from a nearby table to staunch the bleeding. A sound from outside: someone was coming in. Was Il Freccia returning to finish his work? Aldo pulled the stiletto from his boot.

'Hello? Is anyone there?' That voice sounded familiar.

'In here!' Aldo shouted. Moments later Benedetto wandered in. His eyes widened at Aldo clutching the stiletto, and Dante's bloody body. 'Quick, go and fetch Orvieto!'

'Orvieto?' Benedetto didn't move, his gaze still fixed on Dante.

'The Jewish doctor, along the road! Say my name, tell him Malachi Dante is dying. Go! Now!' The recruit backed out of the room, stumbling away.

Dante's eyes had closed. He coughed more blood, red flecking his face. Spasms took hold of his body, his legs kicking the air. Aldo heard shouting voices and running feet.

'In here!' He slid the stiletto back into his boot while keeping the blood-soaked cloth pressed tight against Dante's chest. Orvieto rushed in with a satchel, his face stricken by worry. 'Someone stabbed him,' Aldo said as the doctor crouched by them.

Orvieto nodded, leaning over Dante to listen. 'He's still alive.' The doctor replaced Aldo's hand on the wound with his own. Aldo stood up, both hands and knees wet with blood. Benedetto blundered back in, his face curdling at the red mess on Aldo's hose.

'Is he . . . ?'

'Alive,' Aldo said, 'for now. Go back to the Podestà, find the *segretario*, and tell him another moneylender has been stabbed. Go!' Benedetto nodded, backing out of the room. Orvieto was muttering under his breath in Hebrew. 'What is it?'

'Two of our kind attacked,' the doctor said. 'I thought Florence was safe for Jews, so long as they stayed among their own.'

'Faith wasn't why Levi or Dante were stabbed. This was about money and ambition. They got in the way of that.'

'Joshua should be at my home by now,' Orvieto said. 'Find him, and send him here. I'll need his help.' Aldo nodded, taking a last glance round the room. Two chairs had been turned over, and books were strewn across the floor. Dante had fought with his attacker. That was different to how Levi was attacked. 'Cesare, please,' Orvieto said. 'Hurry.'

Aldo found Joshua knocking at the doctor's door. The young man looked horrified by the blood all over Aldo, but didn't hesitate in going to help Orvieto. Aldo went on to the *bordello* for a wash and change of clothes, his left knee throbbing from where it had been kicked. Il Freccia must have seen him favouring the leg, knew it was a weakness. Robustelli was taken aback by his appearance.

'It's not my blood.'

The *matrona* peered at him. 'Cesare, when did you last sleep, or eat a meal?'

'It can wait,' he said, pushing past her.

'I'm sending Clodia with food,' she called after him.

Upstairs Aldo removed both boots and peeled off his blood-soaked hose, throwing them in a corner. The tunic was dark enough to hide most stains, but his face and hands both needed washing. By the time he'd finished and pulled on fresh hose, Clodia was blocking the doorway. She thrust a plate of meat, cheese and bread at him, plus a half bottle of wine. 'The signora says you're not allowed to leave without eating.'

Aldo gnawed on the food while Clodia watched, using the time to think. Why had the youth stabbed Dante? He was no threat to Lorenzino's plans. The only thing he'd done was— Aldo stopped chewing. He'd taken the ledger to via dei Giudei for translation the previous night. Il Freccia must have been following him all that day, staying out of sight. The youth had realized what Aldo was carrying, and told Scoronconcolo or his master. They sent Il Freccia to find out what Dante had discovered in the burnt ledger. Dante was dying because he'd helped Aldo.

Attacking Dante, the attempt at bribery – it all showed how desperate Lorenzino was becoming, what he was willing to do to stall the investigation. Aldo considered taking what he knew to Bindi, but dismissed that notion. It was unlikely the *segretario* would even listen now after what happened earlier, let alone act on what Aldo knew.

There was still one person who could intervene, one person who could change the course of events. Cibo's help would not come cheap, but Aldo had little choice left. It was his fault Dante was dying. How many more people had to suffer before there was an end to this? Aldo took a mouthful of wine, and spat it back out – it was too bitter to swallow.

Chapter Twenty

Strocchi hadn't meant to fall asleep. He withstood as many sharp comments from Signorina Mula as he could before retreating upstairs. Tucked into the eaves, the attic room was at least warm. Strocchi lay on the bed, wondering how long he'd have to stay on guard duty. With any luck, the Podestà would send another constable soon . . .

A loud noise woke him. It sounded like a door being attacked. Mula was shouting. *Santo Spirito*, the Bassos. Strocchi cursed himself for a fool. He had come straight to Mula's home, instead of stopping by the Podestà on his way for a blade or bludgeon. He scoured the attic for a weapon, finding only a broken chair leg on the floor. It would have to do.

He reached the top of the stairs as Mula's front door gave way. She fled into the house as two men pushed their way in, hooded cloaks masking both faces. But their size left little doubt about who they were. They had no knives or clubs, but the Basso brothers didn't need weapons. After offering a silent prayer, Strocchi shouted at them to stop.

The brothers exchanged a nod. One went after Mula, the other came up the stairs. Strocchi stood his ground. Being above should give him an advantage. But as the intruder got closer, fear was clenching Strocchi's gut. He swiped the chair leg through the air.

'I'm a constable of the Otto di Guardia e Balia. Attack me and you'll suffer the consequences.'

The brother stopped, pushing back the hood to expose his slab of a face. A slow smile split his grim features. 'Only if you live.'

Strocchi's fists tightened round the scavenged weapon.

The brother stormed up the narrow staircase, two steps at a time. Strocchi swung the chair leg downwards, smashing one of those meaty fists. The crack of bone brought a snarl of rage. Strocchi pulled his weapon back for another hit – and the intruder lunged at him, grabbing Strocchi's left leg. One sharp tug and he was down on his back, the impact forcing all the breath out, making him gasp for air.

Somewhere below Mula screamed, her cries cut off by the smack of a fist against skin. Strocchi willed himself to breathe in as his attacker clambered the last few steps, nursing a broken fist. 'You'll pay for that.' He grabbed a handful of Strocchi's hair, lifting and then smashing the constable's skull into the wooden floor. Pain exploded in Strocchi's head, dancing before his eyes. Praying for strength, Strocchi kicked out with both legs.

His boots collided with something soft, crushing it. There was a sudden gasp, and a sound like a tree toppling. The intruder went back down the stairs head first, hitting each one on the way. He slid straight to the bottom and slammed into the broken door. Strocchi whispered a prayer to himself: don't get back up. Please, don't get back up.

Praise be, his attacker didn't.

An angry male voice called out below, but was cut off by a heavy, ringing sound. Strocchi dragged himself to a sitting position, everything still swirling round him. He stumbled down the stairs, a hand against either wall for support, legs almost giving way.

At the bottom, Strocchi kicked the crumpled brother, just to be sure. The *bastardo* didn't move. The constable lurched through the doorway where Mula had fled. She was standing over the second intruder, a thick iron pan in both hands. Her dress was ripped, and one eye swollen shut, skin round it already bruising. She spat blood at her attacker before peering at Strocchi.

'Now I'll swear a *denunzia*.'

Rebecca hesitated at the door to Malachi Dante's home. She hadn't been inside since Father broke from his former business partner, it was forbidden. But Malachi had sat *shiva* almost every day, keeping her company while she mourned. The visits had been a reminder of how much she missed having him in her life. With Father gone, she'd hoped to rebuild her bond with Malachi. Then Joshua brought news of another stabbing, just like Father. If Rebecca wanted to say goodbye, it had to be now.

Still she hesitated, lingering outside. It was shameful to admit, but she didn't want to be there when Malachi died, not after witnessing Mother's death. To watch one person you loved slip away was sorrow enough, surely? Then she heard Malachi's voice. It was weak, but still him – still the man who had loved her without judgement, more than Father had ever seemed to, if truth be told. She could not abandon Malachi, not now. Clutching her courage close for protection, Rebecca went across the threshold.

Malachi was on the table, a pillow under his head, that favourite russet cloak draped over his body, hiding what had happened. His face was pale and tired, the grey shadows beneath his eyes making him look years older. His lips whispered a prayer until he saw her. Malachi smiled, and it broke her heart. '*Ahuva*.' He hadn't called her beloved in months.

Orvieto appeared at her side, facing away from the table. 'Malachi doesn't have long,' he murmured to her. 'Call me if he worsens.' Rebecca nodded, and the doctor slipped away. She went to Malachi's side, ignoring the bloodstained cloths on the floor and the smell of iron in the air. Rebecca took Malachi's hands in her own, giving them a squeeze.

'I knew you'd come,' he whispered. 'You're a good daughter, a loving daughter to your parents. You deserved better from those who were meant to love you.'

'I don't want to talk about Father.'

Malachi shook his head. 'You deserved better from me, dear Rebecca. I should have spoken out for you, made your father be kinder to you, more loving.'

'That doesn't matter now. Tell me, what happened? Why would anyone hurt you?'

'They kept demanding your father's ledger.'

'But it was stolen.'

'Aldo found it or recovered it. He brought the ledger here last night for me to translate, before taking it away again – but that doesn't matter now.' Malachi stared at her. 'I have something I must tell you. I betrayed your father. I betrayed both of you.'

Rebecca let go of his hands. Whatever this was, she didn't want to hear it. Malachi had been the one person she could believe in since Mother died. 'Please, don't . . .'

Now his hands were clasping at her, urgent, desperate. 'I cannot die without you knowing the truth. Your father – I hated him.'

'I know,' she said, closing her eyes. 'So did I, sometimes.'

'But there is more you don't know. I paid a man to kill Samuele, on the road from Bologna.' Rebecca wanted to breathe out but couldn't. She wanted to pull her hands free but Malachi wouldn't let go. 'I tried to stop it, I did try, but I was too late.' Malachi was weeping now. 'When Samuele came back alive, I was so relieved. My sin had not come to pass.'

'Stop telling me this,' Rebecca said, unable to escape his words.

'You deserve . . . You deserve to know the truth,' he gasped, his breaths a rasp of air. 'You deserve better than . . . Than any of us . . .' Malachi's face twisted, his back arching atop the table. Rebecca fought to wrench her hands free but his grip was too tight.

'Doctor!' she cried out. 'Doctor, come quick!'

Orvieto raced back into the room as Malachi collapsed back onto the table, his hands letting go of Rebecca, arms flopping down from his body. She stumbled back, unable to look away from Malachi's last moments. Then Joshua was at her side, his strong arms around her, guiding her away. They got as far as the doorway before Rebecca's legs collapsed. She slid down a wall to the floor, Joshua making sure she didn't fall. Rebecca could still see Orvieto leaning over Malachi, doing whatever he could. Soon the doctor straightened up, his face mournful. Orvieto saw her watching, and shook his head.

Malachi Dante was dead.

Aldo stalked into Palazzo Pazzi, ignoring the pain in his knee. Enough of waiting to be announced, people were dying. He barged into Cibo's *officio*. The cardinal was behind his desk, peering at papers. 'Aldo? What are you . . . ?'

'Alessandro is in danger. Lorenzino plans to overthrow him. Tomorrow.'

Two servants scurried in, apologizing for not stopping the intruder. Cibo dismissed them with a wave. Once they'd gone, he rose from his chair, coming round the desk to Aldo. 'Lorenzino? Are you sure? He's always seemed so weak, so eager to please.'

Aldo revealed everything: the ledger entries, the attempted bribe to step aside, the stabbing of Dante. 'Lorenzino knows his part in all of this is becoming apparent. There's no telling what he will do next to keep that from the Duke.'

Cibo shook his head. 'It's still hard to imagine Lorenzino as a murderer.'

'He gets others to bloody their hands while his stay clean.'

'Like a true Medici.' The cardinal frowned. 'Do you have any direct proof of his involvement, or that the plotters will strike tomorrow?'

'Lorenzino's initials in the ledger, one murdered moneylender and another dying because I asked for his help to read that damned ledger – what more do you need?'

'Have you got this ledger, can you show me the entry?'

Aldo shook his head. 'Bindi has it.'

'Then there's little I can do,' Cibo said, moving away to a window.

'You have to warn Alessandro. Tell the Duke that he's in danger.'

'From what? A ledger you don't have, a possible bribe and some gossip.'

'Some gossip?' Aldo struggled to keep hold of his temper. 'You were the one who told me about the conspiracy. You said plotters were using Levi to fund their insurrection.'

'I said they may have found a way to fund it,' Cibo replied. 'Nothing more than that.'

Realization hit Aldo like a slap across the face. The cardinal had been using him to test whether there was any truth to the rumour. The fact this had put Aldo in danger and looked certain to cost Dante his life made little difference to Cibo. 'What about the stabbings?'

'Neither committed by Lorenzino, it seems.' Cibo stared out at the city. 'I'm sorry, Aldo. Find me proof that can't be so easily dismissed, and I promise to intervene, if I can.'

'If it suits the purposes of the Holy Roman Emperor, you mean.' No reply. 'The Duke needs to know what Lorenzino is planning—'

'I'm expecting Guicciardini and Vettori any moment,' the cardinal said, not bothering to look round. Aldo knew them by sight, and by reputation. Both were leading figures among the Medici-supporting Palleschi faction of the city's Senate. The Palleschi would have a significant role in choosing the next leader of Florence, should anything befall Alessandro. Cibo made a dismissive gesture with his right hand. 'Since you know the way in, I trust you can see yourself back out.'

Aldo glared at him before limping away. Cibo was a political creature, his words made sense most days. But this was no courtly intrigue. The plotters were dealing in blood.

Bindi watched Signorina Mula swear her *denunzia*. There was no hesitation in the words, no evasion in her demeanour. Bruises were blossoming across her face and one eye was swollen shut, but she held herself with dignity and resolve. Benedetto returned from Oltrarno as she finished, confirming the damage to her home. Good. The signorina would make a strong witness if the matter came before the Otto. But the men who attacked her had escaped, leaving behind the ropes Strocchi had used to bind them, the ends torn and frayed.

The *segretario* noticed Mula staring at him.

'Are you in charge?' she asked.

'I am but a humble functionary of the court,' he replied, inclining his head a little. 'I advise the magistrates on matters of law and direct those who enforce it.'

'Your name isn't Cerchi, is it?'

Bindi afforded himself a slight chuckle. 'No, signorina. He is one of our officers.'

'The men who attacked me, they broke into my home once before – last Sunday, after dark.' She scowled. 'I came and swore a *denunzia* the next morning. The constable said he'd pass it along to Cerchi, but nothing happened. How do I know you'll do anything about this?'

Bindi forced a smile. 'You have my word, signorina. That is my bond.'

Mula pushed back her chair. 'We'll see.'

'One of my men can guard your home until the intruders are caught.'

'I can look after myself,' she said on her way out.

Once the headstrong woman was gone, Bindi summoned Strocchi. The constable stumbled in, unsteady on his feet. 'Have you been drinking?'

'No, *segretario*. One of the intruders smashed my head into the floor.'

'Benedetto says both men are gone.'

Strocchi gaped. 'But I tied them both securely before bringing Signorina Mula here.'

Bindi grimaced. 'Can you describe them?'

'I believe they are the same men who beat Corsini to death – twin brothers, called Basso. They work for Girolamo Ruggerio.'

'The silk merchant? Has he something to do with this?'

'It's possible he ordered the attack. It seems he . . . knew Corsini.'

'Ahh.' Bindi shifted in his chair. 'And you have evidence to support this . . . possibility?' The constable looked at the floor. 'Very well, take three men to Palazzo Ruggerio and ask if these brothers are inside. If they are, request that both men be surrendered to you because they stand accused of attacking a woman in her home today. You will make no mention of Corsini or any involvement you think Ruggerio may have in these matters.'

'But, *segretario*—'

'You will make no demands, and issue no threats. Ruggerio is a powerful man among the silk merchants. Two of the Otto's current magistrates are members of his guild. You will make no accusations against him, or about his conduct – is that clear?'

The constable scowled before replying. 'Yes, sir.'

Bindi waited till Strocchi was almost at the door before speaking again. 'Have you seen Cerchi today?' The constable shook his head. 'Then tell the guards at the gate he's to report to me as soon as he arrives. I have questions for him.'

Robustelli had run her *bordello* long enough to know when something was wrong. She did not see Clodia's visitor arrive, but the sounds from her room were worrying. A low, urgent voice was demanding something from Clodia, and her only reply was quiet sobbing.

A sharp knock brought a hesitant response from inside. 'Y-Yes?'

'Come out and explain yourself,' Robustelli called.

A long silence. The *matrona* was preparing to force her way in when the door opened. Clodia peered out, teardrops running down her painted breasts. 'I'm with someone.'

'I'm sure your guest will understand.'

'Yes, *matrona*. I'll just . . .'

'Now.' Robustelli pulled Clodia into the hall and marched her away from the room, speaking in a quieter, soothing voice. 'Are you all right, my dear? I heard you crying.'

'He keeps asking me things I don't know,' Clodia said. Robustelli pressed her for more details. 'He wants to know about the officer who stays here.'

'Aldo?'

Clodia nodded. 'He asked if I had been with Aldo, or seen others in his room.'

Why would anyone ask that, unless . . . 'What did you tell him? What did you say?'

She burst into tears again. 'That I didn't know anything.'

The *matrona* gave her a hug. 'Good girl.'

Clodia managed a weak smile. 'I told him what you told me my first night. That Aldo was an officer of the Otto, and he wouldn't arrest me. That he keeps most trouble away.'

'Yes, he does.' Usually.

Clodia's face crumpled with worry. 'Do I have to go back?'

'No, I'll get rid of your visitor. Wait in my *officio*. Go quietly, yes?'

The young woman nodded. 'Oh, and I told him the other thing you said. That Aldo is a rarity – a man with no interest in women.'

Robustelli kept her smile as Clodia left, but the *matrona*'s mind was racing. To most ears what Clodia had said meant nothing. But if this stranger was looking for ways to hurt Aldo . . . She strode to Clodia's room, but the inquisitive guest was gone. Robustelli hurried back to her *officio*. Clodia was retouching the paint on her breasts. 'Does this look better?'

'Tell me dear, what did this man look like? I want to warn the others.'

'He didn't take his clothes off,' Clodia said.

'I understand. But what did his face look like?'

'Oh! Well, it was thin. He had a patchy sort of beard, and a drooping moustache. Narrow, beady eyes, too.' Clodia shivered. 'He looked like a rat.'

That described plenty of men, but it captured one in particular: Cerchi. He'd been a grasping *merda* while working for the Office of Decency. Robustelli knew Cerchi had since become an officer of the Otto. So why was he investigating Aldo?

Chapter Twenty-One

$\mathcal{T}$he *segretario* was no doubt expecting a report on Dante's
stabbing, but Aldo passed the Podestà gates without a pause.
Better to know if the stabbing had become a murder before facing
Bindi. That meant returning to via dei Giudei. He went to Orvieto's
house first. For once, the door was shut. But the doctor still
answered, rubbing his eyes. 'Cesare?'

'I need to ask about Dante.'

'He's dead. I made him as comfortable as I could, but . . . Please,
come in.' Orvieto stepped aside, allowing Aldo to enter before
closing the door. 'I don't often shut out the world. My patients
expect to call on me at any time, but today . . .' They went through
to the back room. Orvieto took a seat at the table. 'What do you
need to know?'

'Was his stabbing like that of Levi?'

Orvieto shook his head. 'Similar, but not the same. The blade
was driven up into Dante's chest, so whoever held the knife was
probably shorter than him, or stooped over. I'd say the weapons
were similar, but not the person holding them.'

Aldo nodded; that confirmed his suspicions. The stooped youth
Il Freccia had stabbed Dante, but it was Scoronconcolo who
murdered Levi. Would either attacker have kept their blade?
Unlikely, but some men had affections for their weapons that went
beyond reason. Aldo realized Orvieto was studying him. 'What?'

'Do you know who did this to Dante?'

'Yes.'

'You've caught him?'

'No, but I know who's paying him.'

The doctor frowned. 'I don't understand.'

'Good, it's safer that way. I don't want your blood on my hands too.'

'You don't have to tell me names, Cesare. But something is troubling you.'

'Besides my bad knee?'

'I'll see to that if you stop avoiding my questions.' Orvieto went to his shelf of remedies, taking down the bottle of salve. 'Trust me.'

It was tempting to share what he knew with this man. They'd only met a few times, but a bond was forming between them – something Aldo hadn't known with another man in years. It was more than just wanting Orvieto, though that was part of it. 'I do trust you.'

The doctor smiled. 'Roll down your hose.' Soon he was crouched by Aldo's bare legs, rubbing lotion into the aching joint. 'So, what can't you talk about?'

'A conspiracy. I believe those behind it intend to strike tomorrow. I know who some of the plotters are, but don't have enough proof. I've asked those with power to intervene, but nobody will listen.' Orvieto's hands were strong and supple, his fingers soothing away the dull pain. As it receded, more urgent feelings took hold.

Orvieto continued caressing the knee. 'You're used to finding those who have broken the law. But in this you're trying to stop a law being broken. That's much harder. There's no real proof yet because the crime hasn't happened.'

'Tell that to Levi or Dante.'

The doctor rose to wash his hands. 'You didn't push the blade into either of them.'

Not directly, but taking that damned ledger to Dante had led to him being stabbed. Aldo kept that to himself as he pulled up the hose, adjusting his tunic to hide the effects of Orvieto's touch. 'How do I stop something that hasn't happened yet?'

Orvieto wiped his hands on a cloth. 'You're like a doctor who knows his patient is hurting themselves by their choices. Take your knee, for example: that will keep becoming aggravated unless you rest it properly. Eventually you'll have a permanent limp – or worse. Doesn't matter how often I tell you to rest; what happens next depends on you. It's the same with this conspiracy. You can warn those in danger, but they must decide how to respond.'

Aldo nodded. The doctor was right, but that didn't solve the problem.

Orvieto smiled. 'Whatever you decide, Cesare, please – be careful. I would hate to be doing for you what I have for poor Dante.'

Aldo knew he should go, but also knew he might never see those warm hazel eyes again. Too often he turned away from moments like this, leading to too many regrets. Not any more. Instead he pulled Orvieto into a kiss. Mouth to mouth, lips together, tasting him, savouring, feeling his warmth. The doctor didn't respond, and Aldo feared it was a mistake. Then Orvieto was kissing him back, pulling him into a closer embrace, tugging at his . . .

'Doctor Orvieto, are you there?' Joshua called as he opened the front door. Aldo and Orvieto stepped apart as Joshua came in. 'They're gathering to prepare Dante's body.'

'I understand,' Orvieto said, reaching for his satchel. 'Go, I'll be right there.' Joshua left the room, the doctor following. Orvieto paused on his way out to glance back at Aldo. 'I'll leave my door unlocked, in case your knee hurts again tonight.'

Strocchi left the three constables outside Palazzo Ruggerio to stop anyone leaving. It didn't take long to secure another meeting with the silk merchant. Ruggerio even came down to the internal courtyard to meet him, clad in robes of vibrant crimson and darkest black. He welcomed the constable with a smile, but getting answers from Ruggerio was another matter.

'Signor, it's a simple question. Are your guards here or not?'

'Which guards do you mean? I employ a dozen different men to protect me.'

'I witnessed the Basso brothers attacking a woman in her home today – not long after I came here to see you. Don't you know where your men are?'

Ruggerio sighed. 'I am among the city's most successful silk merchants. I cannot be expected to know where all my men are. What the Bassos do with their own time is up to them.'

Strocchi bit his tongue, recalling Bindi's warning: no threats, and no accusations. Shouted voices disturbed the silence, men bellowing at each other. Moments later, the Bassos burst into the palazzo, pursued by the three constables.

'Ugo! Vico!' Ruggerio's voice stopped the brothers where they stood. 'What are you doing?' The pair glanced at each other, their confusion obvious. Ruggerio marched towards them, Strocchi following. 'This constable says he saw you attack a woman. Is that true?' The brothers didn't reply. 'Is that true?'

They hesitated before nodding. Strocchi wasn't sure why Ruggerio was compelling them to confess, but still welcomed it.

The admission meant he could interrogate the brothers – a chance to serve justice, and not just the law. ·

Ruggerio gestured at Strocchi. 'You'll go with this man to the Podestà. I'll be there tomorrow to plead your case.' The pair nodded again, meek as scolded children. Ruggerio raised an eyebrow at Strocchi. 'I trust that meets your approval?'

Strocchi replied with a smile – and he meant it.

Free from pain, Aldo wasted no time in crossing Ponte Vecchio. Butchers' boys were sluicing blood into the Arno as their masters closed for the day. Orvieto's words had rung clear as a church bell. Alessandro could make his own decision about the threat posed by Lorenzino – but only if the Duke knew how close to him the plotters were. That meant getting inside Palazzo Medici and warning Alessandro before it was too late.

But when Aldo approached the Medici residence, a line of men were standing guard outside, with Scoronconcolo moving amongst them. They listened to him, faces resolute and grim. Was this a way to ensure nobody could reach Alessandro before the plotters did?

'Out of the way!' a voice bellowed, a clatter of hooves approaching fast. Aldo leapt aside as Alessandro rode by with two guards. The Duke halted outside the palazzo, jumping from his horse and throwing the reins to Scoronconcolo. All the guards followed Alessandro inside. Scoronconcolo gave the reins to a servant before striding into the palazzo.

When Aldo reached the entrance, it was empty. Inside appeared equally deserted, no Campana waiting to announce visitors to the palazzo. But as Aldo reached the courtyard, Scoronconcolo stepped from the shadows, a sword in his hand. 'Why are you here?'

'To give His Grace my report.'

'He's busy. Come back tomorrow.'

'The Duke insisted I report each day.'

Scoronconcolo raised his sword. 'I said come back tomorrow.' Armed guards came into the courtyard, blocking the stairs up to Alessandro's *officio*.

Aldo lifted both hands to show he had no weapons. 'I need to see him tonight. It was your master who insisted I bring His Grace the name of Levi's murderer.'

'You know who killed the moneylender?' Scoronconcolo asked.

Aldo spied a lone figure striding past windows on the middle level. Curly hair and dark skin – that had to be the Duke. 'Your Grace, I need to speak with you!' But Alessandro didn't seem to hear. Aldo hurried towards another staircase. 'Duke Alessandro, your life is in danger!' More guards filled the courtyard, blocking the way. Aldo turned to find the stooped youth beside Scoronconcolo, dagger in hand.

'Leave now,' Scoronconcolo said, 'while you still can. Il Freccia will see you do.'

The young man smirked at Aldo. 'We gave you a chance. Remember that.'

Strocchi and the constables escorted both Bassos to the Podestà without trouble, locking the pair in separate cells. Strocchi sent word to Bindi about their confessions. He soon emerged, beckoning Strocchi up to the *loggia*. 'Good work. They can go before the Otto next week.'

'The brothers admitted attacking Signorina Mula,' Strocchi said, 'but I believe they also killed Corsini. They look just like the men I saw fleeing from via tra' Pellicciai after curfew on

Sunday. Interrogation on the *strappato* would get the truth from them.'

Bindi's eyes narrowed. 'Perhaps, but is that the best use of our time?'

'Sir, they beat a defenceless young man, left him to die on the street like an animal. Where is justice if we don't find and punish those who unlawfully take a life?'

'We enforce the law and the will of the Otto,' Bindi replied. 'That is all.'

'But, sir—'

'Enough!' The single word echoed round the Podestà. Strocchi's mouth went dry. 'Your prisoners can wait until tomorrow. There are more important matters in hand.'

The constable nodded, bowing low as he retreated to the wide stone staircase. Strocchi risked a glance back as the *segretario* stomped into his *officio*, catching a glimpse of two men inside. One Strocchi didn't recognize, but the other was all too familiar. Cerchi emerged from the *officio*, beckoning to Strocchi. 'Constable, I have an errand for you.'

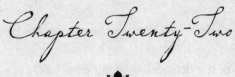

*T*wilight was a shroud lowering across the city as Aldo strode south from Palazzo Medici, the Duomo a brooding silhouette ahead of him. The streets were all but empty, curfew sending most citizens home as the bitter cold of another winter's evening set in. Aldo marched on, certain of the path ahead, no matter how dangerous it would be. Swearing a *denunzia* against Lorenzino would officially expose the conspiracy, forcing Bindi to involve magistrates from the Otto. That should stop or at least impede whatever the plotters had planned for tomorrow, the feast of Epiphany. Repercussions were inevitable, and likely to be bloody.

After passing the Duomo, Aldo turned east towards the Podestà. He pulled Orvieto's cloak closer, but even that could not ward off the cold. Aldo knew there would be retribution for what he was about to do. Exposing the conspiracy meant also exposing the *segretario*'s refusal to take that threat seriously. Bindi hated to be thought a fool, but it was even worse to be seen as incompetent. To reveal he was both at the same time? That threatened his position with the Otto, and would never be countenanced. A sacrifice would be required, and Bindi's gaze would fall on the man responsible for the *denunzia*. So be it. There was no prudence in avoiding danger, because danger always came. Better to calculate the risk and act decisively.

The guards outside the Podestà didn't acknowledge Aldo,

avoiding his gaze as he went inside. Perhaps Cerchi had been shouting at them again. That fool gave other officers a bad name. Aldo headed for the wide stone steps, keen to make his *denunzia* direct to Bindi. But the *segretario* was already coming down the staircase, belly bouncing beneath his robes.

'Ahh, Aldo – you have questions to answer!'

'I apologize for not coming sooner, but I was busy gathering the evidence you ordered me to provide. I now have that proof—'

'Silence!' Bindi thundered. 'You will speak only when I permit it.'

Footsteps approached Aldo from behind. He glanced back and saw the guards from the gate, their blades drawn at him. What was happening?

'A *denunzia* has been sworn against you,' Bindi announced, his voice booming round the cold stone walls of the courtyard. 'It accuses you of beating a citizen after he refused to submit to your threats.' The *segretario* nodded to Cerchi, slouching nearby, who gestured at a doorway across the courtyard. A small, crumpled figure emerged from it: Sciarra.

'That man has evidence of a conspiracy,' Aldo said, pointing at the moneylender.

'Indeed he does,' Bindi agreed. 'He came to me with details of what you said, how you hurt him because he wouldn't submit.'

'I never laid a finger on him,' Aldo protested.

Sciarra pulled back a tunic sleeve to show yellowing bruises round his wrist. 'You did this,' he snarled. 'Pulled my arm so far up my back that it almost broke.'

Aldo turned to the *segretario*. 'When Levi's body was found, Sciarra tried to force his way into the house where the murder happened. I had to restrain him.'

'So you admit giving him those bruises,' Bindi said. 'What about the others?' Sciarra lifted his tunic to reveal fresh black blotches across his bulging belly and chest. 'People in nearby houses saw you beating at his door today,' the *segretario* continued, 'demanding to be let in. You threatened to charge him with Levi's murder—'

'I needed to know if he'd been approached by those who killed Levi,' Aldo said, aware how weak the words sounded. 'He refused to help.'

'He refused to help you,' Bindi replied.

Constables and other guards were spilling into the courtyard now, no doubt eager to watch. Someone must have told them what was going to happen. The smirk on Cerchi's face left little doubt who was responsible. Aldo bit down on his anger. 'I may have been too zealous with Sciarra, but I was seeking evidence of a conspiracy against the Duke.'

'So you admit there's a conspiracy?' a voice interjected. Lorenzino stepped from the room where Sciarra had been. The Duke's cousin sauntered across the courtyard, both hands behind his back. 'Well? Do you admit there is a plot against Alessandro?'

'Yes,' Aldo replied. 'And you're one of its leaders.' The accusation brought a gasp from several of those watching, but Lorenzino just laughed as he stopped by the *segretario*.

'What did I tell you? This man will say anything, invent any lie, to conceal the truth of his murderous scheme. He is utterly without shame.'

Bindi scowled. 'The Duke's cousin has also sworn a *denunzia*, Aldo. He has accused you of plotting to murder Alessandro.'

'But that's madness,' Aldo protested. 'What reason could I have to kill the Duke?'

'You're working for exiles from outside the city,' Lorenzino said. 'I've heard you were in Bologna a few days ago – a perfect opportunity to meet your paymasters.'

'The *segretario* sent me there to guard Levi!'

'And the poor man was dead hours after returning to Florence,' Lorenzino replied.

'Slain by your servant,' Aldo spat. 'Scoronconcolo murdered Levi and took his ledger because it proved you wanted to borrow coin to fund your plot against the Duke.'

'More lies, more duplicity,' Lorenzino said, shaking his head.

'I had the ledger translated,' Aldo insisted. 'The evidence against Lorenzino is still inside that ledger. The *segretario* has it in his *officio*.'

'But where is this translator you claim confirms your story?' Lorenzino asked.

'Dead. Slain by another of your men,' Aldo said.

'Do you have any proof of that?' Bindi asked.

'Not yet, but I will soon,' Aldo insisted. 'I need to ask Dante's neighbours if they saw his killers.'

Lorenzino was struggling to keep the triumph from his face. '*Segretario*, I am sure the Otto will bring all its wisdom to bear on these matters in time, but I urge you to put this man behind bars until the truth of his actions can be determined. If the Duke's life is in jeopardy, you would be the one held accountable should anything happen to my cousin.'

Bindi's dismay was evident, like a fish caught upon a hook. Aldo looked round for an ally, someone – anyone – that might speak for him. Strocchi, where was Strocchi?

The *segretario* took a deep breath. 'Cesare Aldo, I believe there is evidence for you to answer. You will be shackled and kept in a cell until the next meeting of the Otto.'

Aldo resisted the urge to struggle as guards took hold of him, clamping cold metal round his wrists and ankles. So long as he remained here in the Podestà, there would be chances to get a message to Cibo. But a dissenting voice spoke out once the shackles were in place.

'I understand your desire to be merciful,' Cerchi said. 'But Aldo has allies here. He might use one of them to have witnesses coerced. A cell in Le Stinche might be wiser.'

'No!' Aldo cried out, fighting against the guards holding him in place. He wouldn't last a day inside the jail, not once word spread among its most violent inmates. The guards might as well kill him where he stood. That would be a mercy, at least.

'Very well,' Bindi said. 'The prisoner will be taken to Le Stinche.'

'Listen to me,' Aldo shouted. 'The Duke, you have to protect the Duke!' But Bindi turned away, escorting Lorenzino up the steps. Aldo fought his shackles, determined to be heard. He had to make them listen, to make them see sense. 'Alessandro's life is in danger!'

Bindi gave a final, dismissive gesture to Cerchi. He advanced on Aldo, slapping a thick cudgel in the palm of one hand. 'I've waited a long time to do this.'

Strocchi was on his way back to the Podestà, still unsure why Cerchi had sent him to Porta San Gallo. A messenger could have taken the request for a tally of those passing through the north gate. But Strocchi did what he was told, hurrying back with the numbers.

Four guards were dragging a body out through the Podestà gates. It looked like a corpse, maybe a suspect who'd died during interrogation. Shackles were binding the arms and legs. It was a prisoner, not a corpse. Then Strocchi saw the prisoner's face: Aldo!

'What happened?' Strocchi demanded. 'Where are you taking him?'

'Le Stinche.' Cerchi emerged from the gates, his pleasure at Aldo's plight all too evident. 'Captain Duro can deal with him.'

Coming closer, Strocchi saw why Aldo had looked dead. His head rolled to one side, blood streaming down the bruised face.

'You know what happens to law enforcers in Le Stinche,' Strocchi said. 'He won't last a day there, not like that.'

Cerchi gestured at the guards. 'Get moving.' The men staggered away, Aldo a dead weight between them. Strocchi strode towards the Podestà gates, but Cerchi stopped him. 'Wouldn't go to Bindi right now. He's busy with the Duke's cousin, giving an *apologia* for Aldo's lies and accusations.'

Aldo knew pain first, pounding in his head like a dozen horses on cobbled streets. Nausea came next, churning and roiling, before the rasp of shackles on his arms and legs. Fingers dug into his limbs as he was carried through twilight air, swaying from side to side. Aldo opened his eyes, but that was a mistake. A burning stream of bile spewed from his mouth, spattering the boots of those carrying him. They shouted, almost dropping him. He would have enjoyed their curses more if he hadn't recalled where the guards were taking him.

Soon they were outside Le Stinche, the ugly building a brutal silhouette against the darkening sky. Debtors went into the prison and some managed to pay their way back out, but no law enforcer incarcerated inside these forbidding walls had ever emerged again. Not alive. Three guards pulled Aldo to his feet while the fourth pounded on the Porta di Fuori. The door opened, an angry warden with a lantern glaring out. 'What?'

'Prisoner.'

'It's gone curfew. Come back tomorrow.'

'Orders from *Segretario* Bindi. Let us in.'

The warden grumbled before shoving his lantern at Aldo. 'Who's so important they have to . . . ?' His eyes widened.

Aldo forced a smile. 'Cesare Aldo, at your service.'

'Not for long.' The warden waved at the guards. 'Bring him in.'

The four men shoved Aldo towards the low doorway. He saw a stone plaque above the entrance, two words on it: *Opertet Misereri.* He knew what to expect inside Le Stinche, and mercy was never part of it.

Chapter Twenty-Three

Saturday, January 6th

*R*ebecca lay awake, not wanting to move in case she disturbed Joshua. He had brought her home after Dante died. Ruth and her brothers were already asleep, and Joshua was being so kind to her. Rebecca had kissed him to say thank you at the front door. Then one kiss turned into another, and soon they were in her room – alone, yet together.

The temptation to keep kissing, to go further, had been so strong. But the words in Father's last letter filled her thoughts and she'd drawn back. She still let Joshua stay the night, sharing her narrow bed, his hard body pressing against her, his warmth so close – but no more than that. Now it was morning and Rebecca knew they'd been right to stop. The question was, how could she get Joshua out of the house without the others realizing?

A gentle knocking startled Rebecca. 'Are you awake?' It was her cousin, come to say goodbye. Ruth and her brothers had a long journey ahead. Rebecca slid from the bed, grateful Joshua was facing the wall. She slipped a shawl round her shoulders and went to the door.

'Be with you in a minute,' Rebecca whispered. She heard Ruth move away. Rebecca stared at Joshua, his clothes strewn across the floor. In a few days sitting *shiva* would be done. There were so many decisions to make – where to live, and what to do with that life.

Joshua rolled over in her bed, one arm hanging over the side, his nose pressed into the pillow like a child. He was a good man, she was certain of that – but was it enough? Father had forbidden her from being with Joshua, yet never gave any reason for that beyond matters of faith and birth. Were those enough to deny the feelings growing inside her for this man?

She was falling in love with Joshua. There, she had admitted it to herself. Should she stay with him, and become his wife? That would be breaking with Father's final wish, knowing that the shame and guilt of doing so would haunt her for years, perhaps forever. Or should she accept her cousin's offer and move to Bologna, a city she had never visited? Give up everything and everyone she knew here in Florence for the hope of another life, a better life? Whatever she chose, it would mean stepping into the unknown. And that was terrifying.

Aldo woke in more pain than he'd known for years. Someone must have put a block of stone inside his head during the night – it was the only way to explain the dull thudding that met each tiny movement. Shackles bound his wrists and ankles, rough metal edges rubbing and grinding against the skin. Every part of him was stiff and sore in the bitter cold.

He hadn't seen much of Le Stinche when the guards brought him in, still reeling from Cerchi's cudgel. A dark blur of scowling faces and muttered threats were all Aldo could recall. A gruff voice ordered him thrown into the cell for the condemned. That explained why there was nobody else in the cramped chamber, no bedding on the frozen earth floor.

Aldo touched two fingers to his battered head. White stars burst across his vision, even with both eyes closed. When the pain settled back to a dull throb, he peered round the cramped cell. Cold stone walls enclosed a space just big enough to store two coffins side by side. Pale daylight spilled in round the edges of the cell door, revealing a floor of dirt and broken stones. The stench of stale piss left little doubt where the *latrina* was. Pulling down his hose wasn't easy in shackles, but worth the effort to empty a bladder close to bursting. *Palle*, he was thirsty.

Aldo tugged his hose back up as a jangle of keys heralded the door opening. Murky dawn light poured in past a burly guard. 'Captain wants to see you.'

Aldo held out his shackled wrists. 'Get there quicker if you take these off.' The guard stomped away, leaving the door open. Aldo shuffled over to look out, stumbling on a broken stone the size of a fist that had fallen from the crumbling cell wall.

Le Stinche was even bleaker than it looked from the street. Tall walls enclosed the cramped central courtyard, the stones blackened by smoke and damp. Across from the condemned cell huddled a small chapel, a *tabernacolo* beside it for those in need of swifter salvation. Doorways led off the courtyard into the surrounding buildings, most likely wards for the different inmates. Both men and women were housed in Le Stinche, mainly debtors, but the remaining inmates were convicted criminals, suspected criminals and the insane. Looming over them all on the prison's northern side was a watchtower, a brooding stone citadel above the main doorway.

It was early, inmates still in their wards. Outside, dawn was breaking over the city's piazzas and grand palazzos. Citizens would soon be celebrating Epiphany. Lorenzino and his conspirators were doubtless preparing to strike at Alessandro, whatever form that might take. Aldo almost admired the cunning that had turned him from investigator into suspect. But that same cunning was now free to overthrow the Duke, with nobody to impede the conspirators. If Lorenzino succeeded, it would prove Aldo's innocence – but plunge Florence into chaos. Enemy armies, anti-Medici exiles and republican zealots would all be eager to fill the void.

The guard returned with more keys and removed the shackles. Aldo was still rubbing his raw wrists when he was shoved into a cramped room. Behind a plain wooden desk sat Captain Duro, the formidable commander of Le Stinche. A shaved head and grizzled face showed every year of his forty summers, and more besides. Duro sifted through what had been in Aldo's possession the previous night: the gleaming sharp stiletto from his boot, a pouch for paying bribes and informants, plus papers proving his status with the Otto.

'Not much to show for a life,' Duro said.

'I don't carry my whole life around with me,' Aldo replied. Duro looked past him to the guard. A heavy boot kicked Aldo's bad knee, collapsing him to the floor.

'Get up,' Duro said, no feeling in his voice. Aldo reached for the desk, using it to—

Another kick caught him in the ribs, making Aldo cry out.

'No inmate touches my desk,' Duro said. 'Get up, before Bruno kicks you again.'

Aldo struggled to his feet, one hand nursing his ribs.

'Speak without permission and Bruno will hurt you. Do anything to challenge my authority and Bruno will hurt you.' Duro looked up. 'This is my prison. All inmates receive the same treatment, regardless of who or what they once were. Judge, thief, whore or law enforcer, it doesn't matter. Inside Le Stinche you are an inmate – nothing more, nothing less.'

Aldo nodded. Past meetings with the prison's captain had been equally abrasive.

'You've no authority here,' Duro continued. 'You will abide by the same rules as everyone else. Attack another inmate, and you will be punished. Do so again, the punishment becomes more severe.' Duro emptied Aldo's pouch on the desk. 'This will pay your arrival fee, and for the first night. You'll need more tonight. If you want one of our better cells, you'll have to pay extra for that. Assuming you have any coin left.'

Aldo opened his mouth to make a comment about how gratifying it was to see the prison turning a profit but stopped himself, remembering the warning. 'What?' Duro demanded.

'I arrived after dark,' Aldo replied. 'Isn't tonight my first night?'

Duro ignored the question. 'You are now in debt to the city. Every day you remain in Le Stinche – every day you stay alive within these walls – increases that debt. Food, water, lodgings – everything has a price here. You could beg for alms from our charitable visitors, but that probably won't be enough. Family and friends outside can meet your debts, assuming they possess the means to pay. Any other questions?'

Aldo couldn't resist. 'When's lunch?'

It was almost worth the pain.

For once, Bindi had a report rich with incident for the Duke. Yet Alessandro was yawning within minutes. 'Yes, yes, our cousin told us how he helped uncover this conspiracy. One of your men was behind it, apparently – the same man you recommended to investigate that moneylender's murder. Do you have an explanation for that, *segretario*?'

Bindi dared not look up, not with Lorenzino lurking by the Duke. 'No, Your Grace.'

'And we understand there's been a second killing – another Jew?'

'Yes, Your Grace.' The *segretario* hesitated. 'Another money-lender.'

'This isn't good enough,' Alessandro said, slapping a hand on his grand desk. 'The murder of one moneylender is bad for business. The murder of two is bad for the whole city. You promised to catch those responsible. Now it seems they were under your nose!'

Bindi spluttered a response, but the excuses sounded weak to his own ears. The *segretario* fell silent, waiting for the Duke's tirade to resume. Instead, he heard whispering. Lorenzino was murmuring in his cousin's ear. Bindi leaned closer, straining to hear.

'Your Grace has long wished to become acquainted with a particular young woman,' Lorenzino whispered. 'I understand her guardian is away in Naples at present. Now could be the perfect time to meet her. If you wish, I could arrange an *appuntamento* at Casa Vecchia.'

Bindi suppressed a sigh of disapproval. Must he witness the Duke and his cousin discussing the latest conquest being procured for Alessandro? The *segretario* cleared his throat to remind them he was still in the room.

Alessandro waved a dismissive hand. 'Thank you, that will be all.' Bindi bowed on his way to the double doors. But the Duke had one last ignominy to inflict. 'Now that we think about it, there is something else you can do. The officer who plotted against us – what was his name?'

'Aldo, Your Grace. Cesare Aldo.'

'He seemed an unlikely sort of conspirator. We want you to look further into this.'

Bindi noticed Lorenzino's surprise at this intervention. 'It was your cousin who swore one of the *denunzie* against Aldo, Your Grace.'

'True, but there's something curious about all of this.' The Duke arched an eyebrow at Lorenzino. 'Don't you agree?' His cousin gave a gracious nod, but Bindi could see a tightness in Lorenzino's jaw. Alessandro smiled, oblivious to his cousin's feelings or paying them no heed. 'Good, then it's settled. Have one of your officers – your other officers – find out whatever they can about this Cesare Aldo. After all, one man can't be a conspiracy on his own. If he truly planned to overthrow us, he would have needed help. Hunt down the other plotters, *segretario*. This is a matter of urgency. You don't want to disappoint us again.'

Aldo chose a bench against a wall in the courtyard as his place to watch Le Stinche coming to life. Female inmates emerged first, coming from the women's ward in the south-west corner. A water-carrier brought them fresh supplies. Male inmates of limited means were next into the courtyard, stumbling from a ward beside the condemned cell, their ragged clothes a sign of the debt that had brought them to Le Stinche.

Nobody came from the ward in the south-east corner, but sobbing and screams were audible from it. That must be where the insane were kept, hidden from view. Some of the other wards occupied two levels, with windows on the higher floor enabling those inside to look down on the prisoners below. Judging by the quality of their robes, it was mostly merchant families in the upper levels. Le Stinche observed much the same hierarchies as the rest of Florence.

A few wardens moved between rooms, keeping an eye on

inmates, while two guards were visible in the watchtower. There couldn't be more than one sentry for every ten prisoners, yet there was no sign of trouble between captors and captives. The debtors seemed accepting of their fate, with Le Stinche the price they paid for their mistakes or misfortunes.

A church bell chimed beyond the high walls, and a guard opened the sturdy wooden door. Visitors ventured into the court-yard, some anxiously searching for friends or family among the inmates. Others had an easy familiarity with what they would find inside. Two distributed food to those most in need; they were probably people atoning for their sins by attending to the needs of prisoners.

'Bread's always stale,' a wry voice said. 'Our visitors want forgive-ness, but not so much that they give us fresh loaves. Still, it fills the belly, if you've the teeth for chewing.'

Aldo had wondered when Zoppo's brother would approach him. Lippo bore a strong resemblance to the tavern keeper, but was missing an arm instead of half a leg. He'd been the best pick-purse in the city – when he still had two hands. 'What happened to your arm?'

'First night I was in here, another inmate decided I should be his *cagna*,' Lippo replied. 'Show weakness and you become a hole for anyone who wants his *palle* emptied. I put a stop to that, but didn't have enough coin to pay the fine.' He looked at the stump where his right arm used to be. 'The wardens took this instead.'

Amputation was an extreme punishment, even in Le Stinche. There must be more to the story than Lippo was telling, but Aldo didn't pursue it. To survive within these walls meant finding allies, and Lippo was the likeliest-looking candidate so far. 'About your arrest . . .'

Lippo gave a shrug. 'It's your job – well, it was. Word is you're in here for plotting to murder the Duke. Apparently you want to free the city from his tyranny and restore Florence to a glorious republic – or something like that. Didn't know you were political.'

'I'm not. I was –' Aldo paused, knowing how his words would sound – 'framed.'

It took a long time for Lippo to stop laughing.

Strocchi had spent a sleepless night. The charges against Aldo beggared belief. Conspiring to overthrow the Duke? He'd never shown any interest in who ruled the city. Was the murder of Levi somehow part of this? Striding to the Podestà, Strocchi realized how little he knew about that investigation. All his time had been spent pursuing the men who killed Corsini. Marching through the gates, Strocchi vowed to visit Aldo in Le Stinche once the Basso brothers had been interrogated. At least an end to that case was within reach.

Strocchi had no wish to use the *strappato* on either brother, but it might be necessary. Most suspects confessed before guards finished securing the ropes, such was the fear of that infernal device. But the Bassos were muscular and looked familiar with pain – they might not be so easily broken. Once Ugo Basso was secured in the interrogation cell, Strocchi went to find Bindi. The *segretario* had to approve all uses of the *strappato*, often attending interrogations.

Strocchi was crossing the courtyard as Bindi came through the Podestà gates, muttering under his breath. Maybe now wasn't the time to approach him. But Cerchi didn't notice the *segretario*'s mood and stopped Bindi on the stairs. Strocchi wasn't close enough to hear them, but a jabbing finger was never a good sign. Soon Cerchi was stalking from the Podestà as if chased by wasps, taking two guards with him. Ugo and his brother could wait until Bindi was calmer. Maybe now was the best time to visit Aldo after all.

But as the constable was preparing to leave, Ruggerio strolled into the Podestà, flanked by two of the Otto's eight magistrates. The silk merchant was dressed in robes of midnight blue, his head gleaming in the early morning light. Strocchi recognized the magistrates from a recent sitting; both men were members of the same guild as Ruggerio. 'Ahh, constable,' Ruggerio said. 'I would like to speak with my men, if I may.'

'That's not possible.' Strocchi chose his words with care. 'They admitted attacking a defenceless woman and are due to be inter-rogated about another crime – a murder.'

Ruggerio waved a dismissive hand. 'Yes, I know all of that. I've already told these magistrates the details. But I believe a brief conversation with my men would avoid the need for any time-consuming interrogations. That would be for the best, I'm sure we all agree.' He glanced at the magistrates, who dutifully nodded. Of course they did.

'I do not have the authority for that,' Strocchi said. 'You'd need to ask—'

'*Segretario* Bindi!' Ruggerio called, pushing past the constable. Bindi was watching from the *loggia*, his gaze no doubt drawn by the unexpected arrival of two magistrates. Ruggerio repeated the request, his words echoing round the courtyard.

Bindi pointed at Strocchi. 'Have the Basso brothers moved to the same cell, and put a chair in there for Signor Ruggerio. He's to have as long with them as he wishes.'

Aldo watched inmates leaving the small chapel after mass. His head had stopped trying to split open, and slow circuits of the courtyard had put life back into his stiff, sore limbs. A few days of rest and good food would bring a full recovery. But that wasn't very likely in Le Stinche.

Lippo emerged from the chapel weeping, aglow with fervour. Visitors were giving alms to the inmates, and Lippo received twice that of anyone else. When there was no more left, he went to the poor men's ward. Lippo soon reappeared with only a single end of bread.

'You still know how to fleece a crowd.'

'I stole nothing but their hearts, and gave as much as I took.'

Aldo laughed. 'What did you give them?'

'The gift of being a good Christian,' Lippo said, chewing on a crust. 'They return home believing they're better people for helping me. Seems a fair exchange.'

Aldo nodded at the poor men's ward. 'Who'd you make payment to?'

Lippo smiled. 'Nothing gets past you, does it?'

'Answer the question.'

The smile faded. 'This isn't the Podestà. You're not an officer of the court any more, Aldo. You can't make me do anything I don't want in here.'

'Try saying that to the man who's got your alms,' Aldo replied. 'Who is it? Who runs this place when Duro and his men aren't looking?'

Lippo hesitated before replying. 'Used to be a beast called Riccio, but he was getting old. A new inmate came in two, three days ago. Didn't notice him at first, but he put Riccio in the *ospedale* without any wardens seeing. He's cunning, dangerous – you'd like him.'

Aldo counted back the days. 'What's his name?'

'Carafa – Marsilio Carafa.'

'*Merda.*'

'Friend of yours?' Lippo asked.

'He tried to kill me on the road from Bologna. I'm the one who put him in here.'

'Ahh.'

'Yes.' Aldo took a deep breath. 'So long as nobody tells him . . .' Lippo was doing his best to look innocent. 'You've already told him.'

'An officer of the Otto, thrown in here with us? Of course I told him. Didn't matter, he knew. Probably got it from one of the guards. *Santa Madre*, the whole prison will know soon.' Lippo smirked. 'I'm taking bets how long you'll survive. Want to make a wager?'

'Isn't gambling illegal in here?'

'So are brawling, assault, murder, rape, drinking, whoring and plenty more besides. But they all happen. I can get you a blade, for a price. You'll need one.'

Aldo shook his head. 'Nice try. I know the punishment if I'm found with a weapon.'

Lippo saw something over Aldo's shoulder. 'Well, don't say I didn't warn you.'

Aldo turned round, masking the pain that caused. Carafa was strolling towards him, a muscle-bound brute at his side. 'So it's true,' the bandit said, stopping a safe distance away. 'I didn't believe Lippo when he claimed you had joined us.'

'Don't worry, I won't be here long,' Aldo replied. 'I'll be let out in the next few days – or executed.' He nodded at the burly figure shadowing Carafa. 'Who's your friend?'

'Maso. We worked together a while back. Doesn't talk much, but he's loyal to the death. Finding him here was a happy surprise,' the bandit said. 'Of course, I'm only in this *merda* because of you – the accusations of a disgraced officer, it turns out.'

'I'd mention that to your *avvocato* when he visits.'

Carafa stroked a thumb down the pale scar on his cheek. 'Neither of us wants to be here, but since we are . . . If you don't make trouble for me, I won't make trouble for you.'

Aldo paused, as if considering the offer. It was a ruse, of course, but accepting cost him nothing and might mean a few hours without being attacked. 'Agreed.'

Carafa nodded before strolling away, Maso close behind. Lippo let out a sigh of relief. 'Had me worried. I'll lose a fortune if you die today. That truce should keep you alive until tomorrow, at least.'

'Don't count on it,' Aldo said.

Chapter Twenty-Four

Strocchi lurked outside the cell while Ruggerio was meeting the Bassos. It sounded as if Ruggerio was doing all the talking, but his words were too hushed to hear through the door. When he emerged, Ruggerio beckoned to the waiting magistrates. Strocchi joined them, refusing to be omitted from whatever they discussed.

'My guards have confessed to killing an unfortunate young man called Corsini,' Ruggerio said. 'He approached them on Sunday night, dressed as a courtesan. The brothers were taken in, believing he was a woman. When they discovered the truth, Ugo and Vico reacted as any man would, retreating from his perversion. But it seems the *buggerone* persisted, and righteous fury overtook them. The brothers never meant to end this lost soul's life. They've been stricken with grief and remorse ever since.'

'So stricken they couldn't come forward and admit their crime?' Strocchi asked.

Ruggerio's assured manner faltered a moment before he continued. 'Ugo and Vico didn't know the young man had died until this constable brought that sad news to my palazzo yesterday. The brothers have been searching their consciences ever since.' Strocchi fought the urge to laugh. 'Ugo and Vico are ready to face whatever punishment the Otto deems fit for their . . . lapse in judgement.'

The *segretario* had joined them while Ruggerio spoke. 'Signor, thank you for helping bring a swift end to this regrettable matter,' Bindi said. 'I cannot predict the outcome of the Otto's deliberations. But I imagine the court will welcome this freely given confession.' The magistrates nodded their agreement. Strocchi could hold his tongue no longer.

'But none of this makes sense. Why were the Bassos in via tra' Pellicciai? Why were they out after dark? A strong wind would have knocked over their victim, yet we're supposed to believe he pursued them – in a dress, after dark?'

Ruggerio's eyes narrowed. 'Who knows what such unfortunates will do to sate their unholy desires? The fact remains the Bassos are confessing to this crime. There is no need for any interrogations, or a trial. A murder has been solved, and justice can be done.'

Strocchi opened his mouth to reply but Bindi spoke first. 'I can only agree, signor.' He glared at Strocchi. 'And I must compliment you, constable, for your diligence in helping bring this matter to an end. It does you credit.'

Never had praise sounded so sour to Strocchi. 'The brothers must go to Le Stinche until the Otto passes sentence. *Segretario*, I offer my help escorting them to prison. It would be embarrassing if they somehow escaped on the way there.' Embarrassing, but he wouldn't put it past Ruggerio to make that happen.

Bindi turned to the magistrates. 'If the members of the Otto present do not object . . . ?' The pair looked at each other and Ruggerio before shaking their heads. 'Very well – the brothers will be taken from here to Le Stinche, where they shall await sentencing.'

Strocchi watched Bindi usher Ruggerio and the magistrates out. The Basso brothers' punishment would be severe when they came before the Otto. What must Ruggerio have promised to make them confess? At least Corsini's killers were going to prison.

But he was still dead, while the man who condemned him was free, with an unharmed reputation.

Signora Robustelli was preparing a belated breakfast for Piccolo when the tiny dog took to barking. 'It's coming, you ungrateful pup!' But her beloved pup was barking at the hallway, not the *matrona*. 'What's wrong, sweetness?'

Crashing wood answered that question. Robustelli scooped up Piccolo and hustled to the front door. It was tilting off the frame, grim satisfaction on the face of the man beyond it. Cerchi stomped inside, two burly men close behind.

'You've no right!' Robustelli protested, blocking his way.

'I answer to the Otto,' Cerchi replied, 'not some cheap whore.' His men battered on doors, frightening the women. Customers didn't start coming till noon, so most girls were still asleep. Clodia burst from her room in tears, while Matilde hissed curses at the intruders. Piccolo was barking so hard he nipped at Robustelli's hands.

'What are you looking for?' she asked. Even the Onestà at its most bullying did not storm into a *bordello* without good reason.

'Cesare Aldo.'

'He's not here,' Robustelli said, refusing to give this *bastardo* the pleasure of seeing her fear. 'Don't think he came home last night.'

'Which room is his?'

'Upstairs, at the back.' No sooner were the words out of her mouth than Cerchi's men were stalking up the staircase, two steps at a time. Cerchi's previous visit had been secretive. Now he was using his status like a cudgel. What had changed?

'Your tenant's accused of plotting to overthrow the Duke.'

'The Duke? The duke of what?'

Cerchi leaned closer, disdain twisting his narrow features. 'Florence.'

Robustelli burst out laughing. The notion was ridiculous. But laughing in any man's face was not a good idea. Cerchi pulled back a hand—

—and Piccolo launched himself at Cerchi, barking and biting. Robustelli pulled the tiny dog back before it could actually hurt Cerchi, but the attack still startled him. 'Get that little *merda* away from me,' he hissed.

Robustelli thrust Piccolo into Clodia's arms, sending her and the other women out of harm's way. Once they were gone, she tried reasoning with Cerchi. 'You must know Aldo has no interest in anything like that.'

'The Otto already has two *denunzia* naming him as a suspect, more than enough to keep him in Le Stinche. I'm here to find further evidence. One of his informants refused to help. I doubt Zoppo will be reopening that hovel of a tavern anytime soon. You'd be wise not to test my patience any further.'

Le Stinche. So that's where Aldo was. Robustelli could hear his room being torn apart. 'Search all you want, there's nothing to find. He lives like an *eremita*.'

Cerchi's men soon returned with only a handful of books. He glanced at each one before casting them aside. Cerchi dismissed his men. When they were gone, he sneered at Robustelli. 'You can expect life to be different, now there's no Aldo protecting you. Staying open and staying safe comes at a price.'

Robustelli swallowed her anger. 'You don't work for the Office of Decency any more. You have no authority over what happens inside these walls.'

'Don't be so sure about that,' Cerchi replied. His hand flashed sideways, slapping her hard across the face. 'Get every whore working. I expect coin, and plenty of it.'

Escorting the Bassos to Le Stinche was easier than Strocchi expected. Nobody tried to free them, and the brothers went inside without complaint. Captain Duro agreed to let Strocchi see Aldo, but forbade giving him any coin. 'New inmates need to learn how this place works.'

Strocchi expected Aldo to be brought to him. Instead, a ruddy-faced guard opened a heavy wooden door to reveal prisoners huddling in a bleak courtyard. 'No need to worry, they don't bite. Much.' The guard was still laughing when the door slammed shut behind Strocchi.

Most of the inmates were unknown to him. There was a man who looked like Zoppo, but he was missing an arm, not half a leg. He was talking to Aldo. One night in Le Stinche had already taken its toll, etching pain into Aldo's face. Strocchi went to him and the other inmate left them to talk. 'How are you?'

'Imprisoned,' Aldo replied, leaning against a stone wall. 'What's happening at the Podestà? Has Bindi said anything about the charges against me?'

'Not that I've heard. He wasn't happy this morning, took it out on Cerchi.' Aldo muttered something under his breath that Strocchi couldn't quite hear. It sounded like 'Maybe there is a God,' but why would anyone question this? The constable pulled out his pouch. 'Duro told me not to give you any coin. How much do you want?'

Aldo smiled. 'All you can spare. Never knew life in prison cost so much.'

Strocchi emptied his pouch into Aldo's hands. 'You being in

here is madness. They can't honestly think you'd plot against the Duke.'

'Lorenzino made a good case against me.'

'Alessandro's cousin? How is he involved?'

'It's a long story. We'd better sit.' Aldo sank onto a bench.

Strocchi listened with increasing disbelief about the investigation into Levi's murder, the twists and turns leading to the plot against Alessandro. By the end of Aldo's tale Strocchi was shivering. 'Is there anything I can do to help?'

Aldo nodded. 'Alessandro is in danger. I don't know if Lorenzino and the others plan to attack the Duke directly, or his position as ruler of Florence. There are few in the city that could stop them. But Cardinal Cibo has the authority of the Holy Roman Emperor, if he chooses to use it. Go to Palazzo Pazzi, see if you can persuade him into using that power before it's too late. The fact Lorenzino swore a *denunzia* to stop me exposing the plot should help convince Cibo to intervene. He's stubborn, but as it stands the cardinal might be the only hope left of saving the Duke.'

Santo Spirito, Aldo wasn't asking much, was he? But an offer of help was a promise to be honoured. 'I'll do my best,' Strocchi said. The door swung open, a guard gesturing at the constable. Time to go.

A sudden thought hit Strocchi as he strode away: what if this was the last time he saw Aldo? The officer was no saint, far from it, but he'd been the closest thing to a friend Strocchi had found in Florence. He paused at the doorway to look back, but Aldo was gone, lost behind inmates huddling round a burning brazier for warmth.

* * *

Aldo leaned against the wall. Good of Strocchi to visit, but the pity in his face was less welcome. The likes of Carafa would see only an easy target. Spurning Lippo's offer of a weapon didn't seem so wise now. It'd be even less so when the jackals came circling – and they would, sooner or later. The weak and the weakened were always victims in waiting.

A young woman stalking round the courtyard caught Aldo's attention, her face a frown of frustration. She kept glaring at the upper level of the women's ward, muttering to herself. She was plain to the eye, but Aldo knew men's lust and violence cared little about beauty. Several inmates were gazing at her. No wonder female inmates usually went in pairs.

She was passing the condemned cell when Carafa's brute Maso stepped into her path. The woman stopped, and Maso moved closer, leering at her. She looked round the courtyard for help but there were no other women outside. All the other men turned away, refusing to intervene. Disgust twisted Aldo's stomach. He rose and limped across the courtyard, fighting the leaden weight of his legs. Maso clamped a hand across the woman's mouth before she could cry out, dragging her into the condemned cell.

By the time Aldo reached the doorway, Maso was straddling her on the ground. 'Leave her be,' Aldo said, not sure what he'd do if Maso ignored the command. But his words made the assailant look back. The woman took her chance, snapping a knee up into Maso's groin. He rolled away, breath whistling through his teeth, hands between his thighs.

She scrambled over to Aldo. 'Thank you,' she whispered before running out. Maso was back on his feet, a hand nursing his bruised *palle*, the other clenching into a fist.

No point running. Aldo knew his legs wouldn't get far, and nobody was coming to help. Maso flung himself across the cell, his speed surprising for such a big man. Aldo swayed aside, but a flailing arm caught his head, smacking it against the wall. The impact hit right where one of Cerchi's cudgel blows had fallen, fresh pain blossoming.

Aldo staggered away, white spots dancing before his eyes. Fool, don't go deeper into the cell. He twisted round, but Maso was charging again, roaring. Aldo hesitated, letting Maso get close before dropping to a crouch. A pumping knee caught the side of Aldo's temples but the rest of Maso tumbled over him, head first. A crack echoed round the cell.

Aldo put a hand over both eyes, willing them to settle. A warm copper taste filled his mouth. He spat three times to get rid of the blood and tried to stand, but the cell lurched round him. One hand hit a solid shape on the floor. It was the broken stone the size of a fist that he had stumbled on after waking up in the cell—

A crushing weight hit Aldo from behind, forcing the air from his chest. Thick fingers grabbed his ears, pulling his head back before smacking it into the ground. Aldo couldn't see, couldn't cry out. He stretched for the stone, fingers scrabbling at the dirt – but it was gone.

Maso gave a grunt and collapsed on top of Aldo, crushing the air from him again. But someone rolled the bulky body off him. Aldo saw the young woman standing close by, the stone clutched in her hands. '*Grazie mille*,' he whispered.

Rebecca had sent Joshua away to his studies when there was an impatient knock at the door. But it wasn't Joshua returning for something he'd forgotten. It wasn't even Lemuel Volterra from next door, who had promised to sit *shiva* with her today.

A thin, mean-faced man with beady eyes pushed his way past her, two more men following him inside. 'Who are you?' Rebecca demanded. 'What do you want?' The intruder gestured to his men. They ripped open cupboards and drawers, emptying everything onto the floor. 'If you're one of Father's creditors, there isn't any money here.' Rebecca tried to stop the men, but they shoved her aside. 'This house is in mourning. Where is your respect?'

'Your father was involved with a plot to overthrow Duke Alessandro,' the man replied, 'conspiring with a man called Cesare Aldo.'

That made no sense. 'Father was murdered. Aldo is searching for the killer.'

'Is that what he told you? And you believed him?' The intruder laughed at her.

She wanted to slap his smug face. 'Yes.'

'Aldo's been sent to Le Stinche. For all we know, he murdered your father.'

Rebecca shook her head, unable to understand. Aldo couldn't have slain Father, could he? 'If that officer is in Le Stinche, who is looking for Father's killer?'

The other men had finished, with little but mess to show for their efforts. They returned to the street while their master muttered under his stale breath. Rebecca stepped in front of him so he couldn't leave without facing her. 'What's your name?' she demanded.

'Why should I tell you?'

Rebecca recognized a bully when she saw one. Such men were simply cowards with might on their side, Mother used to say. Stand up to them, and they will get bored or fearful. 'I want to be sure Avraham Yedaiah knows who did this,' Rebecca replied.

'He speaks for our people.' She didn't mention that Yedaiah was away, visiting his ill sister.

The intruder scowled. 'My name is Meo Cerchi, I'm an officer of the Otto di Guardia e Balia. Do what you like, I'm here with the authority of the court.' Cerchi pushed past her, slamming the door on his way out.

Rebecca stared at the few things Mother and Father had left her, scattered across the floor as if they had no value, no worth. She sank on to a chair, but refused to let tears come. No matter what men like Cerchi did, they would not break her.

Strocchi went straight from Le Stinche to Palazzo Pazzi but, without an appointment or letter of introduction, getting an audience with the cardinal was challenging. Twice he heard the chime of a distant church bell while pacing the courtyard. Finally a servant escorted Strocchi up to Cibo's *officio*. It was richly decorated: tapestries on the walls and golden ornaments everywhere. A far cry from the modest lodging of Father Coluccio in Strocchi's village. Perhaps the vow of poverty did not apply when a priest became a cardinal.

'I don't have long,' Cibo said as the constable was ushered in, not even looking at him. 'Tell Bindi whatever he wants can wait, at least until after Epiphany.'

'I'm not here on behalf of the *segretario*,' Strocchi replied. 'I work for the Otto, but this is an unofficial matter. I didn't think you would see me if I said so before.'

The cardinal peered at Strocchi. 'Aldo sent you, didn't he? Well, there's nothing I can do. Criminal matters are for the court, not the Church.' Cibo rose from behind his grand desk. A servant draped a cloak over the cardinal's shoulders. 'Now, if you'll excuse me?'

Strocchi had just got into the room and was already being dismissed. Still shivering from his long wait outside, the constable refused to give way. 'Aldo believes you need to intervene before Lorenzino de' Medici moves against the Duke.'

Cibo bristled before sending his servant out. He shrugged off the cloak, draping it over one arm. 'Does Aldo have any new evidence to support this . . . belief?'

'Wasn't Lorenzino swearing a *denunzia* against him proof?'

'No. The implications are worrying, but Lorenzino is no fool, despite his other flaws. He knows that *denunzia* will not stand close scrutiny by the Otto, but it doesn't matter. He sought to halt Aldo's investigation, and he succeeded. That's concerning, but hardly proof that the conspirators are planning any imminent action against the Duke.'

Strocchi shook his head. Praise be he didn't have to deal with the likes of Cibo every day. The cardinal could tie words into knots with that tongue. 'So you'll do nothing?'

'I see why Aldo sent you. He also prefers blunt truths.' Cibo pursed his lips. 'Being only a constable, perhaps you don't understand my role. I represent the Holy Roman Emperor here in Florence. I can advise those who lead this city, but unless I am witness to or have direct knowledge of something that can be deemed a danger to the Emperor, I am not empowered to intervene personally. Florence has its own laws and men who enforce them. It has ducal guards whose job it is to protect the Duke. I'm sorry, but my hands are tied.'

Strocchi stared at a tapestry of winged angels on the wall behind the cardinal. How could a man of God refuse to help others? How could he stand by and let injustice be done like this? There had to be a way.

'Your heart is in the right place,' Cibo said. 'Take comfort from that, constable.'

That wasn't enough for Strocchi. Not nearly enough. 'What if I kept watch over the Duke, from a distance? If I saw something proving he was in danger, would you act then?'

The cardinal put the cloak back round his shoulders. 'It would need to be compelling. I will only step in if you can convince me the threat is imminent and real. I will not be made a fool to satisfy Aldo's allegations, nor will I disgrace the Emperor by my actions.'

It was better than nothing. 'Do you know if the Duke has any public duties today?'

'I don't believe so. There is a joust in front of Palazzo Medici tomorrow that Alessandro is expected to attend – assuming he makes it out of bed in time.'

Strocchi nodded. Aldo had been certain whatever was coming would happen today. Keep watch over the Duke until dark and all should be well.

Aldo and the young woman were summoned to see Duro, while Maso was taken to the *ospedale*, still breathing but senseless. Aldo wasn't feeling much better, but at least he could talk and walk unaided. The captain berated him and the woman – Tomasia – for attacking another inmate. Aldo was going to protest, but she beat him to it.

'Attack him? That devil meant to rape me!' She gestured at Aldo. 'If this man hadn't come in, I'd be the one in the *ospedale*. Or dead.'

Duro glared at her. 'A guard in the watchtower saw you run out of the cell. If Maso was trying to rape you, why return a minute later? Changed your mind about him?'

Tomasia spat on the floor. 'I wouldn't go with that *merda* if he paid me.'

'She saved my life,' Aldo said. 'If Tomasia hadn't returned, Maso would have killed me. She pushed him away from me. He fell, hit his head on a loose stone.' No need to tell Duro what Tomasia had actually done. The captain would suspect, but couldn't prove it – not unless Maso regained his senses. There was little chance of that.

'You're claiming Maso fell?' Duro asked. She nodded. The captain's eyes narrowed but he sent her back to the woman's ward with a warning. Aldo was ready to leave too, but Duro had other ideas. 'Not so fast. Don't think I believe a word of your little fable.'

Aldo leaned against the nearest wall. He'd been admonished, accused and browbeaten many times. Might as well get comfortable. 'Then why let Tomasia go?'

'Maso was imprisoned for rape. Besides, her words sounded true. Yours sounded convenient.' The captain leaned forward in his chair. 'You've been in Le Stinche a few hours and a man is close to death because of you. I can't prove what you did. If I could, you'd be spending the night in an open cage outside. But make no mistake: if anyone else is hurt today, you'll suffer for it – whether you're close by or not.'

Chapter Twenty-Five

'Cesare Aldo is in prison?' Maria Salviati found it hard to believe, but the young constable at the Podestà was adamant. Apparently Aldo had been plotting to overthrow Duke Alessandro, believing this would return Florence to a republic, restore the city to its people. The young constable – Benedetto – confided that the Duke's own cousin was among those who'd sworn a *denunzia*. Bindi was furious about the disgrace this had brought on the Otto.

Maria thanked the constable for his candour before departing the Podestà. There went her chance to get an assessment of the Duke's mood. She'd heard Aldo was reporting directly to Alessandro on some matter. The officer could have been a useful source, but not while he was in Le Stinche. She could pay him a visit in the prison – but what purpose would it serve? They were not friends, and what she knew about him had no value now. A pity.

Talk of a conspiracy to overthrow the Duke set Maria's mind racing. Alessandro was far from being beloved inside Florence. His sexual exploits were notorious amongst the wives Maria had met since arriving in the city. He had helped to resolve some difficult disputes among the people, earning the appreciation of some citizens, but others called him tyrant, *bastardo* – and far worse. So a campaign to overthrow him was not out of the question. But Maria dismissed any notion that Aldo might be a leading figure in such a conspiracy. The man who'd visited her in Trebbio certainly gave no sign of being political. Besides, he was an officer of the court, nothing more. She doubted Aldo had either the alliances or the coin necessary to execute such a plan. No, that was nonsense.

If someone did attempt a strike against Alessandro, it could create instability, perhaps even a chance for Cosimo to shine. Whenever Florence sought to rid itself of the Medici, the family always found a path back to power. Maria quickened her pace, heading for the home of a prominent member of the Palleschi. While the Medici and their supporters still held sway in the city, there remained hope for her and Cosimo.

Bindi was not impressed. He had sent Cerchi away to find evidence of Aldo's plot against the Duke, but the fool came back empty-handed. No proof of a conspiracy. Nothing. Cerchi was far from being the Otto's best officer, but his vendetta with Aldo should have motivated him to find what others might miss.

'We searched Aldo's room, and questioned his informants. I even went to the Jews, the daughter of that murdered moneylender you said was involved.' Cerchi did look ashamed by his failure. Or was that wine colouring his cheeks? The *segretario* hauled himself out of his chair, waddling round the desk to sniff Cerchi's breath.

'Did you think I wouldn't notice that stench?' Bindi asked.

'I was thirsty, stopped at a tavern on my way here—'

'Get out. Now.'

Cerchi retreated from the room, but Bindi's problem remained. Alessandro had asked for – no, demanded – proof. Aldo would have been first choice for that task, if he wasn't in Le Stinche. It would be dark soon. Come morning, the Duke would expect a full report – names, accusations, everything.

There was one faint hope. This might be another of the many ideas that Alessandro mentioned, yet never recalled the next day. If he did indeed spend the night bedding some unfortunate merchant's wife, the Duke probably wouldn't be worrying about this thwarted conspiracy come morning. And it was not uncommon for Alessandro to miss the daily report altogether, especially if he was busy sleeping off a night of drink and debauchery. Such dissolute behaviour usually sickened Bindi, but for once it might be his saviour.

Aldo spied the Bassos as soon as he returned to the courtyard. It was hard not to notice them, standing a head taller than everyone else in Le Stinche. Careful to avoid their eyes, he joined Lippo on a bench outside the condemned cell. 'When did those two arrive?'

'Guards brought them in while you were with Duro. From what I hear they confessed to killing a *buggerone* dressed as a courtesan.'

So Strocchi had brought the brothers to justice. It was typical of the constable not to mention that. Such modesty wouldn't help if he wanted to be an officer. Lippo gave a low whistle when Aldo shared what he knew of the case. 'Better keep away from them. Sounds like they've got good reason to hate anyone from the Otto.'

Aldo had reached the same conclusion. Bad enough he was sharing a prison with Carafa. Now there were the Bassos to watch out for as well.

'Duro must be delighted with you,' Lippo said.

'Overjoyed. If I put anyone else in the *ospedale*, he's promised me a special cell all of my own. More of a cage really, out in the open air.'

The pick-purse paled. 'Last man who spent a night in the *gabbia* froze to death.'

Duro was the least of Aldo's troubles. He doubted Maso's attack on Tomasia had been driven solely by lust. More likely it was a test to see what Aldo would do. The answer cost Carafa a man, but that was one sacrifice in a longer game. Aldo cursed himself for forgetting one of the rules he'd learned as a mercenary while riding with Giovanni dalle Bande Nere: pick your battles carefully, you never know when the next will come.

'It'll be dark soon,' Lippo said. 'You thought about where to sleep tonight?'

'Doubt I'll get much rest,' Aldo replied. 'Not while keeping both eyes open.'

'The guards don't bother locking the wards at night, as there's no way to escape except out through the main door. You won't be welcome in the male wards, Carafa rules them. The women's ward is out of bounds, the guards keep too close an eye on it.' Lippo frowned. 'You'd be safe from Carafa in the ward for the insane, but not from the lunatics.'

'Can't risk the condemned cell again,' Aldo said. 'It's a death trap, in every sense.'

'Running out places to go, unless you want to try the *ospedale*?'

'Not my first choice. Maso might recover.'

Lippo's eyes widened. 'Of course, the answer's staring right at us.' He pointed across to the small chapel. 'Slip in there just before curfew. You could push one of the pews against the door, stop anyone else from getting in.'

'Or me from getting out,' Aldo observed.

'Don't want my help? Fine. But I don't see anyone else offering.'

* * *

Strocchi wished he'd brought a cloak. Lurking in the shadows opposite Palazzo Medici meant he could see everyone coming and going from the Duke's residence, but the cold was fast seeping into his bones. Soon he could see his own breath in the air as it slipped from his lips. At least Florence was far enough south to avoid snow most winters. Strocchi didn't want to think what it must be like in places further north, let alone high up in the mountains. He stamped both boots again, struggling to get warmth into his toes.

There'd been no sign of Alessandro since he returned from a ride. Now twilight was claiming the city. Lorenzino and his fellow conspirators must have abandoned their plan, or else it was happening behind closed doors. Had Aldo been wrong after all? Either way, there seemed little point in staying. Let Alessandro look after himself.

No sooner had Strocchi decided to leave than the palazzo doors opened. Three men slipped out into the gloom. All wore cloaks, but while two were drab and ordinary, the other was lined with silk that shimmered in the twilight. Rumour had it Alessandro spent more on Neapolitan silks and satin than many merchants earned in a year. His companions were burly men with wide shoulders and barrel chests. They must be his guards. Alessandro never went out alone. Good, while those two were at his side the Duke should be safe. But where were the trio going this late? Strocchi followed the three men, keeping well back.

They headed north towards Piazza San Marco. But as they approached the wide square the three turned back, returning the way they'd just come. Strocchi slipped into an alley thick with shadow, holding his breath. He feared the guards must have seen him, but the group passed his hiding place without pause. Had the Duke changed his mind, or forgotten something?

Strocchi followed them south on via Largo, staying even further back. The trio passed the entrance to Palazzo Medici, turning right at the southern corner of the grand building. Hurrying to catch up, Strocchi reached the corner in time to see the Duke knock on a door. Light spilled out when it opened, silhouetting a man in the doorway. The Duke greeted him as a brother, both men laughing. The man inside resembled Aldo's description of Lorenzino, but it was hard to be sure from so far away. The Duke was a public figure, his face familiar to most citizens, but Strocchi had not encountered Lorenzino since coming to Florence. The Duke went inside, gesturing at his guards to stay out on the cold, empty street. Neither seemed pleased by the order, and Strocchi didn't blame them.

Aldo had stolen into the small chapel as darkness fell. Inside was plain, a few wooden pews facing a bare altar, with none of the rich decoration found in most Florentine churches. Two thick wooden candle stands on the altar and a plain tapestry on a wall close by were the only ornamentation. This was a prison, after all. The pew Aldo had shoved against the door wouldn't stop a determined force, but it would slow them down – and give him a warning. He settled on one of the other pews, hoping for sleep.

'Lippo was right,' a voice said.

So much for sleeping.

Carafa emerged from behind the tapestry, stepping through a hidden door – a way out for the priest if inmates turned on him. Aldo rose, studying Carafa. No blade in his hands. Keep him talking. 'About what? Lippo isn't very reliable, in my experience.'

'You dismissed his idea of sleeping in the chapel, but he said you'd still come here.'

'Hard to trust a man who'll betray you to please a killer.'

'He seemed more interested in making you pay for his arm.' Carafa moved in a slow circle around Aldo. 'You're not going to call for the guards?'

'I'm sure you've persuaded those on duty to ignore this.'

Carafa nodded, smiling. 'You think of everything.'

'Come on,' Aldo said, blowing him a kiss. 'Show me what you've got.'

Carafa swung a fist, a clumsy attack. Aldo swayed out of the way, but it'd been a ruse. Another fist punched below the first, into his ribs. *Palle!* He staggered sideways, towards the altar. Carafa followed – another punch, and another. Aldo parried them, but he was gasping for air already. A solid hook thudded into his left ear, ringing bells in his head. Stumbling feet, going backwards. The altar dug into his back, trapping him.

Carafa closed in. 'You'll die in here.' The thick wooden candle stand smacked the smile from his face, the sound of Carafa's nose breaking a whip crack in the chapel. The bandit lurched back, blood streaming. '*Bastardo!*'

'So I hear,' Aldo replied, clutching the candle holder in both hands.

Carafa reached into his boot and pulled out a blade. He swiped it through the air twice, before lunging. Aldo blocked him with the candle stand, but more attacks came. The blade cut upwards, slicing Aldo's left hand. Fight back, fight back! A wild swing. A snarl of dismay, the blade scraping across the stone floor.

Carafa dived for it, Aldo too tired to follow. His left arm hung down, blood dripping from the fingers. He couldn't breathe, sweat was blinding his eyes. Two, maybe three more attacks, then he'd be done. Finished. Was it too late to ask forgiveness for his sins? Assuming he could remember them all.

Carafa rose, blade in hand. 'Why are you grinning, fool?'

'At least now they won't get to execute me.'

Then the chapel door came crashing down. The Basso brothers forced their way into the chapel, shoving aside the pew blocking the door.

'Who are they here for,' Carafa hissed, 'you or me?'

Aldo grimaced. 'Both of us.' Lippo had suggested the chapel as a safe refuge, planting the notion in Aldo's head and laying the trap for Carafa to spring. Then Lippo doubtless made an arrangement with the Bassos to have them kill both men in the chapel. Carafa was the most powerful prisoner in Le Stinche. Murder him and the Bassos could take his place, force other inmates to do their bidding. Killing Aldo made no difference to the Bassos, but it would satisfy Lippo's craving for revenge over his imprisonment and lost arm. Aldo tightened his grip on the candle stand. Fighting Carafa had been a losing battle. Taking on the brothers alone was doomed. 'How about a truce?' he suggested to the bandit. 'A real one, this time?'

'Us against them, till this is over?' Carafa brandished his blade. 'Agreed.'

The brothers lunged at them, hands reaching out. Aldo swung the candle stand up into his attacker's jaw. The brother staggered back, spitting blood and broken teeth.

He grinned. The *lunatico* grinned.

Aldo retreated behind the altar. Across the chapel Carafa was using the blade, cutting and slicing at those huge hands, but it wasn't doing much good. The bandit dived for the doorway behind the tapestry. A bloody hand grabbed his leg, pulling him back.

The toothless brother facing Aldo gripped hold of the altar – and threw it aside. *Palle*, how had Strocchi arrested one of these monsters, let alone two? Moonlight from a high window glinted on the brother's glistening temples, revealing a bruised lump. Maybe that was how Strocchi had stopped this brute? It was worth trying the same.

Aldo beckoned his attacker closer, ignoring cries of pain close by. The brother lunged and Aldo swung his weapon through the air—

—but it hit a muscle-bound arm, bouncing out of Aldo's grasp.

He staggered back, helpless, defenceless.

The first punch was a hammer blow.

The second was worse.

He swung his right arm, more a flail than a punch. It was caught in the air. Twisted. Something popped in his shoulder. Aldo heard a scream of pain – it was his own.

'Aldo,' a weak voice whispered.

The blade scraped across the stones.

Aldo dropped to his knees, bloody left hand searching for the blade.

Where was it? There. There!

Fingers closing, gripping.

Stab it. Stab it deep.

Now – twist.

Strocchi watched the Duke's guards. They looked as bored and frustrated as him. One was dozing, the other picking his nose and eating what came out. Ugh. Neither was paying any heed to their surroundings. Strocchi didn't blame them. The streets were deserted.

No, there was someone else out in the freezing night air. Strocchi could see round the corner of the building into which Alessandro had gone. Three male figures, all in cloaks with hoods hiding their faces, were leaving by a side door. The first had a stoop, but still moved like a young man. That could be the youth Aldo had described, the one who killed Dante. Il Freccia, that was his name. The second also wore a plain cloak, but the hood slipped for a moment, revealing his hooked nose. That must be Scoronconcolo. The third figure was nursing a hand bound in cloth, a dark stain seeping through it. That could be blood. But who was injured? Strocchi glimpsed the man's face – was that Lorenzino? Staying to the shadows, the three men hurried away, leaving the guards none the wiser.

Strocchi wasn't sure what to do. Follow the three men and leave the Duke at risk, or stay and hope the cloaked figures weren't important? He chose to follow. But by the time he'd reached the corner, each of the trio was already on a horse. The last struggled, that wounded hand troubling him. Strocchi watched them ride away, the sound of hooves echoing between the buildings. There was no way he could keep up.

Strocchi returned to his watch. The guards were both dozing against the door, oblivious. Strocchi hoped his life never relied on them. He considered going to Palazzo Pazzi to share what he'd seen with Cardinal Cibo, but how would that sound? The Duke had gone into a building round the corner from his own palazzo, leaving his guards outside. Later three men came out of a side door of the same building and rode away, one of them with a wounded hand. The cardinal had demanded proof, not more specu-lation. What Strocchi had seen was strange, but he didn't know what it signified – assuming it meant anything at all.

No, he would wait a while longer and see if the Duke emerged. There was one thing about which Strocchi could be certain. The city gates were already locked for curfew, so there was no way whoever had ridden away could leave Florence before dawn.

* * *

Aldo's face was being slapped. 'This one's still alive,' a gruff voice announced. 'Can't tell how much of the blood is his. Should we take him to the *ospedale*?'

'No. If he's alive, he can go in the *gabbia*.' Aldo opened his eyes. Duro was looming over him. 'I warned you not to trouble me again. Instead I get pulled out of bed for this.'

The chapel was awash with blood and worse. The toothless Basso brother was dead, a blade jutting from his groin. Four guards were carrying the other brother out, his head rolling from side to side. Carafa had put up an almighty fight. The bandit sat in a corner, smiling. Aldo raised a hand to thank him before realizing there were shoulder blades under Carafa's face. His head had been twisted round, like a cork in a bottle.

Aldo fought back the bile rising in his throat.

Two guards dragged him from the chapel, Duro following. An open metal cage leaned against a wall in the courtyard, thick iron bars enclosing a space no bigger than a coffin, its door hanging open. 'Put him in,' the captain said. The guards forced Aldo inside the *gabbia*. The door slammed shut, a key twisting in the lock. Duro pulled it free, showing the key to Aldo. 'I'll bring this back in the morning, if you're still alive.' The captain and his guards stalked away, disappearing through the door into the watchtower.

What was it Lippo had said? The last man who had spent a night in the *gabbia* froze to death. Aldo had expected to die in the chapel, had been ready to die. But now he wanted to live, just to see the captain's disbelief in the morning.

Duro could get fucked.

Chapter Twenty-Six

❦

Sunday, January 7th

It was cold, so cold in the *gabbia*. The night sky was visible through the open bars of the cage, stars shining bright above the courtyard. There were no clouds, nothing to keep any warmth from escaping. Icy gusts whistled through the prison enclosure, punishing anyone foolish enough to be outside. The watchtower guards had abandoned their posts, retreating indoors. Aldo didn't have that choice.

He'd torn fabric from a sleeve with his teeth, using it to bind his left hand, staunching the cut. Being dragged outside and thrown into the *gabbia* had wrenched his right arm back into place, but the shoulder was now swollen and throbbing with pain.

The first few hours he spent listening to the city, its sleeping silence broken only by distant church bells and the occasional howling of cats. Shaking took hold as the night fell colder. Each breath in chilled his throat and chest, while every breath out left a lingering cloud of vapour. Colder than the air were the metal bars of the *gabbia* – pushing icy numbness through cloth and skin, like a burrowing animal.

Five winters on the streets as a youth had been a brutal *scuola*, but those lessons stayed with Aldo. Falling asleep was tempting, so tempting, but fear of never waking again staved that off. Curling into a ball was the only way to stay warm.

It must be Sunday by now. Had the conspiracy succeeded? If the plotters usurped Alessandro, all those who'd resisted would be dead or exiled within days – it was the Florentine way. Foes from rich families could expect to be banished from the Dominion, skulking away to Venice or Milan, planning for the day they might return. Troublesome officers from the Otto would not be so fortunate.

Aldo knew he could expect a short stay in the cell for the condemned, and a brief visit from two men. One would be a priest, to ensure the condemned man's soul had a chance to save itself. The other would be an executioner, come to deliver extra-judicial justice. Strangling was the preferred method for prisoners that displeased those in power: quick, clean and effective. A cart would take the corpse away to an unmarked grave, a shovel of quicklime waiting to hasten the decay.

Would anyone mourn him? Teresa, perhaps, though Aldo hadn't seen his half-sister in months. Her mother Lucrezia would probably laugh at his fate. Strocchi and Bindi might notice at the Podestà, but few others would. Knowing Cerchi, he'd be at the graveside waiting to piss on the corpse, assuming he hadn't taken the job of executioner.

A pity. Aldo had hoped to do the same to that *merda* one day.

Orvieto. Would anyone tell the doctor, or would Saul be left wondering if he'd done something to push Aldo away? There had been a spark there, and the promise of more. After so long alone, it was galling to think they might never be together, even if only for one night. Aldo pictured the doctor's face – that wry smile, those warm hazel eyes. The deft touch Saul had with his hands, how his strong fingers could ease life into weary limbs and send blood rushing to other parts. What other talents did he possess? It'd be a shame to die not knowing.

Aldo leaned his forehead against his knees. Maybe he'd just rest his eyes. He hadn't slept in days, not properly. What harm could it do to close his eyes?

Strocchi strode through empty streets, wishing for a cloak. It would be dawn soon; dark blues were colouring the sky. Sleep had proven fitful, too many questions left unanswered. He needed to know if the Duke had emerged from the palazzo during the night. Strocchi needed to know if Aldo was right.

If Alessandro had been attacked, then the men who had left on horseback must be part of the conspiracy. The city gates would be unlocked at dawn, giving the trio a way out. That assumed they wanted – or needed – to flee Florence. If Lorenzino and his men planned to seize power, they would be staying to make their claim. Strocchi shook his head. Let rich merchants and senators worry about who was in charge.

The constable turned a corner, boots skidding on frosty stones. The guards were still outside the same door. Strocchi realized it was Casa Vecchia. He'd passed the palazzo before, but hadn't recognized it in the dark. Judging by their surly faces, the guards had been there all night. Strocchi approached, identifying himself as a constable of the Otto.

The guards confirmed what he suspected: yes, the Duke was still inside. No, they'd seen nothing of Alessandro since he went into the residence, leaving strict instructions that they were not to come inside. Yes, the Duke's cousin Lorenzino lived on the middle level. One of the guards – Giomo – thought a widow called Salviati was staying on the upper level. Strocchi could tell the men were losing patience, so he made them an offer. One of them had to remain outside the residence so the Duke's orders were being fulfilled, but the other could come with Strocchi to ask about ending their long vigil.

Saying yes took a moment – choosing who stayed behind took longer.

Aldo knew this was a dream but he couldn't stop shivering. Everything round him was white, a frozen wasteland as far as he could see. Had it snowed in the night? That made no sense, Florence rarely saw snow, even in the coldest of winters. He'd been in a cage, locked in the *gabbia*, left outside in the courtyard of Le Stinche overnight. Now he was huddled naked on fresh snow, unable to stop himself from shaking and trembling. Dream or no dream, he would die if he didn't find shelter soon, that much was certain.

There was a crunching sound, getting closer. Someone was coming, marching across the crisp snow towards him. Aldo looked up, hoping for sympathy, for someone who cared enough to bring him warmth. But the sour face approaching was twisted with disgust. Her scowl he knew well, though they had not spoken in years. She had always resented him, the cuckoo in her loveless nest. His father's body was still warm when Lucrezia Fioravanti had Aldo hurled out into the street. Now she glowered down at Aldo, her thin lips pinched in disdain . . .

'Wake up!' a male voice shouted.

'I think he's dead,' another said.

'He's not dead. He's too stubborn to be dead.'

Aldo opened his eyes, but everything was a blur, whirling around him. He squinted until the shapes became people. Two guards were peering at him through the bars, their stale breath fogging the air. Beyond them, Captain Duro stood with his arms folded.

'Is it morning already?' Aldo asked, teeth chattering together.

'Get him out,' Duro snapped. A guard fumbled the key. The captain hissed a curse, snatching the key and forcing it into the lock. Once the *gabbia* was open, the guards pulled Aldo out and onto his feet. Both legs threatened to give way, no feeling left in them. Duro gave a fresh warning about what would happen if Aldo fought another inmate. Several female prisoners watched from across the courtyard, Tomasia among them.

The captain had fallen silent, waiting for an answer.

When in doubt, agree. 'I understand,' Aldo said.

Duro stalked away, followed by his guards. Aldo staggered, willing his legs to keep him upright. They obeyed, for a few moments. Then everything was lurching sideways and the courtyard stones rose up to claim him.

For the second day in succession, Strocchi waited at Palazzo Pazzi. This time he was with Giomo, one of Alessandro's personal guards, but that didn't persuade Cardinal Cibo to admit them any sooner. Eventually a servant opened a door to the *officio* where Cibo was warming his hands by the fire.

Giomo told the Cardinal how Lorenzino had welcomed Alessandro to Casa Vecchia the previous night, but left both guards on the street. Strocchi revealed seeing the cloaked trio – one with a bloody hand – leave the palazzo by another door and ride away.

'I didn't see the injured man's face,' Strocchi admitted, 'but the other two – they looked a lot like Lorenzino's servants.'

Cibo stopped warming his hands. 'You've seen them before?'

'No, but Aldo described them to me.'

The cardinal studied Giomo. 'Did you see these men leave?'

'No. And I didn't hear any horses.'

The guards hadn't noticed Strocchi watching them either, but he kept that to himself. He needed Giomo as a witness, however limited.

The cardinal wrote a brief note before summoning a servant. 'Take this to Bishop Marzi, fast as you can, and wait for his reply.' Once the servant was gone, Cibo gestured to Giomo. 'If you've been outside all night, you must be hungry. Go to the kitchens. It's warm, and you can eat all you want.'

Giomo didn't hesitate, thanking Cibo on his way out. Once the guard was gone, Strocchi approached the cardinal. 'You believe me, don't you? You think it was Lorenzino and his servants who left by the side door.'

'I believe in being certain,' Cibo replied. 'For now I have other matters that require my attention. You may wait outside until my servant returns.'

Aldo regained his senses as he was lowered onto a straw mattress. A concerned face appeared in front of him – Tomasia. She touched his cheek. 'He's colder than snow.'

'What did you expect?' another woman asked, her voice as gruff as her face. 'Outside in that cage all night, he should be dead. Why even bring him in here?'

'He helped me,' Tomasia said, laying a coarse blanket across him.

Aldo wanted to thank her but couldn't stop his teeth chattering. Female clothes were drying on ropes strung across the room. He must be in the women's ward.

'Are there any more blankets?' Tomasia called out.

'Won't do any good,' the gruff woman replied. 'The cold's got too deep inside him. Blankets will warm the skin, not the bones.' She was right. The *gabbia* hadn't ended him, but death was close now. 'Another person's heat is all that will save him.'

Tomasia stared at Aldo. 'Keep your hands to yourself, or I'll throw you back outside.' Rough hands rolled Aldo onto his back, the gruff woman pulling the blanket away.

She forced Aldo's legs flat, tugging his hose down. 'Do what Tomasia says, or I'll rip your *cazzo* off.' The rest of his clothes were removed, leaving him naked on the straw mattress. 'Roll on your side again.'

Aldo saw Tomasia undressing and closed his eyes, hunching into a ball. She lay down behind him, pressing her warm skin against his exposed back, buttocks and legs before pulling the blanket over them. 'Sleep,' she whispered, reaching over Aldo to take his icy fingers in her own. 'Dream of being anywhere but here.'

Strocchi saw the servant returning to Palazzo Pazzi, a written note clutched in his hand, but it was a while before the constable was summoned to Cibo's *officio*.

'You can read?'

Strocchi nodded, and the cardinal gave him the note. A florid hand revealed the Duke's cousin had visited Bishop Marzi the previous evening. Lorenzino had sought and obtained a letter granting passage through the city gates during the hours of curfew because his brother Giuliano de' Medici was gravely ill at the family villa in Cafaggiolo – or so he'd claimed.

'I didn't know anyone could get such a letter.'

'Only those of particular importance,' Cibo replied.

Marzi had seen no reason to deny the Duke's cousin. Lorenzino and his servants were also given three post horses for the journey, the fastest means of travel outside the city. Marzi confirmed Lorenzino had presented the letter at Porta San Gallo during the night. The gate was opened, and the trio had ridden north in haste towards Bologna.

Strocchi couldn't read the final sentence. 'What does this say?'

'Marzi's writing gets worse every day,' Cibo replied, taking back the message. 'Guards at Porta San Gallo claim Lorenzino had a bloody bandage on one hand.' The cardinal threw on a crimson cape. 'I need to find the Duke. Come with me to Palazzo Medici.'

Strocchi shivered. Somehow he'd got caught up in matters far beyond a simple constable. Aldo was an officer, and look what had happened to him.

Sandalwood and decay, Aldo knew them both well. One was the scent of the house where he'd been a boy. The other was the stench of death, seeping out through sores and skin and holes and wounds. The two smells together could only mean one thing: he was back in Palazzo Fioravanti. He was waiting for Papa to die.

Aldo caught his reflection in a burnished bronze bowl. He'd been twelve when Papa perished, but already aware of what his heart desired and his *palle* craved. But the face staring back at him was that of a grown man, wrinkled round the eyes, greying stubble along the jawline. This was not real. 'Come in, my boy.' There was no ignoring that voice.

The bedchamber was barren, just a high bed, and the dying man atop it. Papa had been strong and vital. Now a husk lay in his place, yellow as a melted candle, skin stretched taut over jutting bones. Being a child in this palazzo had taught Aldo how to hide his feelings. He smiled for the man made old by illness.

'You grew up. You got so big.'

'I'm older than you were when you died.'

A thin smile. 'You and I, we're dreams now. Nothing more.'

'Am I . . . ?'

'You're not dead. Not yet. But you will be if you don't remember what I said.'

Aldo nodded. 'To survive, you must endure what others cannot.'

Papa shook his head. The skin across that cadaverous face split open, revealing the skull underneath. 'Find someone to trust, to love.' Aldo staggered back as the bones became dust, a breeze blowing them away. 'In the end, that's all we have. That's all we ever are . . .'

'Thank you for coming,' Rebecca said, letting Orvieto inside.

'It's the least I can do,' the doctor replied, concern in his eyes. 'I heard about what happened yesterday. Men searching through your things, it's disgraceful. The officer in charge of those men, what was his name?'

'Cerchi.'

'He should be made to pay for that intrusion.' Rebecca motioned for Orvieto to sit with her at the table. 'Tell me, how are you?'

'Tired. I'm not sleeping.'

'Have you eaten today?'

She shook her head, gesturing to food nearby. 'People keep bringing more, but . . .'

The doctor nodded. 'So, why did you want to see me?'

Rebecca hesitated. If only Ruth hadn't gone back to Bologna. 'Whatever you want to say or ask, I won't judge.'

'It's about Joshua.'

'Ahh.' Orvieto pursed his lips. 'That young man has great affection for you.'

'I know. And I have feelings for him, too. But Father forbade me from ever being with Joshua.' Rebecca struggled to keep hold of herself, the turmoil inside her. 'If I tell Joshua I love him, I will be breaking with Father. But if I do as Father wished . . .'

'You fear your own heart will be broken – and so will Joshua's.'

She nodded.

Orvieto sighed. 'I know bodies and how they work,' he said. 'But I'm no sage when it comes to who we do or don't love. The heart wants what it wants. Learning to accept we can't always have that is no easy lesson.' He gave a sad smile. 'No matter how old you get.'

Rebecca looked at the doctor, seeing him with new eyes. Many a daughter had been put in his path, without success. A few women whispered about the reasons why. Some said his heart was broken, others that he had little time for women. But the doctor had only ever been kind to Rebecca. She nodded her understanding.

'Whatever you decide to do, I could be there when you share your choice with Joshua,' Orvieto said. 'To congratulate you both, or to help him understand.'

'Thank you,' Rebecca said, feeling as though she could breathe again. A knock at the door had her up and crossing the room without thinking. No doubt it was another neighbour, come to sit with her. But she paused at the door to look back. 'Doctor, you do so much for everyone else. Is there anything I could do for you?'

Orvieto rose. 'Actually, yes, there is. An officer of the Otto – Aldo, I think his name was – came to see me about your father. Is he any nearer to discovering what happened?'

'I don't know,' she admitted. 'The men who broke in, they said Aldo had been accused of plotting to overthrow the Duke. Apparently he's in Le Stinche.'

Chapter Twenty-Seven

*B*indi had come to Palazzo Medici with his morning report, fearful at having no answer to the question of Aldo's fellow conspirators. It was a relief to hear the Duke wasn't ready for him yet, but the *segretario* was still obliged to remain should Alessandro appear. After a fruitless hour in an antechamber, Bindi realized nobody at the palazzo was sure where the Duke was, or when he might return, so the *segretario* abandoned his vigil.

On his way out Bindi spied Francesco Campana pacing the courtyard. The Duke's administrative secretary was a man of considerable guile, known for having the ear of those in power. He bent with the breeze no matter how the wind was blowing, a strong trait in uncertain times. Campana could be trusted never to betray a confidence, so his agitation was intriguing. Bindi approached, bowing a respectful head. 'I came with a report for the Duke, but he's not here.'

Campana studied the windows overlooking the courtyard. Was he worried they might be overheard? 'The Duke made plans for a . . . private visit last night and has yet to return. I've no doubt he'll be back soon.' It was an obvious lie. Bindi sensed a chance to be useful.

'If you thought it might be helpful, I could have one of my officers – one of the Otto's officers – make discreet enquiries.'

Campana appeared tempted, but shook his head. 'I'm sure that will not be necessary,' he replied, rather too fast. 'But thank you for the offer.'

Before the *segretario* could respond, Cardinal Cibo strode into the courtyard, his crimson cape billowing. As the Emperor's representative in Florence, Cibo was a man of considerable importance. His brisk arrival suggested there was more to the Duke's absence than Campana had admitted. Even more surprising was the figure beside Cibo. What was Strocchi – one of the Otto's constables – doing at the cardinal's side?

Campana repeated his explanation about the Duke, but Cibo dismissed that. He revealed Alessandro had likely spent the night at Casa Vecchia, for reasons unknown.

'I might have the answer,' Bindi volunteered. 'Yesterday I witnessed the Duke and his cousin discussing a woman whose guardian was away in Naples. Lorenzino suggested it was the perfect time for the Duke to become acquainted with her. I did not hear all that was said, but mention was made of an *appuntamento*. The Duke was most . . . enthusiastic.'

Cibo and Campana exchanged a weary look. 'Unfortunate,' the cardinal said, 'but better than the alternative. I shall visit Casa Vecchia.' Cibo caught Bindi glaring at the constable. '*Segretario*, I believe Strocchi here is one of your men. He has been assisting me this morning. It may be useful to have his help a while longer. By your leave, of course.'

'Of course, Your Eminence.' Bindi forced a smile. As if there was any choice in the matter. 'I'm sure the Otto can endure a day without one of its more junior constables.'

'Most kind. Now, if you'll excuse us . . .'

'Forgive me, but there is another matter,' Campana said. 'The Duke was to host a joust this morning. It will be noticed if that doesn't go ahead.'

'His Grace is sometimes unwell on such occasions,' Bindi observed. 'So long as the joust takes place, the citizens will still be happy.'

'Well said,' Cibo agreed, his words a balm to the *segretario*. 'Have sand put down outside, and all other necessary preparations made. If the Duke does not return in time to attend, you can announce he's unwell. As Bindi says, it is not uncommon.'

Strocchi followed Cibo to Casa Vecchia. The constable was uncertain of his role, so stayed a respectful two steps behind the cardinal. Giomo was waiting outside with the Duke's other guard, having been sent ahead to ensure the palazzo remained closed to visitors. Hammering at the door brought a wary servant with thinning hair and a silver beard.

Cibo swept inside, Strocchi following close behind. The servant confirmed the Duke had visited the previous night, but begged them not to go near Lorenzino's bedchamber on the middle level. Lorenzino's servant Scoronconcolo had made terrible threats about what would happen to anyone who dared enter the room without his permission.

The cardinal marched to the door, but it was locked. Lorenzino had the only key, the servant confessed. Strocchi noticed boot marks on the floor, a crimson so dark it was close to brown. 'How often is this cleaned?' he asked, crouching to rub a finger through the marks.

'Every day,' the servant said, taking offence. 'But not yet today.'

Strocchi dabbed the fingertip to his tongue, then spat out – blood. Cibo dismissed the aged servant, warning him to keep others away. Once they were alone, Strocchi studied the boot marks. They led away from the bedchamber, becoming less distinct the further they went from the door. There were more than one set – two, perhaps three. The constable noticed Cibo beside the locked door, breathing in deeply, his face twisting with distaste. Yes, there was an ill odour outside the bedchamber, one Strocchi knew. His uncle had died alone at home one winter, but the body wasn't found for days. The stench had been overwhelming.

'Do you wish me to break down the door, Your Eminence?'

The cardinal shook his head. 'Not yet.'

'Could somebody please explain what is going on?' A woman in the robes of a widow bustled into the hallway behind Cibo, her face pinched and impatient. 'Well?'

The cardinal turned. 'Signora Salviati, I did not realize you were staying here at present. Please, forgive the intrusion.'

The widow gave Strocchi the briefest of glances before glaring at Cibo. 'Cardinal, the servants are keeping me confined to the upper level. I'd plans to travel home to my *castello* soon. I never enjoy being away from my son for long.'

No wonder the servant with the silver beard looked so wary, Strocchi realized. Keeping this widow confined to one place must have taken all his efforts.

'Your affection for Cosimo does you credit,' Cibo said, in a soothing voice. 'I'm sure the household staff here can assist if you wish to depart.'

Strocchi noticed the widow gazing at the boot marks on the floor, her eyes narrowing. 'Perhaps you are right,' she said as Cibo led her away. Once they were gone Strocchi went to the bedchamber and peered through its keyhole. The room was dark, shutters across the windows. But a shaft of light fell on the floor, revealing thick scarlet stains. The stench of death was almost overpowering. Strocchi clamped a hand over his nose and mouth.

Why didn't Cibo want the door opened?

Everything suggested the Duke was inside Lorenzino's bedchamber – dead or dying, most likely murdered by his own cousin. Opening the door would remove any doubt . . .

Ahh. That was why.

So long as nobody knew for certain the Duke was dead, life in the city would carry on. People would go to mass, courtesans would strive to catch the eye of lusty men. Families would gather for meals, giving thanks for their good fortune or comforting each other over tragedies. Everything would continue as it did on any other Sunday. But once Alessandro's murder was known, it would create an unstoppable cascade of events.

By keeping the door closed, Cibo hoped to delay those events for a few hours more. It would give him time to prepare, to shape what came next. The secret could not stay secret long, there were too many people who knew a little of what had happened. Strocchi shivered. He knew more than most, and that put him in danger. The sooner he got away—

'Constable, I need you to stay where you are.' Cibo advanced on him. 'I have certain tasks to complete before the bedchamber can be opened. I'm sure you understand.'

Strocchi nodded, unsure what was coming next.

'I must ask you to remain by this door, ensuring nobody goes in. It may be a few hours before someone can take your place.' The cardinal paused on his way out. 'Alessandro's guards will also remain, one at each entrance.'

Even if Strocchi wanted to leave, he couldn't.

Aldo woke in all kinds of pain, but it was good pain – or as good as pain could be. His shoulder was throbbing, the cut hand just as bad, along with stiffness from bruises. But he could feel his fingers and toes. Most of all, he was warm. Aldo rolled on his back, and groaned. Maybe all the pain wasn't so welcome. Not when it hurt this bad.

The gruff-faced woman sat with her back against a wall, staring at him. 'Awake?'

'Alive, at least,' Aldo replied.

'You've Tomasia to thank for that.' The woman smirked. 'I took a turn as well. Been a while since I lay with a man.'

It'd been even longer since Aldo lay with a woman, but she needn't know that. 'Thank you.' He pushed himself up onto an elbow.

Her smirk widened. 'My pleasure.' She threw Aldo's clothes across, and watched him dress. He went out into the courtyard and nodded to Tomasia, who was talking with another female inmate. Tomasia joined him on a bench against one of the walls. 'You look better.'

'Thanks to you,' Aldo replied. 'Most people would have left me to die.'

Her gaze flickered to the condemned cell. 'Most people would have left me to suffer.' She looked round the courtyard. 'Where's your friend with the one arm?'

'Doing his best to stay out of my way.' Aldo flexed his injured shoulder, wincing. 'Why are you here, in Le Stinche? You needn't say, but I may be able to help.'

'How? You're an inmate, not an officer.'

True, but Epiphany was over. No executioner had come for him. If the plotters had sought only to end the Duke's life, the fate of a troublesome officer from the Otto was likely to be of little consequence. And there was another possibility: the plot had failed. If so, Lorenzino's *denunzia* would be worthless. The danger was passing.

Aldo smiled at Tomasia. 'Indulge me.'

'My brother Sandro worked for a silk merchant, but he fell ill. What I made at the *mercato* wasn't enough for both of us. The landlord offered me another way to pay, but I wouldn't be his whore. When Sandro died, I couldn't meet the debts. And the longer I'm in here, the more I owe.'

The entrance door opened, admitting visitors to the courtyard. Aldo smiled when he saw who was among them. 'Maybe I can do something about that.'

Maria remained at the palazzo most of the morning, finding out more about what had taken place in Lorenzino's bedchamber. If servant gossip was true, it seemed a chance might be arising for Cosimo to take his rightful place in the city. No more would her son be left in the country, an occasional companion for hawking and hunting with the Duke.

When she could learn no more from those inside the palazzo, Maria announced she was going to church. By the time she reached San Lorenzo, mass was concluding. The doors opened, letting the faithful and their servants into the piazza. Maria spied the notorious gossip Cecilia Paoletti whispering behind her hand to a maid. The Paoletti were a minor merchant family, but Cecilia's husband was close to the Palleschi. If Maria's suspicions were correct, Cibo might have already sought help from the Palleschi – if so, Cecilia would know.

'My dear, what a pleasure to see you,' Cecilia gushed when Maria caught her eye.

'And you, my dearest.' They exchanged pleasantries, Cecilia taking the lead with talk of her new gown – Renato Patricio was performing wonders, as ever – and the latest courtly intrigues.

Maria let her prattle on, giving nods of agreement and making surprised noises when appropriate. Eventually Cecilia paused to breathe, and Maria seized the opportunity. 'My dear, you will never believe who I saw this morning.'

Cecilia's eyes widened, a predator spying a fresh morsel. 'Who?'

Maria gave a brief description of her encounter with Cibo. The locked bedchamber, the bloody boot marks on the floor – they hadn't escaped her notice, oh no – and the fear in the cardinal's eyes. 'Whatever can it mean?'

Cecilia licked her lips, ushering Maria away from the maid. 'I believe I know the answer, dearest. The cardinal has been very busy this morning, talking to friends of the Medici. My beloved just happened to be visiting Guicciardini when Cibo arrived, quite unannounced. You will never guess what he had to say. Go on, guess!'

This woman and her parlour games would be the death of Maria's patience, but she played along as Cecilia recalled her husband's boastful tale. It seemed the Duke was missing, and nobody knew where to find him. There were rumours of a conspiracy, even of an attempt on his life. Cibo planned to summon militia from different communes to protect the city. There was even talk of a special Senate session of the Forty-Eight for the next day.

If half that was true, it was still extraordinary. Should the Duke die without a legitimate heir, Florence would be vulnerable to threats from inside and outside the city. Cecilia babbled on, but Maria was no longer listening. So, this could be Cosimo's moment. He was still at the *castello*. She would send a messenger once she was certain, summoning him to Florence. Yes, that was the next step.

Maria noticed Cecilia staring at her. 'Sorry, dearest, I missed that.'

'I asked if you knew what Guicciardini said after the cardinal revealed they had searched and searched, but nobody could find the Duke?'

'Pray, tell me.'

'"Search better!" Isn't that just so Guicciardini.' Cecilia burst into loud, braying laughter, and Maria smiled along. But she suspected Cibo already knew where Alessandro was. When the Duke's body was finally found, Maria would be ready.

Aldo was so happy to see Orvieto, he let himself be persuaded into the *ospedale*. 'You look like you've been run over by a coach and horses,' the doctor said. Fortunately, Maso was still senseless after having his head caved in by Tomasia, while the surviving Basso brother looked equally bad. Neither man was a threat for the moment. Aldo sat on a bench, away from other patients.

Orvieto helped Aldo undress to the waist, carefully pulling his torn tunic over his head. The right shoulder was swollen, while his torso was mottled with bruises, the most recent blue and black, the others yellow and purple. The doctor unwrapped the bloody fabric round Aldo's hand, wincing at the deep wound.

'How did you know I was here?' Aldo asked.

'Levi's daughter,' Orvieto replied while tending to the hand. 'An officer from the Otto and two other men ransacked her home, searching for evidence.'

'Somebody is still investigating her father's murder?'

'No, they were looking for evidence of your conspiracy against the Duke.'

'Did this officer have a name?'

'Cerchi, I think she said.'

Of course. 'Has he approached you yet?' Orvieto shook his head.

'Be careful if he does. Cerchi is a devious little *merda*. Tell him nothing he doesn't need to know.'

The doctor nodded, tying a fresh bandage round Aldo's hand. 'There's not much I can do for your shoulder. Try not to make any vigorous movements with your right arm. No horse riding, and no fighting. Sleep on your left side, if you can.' He examined Aldo's head. 'You must have a skull like an anvil. These blows could've killed you.' Orvieto closed his satchel. 'That shoulder will be weakened from now on. But stay out of trouble the next few days and most of your injuries will heal. Can you manage that?'

'Probably not,' Aldo admitted.

Bindi enjoyed making those who knocked at his door wait. It reminded them who held power within these walls. Men of importance rarely visited the Podestà, and those that did sent ahead with word of their arrival to ensure the proper deference and ceremony was waiting. The *segretario* was ill prepared for the impatient fist hammering at his *officio* door, and even less ready for Cibo bursting in, the cardinal's face as crimson as his cape.

'Y-Your Eminence,' Bindi stammered, struggling to his feet. 'I'm sorry, I did not realize it was you.'

'I don't have time for your apologies,' Cibo said, striding towards the desk. 'You will release Cesare Aldo from Le Stinche immediately.'

'May I ask, on what grounds? Aldo faces a serious allegation—'

'Yes, I know about the *denunzia* made by Lorenzino de' Medici. But he subsequently fled the city, and the Duke is missing. When was Aldo incarcerated?'

'Two nights ago – Friday.'

'Aldo can hardly have led an attempt to overthrow the Duke

from inside a cell, can he? Or is Le Stinche so lax prisoners can come and go as they wish?'

'Of course not.' The *segretario* struggled to swallow, his mouth and throat gone dry. 'I simply . . . The Otto would have to . . . It is beyond my authority . . .'

'Enough!' Cibo slammed a fist down on Bindi's desk, making the inkpot jump. 'With the Duke missing, it falls to me as the Emperor's representative in Florence to ensure that everything possible is done to find Alessandro.'

Bindi had never seen the cardinal so angered before. It made the *segretario* wonder what was driving Cibo to act in such a manner. If something had happened to Alessandro – and the Emperor discovered it was due to negligence or apathy on the cardinal's part – the consequence would be ruinous, at best. Cibo knew he was at fault, and he was pouring his guilt out onto anyone else he could blame. Yes, that would explain . . .

'Are you even listening to me?' the cardinal demanded. 'Is it true that Aldo warned you of an imminent threat to the Duke's life, a warning that you ignored?'

Bindi wanted to shake his head, but dared not deny the truth.

'I thought as much.' Cibo drew back. 'Should you wish to continue as *segretario* – or, indeed, hold any other administrative position in this city – you will release Aldo. Now.'

Bindi nodded, conscious of the sweat soaking his collar.

'Have him meet me south of Palazzo Medici within the hour.' Cibo swept away, and Bindi sank into his chair, hands trembling. But the cardinal was not done yet. He paused at the door. 'I don't like to be kept waiting, *segretario*. Remember that.'

Chapter Twenty-Eight

*A*ldo stayed inside the condemned cell, waiting for Lippo to creep along from the poor men's ward. He finally appeared when the late afternoon visitors were admitted, bringing alms. Lippo scuttled across the courtyard, his pitiable face securing half a tired loaf. But when he retreated towards the safety of the poor men's ward, Aldo was waiting.

'Th-there you are,' Lippo stammered. 'I wasn't sure if—'

'If I'd survive? Unfortunately for you, my time in here isn't over yet. But I have to thank you.' The pick-purse stumbled back, still clutching the half-loaf of bread.

'W-Why? I haven't done anything.'

'But you did. You arranged for Carafa to come after me in the chapel last night, and for the Bassos to follow him in and kill both of us. Carafa must have humiliated you once too often. But for the Bassos, I might not still be alive. Of course, you expected the guards would find me dead in the morning, alongside Carafa. Didn't plan for this, did you?'

Lippo tumbled over his own feet, losing hold of the loaf. 'No, you're wrong. I would never do that. I mean, how could I?'

'Carafa would have killed me if the brothers hadn't come in. Their arrival forced us to work together. I survived, he didn't. Lucky me. Not so lucky for you.' Aldo loomed over Lippo, ready to kick him. The pick-purse curled into a ball to protect his *palle*.

'Don't hurt me,' Lippo begged.

'You don't have anyone's protection. Nobody to keep you safe.'

'Aldo!' Duro emerged from the main doorway into the court-yard, two guards flanking him. 'Come here. Now.' Aldo made sure to stand on Lippo's bread while passing. The captain studied him. 'You're recovered from what happened in the chapel?'

Why was Duro asking that? Unless . . . 'I'm being released?'

A nod. 'Orders from *Segretario* Bindi. You're to meet with Cardinal Cibo, south of Palazzo Medici, before curfew.'

Bindi would not have ordered the release unless required to by someone of power. The direction to meet with Cibo told Aldo who was responsible. The plotters must have struck against the Duke – but whether they'd succeeded was less clear.

'Just as well I survived my night in the *gabbia*, isn't it?'

Duro bristled. 'One of my men can escort you there, if you wish.'

'I've had more than enough help from your men,' Aldo replied. 'But they can fetch the things you took from me when I arrived – my stiletto, my coin.'

The captain nodded, stepping aside to let Aldo out of the courtyard.

Aldo paused to look back round the courtyard. Lippo was gathering his crushed loaf, while Tomasia watched from the women's ward. Aldo gave her a brief nod. He wouldn't neglect his promise, not if he could help it.

Dusk was approaching as Aldo neared Palazzo Medici. Cibo waited by the south corner with Francesco Guicciardini, a blue *berretto* casting heavy shadow on the senator's jowly features. Guicciardini was a key member of the Palleschi. His presence underlined the significance of this meeting. The senator looked down his hawkish nose, but Aldo ignored that. He'd come directly from Le Stinche, still in the same clothes he'd had since Friday. Let Guicciardini spend two nights in the prison, then he could judge.

Cibo made introductions. 'This was the officer who first suspected the plot. Lorenzino had Aldo imprisoned to silence him.'

'You've yet to produce any proof of this supposed plot,' Guicciardini sniffed.

'Follow me,' the cardinal replied. 'I fear we'll find all the proof you need.'

Aldo fell in step as they strode away, Cibo outlining recent events: the Duke being lured to Lorenzino's bedchamber in Casa Vecchia; Alessandro's guards left outside all night; Lorenzino and his servants fleeing Florence that same night, the Duke's cousin with a wounded hand; and the locked bedchamber, bloody boot marks leading away from it.

A guard remained outside Casa Vecchia, blocking the way in. Cibo led Guicciardini and Aldo inside and upstairs, urging both men to silence. But the constable standing sentry outside the bedchamber did not stay quiet.

'Aldo?' Strocchi gasped. 'What are you doing here?' Aldo clasped his hand, pleased to see a trustworthy face. 'I've been here for hours,' Strocchi whispered in his ear. 'You know who's in this bedchamber, don't you?' Aldo nodded, putting a finger to his lips.

Guicciardini sighed. 'Can we finally see this evidence you keep promising, Cibo?'

'Very well.' The cardinal gestured at Aldo. 'Open it.'

He considered putting a shoulder to the heavy wood, before recalling Orvieto's words. Instead Aldo braced one leg on the floor and kicked out with his other. The wood splintered, but held. Another kick and the door gave way, swinging inwards.

The bedchamber was dark, but the stench of blood and shit and death left little doubt as to what was inside. Aldo paused in the doorway, letting his eyes adjust to the thin light creeping between closed shutters. Dark boot marks converged by the door. Whatever had happened in here had not been the work of a single attacker.

A four-poster bed dominated the chamber, but scarlet curtains draped round it hid whatever was on the mattress. Sheets spilled out from beneath the curtains, stained with dark fluids. Was that a hand, stretching from between the curtains, clawing at the air? A memory shook Aldo, the sight of his dying father. No, that was a fever dream, born of delirium and regret. Papa was not here.

Guicciardini muttered a curse. 'That smell! What is it?'

'Death.' Aldo stepped aside so the others could enter. Cibo was first through the door, a cloth over his nose and mouth, eyes wide. Guicciardini followed, his face twisting with disgust. Strocchi was last, seeming least affected by the ripe, thick air. Perhaps he'd grown used to it while standing outside the door. 'Open the shutters,' Aldo urged.

Strocchi crossed to the windows, stepping round a sticky crimson puddle on the floor. As he opened the shutters, light poured into the bedchamber, revealing the full violence of what had happened. There was blood, so much blood – on the floor, the rugs, spattering the plaster wall beside the bed, even on the scarlet curtains round the mattress.

A dagger had been left behind, its blade stained red, with fingermarks on the hilt. A breastplate lay by the bed, unbuckled and set down carefully. Aldo recognized the design adorning the metal, he'd seen it while visiting Palazzo Medici. Alessandro wore the breastplate for protection, even inside his own residence. Yet the Duke had been persuaded to remove it, anticipating the arrival of a beautiful young woman, no doubt. That had been his undoing – that, and the folly of trusting his cousin.

Aldo approached the bed, careful not to step in the worst of the blood. Reaching for the closed curtains, he glanced at the cardinal. Cibo nodded, his face pale. Aldo flung them open, staggering back from what was revealed. Alessandro's pale body sprawled across blood-soaked sheets, his mouth wide as if to scream, eyes staring in accusation. The Duke's throat had been sliced open, silencing his cries and likely ending his life. There were at least a dozen more wounds on his hands and chest.

It had been a brutal attack. Cuts to Alessandro's hands showed he fought back, despite having no weapon. Was that skin caught between his teeth? Had he bitten one of his attackers? It would explain the bloody hand Lorenzino was seen nursing. The Duke was dead, but he'd left a lasting mark on his cousin. No matter where Lorenzino went, or how others might celebrate his boldness here, the Duke's cousin would always bear that scar, always be reminded of what had truly happened.

Cibo whispered a prayer while Guicciardini swallowed hard, unable to stop staring at the bed. Aldo could see Strocchi's discomfort too, but the constable was better at keeping hold of his horror. Good, that would help with what must come next. If Benedetto had been guarding the bedchamber, the floor would bear fresh stains by now.

'What do you want us to do with him?' Aldo asked.

Cibo ignored the question, continuing his prayers. Guicciardini recovered enough to study his surroundings. 'How long has Alessandro been dead?'

Aldo put a hand to the Duke's outstretched arm. The skin was cold as the room, the limb rigid. 'All day, and much of last night too.' Guicciardini arched an eyebrow at such certainty. 'I've seen more than my share of death,' Aldo said. The cardinal finished, Strocchi nodding respectfully. 'What do you want us to do?' Aldo asked again.

'His body can't be found here,' Cibo replied. 'The widow Salviati is staying on the level above. She came by earlier, inquisitive about what was in this room.' Aldo didn't doubt that. Salviati was a woman with an eye for opportunity.

'No doubt the servants already know something is awry,' Guicciardini said. 'They will have been gossiping among themselves, at church today, or at the markets.'

'Where do we take the body?' Aldo asked.

The cardinal and Guicciardini exchanged a look. 'The family crypt at San Lorenzo would be a fitting place,' Cibo suggested.

'He could be put inside his father's sarcophagus,' Guicciardini added. 'Until a more permanent place – one suitable for a Duke – can be found.'

Aldo pondered how to get the body there. They'd have to carry the body, without anyone noticing. Guicciardini and Cibo wouldn't be bloodying their hands, and fetching a cart would invite unwanted questions. 'Strocchi, choose the largest rug and bring it to the bed,' Aldo said. 'We'll roll him in it.' Cibo looked aghast. 'You have a better suggestion, Your Eminence?' The cardinal considered a moment before shaking his head.

The body was as rigid as a length of wood. Good, that'd make moving it easier. Both legs and one arm were close to the torso, but the right arm was clawing at the air. Aldo pushed the limb against the body, but it sprang back. He'd have to break the arm.

Aldo clambered on the mattress while Guicciardini and Cibo were muttering strategy. 'Word will spread,' Guicciardini warned, 'no matter what we do. Hiding him gives us a few hours, maybe a day, but we need a new leader. If the city doesn't have a Medici in charge, others will try to take Alessandro's place. By force of arms, if necessary.'

Guicciardini's words were wise, but Aldo noticed the senator was already shaping the path ahead. Florence had seen many leaders, not just the Medici, yet Guicciardini was intent on that family continuing its hold over the city. No surprise from a leading Palleschi. Men like Guicciardini had grown rich under the Medici, acquiring influence at court in exchange for their loyalty. The Palleschi helped ensure any rebellious elements within the Senate, those among the Forty-Eight with sympathies for the old Florentine Republic, were kept quiet or persuaded to leave the city. But the cardinal was an imperial representative with other loyalties to consider.

'I've sent word to militia out in the Dominion,' Cibo said, 'and despatched a rider to hasten Captain Vitelli's return from his country residence, bringing all the troops he can muster. They can keep peace on the streets, and defend the city if needs be.'

'You fear an uprising?' Guicciardini asked.

'It's happened before.'

Aldo grabbed the dead man's protruding arm and snapped it in two at the elbow. The crack echoed in the bedchamber, shocking Cibo and Guicciardini into silence. 'We couldn't carry him with one arm sticking out,' Aldo said. He had Strocchi place the rug by the bed, before rolling the body onto it. Alessandro hit the floor with a thud, a long sigh escaping him. Strocchi stepped back, startled.

'Don't worry,' Aldo reassured the constable. 'It's just the body settling.'

He rolled the rug around Alessandro, while Guicciardini and Cibo concluded their planning. 'The Senate meets tomorrow to appoint a successor,' the cardinal said. 'The Forty-Eight shall ensure that the will of the people is respected.'

Aldo suppressed his disbelief. The people could have all the will they wanted, but the future of Florence would always remain in the hands of the few.

Strocchi was exhausted by the time he and Aldo reached San Lorenzo. Helping carry the body to the Medici crypt took all his strength. How Aldo kept going was beyond the constable. It was doubtful Aldo had slept much while in Le Stinche. At least Cibo had sent word ahead so the crypt was already open. A priest with a lantern ushered them down stone steps to the vault, their breath misting the air. Aldo took the lantern, sending the curious priest back up into the church. 'Let's stand the Duke in a corner,' Aldo said when the priest was gone.

It seemed wrong to treat the body like a tiresome fallen branch, but Strocchi was grateful to shed the dead man's weight. Aldo kept rubbing his right shoulder, muttering blasphemous curses. Strocchi chose not to listen, not here, not in this place. Instead he looked at the sarcophagi, struggling to read inscriptions in the gloom. Aldo found the right one, on the other side of the crypt. 'You'll have to open this for me.'

Strocchi pushed a shoulder against the sarcophagus lid, but it didn't move.

'Harder,' Aldo urged.

Strocchi put all his anger into the stonework. Pushing and straining, the top of the sarcophagus shifted sideways. Foul air blossomed out, forcing him to stagger back. 'We can't put him in there, can we?'

'Dead is dead,' Aldo replied. 'Doesn't matter whether you feed worms in a pauper's grave or rot away in a grand crypt, the end is the same.'

Strocchi prayed the cardinal would ensure Alessandro got the interment he deserved. After rolling the corpse into the sarcophagus, rug and all, Strocchi pushed the lid back into place. 'What happens now?'

'Go get some rest.' Aldo picked up the lantern. 'We've both earned it.'

'I meant – what happens to the city?'

'There was war when the Duke of Milan died without an heir. Plenty of fools dream about Florence becoming a republic again, and many exiles are eager to reclaim the city. From what I know of Guicciardini, the Palleschi will fight to keep the Medici in charge. But Cibo's loyalties are more divided.'

Strocchi frowned. 'But what about the citizens, what happens to people like us?'

'We do what those like us have always done. We live, we drink, we love, we fight, and we endure. The fools in charge do their worst, and we try to survive.' Aldo smiled at the constable. 'Tomorrow will come, whether we welcome it or not.'

Much as Aldo craved sleep, there were things that couldn't wait for the morning. He returned to Casa Vecchia after sending Strocchi home. Cibo had posted fresh guards at the entrance. Inside, a beady-eyed servant with a silver beard stood outside Lorenzino's bedchamber, the splintered door pulled shut. 'The cardinal asked me to make sure nobody goes inside,' the servant confided. 'Anyone who does could face banishment, even excommunication.'

'Including you,' Aldo said.

'What do you mean? I haven't—'

'Go and wash your hands, before anyone else sees the dried blood under your nails.' The servant paled as he noticed the dark crimson stains. 'I'll keep watch until you return.'

When the servant had scuttled away, Aldo went into the bedchamber. Someone had drawn the curtains and closed all but one shutter. The Duke's breastplate was gone, along with the bloodied knife. Guicciardini and Cibo were wasting no time shaping how this murder would be known, all too aware of the effect it could have on Florence.

What about Alessandro's killers – what of Lorenzino, and his servants? It seemed certain the Duke's cousin had been in the bedchamber when the murder took place. Had he inflicted the fatal wound, or did he leave that to the others? Three men left the room alive, with blood on their boots. Three men had fled Casa Vecchia, and Strocchi's description suggested two of them were Scoronconcolo and Il Freccia. The last was Lorenzino, judging by the report from guards at Porta San Gallo. It didn't matter who cut Alessandro's throat and who stood watching. In the end, all three of them were partners in the killing.

Lorenzino and his *complici* were a full day and much of a night's ride away. They could be in Bologna by now. Would Lorenzino be bragging about what he'd done, seeking glory for striking down Alessandro? Or would he be skulking in the shadows, fearful of retribution when his crime was discovered? Lorenzino would certainly need allies, a place to stay. Was that why he had sought the loan from Levi, to buy safe passage? Had the plan to overthrow the Duke been no more than a ruse hiding Lorenzino's plans to murder Alessandro?

Aldo leaned against a wall, weariness close to claiming him. With each hour Lorenzino was likely to be further away. Someone would have to go after him, and Aldo knew where that task would fall. But there was nothing more to be done tonight. Lorenzino's crime would catch up with him eventually. The Medici had a long reach.

The creak of a floorboard warned of someone lurking outside the door. But it was Maria Salviati in the hallway, not the servant. 'Aldo? I heard you were in prison.'

'I was,' he replied. 'What are you doing here?'

The widow drew herself up as if to protest, but smiled instead. 'We've no secrets, you and I. Let us be honest with one another.'

There it was. Aldo had wondered when she would use what she knew about him. Better to his face than someone else's ear. 'We can try.'

'Is it true? Is Alessandro dead?'

No one had forbidden Aldo from confirming that. Gossip must already be spreading. By tomorrow much of the city would know. 'Yes. Murdered by his cousin, it seems.'

The widow nodded. 'I've heard the Senate meets in the morning to appoint a successor. Alessandro doesn't have an heir – not a legitimate one, at least.'

'Florence has been led by a *bastardo* before.'

'But the Duke's son Giulio is four summers, if that – too young to rule.'

Aldo smiled. 'How old is your son?'

'Cosimo is not yet eighteen,' she replied, affecting an air of innocence. As if she hadn't already been thinking of him as the solution to Florence's need.

'Old enough to be appointed,' Aldo said, 'but young enough some might believe he can be guided. Led. Manipulated.'

Now it was her turn to smile. 'They don't know my boy.'

'If Cosimo is his father's son, he should enter Florence like a lamb so that those with the power to make him duke only discover his true strength later.'

'I will send for Cosimo tomorrow,' the widow said. 'Thank you for being so honest – not many men share what they know with me. My son will reward that, if he becomes duke.'

Chapter Twenty-Nine

Monday, January 8th

Signora Robustelli didn't believe in ghosts. She'd spent enough years as a *matrona* to have few illusions. When Clodia ran into the *officio* sobbing about unnatural noises coming from Aldo's empty room, Robustelli dismissed it as nonsense. But the silly girl was inconsolable, leaving little choice. She had to go look before anyone else believed Clodia.

There were noises coming from Aldo's room – but no ghost was making them. Someone was hurling things against the door. Had that *bastardo* Cerchi come back? Would he tear the place apart, one room at a time, until she paid him? The answer was yes – and he'd think it righteous. Men like him enjoyed using women, and then sneering at them elsewhere. Hypocrites.

Robustelli shoved the door open – and found Aldo slumped on the floor, his clothes askew, revealing a body mottled by bruises. 'Finally. I can't seem to get back into bed.'

She hefted him up on to the mattress. 'Thought you were in Le Stinche.'

'They released me.' Aldo winced, rubbing at his swollen right shoulder. 'The other inmates didn't welcome me with open arms.'

'More like open fists,' she said. 'Wait here.' She fetched liniment from downstairs, pausing to reassure Clodia that the house wasn't haunted. She returned to rub the foul-smelling salve into Aldo's shoulder, ignoring his protests. 'My girls take worse and they don't complain this much.'

'They lack my natural sensitivity,' he replied, looking round the room. The few pieces of furniture were turned over or broken. 'I hear Cerchi has been asking questions about me. Can I thank him for this?'

Robustelli nodded, wiping her hands on a cloth. 'He's been here twice, brought help the second time. Promised to shut us down unless I pay him half of what we make.'

Aldo scowled. 'That won't happen again.'

'You be careful. The first time Cerchi came, he was asking questions about what you like – who you like.' She didn't say more. She didn't need to.

'If Cerchi had proof, I'd still be in Le Stinche.'

But Robustelli could see doubt in his eyes.

Aldo marched into the Podestà, enjoying the surprise of the gate guards. Dragged out in shackles, now he was returning a free man. Better still, he'd been proved right. It didn't stop his shoulder aching, but the satisfaction still gave a warm glow. Cerchi was swaggering round the courtyard as if it was his domain. 'You should be careful about using the Otto to fill your own pouch,' Aldo said, loud enough for anyone nearby to hear. 'There's a name for men who take coin from the work of women.'

Cerchi's face darkened. 'I'd be careful about making accusations without proof. Only a fool starts a fight he can't win.' The man was a grasping *merda*, but something new was behind that smug face. Cerchi seemed more certain of himself.

Somebody must have surrendered what they knew to save

themselves. Not Zoppo – the tavern keeper couldn't be trusted, but he knew nothing that could make Cerchi so bold. Robustelli had revealed what that girl with the painted breasts had said to Cerchi, but it was little more than gossip. Renato, it must be Renato. He had the courage of a mouse. There was nothing to be told there, but Renato knew others and if they talked . . .

'Aldo!' Bindi shouted down from the *loggia*. The *segretario* made a single gesture, summoning Aldo before disappearing from view. Had Cerchi already made a *denunzia*? No, he looked surprised, even disappointed.

'When Bindi's done with you,' Cerchi said, 'we have unfinished business.'

Bindi didn't bother making Aldo wait – the cardinal had made it clear any delay would be punished. 'You're limping,' the *segretario* said when Aldo came in.

'An old wound,' the officer replied. 'Got twisted during a scuffle in Le Stinche.'

'Duro tells me you killed one inmate and left another fighting for his life.' Aldo shrugged. Two nights in Le Stinche had made him no less elusive. 'Are you able to ride a horse? For hours at a time, if need be?'

Aldo's eyes narrowed. 'You want me to go after Lorenzino.'

The *segretario* leaned back in his chair. 'Cardinal Cibo and certain members of the Otto believe it would be wise to question potential witnesses regarding recent events.'

'Such as the murder of Duke Alessandro de' Medici at Casa Vecchia?'

Bindi ignored the question, reaching into his desk for a parchment sealed with red wax. 'This grants you unquestioned authority across the Dominion. You can requisition horses or whatever else you may need.' He pulled a pouch heavy with coin from the drawer, tossing it beside the parchment. 'This should pay for anything else.'

Aldo took both. 'Lorenzino has two servants with him. Both have killed at his command. I'll need somebody I can trust.'

The *segretario* bristled, but had no choice. 'Who?'

'Strocchi is honest – and no fool.'

Strocchi was the constable Cibo had used the day before; now Aldo was requesting his services too. That couldn't be chance, but Bindi's hands were tied. 'Agreed. The Otto is scheduled to meet this Friday, and the murder of Duke Alessandro will be foremost in the mind of the magistrates. That means you have four days to be back here with answers. When you do, report to me first. Understand?'

Aldo nodded. 'Strocchi and I will leave within the hour,' he said before withdrawing.

The *segretario* leaned back in his chair. The chances of finding Lorenzino were few, let alone of bringing him back to face justice from the court. If Aldo did at least return with answers, that would reflect well on Bindi. If the officer did not make it back alive, well, the Otto would have one less troublesome officer. So be it.

Aldo strode down the staircase to the courtyard, struggling not to limp. But Cerchi was nowhere to be seen. Instead Strocchi was waiting at the foot of the steps, concern evident in his face. He ushered Aldo to one side. 'Word is spreading about the Duke,' the constable whispered. 'I was at the *mercato* and traders were gossiping about it.'

'They know he was murdered?'

Strocchi shook his head. 'But people know something's happened. They're already talking about who – or what – might replace him.'

'It's a small city. Rumours run through Florence faster than the Arno, and secrets never stay secret for long.' More's the pity.

'What do we do about it?'

'Nothing. Senators and cardinals decide who rules Florence. Trust me, you're safer not getting involved with such things. I've got the bruises to prove it.'

The constable nodded, his unease still obvious. Aldo briefed Strocchi on their orders. Four days away meant taking clothes and supplies, not to mention good horses. After the first leg they'd be relying on whatever could be secured on the road.

'Four days?' Strocchi frowned. 'Lorenzino and his men have been gone two nights, they could be halfway to Venice by now. What chance have we got of finding them in four days, let alone of getting a confession?'

'We're not expected to succeed. But Alessandro's murder is still a crime, and the Otto has to be seen to pursue those responsible for it.'

The constable nodded. 'I'll pack a satchel.'

'We leave at noon.' Aldo reached into the pouch Bindi had handed over. 'But first there's something I need you to do for me.'

Maria waited in the courtyard of Palazzo Pazzi, her patience untroubled. A minute, an hour, or longer – she would wait till the day of judgement, if need be. A patient woman was a dangerous woman, and Maria prided herself on having all the patience in the world. She smiled when Cibo bustled in from outside. He seemed beset by worry. Good.

'Your Eminence, you appear troubled. The Senate did not do as you'd hoped?'

'How did you . . .?' Cibo stopped himself, dismissing those at his side. The cardinal waited till they were gone before speaking again. 'How are you aware of this morning's events? The gathering at Palazzo della Signoria . . .'

'It's well known among the wives of the Palleschi,' she said. 'Men discuss much in bed, especially those with ambition. I've heard you proposed that Alessandro be replaced by his young *bastardo*, Giulio. You should have known the Forty-Eight would never accept a four-year-old as ruler, not with you as his keeper.'

'These are matters for the Senate,' Cibo insisted, moving away.

'There were rumours the senators might offer you the post as ruler, if your *stratagemma* with the child fell short. Was that not to your liking?' Maria took hold of his arm, refusing to be easily dismissed. 'There is another option. A true Medici, born into wedlock. Young, yes, but with an open mind. Willing to be guided. Trained. Led.'

Smiling without sincerity, the cardinal removed her fingers. 'Thank you for your counsel, signora – it will receive all the consideration it deserves. *Buon giorno*.' He strode up the marble steps, two at a time.

Maria had expected little from Cibo and had got less. But his silence confirmed the whispers she'd heard. There was still a chance for Cosimo to become duke.

It was kind of Joshua to come and sit *shiva* with her again, there was no denying that. But his presence was as much a shroud as a comfort for Rebecca. She had been re-reading Father's letter, his final wishes. She needed to decide what to do once the days of mourning were over. When Mother was dying, the house had still been a home. Now all it held were death and sour memories.

The knock at the door was a relief, stopping her from blurting out what was troubling her. A visitor meant she could delay the choice she must make a while longer. Joshua opened the door, stepping aside to reveal Aldo on the doorstep. He looked frayed, a man trying his best to hide his exhaustion. Wasn't he meant to be in Le Stinche?

'May I come in?' Aldo asked, his voice quiet.

'Please,' Rebecca said, rising from the floor.

Aldo entered. 'I won't stay long. I came to say that the men we believe killed your father have fled the city. I'm leaving to pursue them, though the chance of catching them is slight. Nonetheless, you should know the danger to you has passed.'

Rebecca had assumed whoever had killed Father had done so because of his business – not for any reason that might threaten her. To hear she had been in peril all this time was a shock.

'Where do you believe these men are now?' Joshua asked.

'They rode north, towards Scarperia,' Aldo replied. 'They may be bound for Bologna.'

A dark notion took hold of Rebecca. Were Ruth and her family in danger? 'If you go there, you must visit my uncle, and my cousins. They shared the risk for all Father's loans.'

'I'm sure they are safe, but if I do go to Bologna I will visit them.'

Rebecca went to the table and wrote a brief note in Hebrew for Ruth. 'Pass this to my cousin, she will give you any help you need.' As Aldo was leaving, something occurred to her. If she decided to stay in Florence and marry Joshua, she would need a way to support herself until the wedding, to provide for a dowry. 'Before he died, Dante said you'd found Father's stolen ledger. Do you still have it?'

'No, it's at the Palazzo del Podestà. *Segretario* Bindi is keeping the ledger, in case of a trial. Whoever stole it tore out many of the pages, and burnt what was left.'

'I understand. Do you think the ledger might be returned to me?' Rebecca was aware of Joshua close by. She didn't want him to know of her reasons for wanting the ledger, not yet. Not until she had made her choice. 'Things were never easy with Father. But that ledger was his life's work. To get it back would be like still having part of him here, with me.'

'I'll see what I can do when I return,' Aldo said, closing the door on his way out.

Once Aldo was gone Joshua grabbed hold of Rebecca's hands, kissing both of them, his face full of relief. 'Did you hear that? You're safe. The Otto believes the men who killed your father have fled the city. It's over. It's finally over.'

Rebecca looked at the joy in his face. In that moment, her mind was made up. She knew what she was going to do with the rest of her life.

Strocchi hadn't been outside the city walls since coming to Florence. He'd expected his first journey beyond them would be to return home. Instead he was preparing for four days and nights in the Dominion, helping Aldo hunt murderers. That meant riding at speed, and travelling light. Strocchi shoved a handful of clothes in his satchel, and threw a cloak across his shoulders. That would have to do.

He went to a market for food, and a trustworthy stable for two strong, fast horses. Going long distances meant they'd have to change rides, taking whatever was available, but at least the first leg would be assured.

Preparations complete, Strocchi went somewhere he'd hoped to avoid revisiting. The Podestà was a brooding presence, but he found Le Stinche far more intimidating. The tall stone walls bore no ornamentation, and no windows. Once inside, he met with Duro. The captain was surprised to see him, and more so when the coin was handed over. 'You're sure?'

'It's not my money. I'm paying for someone else.'

'As you wish.' Duro opened a desk drawer and swept the coin into it. 'There are certain formalities to be completed; it may take a while.'

'I'll wait outside,' Strocchi replied, grateful to escape the cramped *officio*.

Back on the street, people scuttled by, eyes cast down, ignoring the prison. Le Stinche cast a cold shadow, forcing Strocchi to rub his hands together for warmth. Finally the small door opened and a young woman stepped out. She was more handsome than beautiful, long dark hair down to her thin shoulders. But there was strength in the way she stood. She had a proud face yet her eyes were warm. She looked round, as if expecting to see someone she knew.

'Tomasia?' Strocchi asked, introducing himself. 'I paid to have all your debts settled.'

'Do I know you, sir?'

'Please, I'm no gentleman. I mean, I'm not a scoundrel, but . . .' He shut his mouth to stop the babble spilling from it. Tomasia smiled, and it lit up her face.

'Well, whoever you are, thank you.'

He recovered enough to speak. 'Cesare Aldo sent me, he's your true benefactor.'

She looked surprised. 'He said he would help, but I didn't . . . You hear men say so many things, but few of them prove true.'

Despite being a free woman, Tomasia seemed slow to leave. If Strocchi had been released from Le Stinche, he would have been running by now. 'Is something wrong?'

'My debts being cleared is a miracle, beyond anything I could ever have hoped – but what do I do now? I have no job, nowhere to stay, and no family left alive.'

Aldo hadn't mentioned any of that. Solving one problem had created another, and Strocchi had little coin left. There must be something he could . . . Of course! 'It's not much, but you can sleep in my bed the next few nights.'

Tomasia's face soured. 'I will be no man's whore. I would rather go back inside Le Stinche.' She stalked away, muttering under her breath.

What had he said to make her—? Strocchi's stomach lurched. *Santo Spirito*, he hadn't meant . . . The constable hurried after Tomasia. 'You misunderstand . . . I wasn't . . . Please, stop!'

She whirled round, fists clenching. 'Touch me and I hurt you.'

Strocchi raised both hands. 'I'm leaving the city for the next four nights on behalf of the Otto. The room I have, my bed – it will be empty. That was all I meant. I would never . . .' He shook his head, unsure what else to say. Did she believe him?

Eventually, finally, she spoke. 'It's difficult for me to trust anyone, especially any man, after . . .' Tomasia fell silent. What had happened to her in Le Stinche?

Strocchi lowered his hands. 'I lived in a village all my life before coming here. I knew everyone, trusted everyone. But this city . . . It can be hard to survive.'

Tomasia nodded. 'Where is this room?'

He told her how to find it, where the key was hidden outside his door. 'Forgive the mess. I didn't know, that, well . . .'

The edges of a smile reappeared at the corners of her mouth.

'I understand. But I have one more question. Why are you trusting me with your home?'

Strocchi hesitated. 'Aldo trusts you, and he's mostly right. About people, at least.'

'Well, thank you.' She leaned closer – and kissed him on the cheek.

It was only after Tomasia had gone that Strocchi realized he was blushing.

'You need treatment again?' Orvieto sighed. 'There are other healers in this city.'

'Illness is a weakness in my job,' Aldo said, following the doctor through to the back room. 'I prefer to see someone I can trust.'

'How's the shoulder?'

'It hasn't got worse. I've been trying to do as you said, but . . .'

Orvieto gestured at his table. 'Sit on there, take off your tunic.' He examined the joint, probing fingers forcing grunts of pain from Aldo. 'I can give you a herbal mixture to ease the swelling, that will help a little. But rest is what you need.'

'What I need and what I get don't often share a bed.' Aldo explained his trip away from Florence, riding fast for hours, even days. 'Something for the pain would help.'

Orvieto opened a drawer and pulled out several twists of paper. 'Put these powders in your drink, one first thing, and another at night. Too many and they become your master.'

'Thank you.' Aldo let Orvieto ease him back into the tunic, enjoying their closeness. 'I'm not sure when I'll be back. Several days, at least – or not at all, if the worst happens.'

'You seem to attract pain, yet are very good at surviving it,' Orvieto replied. He rested a gentle hand on Aldo's good shoulder.

'There's something I need to say. Last time you were here, you were . . . bold.'

Aldo couldn't bring himself to look Orvieto – Saul – in the face. Was this to be a kind but final farewell? They'd only known each other a few days. He'd no right to hope this man would risk all he had, all that he was for what – lust? Passion? A chance of something more?

'Cesare, look at me.'

Aldo forced himself to stare into those warm hazel eyes.

'I liked it. I liked you being bold. I don't know what to expect with you, and I haven't felt that for a long time. So, make sure you do come back, yes?' He slipped a hand behind Aldo's head, pulling him into a long, deep kiss.

The first time they'd kissed had been urgent, hurried. This was slower, more assured. Aldo reached both hands to Saul's head, fingers in his hair, pulling him closer, their lips parting. Aldo breathed Saul in, savouring his scent, his closeness. Their hands found one another, holding, embracing and exploring each other's muscles and limbs and warmth. When at last Saul broke the kiss, he was smiling. 'Think about that while you're away.'

S trocchi got down from his horse on the approach to Porta San Gallo, following Aldo's example. The city wall stretched away on either side of the north gate, less impressive than Strocchi remembered it. Coming to Florence, the wall had seemed vast, a great barrier capable of keeping out all those who did not deserve to go within. But from this side, it was not so imposing. Had the city altered him, what he saw? Strocchi did not wish to believe that.

They neared the gate, Aldo nodding to the guards. A few questions confirmed previous reports. Lorenzino and his servants had passed through Porta San Gallo well after dark on Saturday, the Duke's cousin nursing a wounded hand. But the guards had questions of their own. Was it true Lorenzino had murdered the Duke? Aldo shrugged, and Strocchi kept his counsel. The truth – or some of it – would be known soon enough.

They walked their horses through the gate, mounting again once outside the city walls. The effort caused Aldo to groan, but the constable knew better than to offer help. Once in the saddle, Aldo glanced across. 'Ready?'

Strocchi gave a nod, resisting the urge to look back through the gates.

Aldo urged his horse forwards and it sprang away, eager to

escape the city. Strocchi did the same, the two of them gathering speed as they raced towards the hills.

The invitation from Guicciardini came as no surprise. Maria had been generous with her coin, making sure his household servants were just as generous in sharing what they knew. A man of importance should know to pay his staff more if he valued their silence. She took her time going to his palazzo, careful not to seem eager. This was the chance she'd sought so long. Meet it with poise, and Cosimo would have the measure of them all in no time. Stumble, and she would see out her days in a crumbling *castello*, knowing it was her fault.

Maria practised her words, prepared speeches to convince Guicciardini. But she needed no words to win the favour of the leader of the Palleschi. Instead, he did all the talking. The city stood at a precipice. The death of Alessandro – not murder, Guicciardini wouldn't call it that, not yet – had left an absence. The Duke's *bastardo* boy could not fill that, and it was quite the understatement to say that Lorenzino had shown his unsuitability for the role.

She feigned a cough to hide her laughter, blaming some ailment. Guicciardini pressed on. Word of Alessandro's fate was already across the city, and no doubt spreading throughout the Dominion too. There were those who would see Florence fall into the wrong hands, or into darkness. And there were others who held republican ambitions. None of that could be allowed, but preventing it required someone untainted by the intrigues of court and the politics of the past.

Finally, Guicciardini got to his question: did Maria believe that her son Cosimo might be the man Florence needed, and would she consent to him being proposed as its leader?

It took all of her restraint not to say yes before the question was even complete.

Aldo didn't recognize it at first. They'd been riding all afternoon, eager to reach Scarperia before dusk. The last time on this road, he had come in the other direction, headed south. But that familiar clenching in the *palle* made him pause. The road ahead narrowed, passing between two steep stone slopes. Birdsong died away, the sounds of the horses' hooves echoing around him and Strocchi.

This was the place. This was where Carafa and the bandits had tried to kill Levi. The attack had been what – seven, eight days ago? Levi survived only to be slain the next night. Was dying at home a comfort for the moneylender? Doubtful.

Dead was dead, whatever priests might say.

'Are we stopping here?' Strocchi asked.

The horses were uncertain, skittish. Was there a reason? There, the sound of another rider, coming from the north. Aldo reached for the stiletto in his boot. He wouldn't be caught unawares this time. But when the rider came over the hill, Aldo was still surprised. 'Cosimo?'

The widow Salviati's son was alone, no guards or escort at his side. He slowed to a halt as he reached them. 'Aldo, isn't it? You rode with my father.'

'This is Carlo Strocchi, a constable with the Otto. Strocchi, this is Cosimo de' Medici, son of Signora Maria Salviati. His father was the *condottiere* Giovanni dalle Bande Nere.'

The young man nodded to Strocchi. 'It's not often we see two representatives of the Otto together out here in the Dominion.'

'We're riding to Scarperia,' the constable replied, but said no more. Good, he was learning not to offer information needlessly. Cosimo leaned forward.

'I've just come from Scarperia. The town is alive with rumours. Militia are being mobilized, with orders to ride to Florence. I'm bound for the city myself to see if everything being said is true. Some are claiming Duke Alessandro is dead.'

'For once, the gossip is correct,' Aldo replied. 'The Duke died two nights ago, murdered by men who fled the city afterwards, but his body was not found until yesterday. We are pursuing those believed to have killed Alessandro.'

Cosimo sank back in his saddle, as if struck in the chest. 'So it's true. He is gone.'

Strange to see someone made sad by this killing. Aldo had witnessed shock and dismay, but most seemed to regard the death of Alessandro as a threat, or an opportunity. Nobody mourned the man. But here was Cosimo, not yet eighteen summers, grieving for Alessandro.

'Forgive me asking,' Aldo said, 'but why were you in Scarperia? Trebbio is south of here, as is your family's *castello*.'

'I heard my cousin Lorenzino had been seen galloping into Scarperia, with two servants. Some claim he had one hand jammed in a bloodstained glove. He spent time with a doctor, before going on north, towards Bologna.' Cosimo frowned. 'I went to Scarperia to see if the rumours were true. Tell me, what can I expect to find in Florence?'

Aldo hesitated. Whatever he said now could lose or gain the trust of a young man who could soon be ruler of Florence.

Strocchi watched Aldo and Cosimo talking, the two men at ease despite their differences. Aldo having ridden with Cosimo's father seemed important to the young Medici. Strocchi reminded himself that he was only a few summers older than Cosimo. But he could see how that young face might fool some into dismissing Cosimo.

'The city faces a grave decision,' Aldo said, 'though most of its people do not know that yet. The Duke must be replaced soon, or those with their own interests will intervene. Whoever takes Alessandro's place faces many challenges in the days and months ahead. To lead the city will require courage and a resolve that few possess.'

Cosimo listened, gripping the reins of his horse tight. 'Do those who decide the city's fate have someone in mind for that burden?'

Aldo glanced at Strocchi before answering. 'A Medici is favoured by many.'

Strocchi felt the hairs on the back of his neck rising at Cosimo's next words. 'How should a Medici little-known in Florence enter the city, this of all days?'

'Respectfully,' Aldo said. 'Some might perceive him as meek. There are men who will see the new leader's youth as a sign of weakness. He will know better, but need not show that yet. He is patient – much like his father.'

Cosimo gave the slightest of nods, as if Aldo's words confirmed his own thinking. 'Come closer, and I will give you a message for Lorenzino, should you find him.' The young man murmured into Aldo's ear, the words too quiet for Strocchi to hear.

'I understand,' Aldo said. 'May your journey lead you to what you seek.'

'And the same for your journey north,' Cosimo replied. He nodded to Strocchi before riding away. Once Cosimo's horse was out of hearing, Strocchi moved alongside Aldo.

'What did he say to you? What message did Cosimo have for Lorenzino?'

'I'll tell you if we find him,' Aldo said. 'Let's get to Scarperia. I don't want to be out on this road at night.'

Chapter Thirty-One

Tuesday, January 9th

Finding fresh horses in the village of Scarperia proved all but impossible. Strocchi and Aldo had arrived not long before dusk the previous night, riding between beech and chestnut trees, the scent of spruce thick in the air. In such a small settlement it didn't take long to confirm much of what Cosimo de' Medici had told them. But the militia preparing to ride south meant there were no fresh horses available, despite brandishing the Otto's letter of authority and offering plenty of coin. Staying on the horses they had ridden north from Florence would mean travelling at a slower pace today.

Strocchi expected sharp words from Aldo at this, but he seemed untroubled. 'You've worked with Cerchi too long.' While their horses were being readied, the constable helped Aldo discover the doctor who had treated Lorenzo. Coin put in the right hands led them to Barbani, a keen-eyed man who licked his lips whenever payment was mentioned.

'Yes, the Medici was here,' Barbani admitted. 'He claimed a wild dog savaged his hand. I did find a tooth lodged in the wound – but it was a human tooth.' Looking past the grasping healer, Strocchi noted a rich, colourful rug taking pride of place among Barbani's tired furniture, the floor around it freshly swept.

'We heard they went west from here,' Aldo said. Strocchi kept his silence at the lie.

'You heard wrong,' Barbani replied. 'Lorenzino was in pain, snapping at both his men. The younger one went to fetch supplies for a long ride.' The healer hesitated, licking his lips. Aldo obliged him with a coin. 'They were bound for Bologna.'

More coin was offered, but withdrawn again before Barbani could snatch it away. 'Bologna's a big place,' Aldo said, 'and it doesn't welcome many Medici these days. Who did Lorenzino think would give him sanctuary there?'

Barbani's tongue wet his lips once more, reminding Strocchi of tiny lizards that emerged on hot summer days back in his home village. 'Strozzi – Filippo Strozzi.' Barbani grabbed the coin, grinning at his reward. Aldo asked more questions but the doctor had nothing further to add. Strocchi was grateful he'd never have to visit Barbani for treatment.

'Did you see that rug?' Strocchi asked, following Aldo away. The sound of iron being tempered rang out in the air, and smoke billowed from artisans' chimneys. Scarperia was well known for the quality of its blades and knives. 'Barbani was well paid for his services.'

'Probably for his silence too.'

'We've no way of knowing for certain that Lorenzino and his men are riding towards Bologna. He might have bribed Barbani to lie if anyone came asking questions.'

'I'm not convinced Lorenzino was thinking that far ahead. Besides, it makes sense for him to go to Bologna. There are plenty of Florentine exiles living there, driven out by the current Medici and past generations of the family. Strozzi in particular is known for giving shelter to the banished. Lorenzino can expect a warm welcome for killing Alessandro.'

Strocchi noticed Aldo was moving well this morning, and his mood was lighter too. Perhaps it had something to do with the powders he was taking. Whatever the reason, the result was welcome when they had a long ride ahead of them.

Maria had feared it would be a struggle to keep Cosimo calm when they arrived at Palazzo della Signoria, but her own temper was close to fraying. Why were the Forty-Eight taking so long to confirm him as the next duke? What caused the raised voices she could hear from the senate chamber, even with the doors closed? The Forty-Eight were all men, of course. No woman had a voice in such matters. Indeed, it was possible she was the first woman ever to venture this close to the senate chamber. But wives and mothers still held sway in homes and bedchambers. The decision about who should lead the city had already been taken, or so Maria had heard. The Palleschi were of one mind that Cosimo be made ruler of Florence and its Dominion. Yet convincing the rest of the Senate was taking far too long.

Cosimo had arrived the previous afternoon, entering the city with a humility that made her proud. Not that she wanted her son to be humble – or, worse still, humbled. But his arrival showed how much he had learned: how to behave when all around you were watching, how to win favour from those whose approval would be important in the days to come. He looked a simple country boy who could easily be guided. Let them believe that. They didn't know her son.

Cosimo stood at a tall window, watching the piazza below. In this light he looked so much like his father. Noticing him frown, Maria went to his side. 'What is it?'

A crowd was gathered outside. Alessandro's murder was no

secret any more, and the citizens had come to see who would succeed him. But the long deliberations seemed to be trying everyone's patience. Arguments and scuffles were spreading through the throng. Was it her imagination, or were militia moving among the crowd? Did they hope to force the Forty-Eight into a decision – or were they coming to stop it? Cosimo opened the window to hear what was being shouted.

'Cosimo! Cosimo!' Maria's breath caught in her throat. 'Cosimo, son of the great Giovanni, must become Duke of Florence!' More voices joined in. The shouts became a chant, the crowd calling with one voice for her son. Maria could see those shouting loudest were militia, urging the others into chanting for her son. No doubt one of the Palleschi had arranged for that to happen, adding to the demands for Cosimo's selection.

Pounding boots approached the antechamber, and Captain Vitelli of the Duke's guard burst in. Stern-faced, with a breastplate worn over his dark clothes, he nodded to them before striding to the meeting room entrance. 'Hurry,' Vitelli shouted, throwing open the doors. 'The soldiers can't be held any longer!'

Cosimo straightened, his chin rising to meet the challenge ahead. This was the moment when the boy became a man. All her sacrifices had not been in vain. She wanted to hold him close one last time, but he belonged to the city now – and the city belonged to him.

Rebecca was outside for the first time since Dante's death. She felt ready to face the world, her week of sitting *shiva* complete. It was strange to stand on the narrow stones of via dei Giudei again. People brushed by on their way to the *mercato* or to visit family. All had a reason for their journey. What purpose did she have?

No longer did Father need her to cook and clean for him, she was free of that. But no longer would he be putting food on the table, or fire in the hearth. She could not expect the charity of neighbours to last much longer. They had worries and cares of their own.

A young mother passed with two infant boys, holding their hands tight. She wasn't much older than Rebecca, but already had a family. Not long ago Rebecca had believed that becoming a wife and mother was the only path ahead. Ruth's offer of a new life in Bologna had shown there were other ways, other paths for the taking. An old head on young shoulders, that was how Father had always described Ruth. He'd been right about that, at least.

Rebecca looked up through the narrow gap between buildings to the sky. It felt good to be back outside, to rejoin the world. It felt even better to have made her choice. Yes, it would disappoint, perhaps even shock others. But the decision was for her to make alone.

She breathed in. The air was cold and fresh, especially after so long indoors, so long with nothing but grief and guilt and tears. Rebecca strolled away from her front door, away from the house of her parents, heading north towards the Arno. That house would be her home a while longer, until everything could be arranged. But she would not be spending the rest of her days there, as they had. There was another path ahead of her.

Rebecca smiled. She was at peace.

Men came and went, but Maria still waited for Cosimo to emerge. His name had been acclaimed behind the doors, the voices of the Forty-Eight echoing into the antechamber, so she had no fear for him. But she wanted to share this moment with Cosimo – she was his mother, after all.

The arrival of Francesco Campana did put a flutter of fear in her heart. She knew the ducal adviser by sight, despite his face being rather forgettable. He was someone of quiet importance, someone who had had the ear of Alessandro. That duke was dead, but men like Campana endured. It was the city's way, administrators serving one leader and then the next. How else could commerce continue? Rulers rose and fell, but Florence endured.

Campana had nodded on his way into the chamber, acknowledging her presence. No doubt he was now whispering in her son's ear, advising Cosimo on what to say and whom to trust. How long before she was left in the shadows? The wife of a ruler had influence and importance – his mother far less.

The doors opened and Maria watched Campana usher her son from the chamber. Cosimo saw her and smiled. Bless him. He took both her hands, leaning close to kiss a cheek. 'Smile,' he whispered in her ear. 'Don't let them see anything but joy in your face.'

'Of course.'

'They refused to name me duke,' he said, venom cloaked in his voice. 'The Forty-Eight elected me as leader of Florence and the Dominion, if recognized by the Emperor. But I must leave a Florentine in charge whenever I leave the city. And I'm to be paid only twelve thousand *scudi* a year – Alessandro got half as much again.'

Maria pulled him closer, beaming over Cosimo's shoulder at Campana and the Palleschi. 'These fools think they can shackle you,' she whispered. 'They believe you're a child without the *palle* to challenge them. These men do not know you, Cosimo. You will outlive them – but first you will outwit them. You shall serve this city well, and make you father proud.'

Cosimo's embrace tightened. When he let go, he was smiling.

'I shall not forget this.' He strode from the antechamber, Campana and the Palleschi in step behind him.

Maria turned to the window, smiling to herself. Her son never forgot a slight, however small. To belittle him at the start of his rule was foolishness. But for her, it was a boon. By treating Cosimo this way, the Forty-Eight had bound him to her a while longer. He would be duke, perhaps even grand duke one day – and she would remain safe in his shadow.

The journey north was arduous, made worse by having to ride the same tired horses all the way. It was late in the afternoon when Aldo and Strocchi finally approached the walled city of Bologna. For Aldo, Bologna lacked the majesty of Florence or the simple village beauty of a settlement like Scarperia. Yes, it had the impressive Due Torri, twin towers that loomed over the city, but they were brutish fingers of stone stabbing at the sky – nothing to match the wonder that was the Duomo. Strocchi admitted he had never been to Bologna as they dismounted and led their horses through the southern gate. 'Should I be worried?'

It was a good question. The more Strocchi knew about what they were likely to face here, the more useful he could be. The constable certainly needed to know what not to do while they were in the city, if nothing else.

'Bologna is a papal state,' Aldo said, keeping his voice to a murmur to avoid being overheard as they went to the nearest stable. 'That means our letter of authorization holds little meaning here. If we get in trouble, nobody is coming to save us. Word of Alessandro's death may well have reached here already, and many Florentine exiles will rejoice in that.'

'Celebrating a man's murder is barbaric.'

'Perhaps, but the Medici have driven many families out of Florence over the years, and more than a few lost all their wealth as a consequence. It's no surprise that they long to see those who banished them from Florence fall. We can expect few welcomes here.'

After stabling the horses, Aldo led Strocchi on foot deeper into the city, trying to recall the way to Bologna's Jewish commune. This far north it was much colder than in Florence, their breath forming a cloud in the air. One thing the city did have in its favour were the many porticos, the walkways beneath vaulted ceilings saving those on foot from have to traipse through so much mud and *merda*. Would that Florence had the same.

Aldo explained to Strocchi how Bologna had long been a seat of learning. Becoming a papal state had naturally increased the influence of the Church over the city. 'You say that like it's a bad thing,' the constable muttered.

Aldo pointed to the many churches being restored and the new ones being built as they pressed on, early to reach their goal before curfew. 'Does even God require this many places built to worship him? Could not that coin be spent on helping those in need of alms?' The constable grumbled under his breath, and Aldo chided himself for breaking his own rule: never argue with men of true faith, as changing their minds was almost always a lost cause.

Aldo led Strocchi to the home of Rebecca Levi's uncle and cousin, tucked away in a minor street of the Jewish commune. Aldo banged a fist on the door. There was no reply at first, but shuffling feet could be heard approaching from inside. 'Who is it?' an uncertain, frail voice asked. That must be the father.

'I was here with Samuele, the last time he came to Bologna.'

The feet shuffled closer. 'If that's true, what did my brother take with him?'

'He carried away no coin. But Samuele did leave a letter with you in case he died.' Strocchi opened his mouth to speak, but Aldo silenced him. 'It was Samuele's *zava'ah*.'

Bolts were undone and the door swung open, revealing an old man with a silver beard and milky eyes. He squinted at Strocchi and shook his head, but nodded after staring at Aldo. 'You I remember. You were meant to guard Samuele, keep him alive.'

'I did, all the way to Florence. Your brother was murdered in his own home, after he left my protection.' Aldo introduced the constable. 'Strocchi, this is Shimon Levi.'

'Father, who is it?' Ruth appeared behind Shimon, wiping her hands on a cloth. She paled at seeing Aldo. 'Has something happened to Rebecca?'

'No, she's safe. Your cousin gave me this note for you.' Aldo handed over the Hebrew message, which Ruth read.

'She asks us to give whatever help we can. She says we can trust you.' Ruth studied them. 'You must be tired, if you rode here from Florence.' She put a hand on her father's shoulder, moving him aside. 'Please, come in.'

Ruth was only a summer or three older than Rebecca, but seemed far more mature. She gave them simple food and wine while Aldo explained their task. Ruth offered directions to Strozzi's palazzo, describing landmarks that would help them find the way through the city. She also offered a room for the night, which Aldo accepted. Word of two Florentine law enforcers staying the night in a tavern would soon reach the ears of curious exiles.

After eating, Aldo took Strocchi aside. 'We need to be sure Lorenzino is still here. We don't want him slipping away again. That means finding a way inside Strozzi's palazzo.'

'We won't see much if we go now, it'll be dark soon.'

'Exactly. Strozzi won't invite us in during the day. This is our best chance of getting to Lorenzino.' Aldo adjusted the stiletto in his boot. 'Then I can deliver Cosimo's message.'

The afternoon had been spent in meeting after meeting, Campana introducing Cosimo to the worthy men of Florence, all the while whispering in his ear. Maria followed, dutifully staying two steps back. Enough distance to be respectful, but close enough to hear whatever was said. Her back and feet ached, but she refused to sit or rest. Not while she might be needed.

It was almost dusk when it came time to enter Palazzo Medici. They'd been to the ducal residence before, but now Cosimo was arriving as head and leader of the city. Maria knew that title was vexing him; she recognized the anger lurking behind his gaze. But her son was also wise enough to mask his anger. She had readied Cosimo for this moment should it ever come, more in faith than expectation. Years spent under the tutelage of Pier Francesco Riccio, visits to Bologna and Venice to train Cosimo in the ways of diplomacy. He might be nervous, even fearful inside, but her boy knew better than to let that show.

Cosimo stopped at the threshold of Palazzo Medici, Campana going ahead of him. Maria went to her son's side, keeping her voice hushed. 'What is it?'

'Alessandro's dead, but what of his wife?' Cosimo asked. 'Will she be inside?'

Maria hesitated. In the tumult of the last few days, she had all but forgotten young Margaret. The Duke's wife – widow, now – was only fourteen, but Margaret was also the illegitimate daughter of the Holy Roman Emperor. What happened to her could have profound importance for the city and Cosimo's future as its leader.

'She was residing at the home of my late sister Francesca, with your uncle Ottaviano. I'm sure Campana will have made suitable arrangements for the widow,' Maria said. She left that to fester. If the adviser had failed to do so, it showed his reputation was unwarranted. If Campana had done so, it showed he was capable at his job – but no more. Maria slipped her hand through the crook of Cosimo's arm and they went inside.

Campana was arguing with a courtier in terse whispers. Something was amiss. He sent the courtier away before facing Cosimo. 'Forgive me, but it seems that there has been a disturbance within the palazzo while you were occupied elsewhere.'

'What do you mean – disturbance?' Cosimo asked.

'Soldiers entered the palazzo and took whatever they could carry – coin, jewels, silver plate and other valuables. I will need to undertake a full inventory to know what has been removed, but it seems the loss was . . . considerable.'

Maria saw Cosimo's fists clenching tight. 'Who? Who did this?' he demanded.

Campana stared at the marble floor. 'There seems to be some confusion about that. Some of the servants are suggesting it was Vitelli, and his men.'

The captain of the ducal guard had led the ransacking of the Duke's home? If true, it was outrageous – Vitelli spitting in the face of the city's new leader. Yet Cosimo showed a restraint Maria had not always witnessed before.

'Where is the late Duke's widow?' Cosimo asked.

Campana hesitated. 'Captain Vitelli has taken her to Fortezza da Basso. He suggested her life might be in danger, following the murder of Alessandro.'

Clever. Any attempt to strike back against Vitelli would never breach the fortress walls. Besides, no one was foolish enough to attack those guarding the Emperor's daughter. To do so would be an act of war, a war Florence would surely lose.

Cosimo took a deep breath before nodding. 'Send a message to Vitelli. Commend him on this bold action. The Emperor will be grateful to know his daughter's well-being rests in the hands of such a skilled soldier.'

Maria permitted herself a smile. Vitelli had won this battle. But Cosimo's words made it plain that if anything happened to Margaret, it was the captain who faced the Emperor's wrath – not Cosimo, not the city. Campana nodded. He too saw the *strategia* behind the bland words. Good. The sooner all Florence knew her son was no foolish boy, the better.

Strocchi was relieved when they discovered Strozzi's palazzo was vacant. A few servants remained in residence, but the exiled banker was not there – and neither was Lorenzino. The constable's conscience had been uneasy since he and Aldo had met with Cosimo north of Florence. Aldo still refused to reveal the message he had promised to give Lorenzino, but Strocchi feared the sharp end of a stiletto was involved. The constable could not – and, given the choice, would not – be a *complice* to murder.

For a handful of coin one of Strozzi's servants confirmed Lorenzino had come to the palazzo on Sunday afternoon. Having been told Strozzi was in Venice, Lorenzino sought directions to another address. That set Aldo and Strocchi on a trek around Bologna, trying to find where Lorenzino had spent Sunday night. Eventually they found Francesco Dall'Armi, a tall exile with a weak chin and weaker will, who admitted giving the fugitive and his men shelter. By then pain was twisting Aldo's face and his patience seemed spent. He shoved his way inside, demanding answers. Dall'Armi described the Duke's cousin as desperate, a man near afraid of his own shadow. But wine had soon set Lorenzino bragging about what he'd done.

'And what was that?' Aldo asked.

'Lorenzino claimed he had murdered the Duke of Florence.' Dall'Armi shook his head. 'I didn't believe him at first, but the way he described it was quite compelling. He even showed me the wound on his hand where Alessandro bit him to the bone.'

'Did Lorenzino say why he murdered the Duke?' Strocchi got a glare from Aldo for interrupting, but it was still a question worth asking.

Dall'Armi frowned. 'Lorenzino called his cousin a tyrant, a despot who used the city for pleasure when it had once been a great republic. Lorenzino seemed to believe the people would rise up and reclaim Florence, all while giving thanks to him. I thought his words were fanciful, but . . .'

'Where did Lorenzino and his men go after staying here?' Aldo demanded. 'Where are they now?'

'Venice,' Dall'Armi replied. 'Filippo Strozzi has his other palazzo there. Lorenzino and his men left early the next morning, riding hard. They'll easily be there by now.'

Aldo marched from the exile's home, muttering curses under his breath. Strocchi hurried after him. Dusk was falling on Bologna and the constable wasn't sure he could find the Jewish commune again on his own. 'Where are we going now? Venice?'

'Not tonight.' Aldo stomped onwards, favouring his left knee. 'I need sleep.'

'But we're leaving for Venice at dawn?'

'Stop asking fool questions if you still want to have all your teeth in the morning!'

Strocchi hesitated. Whatever he did or said seemed to infuriate

Aldo, but he needed to know. 'I've been patient as long as I can, but I want to know what you plan to do next.'

'Don't you understand?' Aldo hissed at him. 'It's over.'

'What is?'

'This, this fool's errand! If we go to Venice, the odds on us finding Lorenzino are much the same as for us getting killed. Our coin will buy us no favours there, and certainly no friends. Even if we did find Lorenzino, he'll be the hero of every exile in that city by now. Protected by Strozzi and all his allies, safe from harm. Safe from us.'

Strocchi swallowed hard. He'd never been on the wrong side of Aldo's anger.

'Don't you understand? We've failed.' Aldo stalked away from Strocchi. 'It's over.'

Chapter Thirty-Two

Wednesday, January 10th

Aldo woke early, his right shoulder throbbing. The powders had been numbing the worst of the pain, but only one dose remained. He didn't want to use that until they turned for home. Bad as his shoulder felt, worse was the memory of bullying Strocchi. Pain was part of why he'd snapped, but frustration was most of it. To come so far and find Lorenzino was already in Venice – maddening. If Bindi and others had listened, Alessandro would still be alive.

Did it matter who led Florence? One ruler was little different from the next. No, it was the injustice of what had happened that rankled most. He could have died in Le Stinche because of Lorenzino's *stratagemma*. Instead, he'd survived to be sent north on a wasted journey when every part of him wanted to be back in Florence, getting to know Orvieto. Was wounded pride part of his frustration too? Yes. To be right but not to be believed was like a burr beneath a saddle, scratching at the skin.

Aldo rolled over, expecting to see the constable asleep across the borrowed room. But Strocchi was gone, his mattress stripped bare. *Palle*. Strocchi hadn't said a word when they got back to the Levi home. Aldo wouldn't blame the constable if he'd chosen to leave for Florence already. Making the long ride together in bitter silence was not a welcome prospect.

Aldo rose, washing in haste. Dressing took longer thanks to his shoulder, with plenty of cursing for company. He found Ruth in the kitchen, dropping herbs and stale crusts into a steaming pot of *ribollita*. Baking smells mingled with the broth's warming aroma. She halved a lemon and squeezed its juice into the liquid. 'Hungry?' He nodded, stomach aching. It'd been too long since his last warm meal. She gestured for him to sit at the plain table.

'Have you seen Strocchi?'

'He left early.' Ruth lifted a cloth from a fresh loaf of black bread, and put it on the table with a gleaming knife. 'Cut that for me.'

Aldo did as he was told. 'Did Strocchi say where he was going?'

'No, but he left his satchel.' She pointed at the bag hanging on the back door. That was something, at least. Ruth filled two bowls with broth, sprinkling salt on each. She handed one to Aldo and carried the second away with two slices of bread.

The *ribollita* was good, the tomato broth thickened with beans and offcuts of dried meat, brought to life by the herbs and seasonings. When Ruth returned, Aldo was using his bread to mop up the last few mouthfuls. 'We should pay you,' he said.

'There's no need,' she insisted. 'You brought Rebecca's note, I'm grateful for that. But you can tell me how she is. I worry about her.'

Aldo hesitated. He had devoted so much time to investigating the conspiracy against Alessandro – all to no avail – that the consequences of Levi's murder had been neglected. 'I'm not sure,' he admitted. 'Joshua Forzoni was there when I've visited. They seem close.'

Ruth frowned. 'If I give you a letter, would you deliver it to my cousin?'

'Yes, if I can have more of that *ribollita*.'

He was finishing a second bowl when Strocchi returned,

red-cheeked from the cold but with a gleam in his eyes. Ruth brought him food, before going back to her father. Aldo let Strocchi eat before asking where he'd been.

'Thought if I found out where Strozzi lives in Venice, we could take the address back to Bindi. Then it's up to the *segretario* to decide what should be done next.'

The constable was learning fast. 'You'll make a good officer one day, Carlo. And I'm sorry for what I said last night, you didn't deserve it.'

Strocchi accepted the apology with a simple nod. 'You were frustrated, we both were.' He dropped pieces of black bread into the broth. 'I did learn where Strozzi lives in Venice, but it doesn't matter now. Seems he's coming back to Bologna. Took most of our remaining coin, but one of the servants told me Strozzi is leaving Venice this morning. He's due here tomorrow, bringing someone called the Brutus of Florence with him.'

'That's got to be Lorenzino.' Alessandro's killer had just ridden to Venice; why was he coming all the way back again so soon? 'Strozzi must be hoping to convince all the other exiles here in Bologna to join him in funding an attempt to reclaim Florence,' Aldo said. 'No doubt he believes the city is vulnerable after what Lorenzino did. But why isn't Strozzi due back here today? It's possible to ride from Venice to Bologna in a day with good horses.'

'Apparently Strozzi finds the journey too much for a single day. He always stops and spends the night at a coach house in a small village called Le Casette, near the Po.'

Aldo smiled. 'If we ride north-east today, we could meet Strozzi and Lorenzino when they stop for the night.' He stood up. 'The sooner we leave, the better.'

* * *

Bindi stood outside Palazzo Medici, preparing himself for the ordeal ahead. Days had passed with no call to offer a report to the Duke. Indeed, days had passed when the city had no duke. If the gossip was true, Florence still did not. Instead, the Forty-Eight had seen fit to elect the widow Salviati's whelp as leader and head of the city.

Cosimo bore the name Medici – legitimately, unlike his predecessor – but giving some pock-faced youth charge of the city was dangerous. The purposes of the Palleschi might be met, but what of the people? What of those who faithfully served Florence? The answer came at dawn, a summons from Francesco Campana. Bring everything about the Duke's murder, especially the Otto's investigation. Bindi had gathered what he had, grumbling to himself.

As ever, the city's latest leader had no grasp of how the Otto worked. First and foremost it was a criminal court, entrusted with the prosecution of particular laws. Yes, it had men to enforce those laws and bring to justice anyone who broke them, but resources were limited. This was Florence, after all, and the Otto was expected to turn a profit. If that couldn't be done, the court was certainly not allowed to lose money.

Bindi realized he had no idea what to call the new leader. The Duke had been Your Grace, but how did one address the head and leader of a city? He had to hope Campana would be present for the briefing and could offer some guidance. Failing that, Bindi would have to respond as best he could once in the room with the newly elected Medici.

The *segretario* strode into the palazzo, nodding to the guards by the doors. There seemed little value in having sentries outside if the threat came from within your household, but the need for such a display was understandable. The city's leader should be guarded, seen to be deserving of protection. The true worth and value of Cosimo to Florence would become apparent – or not – soon enough.

In the courtyard Bindi found Campana arguing with a woman dressed for mourning. The *segretario* had encountered Signora Salviati twice before, each a bruising occasion. She was a forceful creature, with a stubborn streak that could outlast stone. How much sway did she have over her son? Better not to test that by interrupting them. Bindi caught Campana's eye and the adviser nodded, gesturing for the *segretario* to go up. Cosimo was using the same *officio* as his predecessor, it seemed, but Campana was too busy to attend the meeting.

Bindi made his way along the corridor to the *officio*. Gaping absences were apparent where rich tapestries and silver plates had adorned the walls and cabinets. So the tales of ransacking and pillaging were true. Fools. Goading a new leader was asking for trouble. Bindi had no intention of making the same mistake.

The *segretario* knocked at the double doors, and was commanded to enter. Inside was much as it had been in Alessandro's time, though the imposing desk and throne were absent. Cosimo stood alone in the centre of the chamber, facing away from the doors.

'Sir, my name is Massimo Bindi, and I'm—'

'*Segretario* to the Otto di Guardia e Balìa,' Cosimo said, turning round. He was older than Bindi expected, though that attempt at a beard still betrayed his youth. 'Campana says someone in your position is the most powerful individual at any court. Magistrates come and go, but the *segretario* remains – is that correct?'

Bindi feigned a modest smile. 'Campana flatters those of my position. We have some minor influence, but it is magistrates who pass judgement.'

Cosimo did not reply, standing quite still. Bindi knew this *stratagemma* well, but that didn't stop beads of sweat forming on his brow. Finally, blessedly, Cosimo strolled away to look out of a closed window. 'Tell me, how goes the quest to find my predecessor's killer?'

Bindi let himself breathe. 'Evidence suggests your cousin Lorenzino was responsible for the murder, assisted by his servants. They fled the city after dark on Saturday, riding north. I sent two of my men into the Dominion to pursue Lorenzino.'

'Cesare Aldo and a constable – Strocchi, that's his name, yes?'

How did . . . ? The *segretario* put the question from his head. Focus on what was being asked, not on how this youth knew so much. 'Yes, sir.'

'Aldo's a good man,' Cosimo said, turning round. 'He rode with my father.'

Bindi nodded, as if this was familiar knowledge. It seemed Aldo had Cosimo's ear – or his confidence, at least. 'If anyone can bring Lorenzino back to face justice, it's Aldo.' And if he failed, that would reflect only on him, not the Otto.

But Cosimo was shaking his head. 'I've already given Aldo instructions on how to deal with Lorenzino, should he get close to that traitorous *bastardo*. While I have breath in my body, Lorenzino will not be returning to Florence. Not alive.'

Progress was slow on the ride north-east. The horses Strocchi had hired in Bologna were tired before leaving the stable, and the road was rough and uneven. Aldo's knuckles whitened on the reins with each jolt, but he was keeping his pain to himself today. His mood seemed lifted by the prospect of facing Lorenzino. But the closer they got to Le Casette, the stronger Strocchi's misgivings became.

When they stopped to eat a simple meal provided by Ruth, the constable knew he had to say something. It might not change what happened, but his conscience demanded a voice. 'I won't be a *complice* to murder,' Strocchi said as Aldo chewed a mouthful of food. 'I didn't hear the message Cosimo de' Medici asked you to deliver to Lorenzino, but I can guess what it was. If you plan to kill Lorenzino tonight, I can't be part of that.'

The constable watched, waiting for a response. Aldo swallowed and wiped his mouth before finally replying. 'Why not?'

'It'd be murder. What Lorenzino and his men did to the Duke was a crime, just as what happened to Corsini was a crime. But that doesn't give us the right to murder Lorenzino if we get the chance.'

'And who gives you the authority to judge what's right and wrong?' Aldo asked. 'I killed one of the Bassos in Le Stinche, when he was going to kill me. Was that wrong?'

Strocchi frowned. 'You were defending yourself. That's different.'

'I believed he would kill me, yes, but he never said so. Not out loud.'

'Your injured shoulder is proof of what he intended.'

'That only proves he meant to hurt me.'

Strocchi shook his head. 'You're kicking mud into the water. I'm talking about you and Lorenzino, what you plan to do to him tonight.'

'I haven't said what I plan to do.'

'Lorenzino killed the Duke, and the Duke's cousin wants you to strike back. You might be able to kill a man in his bed, I can't,' Strocchi insisted. 'It is for God to take a life.'

'What about during war? Would you take a life then?'

'We're not at war. I've never been a soldier, and I hope I never will be.'

'You can turn back if you don't wish to come any further.'

'That's not what I said. You're twisting my words . . .'

'I'm testing your loyalty,' Aldo replied. 'Lorenzino will have servants with him, not to mention Strozzi and his men. If I can get close to Lorenzino tonight – and that's far from certain – I'll need someone by my side I can trust.'

'You know you can trust me,' Strocchi insisted, 'but you choose not to. If you did, you would share Cosimo's message with me. Trust me to use my own judgement, to make my own choice. I want to help if I can, but I won't do that unless you tell me.'

Aldo rose and strode away, towards the horses. He stopped short of them, hands on his hips. Strocchi offered up a silent prayer for the officers to see sense. Eventually Aldo spat at the ground before turning back. 'You're right. I don't trust people easily, because plenty have given me reason to be careful. So I'm not going to apologize for keeping my own counsel, Carlo. But if you are coming with me, you deserve the truth.'

Strocchi's eyes widened as Aldo kept talking.

Rebecca was jolted awake by shouting outside. 'Samuele's daughter! I know you're in there!' She stumbled to the front door, dazed from sleeping late. It was the first good rest she'd had since staying the night with Joshua's family, the night Father died. It was dark in the house, shutters still closed over the windows, all the candles burnt down.

'Who is it?'

'I am – I was – a colleague of your father,' the man replied. 'A friend.'

Rebecca didn't recognize the voice. Father had driven away almost anyone who ever cared about him. But if this man did consider Father a friend, she had a duty to welcome him, even now. Rebecca slid back the bolt and opened the door. Sciarra shoved his way in. 'You were no friend of Father,' Rebecca protested. 'He despised you, said you had no honour.'

Sciarra strutted round the room, his swagger belying his lack of height. 'Samuele had no right to judge me. He was little more than a thief, stealing others' business.'

Rebecca didn't reply, knowing what Father had done to Dante. She opened shutters to let some light into the house. Sciarra was as unpleasant as she recalled. His sour expression softened when he looked back at her.

'But my quarrel was with Samuele, not with you. So I've come to make a proposition to you, my dear, one that will put food on your table.'

'A proposition,' Rebecca said, queasiness stirring in her belly.

'I intend to take over your father's business. Now, I could do that without giving you a *giulio*. Samuele is dead, so is Dante. Sooner or later anyone who lives south of the Arno will be coming to me for a loan. But I'm prepared to be generous and pay you a small fee in return for your father's list of debtors.'

Rebecca struggled to grasp what this vile man was saying. 'A fee?'

'Yes, in exchange for your father's ledger.' Sciarra acted as if he was dealing with an *idiota*. 'The ledger contains the names of his debtors and what they owe. I assume you've been too busy to collect since he died, my dear?'

Sciarra's arrogant presumption was too much for her. This *merda* seemed to believe he could march into her home and decide her future. 'Of course I haven't been collecting debts. I was sitting *shiva* for Father. If you had any respect for him, you would know that. And I am certainly not your dear, or your anything else for that matter.'

Sciarra reached inside his tunic for a folded piece of paper, and offered it to Rebecca. 'I think you'll find this offer more than generous, in the circumstances.'

She took the paper, hands shaking as she unfolded it. The number was small, an insult to Father's memory. Enough to live on for a month, if she was careful.

'We have an agreement?' Sciarra asked.

'I need to think about this.'

'Why? I won't be increasing my offer.' He arched an eyebrow. 'Don't tell me you're thinking of running the business yourself? A woman, working as a moneylender?' Sciarra laughed, he actually laughed at her. 'The ledger – fetch it for me.'

'I'm not your servant,' Rebecca replied, anger rising like a fire in her. 'If you want Father's ledger, come back tomorrow. But I will not hand it over until you pay what his ledger is worth – not this insulting amount.' She threw the piece of paper aside.

Sciarra's face curdled. 'Like father, like daughter? Very well. I will return at noon tomorrow. But if our bargain is not made then, you shall get nothing from me.' He stalked out.

Only when he'd gone did Rebecca remember what had happened to the ledger.

Riding hard, Aldo and Strocchi reached Le Casette well before dusk. It was little more than a huddle of simple, single-level houses by the Po. The village probably wouldn't have survived if it hadn't stood beside an easy place to ford the river. The tallest building was the church with its bell tower, while the coach house and stables stood across the dirt road from it. Salvation and God on one side, drink and the potential for devilment on the other – it was often the way.

Aldo wanted to confirm Strozzi and Lorenzino were expected before sundown, but didn't dare go asking questions at the coach house. Instead he sent Strocchi. The constable was unknown to Lorenzino, so the Medici fugitive would be none the wiser if any of the coach house workers described Strocchi. The constable did well, charming a servant girl with flattery and giving a coin for her to stay silent later.

As dusk approached, Aldo and Strocchi found a vantage point inside the church bell tower, looking down at the coach house and stables across the road. Strozzi and Lorenzino arrived soon after, with half a dozen men following on horseback. Scoronconcolo and Il Freccia were at the back, while Lorenzino was at the front alongside Strozzi.

Stable hands came to greet the arrivals and tend the horses, welcoming Strozzi with easy familiarity. That gave Lorenzino's servants a chance to approach their master, but he dismissed them with a gesture. Aldo smiled. Good. Getting to Lorenzino would be much easier without Scoronconcolo and Il Freccia close by. The travellers went inside to feast. The aromas from the coach house kitchen were delicious, but Aldo and Strocchi had to make do with the last scraps provided by Ruth while they waited.

Dusk brought a bitter chill. Aldo and Strocchi remained in the bell tower, listening to laughter from the coach house. Aldo folded both hands beneath his arms to stop the fingers going numb, clenching and unclenching his toes for warmth. At long last the meal ended, the travellers going to their rooms upstairs in the coach house. Lorenzino's servants stomped off to the stables, forced to spend the night with the horses.

When the last sounds below had ceased, Aldo set to work rubbing life back into his limbs, Strocchi doing the same. They clambered down the creaking wooden ladder and crept through the church to a door facing the coach house. Nobody was standing guard. Strozzi had no reason to believe he or Lorenzino were in any danger. Let them believe that.

Pulling the stiletto from his boot, Aldo stepped from the church, waiting for a shout or a cry of alarm – but none came. He hurried to the coach house door, Strocchi close behind. They slipped inside, climbing up to the humble bedchambers, testing each step for creaks before putting any weight on it. Along the narrow corridor, passing the first door, on to the second. The servant girl had said that Strozzi always took the first bedchamber. On the rare occasions when the Signor brought guests, they were given the second bedchamber, which was almost as good. Strocchi believed she could be trusted.

Aldo closed his fingers round the door handle and opened it, letting his eyes adjust to the darkness within, listening for any change of breathing. Whoever was in bed kept snoring. Aldo slipped inside. Strocchi came too, but remained on watch at the door, looking out. Aldo went to the bed, staying on the balls of his feet, blade in hand. A shaft of pale moonlight fell across a single figure beneath the covers: Lorenzino. Aldo placed the tip of his stiletto into the notch below Lorenzino's neck, before clamping the other hand across his mouth. Lorenzino jerked awake, his arms flailing and thrashing, calls for help stopped by Aldo's palm.

'Cry out, and I bury this blade in your throat.'

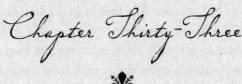

Chapter Thirty-Three

*A*ldo pressed the metal against Lorenzino's neck and his struggling stopped. The Medici fugitive glared as Aldo slowly removed his hand from the sneering mouth.

'I had you sent to Le Stinche,' Lorenzino said, voice hushed. 'How did you get here?' Aldo pushed a thumb into Lorenzino's bandaged hand. He gasped in anguish.

'I ask the questions,' Aldo said. 'Understand?' No reply, so he pushed harder, forcing a fresh sob of pain. 'Understand?' Lorenzino nodded, his face contorting. Aldo eased the pressure, but only a little. 'Why kill the Duke? Why murder your own cousin, a man you served?'

'I was never Alessandro's servant,' Lorenzino replied. 'He was no kinsman of mine. He proved that by ruling against my branch of the family in a dispute. His decision cost us dear, but he never showed a moment of regret. Alessandro was not one of my family.'

'You deny the Duke was your cousin?'

'He had nothing in common with me. He was nothing more than the son of a servant woman from Collececchio who happened to work for the Medici family. It shamed all of Florence to have a *bastardo* as its leader. The city deserved a true-born Medici, not that pretender.' Lorenzino was already creating justifications for the murder. No doubt he'd been practising them among the exiles in Venice. A sharp squeeze of the thumb put an end to that.

'Answer the question: why did you kill the Duke?'

Lorenzino whimpered, the pathetic noise of a snivelling child. 'He was a tyrant. No one doubts that Alessandro – so-called de' Medici – was a tyrant, apart from those who grew rich through flattering and supporting him. In whatever way they are toppled, tyrants should be slain.' Recovering himself, Lorenzino affected an air of nobility. 'My aim was to liberate Florence. Killing Alessandro was a means to that.'

'If you believed you were freeing Florence, why flee the city after killing the Duke? Why hide the body by locking your bedchamber, except to gain time for your escape?'

'What would you have me do?' Lorenzino protested. Aldo pressed the stiletto against Lorenzino's neck, straining the skin. 'What would you have me do,' Lorenzino repeated, his voice now a whisper. 'Should I have shouldered that body like a porter, and gone shouting through Florence like a madman? Did I not have to fear I might be attacked and killed before I had taken three steps outside those doors?'

This tale of woe might convince those who hadn't seen the bloody bedchamber, who didn't know the treachery behind the story Lorenzino was crafting to justify his flight from the city under darkness. But there was more. 'I hoped the tyrant's body would not be found until exiles were on their way to win back the city's liberty. It was not my fault that didn't happen. Not only did I slay the tyrant, I myself went out to exhort those I knew willing and able to fight for their beloved city. I did more than enough in killing him – and saving myself.'

There was the truth. Lorenzino ran to save himself. But Aldo still needed answers before he could deliver Cosimo's message. 'Why did your men murder Levi?'

'The moneylender? I had nothing to do with his death.'

Aldo pushed the stiletto deeper, a bead of blood forming at the tip. 'Don't lie to me.'

'You'll kill me no matter what I say,' Lorenzino replied, eyes wide with fear.

'Everyone dies eventually.' Aldo pushed his thumb deeper into the wounded hand. 'But how much you suffer before I leave this room is up to you.'

'Please don't,' Lorenzino begged. Aldo eased the pressure he was applying – for now.

'Why did your men murder Levi? Was it because he didn't bring the money you wanted from Bologna?'

'Why do you keep asking about him? Levi was dead when my man got there that night. Well, he was dying. There was a knife in his chest.'

'Don't lie to me!' Aldo hissed.

'I'm not,' Lorenzino insisted. 'I've already confessed to murdering the Duke of Florence. Why would I lie about one of my servants killing a Jew?'

What Lorenzino said unlocked a realization for Aldo. 'The coin – that's why you wanted Levi's murderer found. You believed whoever killed Levi must have taken the coin he brought back from Bologna. You didn't know he'd left it with his brother.'

Lorenzino grimaced. 'I sent Scoronconcolo to get the coin. He found Levi dying and took the moneylender's ledger, in case I was named in it. I was the one who urged the Duke to make investigating Levi's murder a matter of importance. It was safer to lead events than leave them to chance. I hoped you'd find whoever killed the Jew, so my men could intervene to take the stolen coin. I had a servant follow you from the first time you visited the palazzo.'

'Il Freccia.' Aldo cursed himself for not paying attention to his own instincts sooner.

'While you were hunting the killer, we tried to have the ledger translated. When that failed, I told Scoronconcolo to burn it.' Lorenzino frowned. 'How did you get that ledger?' Aldo shoved his thumb deep into Lorenzino's bandaged wound, making him gasp in pain.

'I said I ask the questions.'

A floorboard nearby creaked. Aldo clamped his hand back across Lorenzino's mouth, listening for more noises. Another creak, then the sound of liquid pouring into a bowl from a height. It continued for what seemed an eternity before pausing. Two more splashes, then the creak of a floorboard, and finally silence once more.

Aldo glanced at Strocchi, who nodded. Nobody was coming, all was well. The sounds had been somebody getting up to empty their bladder, nothing more. It was safe for now, but the longer they lingered here, the greater the chance of being trapped. Aldo took his hand from Lorenzino's mouth. 'Why insist I find the killer by Epiphany, why the urgency?'

'Captain Vitelli and most of the ducal guard were returning after the feast day. To have any chance of overthrowing Alessandro, it had to happen before then.'

Strocchi was becoming restless at the door. 'We should leave.'

Aldo nodded his agreement. 'One last question. Why were you borrowing a small fortune from Levi? To pay for men at arms, or to fill your pouch for a new life outside the city after stabbing your cousin in the back?'

Lorenzino sneered. 'I don't have to explain myself to you.'

'I beg to differ,' Aldo said, pushing all his weight into the wounded hand. The Medici fugitive cried out, his pain subsiding into weak sobs. Aldo released the hand. 'Tell me.'

'The coin was for me,' Lorenzino admitted. 'An armed revolt might have succeeded at first, but the Emperor would never release his hold on the city. I chose to kill the man I hated instead, and give the people a chance to reclaim their freedom.'

'While you fled in the night, with a pouch full of coin and a belly full of vengeance.'

'You're wrong,' Lorenzino hissed. 'I brought down a tyrant. I freed Florence.'

'You killed one Medici, but the Palleschi are already replacing him with another.'

'So soon? Who? Who is it?'

Aldo enjoyed Lorenzino's dismay. 'I expect it will be Cosimo, the son of Maria Salviati.'

'But he's just a boy! He'll never rule Florence.'

'That's what the Palleschi are banking on, but he might surprise them.' Aldo pressed the stiletto against Lorenzino's neck again. 'We met Cosimo on the way here. He gave me a message for you.' Leaning closer, Aldo could see terror in Lorenzino's eyes. 'You can never return to Florence, never walk its streets again. If you do, you will be arrested, you will be tried and you will certainly be executed. You are banished from the city for the rest of your natural life. Do you understand?'

A hurried nod.

'One day, your rightful punishment will find you. It might be poison in your food, a knife in your back, or a serpent in your bed. You'll never be sure when that punishment is coming to claim you, but know that it will. So spend the rest of your days – however few they might be – looking over your shoulder, waiting for vengeance to find you.'

'Y-You're not going to kill me?'

Aldo gestured to Strocchi, who joined Aldo by the bed. They used sheets to bind Lorenzino round his ankles, wrists and elbows. A sour smell reached Aldo – at some point Lorenzino had lost control of himself. Aldo tied a gag across Lorenzino's mouth, silencing him. 'We'll be halfway to Florence when you're found in the morning, lying in your own piss.' Aldo spat in his face. 'That's for killing Dante because he helped me, and for putting me in Le Stinche. Be grateful Cosimo said to leave you alive, otherwise I'd do far worse.'

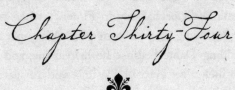

Chapter Thirty-Four

Thursday, January 11th

*B*indi arrived at the Podestà later than usual. Florence's new leader had decreed daily visits from the *segretario* were not necessary unless there was something exceptional to report. Two briefings a week would suffice. So be it. Bindi allowed himself the luxury of rising after dawn, lingering over his morning meal. After the ignominy of being mocked by the former Duke, this new leader had been a welcome relief. It was all quite pleasurable.

Less of a joy was finding a young constable – Benedetto, that was his name – pacing back and forth in the courtyard. '*Segretario*, I feared you must be ill.'

'Clearly, I am not,' Bindi replied, dismissing him with a gesture. But the constable followed him up the stairs, darting about as though he was an overeager pup.

'A young woman came to see you. I explained you weren't here, but she insisted.'

'I trust you had the good sense to send her away.'

'Oh. Is that what I should have done?'

Bindi paused at the top of the stairs, catching his breath. Each day the climb seemed steeper. 'Where is she now?'

'In your *officio*.'

The *segretario* stalked to the door and threw it open. A young woman of some twenty summers was sitting in front of his desk. She waited till he sank into his chair before speaking. '*Segretario*, my name is Rebecca Levi. I come seeking my late father's ledger.'

Levi, Levi, how was that name familiar? The moneylender, slain in his home. This must be the daughter. But why was she asking for a ledger? Ahh, the book Aldo presented as proof of a conspiracy against Duke Alessandro. The less said of that, the better. The stench of burnt leather billowed out every time he opened the desk drawer it was lurking in. 'I'm sorry, but the ledger is evidence in a matter before the Otto.'

The young woman's face crumpled. What on earth was the matter with her? 'Is it important evidence?' she asked, sniffing a little.

'All evidence is important,' Bindi lied. Having examined the ledger, he believed there was little of value inside – especially as the person it implicated had fled the city. All the ledger proved was that the *segretario* had failed to give Aldo's talk of a plot enough credence.

'I understand.' Her eyes were brimming now. 'It's just the ledger has great personal significance. It is one of the few examples of Father's writing left. To have it back would be . . .' She burst into tears, sobbing openly in front of him.

What on earth was he supposed to do? Bindi considered his options. The ledger was of no practical use to the Otto. There was an argument for having it gone from his *officio*, so nobody could use it as proof of negligent judgement. And surrendering it would rid him of this weeping woman. He pulled a key from his pocket and unlocked the desk drawer. The stomach-turning stench rose from the book, despite the rough cloths encasing it.

'The ledger was already damaged when it came into my posses-sion,' the *segretario* said, removing it from his drawer. 'If you have any complaints about its condition, I suggest you address those to Cesare Aldo, the officer who brought it here.'

The young woman nodded, wiping away her tears. 'Thank you.'

'I give this evidence into your safekeeping on the understanding it be made available if the Otto should require the ledger in the next few months.'

'Of course.'

Satisfied, Bindi let go of it. She clutched the ledger to her chest and rose, bowing to him, showing the respect his position deserved. Would that others did the same. Bindi nodded in magnanimous acknowledgement, watching her leave. Once she was gone he went to the shutters and threw them open, hoping to banish the acrid aroma the ledger had left behind.

Good riddance to the damned thing.

By the time dawn broke, Aldo and Strocchi were far enough away from Le Casette to stop worrying. They had ridden through the night, but much of that was at walking pace, letting their horses find a way in the thin moonlight. Aldo kept expecting to hear pursuers, but none came. He and Strocchi stopped in Bologna to eat and managed to find fresh horses. Aldo took the last of Saul's powders before they continued south. That would have to see him home.

He didn't want to consider what was waiting in Florence. Cerchi was full of bluster, but his most recent dark threats had sounded different. Setting those aside was easier while hunting for Lorenzino, when there'd been a chance of not making it back. Now the journey home had begun, Aldo knew he must face whatever evidence that *merda* had.

'Do you think we'll make it back today?' Strocchi asked.

'Perhaps.' The pain was ebbing away, the powders doing their job. Aldo could ride faster now, though he would suffer for it later.

'Didn't think we'd be home so soon. Tomasia has my bed until tomorrow.'

'Having met her, I suspect you'll be sleeping on the floor tonight.'

The constable frowned. 'There's something I've been wanting to ask.'

'If it's about Tomasia, you know as much as I do.'

'No, it's Lorenzino. Did you believe what he said about not having Levi slain?'

'He'd already confessed to killing the Duke. There was no reason for him to deny involvement with Levi's stabbing. One murder or two, the punishment's the same. But his conspiracy did succeed in distracting me from finding Levi's true killer.'

Strocchi nodded. 'So if Lorenzino's men didn't murder the moneylender, who did?'

The answer was obvious, but Aldo didn't want to give it voice. Not till he was certain.

Rebecca let Sciarra hammer at the door a while before opening it. The little moneylender shoved his way inside, coin jangling in his pouch. 'Well, where's this ledger then?' Sciarra demanded. 'I'm not giving you a single *giulio* till I see it.'

She went to a cupboard and retrieved the book, wrapped in several layers of fresh cloth to mask its burnt aroma. 'I'm not a fool, despite what you may think. Father spent a lifetime gathering the names in here. I know it has value far greater than your offer.'

Sciarra huffed out his cheeks, making a show of considering. 'I could give you . . . half as much again. But no more than that.' He folded his arms, trying to show certainty. Fool.

'For that amount I might as well keep it,' Rebecca replied, reaching to put the ledger back in the cupboard. She glimpsed panic in Sciarra's face. He would pay anything for it.

'Two thirds,' he said, the words hasty. 'But not a *giulio* more.'

Where were Joshua and the doctor? She would have to delay this grasping *bastardo* till they arrived. 'I want five times what you first offered.'

Sciarra sucked in breath between his teeth. 'Five times?'

'That's my final offer,' Rebecca said, enjoying his discomfort.

'I'd have to double my rates for a year to cover that.' He was still squirming as Joshua and Orvieto arrived. Sciarra protested their presence, but Rebecca ignored his whining.

'Are we agreed, or not?'

'Five times is too much,' Sciarra insisted. 'I could pay twice what I offered, here and now – with half as much again in three months. Is that not fair?'

'For what's inside this? No. But to be rid of you I'll accept it. Count your coin onto the table and you can have Father's ledger.' The moneylender did as he was told, his eyes never leaving the well-swaddled book. Finally, he reached out a hand for the ledger.

Rebecca hesitated. It was possible the Otto might demand the ledger back, if those who had killed Father stood trial. The chances of that ever happening seemed remote but, should such a day come, she would need a plausible tale to explain the ledger's absence. She could worry about that later, there was business to be done. She gave the ledger to Sciarra while Orvieto swept the coin from the table. Sciarra undid the wrappings, letting them fall to the floor, his eyes gleaming. But when he saw the ledger, disbelief clouded his face.

'What's this?'

'The ledger was stolen the night Father died. The thief tore out many pages and burnt the rest.' Rebecca didn't mention damaging the pages that had remained with her own hands.

'But this . . . this is useless! I can't read any of the names, the entries.'

'You bought the ledger. You never said it had to be intact.'

'You tricked me.' He reddened. 'I want my coin back – every last *giulio*!'

Joshua stepped in front of Sciarra, hands clenching into fists. 'Don't think you can threaten Rebecca. Anyone who hurts her will answer to me.'

Orvieto cleared his throat. 'What would it do to your reputation, Sciarra, if debtors heard you had reneged on a deal, properly made? How could they ever trust you?'

Sciarra seethed and spat curses before leaving, the ledger still in his grasp. Joshua shut the door as Rebecca burst out laughing. 'That's the first time I've been truly happy in days.'

'I hope you will find more to make you happy soon,' Joshua said.

'It's time you got back to work,' Orvieto said, guiding Joshua to the door. He left, but the doctor lingered. 'Have you made a decision about your feelings for Joshua?'

'I have,' Rebecca replied.

He nodded. 'I'm glad. Joshua will be studying with me for the rest of the day. Come and see us later. Let Joshua know your true feelings. No matter what you've decided, I'll be there to support both of you.'

It was late afternoon when Strocchi and Aldo crested the hill to see Florence below. They'd ridden hard and fast, racing to get back. The constable was surprised to realize he was happy to see Florence.

It wasn't home, not yet. But three days and nights on the road certainly had him craving his own bed.

'Once we get through Porta San Gallo, make sure you get the horses looked after,' Aldo said. 'We've ridden them too hard, they deserve to rest.'

'Of course. Where will you be?'

'Reporting to Palazzo Medici. Meet me at the Podestà after, and we'll go to via dei Giudei together.' Aldo urged his horse forwards. 'This ends tonight.'

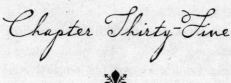

Chapter Thirty-Five

*M*aria had found the perfect place to watch those coming and going from Palazzo Medici. A comfortable chair on the middle level – opposite the main entrance – gave her a clear view of each arrival as they paused by the courtyard. Campana might decide who got an audience with her son, but Maria liked to see their faces. Most were court functionaries, or members of the Palleschi, men of little interest to her now Cosimo was the city's leader. But the arrival of Cesare Aldo, looking haggard and weary, was another matter.

She swept round the corner to meet Aldo on his way to Cosimo's private *officio*. 'I'd heard you weren't expected for another day. It seems the gossip was wrong, for once.'

'Congratulations on Cosimo's election,' Aldo replied. 'You must be proud.'

'What mother wouldn't be?' She stopped him outside the double doors, a hand on his arm. Aldo looked even more tired this close, and his clothes were ripe with the stench of horse. 'It's remarkable how quickly things can change, isn't it? Twelve days ago Cosimo and I were living in a crumbling *castello*, without prospects.'

'Now he's leader of Florence and its Dominion – a remarkable turn of events.'

Maria smiled. 'Cosimo won't forget your part in all of this.' She leaned closer to whisper in Aldo's ear. 'And your secret is safe with me.'

'And your secret is also safe with me,' he replied.

'My secret?'

'That while Lorenzino and his servants were murdering Alessandro, you were in the rooms directly above. You must have heard the Duke cry out for help, yet you did nothing.' She stepped back. 'I'm sure you had nothing to do with the murder,' Aldo continued. 'It was mere chance, a quirk of happenstance that you were so close by when the Duke was killed, leading to Cosimo – your son – replacing him. But there may be some who do not believe in such things as coincidence. Not in Florence.'

Maria saw him with new eyes, how ruthless he could be.

Aldo smiled. 'As I said, your secret is safe with me.' He glanced down at her hand, and she took it away, stepping aside to let him pass.

The *officio* was emptier than Aldo remembered, the walls where rich tapestries had hung now bare. No doubt that was a result of the looting Campana mentioned as Aldo arrived at the palazzo, but perhaps Cosimo had welcomed the chance to sweep away past excesses. Alessandro's grand desk was gone, replaced by something plainer and far less ornate.

Cosimo was wearing none of the silks and satins favoured by the dead Duke, opting for simple robes without ornamentation. The new leader of Florence stood at a window, staring out at the city that was now his to command, while Aldo described the encounter with Lorenzino. By the time Aldo finished his report, the last of the powders were wearing off, pain creeping into his voice and posture. Cosimo noticed the change.

'Is something troubling you?' he asked.

'It was a long ride back, and my shoulder is still sore from a recent injury.'

'I trust you can rest after this.'

'I hope so.'

'And what of Filippo Strozzi?' Cosimo stared out a window at the city. 'You said he was on his way to Bologna. Do you believe Strozzi plans a strike against Florence?'

'Perhaps. The death of Alessandro offers exiles like him a chance to reclaim the city.'

'True, but raising an army takes time,' Cosimo said, 'not to mention considerable funds. And winter is no season for launching an assault against a fortified city.'

'Your father taught you well,' Aldo observed.

The young man smiled. He gestured to a jug of wine on a table. 'Will you drink with me? To celebrate your return, and the success of your journey.'

'Thank you, but there are other matters I must attend before this day is done.'

Cosimo nodded his understanding. There was something else in his eyes – sadness, perhaps? To become leader of a city in such brisk circumstances would daunt any person of sense. Aldo did not doubt that Cosimo's mother had done everything she could to prepare her boy for this day, but he was less than eighteen, still becoming a man in many ways. Ruling Florence could be the making of Cosimo de' Medici – or the breaking of him.

Only time would reveal which awaited the city and its new leader. Aldo departed the *officio*, mustering what strength and will he had left for what lay ahead.

* * *

By the time Aldo reached the Podestà all relief from the powders was gone. Tired and sore to the bone, he found Strocchi and took him to Bindi's *officio*. The *segretario* was preparing to leave for the night, but agreed to hear their report, if brief – the shorter the better. Aldo wasted no time revealing Lorenzino's proud confession to murdering the Duke.

'Of course this matter will need to come before the Otto,' Bindi said, 'but that may take weeks, even months. If need be, Lorenzino and any *complice* can be judged in their absence. But it might be wise to let things settle first.' Knowing Bindi, it would be a private hearing. An official record would be kept, of course, because justice must be properly administered. But the citizens did not need to know. So be it.

Aldo bowed to the *segretario* on the way out, Strocchi following his example. As ever, Bindi had to have the final word. 'Good work, both of you. It's a shame you couldn't bring Lorenzino back to face the Otto himself, but there could still be a reward for this.'

'The *segretario* didn't ask about Levi's murderer,' Strocchi said as he and Aldo walked down the steps to the courtyard. 'He only wanted to know who killed Alessandro. He never even mentioned the other moneylender.'

'The killing of a Duke is important,' Aldo replied. 'The stabbing of two Jews matters far less to Bindi. I was only investigating Levi's death because Alessandro demanded it.' A familiar figure was lurking at the bottom of the stairs: Cerchi. Aldo stopped. 'You must be hungry. Go get something to eat. I'll see you at via dei Giudei by nightfall.'

Strocchi went on, nodding to Cerchi. Aldo waited till the constable was gone. He couldn't avoid this any longer, but there was no need for Strocchi to witness it.

* * *

Rebecca stepped from the house as dusk approached. Victory over Sciarra had been sweet, and the coin she took from him would make her choice of path easier. She strolled along via dei Giudei to the doctor's home. The door was open as usual, a murmur of voices drawing her to the back room. Orvieto was lighting a lantern while Joshua cleaned the doctor's knives.

'Good, you're here,' Orvieto said. 'Joshua has been applying himself well, we might make a healer of him yet.' The doctor leaned closer to her. 'Now is as good a time as any.'

Rebecca nodded, maintaining her smile despite a flutter of fear in her belly. Joshua wiped the last blade clean and placed it on the table by the others, before smiling at her with those beautiful warm brown eyes. 'Joshua, there's something I've wanted to say—'

'But you haven't had the chance,' he interrupted, taking her hands in his. 'We've hardly had a moment for us in days.' Joshua glanced at Orvieto watching them across the room.

'Don't mind me,' the doctor said, turning away to grind herbs with a pestle.

'But now seems the right time,' Rebecca began. 'I think we should—'

'Be my wife.'

'What?'

'Be my wife,' Joshua repeated. 'I want you to marry me.'

Rebecca couldn't speak for the roaring in her ears. She opened her mouth to speak, but nothing came out. No sound, nothing.

'I know it's too soon after your father's death,' Joshua continued, pacing back and forth in front of her. 'I know what people will say about us, but I don't care. I love you.' Still no words escaped her. 'All I need to know is that you want the same.' He stopped to look at her with those warm, brown eyes, those beautiful eyes. 'Well?'

Rebecca couldn't hold back her feelings any longer. 'Yes,' she gasped, bursting into tears of joy. 'Yes, I will marry you, Joshua. That's what I've decided too, that's what I came here to say. I want to be with you. I want to be your wife.'

'You look tired,' Cerchi said, his expression triumphant. 'Exhausted. Beaten.'

Aldo rubbed his right shoulder to ease the swollen joint. They were near the well in the centre of the Podestà. A few guards wandered the edges of the courtyard but were out of hearing. 'If you've something to say, spit it out. I have a murderer to arrest tonight.'

'That will have to wait.' A smirk curled Cerchi's thin lips. 'There was always something about you that bothered me, but I never knew what it was – until now.'

'Is it that I'm smarter than you, or a better officer than you'll ever be?'

'Enjoy your clever remarks while you can. From tonight you'll never sneer at me again. Not unless you wish to be revealed for what you are – a pervert. A *buggerone*.'

'Accusing a man without proof is a dangerous game.'

'I'm not playing,' Cerchi hissed. 'I have all the evidence I need, Aldo. Perverts like you and Corsini are a sickness that should be cut out of this city. Using other men or playing the woman for pleasure. You disgust me.'

Aldo had always known this day would come. But did it have to be Cerchi? 'What evidence? Have you beaten and tortured some poor soul into lying for you?'

Cerchi grinned, and Aldo knew all hope was lost. 'I didn't need to torture or beat anyone. They both made a *denunzia* against you of their own free will.'

One *denunzia* could be denied. But two – that was proof in the eyes of the law. Aldo's stomach was churning, threatening to empty itself. He needed to know who had accused him. Could Renato have succumbed to threats to protect himself? It was possible. But who else? There weren't that many who knew for certain what kind of man Aldo was. Robustelli would never break that confidence, but one of her women might say something without grasping its significance. To demand the names of his accusers would be seen as an admission of guilt. Better to maintain the pretence, and search for a way to escape this noose. Worry about who had signed the *denunzie* afterwards, assuming there was an afterwards. 'If you have the evidence you claim, why not take it to Bindi? Why haven't you arrested me?'

'I almost did a few days ago, but Lorenzino got you sent to Le Stinche before I could. No sooner were you released from prison than you got sent out into the Dominion. But your absence gave me time to consider, to think of a different *stratagemma*. I will arrest you one day, Cesare Aldo, but not yet. Instead, you're going to work for me. From this day you will give me half of every reward you earn, half of every bribe you take, and half of everything you make. You're mine now – and so are all the whores at that place you call home.' Aldo swallowed hard, mouth too dry even to moisten his lips. 'Don't think you can steal the *denunzie* from me,' Cerchi said. 'I've learned my lesson, after what happened with that diary. The *denunzie* are with someone you don't know. Challenge or threaten me in any way, and those documents will be given to the Otto. When the magistrates read them, you'll be hung from the gates, your body set on fire, and your ashes hurled into the Arno. That's what the likes of you deserve. But before that happens, I'm going to make your life a misery – and you're going to make me rich. Starting tonight.'

'Tonight?'

'I want my first payment.' Cerchi folded his arms, full of self-importance. 'It needn't be much. Just all the coin you have, and everything those whores earned today. Bring it to me on Ponte Vecchio, after dark – and come alone. I don't think you want Strocchi or anyone else knowing what kind of man you truly are, do you?'

Aldo hesitated before shaking his head.

'Ponte Vecchio.' Cerchi swaggered away. 'Don't make me wait.'

Chapter Thirty-Six

Joshua ran home to fetch his late grandmother's ring, leaving Rebecca with Dr Orvieto. He came to her, concern in his kind face. 'Are you sure this is what you want?'

'Yes. Yes, it is.' She couldn't seem to stop smiling. After being so unhappy for so long, to know such joy – it was making her head dizzy. Her legs seemed close to collapse, but Orvieto got her to a chair in time. He crouched in front of her, taking both hands in his. 'I made my mind up on Monday, but I wanted to be sure before saying anything. And I wanted to wait until I finished sitting *shiva*, out of respect for Father.'

The doctor nodded. 'You didn't wish to break with his wishes while mourning him.'

Rebecca frowned. 'What I'm doing, is it wrong? Am I being selfish?'

'It may sound harsh, but your father is dead and gone. This is your life now. You must decide what is best for you. I saw how happy you were when Joshua asked you to marry him. This is the right path for you. He's a good man with a good heart. He would do anything to protect you.'

'I know.'

Time passed yet Joshua didn't return. Had he changed his mind? It seemed unlikely, but anything was possible. Marrying him had seemed out of all question a few days ago, and now . . . The sound of footsteps approaching quelled Rebecca's fear. She stood to face him, but it wasn't Joshua in the doorway.

'Cesare? You look terrible,' Orvieto said. He was right, the officer seemed spent, pain and worry etched in his face. The doctor helped him to a chair.

'I've brought something for you,' Aldo said, pulling a letter from his tunic. Rebecca realized it was for her. 'From your cousin in Bologna.'

She took the letter, reading it while Orvieto tended to Aldo. Her cousin was worried about Rebecca being alone in Florence. Ruth had spoken with her father and convinced him that Rebecca should move to Bologna and learn to run the family moneylending business alongside Ruth. Shimon was more than ready to step aside. Together the two cousins could make a success of things, Ruth felt certain of that – if it was what Rebecca wanted.

She would have to write back to Ruth with her own news. There would be no new life in Bologna, not when a life of happiness with Joshua was beckoning.

Aldo rose from the chair. He wanted to tell Saul about the Cerchi's threat, to seek counsel, but that wasn't possible with Levi's daughter there. Instead he'd have to put an end to all the questions about what had happened ten nights ago. It was past time for that.

'When I was guarding Samuele on the road back from Bologna,' Aldo began, 'I asked who wanted him dead – but he wouldn't say. When we got back here to Florence, Samuele insisted he was safe inside the city – but he was murdered a few hours later. That happened not long after he argued with you, Rebecca. Dante witnessed you leaving the house.'

'I didn't see him,' she said, confusion on her face.

Orvieto put an arm round her shoulders. 'You were probably upset.'

'Dante had hired bandits to kill Samuele on the road from Bologna,' Aldo continued, 'but they failed. Dante was relieved to discover Samuele had made it back alive.'

Rebecca nodded. 'He told me that, and how sorry he was for what he'd done.'

'After you told Joshua about the argument, he chose to confront Samuele. Joshua saw a man carrying your father's ledger away, and then found Samuele's body inside the house.'

'That's when he stepped in Father's blood.'

'Yes,' Aldo agreed, 'but the man who stole the ledger didn't murder Samuele. I believe Samuele was already dead or dying when the intruder entered your home. I didn't realize that for a long time, and my mistake had me chasing the wrong men for days.'

'If the thief didn't kill Samuele, who did?' Orvieto asked.

Aldo paced the room to keep his weary legs moving. 'Before I could answer that, there were other questions that needed asking. For a start, who had a reason to kill Samuele? Who had the opportunity to murder him, and who gained from his death? Rebecca, you were angry at your father – but you were with Joshua's family when Samuele was murdered.'

'I could never have killed Father,' she said. 'You should be talking to Aaron Sciarra. He hated Father and coveted his business. Sciarra stands to gain from Father's murder.'

'Yes, he does, and he had reason to kill your father – but Sciarra lacks the courage. And there's another reason why Sciarra wasn't the killer: whoever murdered Samuele had considerable skill with a blade.' Aldo stopped, staring at the knives laid out on the table.

Rebecca laughed. 'You can't think Dr Orvieto had anything to do with it.'

Aldo looked at him. 'No. Saul fights to save lives, not to take them.'

'Besides, I was tending to Moise Bassano all that night, so . . .' Orvieto's face fell. He must have realized what was coming. 'Cesare, stop. You need not go any further with this.'

'I'm sorry,' Aldo replied. 'Truly, I am.'

'Sorry about what?' Rebecca asked.

Orvieto came to Aldo, anxiety in his eyes. 'Let me take Rebecca home before you say anything else. Please, she doesn't need to be a witness to this.'

Joshua burst into the room, carrying a silver ring. 'Sorry I took so long,' he gasped between breaths. 'I couldn't find it, until one of my sisters reminded me—' He stopped, everyone staring at him. 'Is something wrong?' Aldo went round Orvieto to face Joshua.

'Tell me, what happened the night that Samuele was murdered?'

'I-I've already said. Rebecca came to see me, upset about an argument with her father, the hurtful things he'd said. I went to talk with him, but when I got there—'

'Samuele was already dead.'

'Yes.' Joshua appeared innocent, but there was a tremble in his voice.

'I don't believe you,' Aldo said. 'Samuele was already spoiling for a fight when you arrived to confront him. There was an argument, it got out of hand – and you stabbed him. Maybe you didn't mean to, maybe it was an accident. You panicked and fled from the house. It was after curfew, so nobody saw. But then you remembered the knife. Was it one you had borrowed from here, or one you always carried? Either way, you realized that the knife would betray you, so you went back for it. That's when you saw the thief leaving with the ledger.'

'This is . . .' Joshua spluttered, turning to Rebecca. 'You can't think . . .'

'You went back inside to get the blade,' Aldo continued. 'That's when you stepped in Samuele's blood. What happened to the knife, Joshua? Did you throw it in the river?'

Orvieto was staring at the blades on the table, unable to look at his student. 'You told me you'd lost it.'

Joshua knelt down in front of Rebecca, taking her hands in his own. 'They're wrong. You know that, don't you? I could never hurt anyone you love. You have to believe that.'

She didn't speak, perhaps she couldn't speak. Aldo doubted he would know what to say if he was in her place. Joshua stood, twisting round to face Aldo.

'It was an accident, I swear it. I never meant to hurt Samuele. I stopped here on my way to confront him, hoping Dr Orvieto would talk me out of it – but he was elsewhere, busy with a patient I suppose.' Joshua went to the table covered in blades. 'The knife was to make Samuele see sense, that's all. But he came at me and—'

'It'll be a cold night out there tonight,' Strocchi said as he strolled in. 'Some of the stones in the street are already icy.' He stopped in the doorway. 'Am I late?'

Joshua grabbed a blade from the table and swung it round, slicing the air. Rebecca screamed as Orvieto shielded her. Aldo raised both hands, voice hushed. 'Strocchi, step aside. Let Joshua leave, if that's what he wants.' The constable glared at Aldo. 'Carlo, do as I say.'

Strocchi moved to one side. Joshua hesitated, sorrow twisting his face.

'Rebecca, I'm so sorry,' he whispered. Then he bolted from the room.

Strocchi raced after Joshua without hesitation, ignoring voices shouting behind him. They couldn't have a madman roaming the city with a knife. Thankfully it was close to curfew, and via dei Giudei was near empty. Joshua was ten paces ahead, racing north towards the Arno, close to reaching the junction with Borgo San Jacopo.

Strocchi yelled at people to clear the way. Nobody else need get hurt. He was closing the gap – eight paces, six. Joshua glanced back, panic in his eyes. He didn't see the cart rolling across Borgo San Jacopo in front of him, pushed by a butcher's boy.

'Look out!' Strocchi yelled.

Joshua slipped and fell, legs going out from underneath him on an icy puddle. There was a fearful crack and Joshua screamed, grasping at his right leg. Even in the dim light, Strocchi could see stark white bone stabbing through Joshua's hose. The fugitive tried to get back up but collapsed to the stones again, crying out in pain and anguish, the knife still in his grasp.

Strocchi moved closer but Joshua brandished the blade at him. 'Stay back!'

The butcher's boy was staring in horror. Strocchi sent him to the doctor's house. 'Tell them Joshua's hurt! Hurry!' By the time Aldo arrived with Orvieto, Joshua was weeping and howling, overcome by pain or something worse.

Aldo approached Joshua, empty hands raised. 'You don't have to suffer like this. Put the knife down so Saul can tend to your leg.'

A young woman came hurrying along via dei Giudei, the same

young woman who had been in the doctor's home. Strocchi moved to stop her getting any closer. She saw what had happened to Joshua and howled in anguish.

'It's what I deserve,' Joshua sobbed at her. 'Rebecca, I'm sorry . . .'

A strange calm fell across his face, the same calm Strocchi had seen in Agnolotti Landini before the merchant jumped to his death. 'No,' Strocchi shouted, 'don't do it!'

Joshua stabbed the blade into his own neck, slicing up to the jawline. Strocchi heard the young woman screaming, and the cries of dismay from Aldo and Orvieto, but he couldn't take his eyes from Joshua. Blood spurted from the wound, soaking Joshua's tunic a vivid crimson within moments. He gasped wordlessly before slumping over.

Strocchi turned away. Another senseless death.

What was wrong with people in this city?

Aldo watched Saul lead a distraught Rebecca away before dealing with Joshua's body. The butcher's cart held only a few barrels; the boy had been fetching water to wash waste from the butcher shops on Ponte Vecchio into the river. Aldo sent the pale, shivering youth home before helping Strocchi load Joshua's corpse onto the cart. 'Take him to the Podestà, and leave the body there. Bindi will no doubt want a full report, but it can wait till tomorrow.'

Strocchi nodded. 'So this man was the one who stabbed Samuele Levi.'

Aldo nodded. At least Joshua's death had been swift. 'Don't go over Ponte Vecchio, it'll be bloody enough by this time of day. Ponte alla Carraia should be clear.'

'You're not coming with me?'

'There's something else I need to do.' As Strocchi had pushed the cart away, Aldo strode in the other direction. He had to make things right before facing Cerchi. He had to try.

Aldo knocked at the Levi home, and Orvieto answered the door. He looked exhausted, his face strained, anger all too evident in those hazel eyes. 'You can't see Rebecca. I've given her something to help her sleep, though I doubt she will. Not after what's happened.'

'I came to see you, Saul.'

'Why?'

'To say I'm sorry. I never meant for that to . . .' Aldo stopped, unable to hold the doctor's stern gaze. 'I never meant to hurt Rebecca, or you.'

'I asked you to stop. I pleaded with you to let me bring Rebecca home before you accused Joshua. She didn't need to see his shame. She didn't need to see him die.'

'I couldn't know that would happen—'

'But it did!'

Aldo stepped back, stung by the fury in Orvieto's voice. Maybe this was for the best. Maybe the two of them had been a foolish whim from the start. At least if they were apart, Saul could be in no danger from what was to come. He would be safe.

That was something.

'She was going to marry him,' Orvieto said. 'Joshua asked Rebecca to be his wife not long before you arrived, and she agreed. I'd never seen her so happy. But this . . .' The doctor straightened his shoulders. 'Her cousin was offering a new life, a new beginning in Bologna. I imagine she will go there, once all this is settled. There is certainly nothing left here for Rebecca, nothing but sorrow and unhappy memories. Not after tonight.'

Aldo nodded. He heard a sound behind him. No doubt neighbours were watching, listening to what was being said. He looked at Orvieto one last time, before limping away.

It had gone curfew.

Cerchi would be waiting.

Aldo went to the *bordello*, retrieving a pouch of coin hidden in the wall behind his bed. He didn't ask Robustelli or her women for their earnings – they shouldn't pay for his mistakes. Then he limped towards Ponte Vecchio, dread gnawing at him.

He'd brought this on himself. No, that wasn't true, not completely. But no matter what he did, no matter whom he loved, this day had always been coming. Enforcing laws in a city where how he loved made him criminal had been a stone in his boot for too long. It was galling enough to face punishment for that. For Cerchi to be the executioner, that was what bit and tore and ate at him most.

Aldo staggered onto the bridge, boots slipping on the blood as cold air hardened the crimson swill to ice. Cerchi was waiting at the highest part of the bridge. Thumbs tucked into his belt either side of the silver buckle, one foot tapping the stones. 'Where have you been?'

'There was a death in Oltrarno—'

'Show me my coin.'

Aldo's shoulders sagged, the last twelve days weighing heavy. Going to Bologna to guard Levi, and the bandit attack on the way back. Sleepless nights struggling to solve the moneylender's murder, when his killer had been in plain view. Those failed efforts to stop Lorenzino's conspiracy, and the bloody, painful days in Le Stinche. Another journey north, more frustrations, more exhaustion – all for nothing, yet all leading to this.

He pulled out the pouch and Cerchi snatched it away. 'Is that all you've got?' Cerchi shoved the pouch into his tunic. 'I expect at least this much again tomorrow.'

'Tomorrow?'

'Unless you want those *denunzie* given to Bindi, you'll do whatever it takes.'

Aldo shook his head, letting all his exhaustion show. 'Please, you mustn't . . .'

Cerchi placed his hands on Aldo's shoulders. 'You don't want anyone seeing you like this, do you?' Aldo shook his head. Then the *bastardo* slammed a knee into Aldo's stomach, doubling him over. He crumpled to the bloody stones, coughing, choking. If he'd eaten in the last few hours, it would be spattered all over the stones. Cerchi strutted past.

'I should have guessed what kind of man you are much sooner, I suppose, but you did a good job of hiding your perversion. Then I heard how your name was the last thing that *buggerone* Corsini said before he died, and it put the idea in my head. The more I thought about it, the more things made sense.'

'Corsini was only ever my informant,' Aldo gasped.

'I don't care,' Cerchi snarled. 'And you certainly have more urgent things to worry about. More than your pathetic life is at stake now.'

Keep him talking, find out what he knows. 'What do you mean?'

'I've been talking to young Benedetto. He doesn't seem like much, but he watches and listens. It was Benedetto who noticed how fond you are of that Jewish doctor, what's his name – Orvieto?' Cerchi loomed over Aldo. 'The doctor – he's like you, isn't he? Tell me, does the Jew like to put it inside you, or do you put it into him?'

'You're wrong about him,' Aldo insisted, his voice sounding

feeble in the cold night air, his body still hunched over on the bloody stones. Cerchi strolled away again.

'Maybe, but a *denunzia* directed against the doctor would certainly destroy him. Do you want that on your conscience? Assuming the likes of you even has a conscience?'

Aldo had heard enough. More than enough. Bad enough to be abused like this by Cerchi, but nobody else should have to suffer the same. 'Please, don't do this,' Aldo said, sounding as weak and vulnerable as possible.

Cerchi returned, stopping in front of him again. 'I'll do whatever I want. And as of tonight, you'll do whatever I say, whenever I say it. From now on, you're my whore.'

Aldo slid the stiletto from his boot and buried it in Cerchi's torso.

The *merda* gasped, disbelief filling his face. Aldo rose, abandoning all his pretence, one hand still gripping the stiletto. Staring Cerchi in the eyes, Aldo twisted the blade a quarter turn. 'You didn't think I was actually going to let the likes of you control me, did you?'

Cerchi staggered back, freeing himself from the blade, hands clutching at his ribs. Blood was soaking through his tunic. Cerchi lurched to the side of the bridge, leaning on the parapet for support. Aldo followed, glancing round to be sure no one was watching. Curfew had emptied the streets, and clouds covered the moon.

Aldo grabbed hold of Cerchi, wiping the bloody stiletto on his tunic before reaching inside to reclaim the money pouch.

Cerchi shook his head, that ugly mouth gasping for air. 'But you—'

One hard shove in the chest, and Cerchi toppled over the side of Ponte Vecchio, arms flailing. He fell into the water below and sank beneath its surface. The river claimed him. Aldo returned the stiletto to his boot before strolling away, stepping around the spilled blood and rancid offcuts that littered the bridge. Come morning, the butchers' boys would wash all of it into the Arno, along with any evidence of what had happened here tonight.

Cesare Aldo took no pleasure from killing, but sometimes it was necessary.

Historical Note

City of Vengeance is a work of fiction, but the story is based in part upon real incidents and people. Lorenzino de'Medici did murder his cousin Alessandro, the Duke of Florence, though historians disagree whether it happened on Saturday, January 6th, or the night before. According to several accounts of the killing, Scoronconcolo helped Lorenzino, while some versions of history suggest the pair were assisted by a young man known as Il Freccia.

Scoronconcolo stayed at his master's side for several years after the murder, until Lorenzino dismissed Scoronconcolo and his other companions for insolence. Lorenzino never returned to Florence, living in exile for eleven years and publishing his *Apologia* about the murder of Alessandro. The Duke's killer was himself murdered in Venice, though on whose orders is still disputed.

Cosimo de' Medici moved the official ducal residence out of Palazzo Medici within three years of his election, and the building was sold to the Riccardi family during the seventeenth century. Like many other grand buildings in Florence, the Palazzo Medici Riccardi is now a museum open to visitors most days of the year.

The Jewish community was relocated from via dei Giudei across the Arno to a ghetto near the centre of Florence in 1571, decades after Jews in other Italian cities were forced into such enclosures. The street in Oltrarno that was via dei Giudei is now called via de Ramaglianti.

The Palazzo del Podestà became known as the Bargello in 1574 when the city's Capitano di Giustizia was stationed there. Large sections of the building were converted into prisons that remained in use until the nineteenth century. The Bargello became a museum in 1865, and now houses a collection of sculptures by Donatello and other artists among its treasures.

The prison called Le Stinche stood for five hundred years in the eastern quarter of Florence, before being demolished in the nineteenth century. Teatro Verdi theatre now stands on that site.

If you would like to read about Duke Alessandro de' Medici, Catherine Fletcher's book *The Black Prince of Florence* is without equal. To discover more about his killer, *The Duke's Assassin* by Stefano Dall'Aglio is the comprehensive work on Lorenzino.

Acknowledgements

*T*his novel has been a long time coming, so there are too many people to thank – apologies in advance to anyone I omit. The initial spark for *City of Vengeance* came from a monograph by historian John K. Brackett, *Criminal Justice and Crime in Late Renaissance Florence 1537–1609*. I was struck by its compelling description of how the Florentine criminal justice was similar to modern police procedure in many ways, and yet still starkly different.

Brackett's work inspired years of further reading. Eventually I realized my research had become as much an excuse to delay writing as a means for enabling it. Two things helped overcome that inertia. The first was starting a PhD in Creative Writing at Lancaster University. My supervisor until 2020 was Professor George Green, who helped bring rigour and discipline to this narrative, asking difficult questions and nudging me to dig deeper.

The second event to accelerate my efforts was a Robert Louis Stevenson Fellowship award from the Scottish Book Trust and Creative Scotland. That gave me a month in France during the summer of 2017, where I drafted the first fifty pages of this novel. Without that opportunity, I fear it would have taken me much longer to finish *City of Vengeance*.

I also must thank the Bloody Scotland crime fiction festival in Stirling. I won its Pitch Perfect competition in 2018, using the pseudonym C. O. Vollmer to spare any blushes. That early vote of encouragement gave a welcome boost as the first draft neared completion.

Numerous friends have helped by giving advice, reading sections of the manuscript, or simply offering encouragement along the way. Special thanks go to Nell Pattison and Liz King from Creative Thursday at the 2016 Theakston's Old Peculier Crime Festival in Harrogate; to my colleagues Laura Lam and Daniel Shand on the creative writing programme at Edinburgh Napier University for their patience; to Tamar Hodos for reading and reassurance; and to my former colleague Sam Boyce for being part of this journey over many, many years.

I am indebted to everyone at Pan Macmillan for making *City of Vengeance* look so resplendent, and read so well – any errors that remain are my fault alone. Special thanks to editor Alex Saunders, whose insightful notes made the novel so much the better.

Being represented by the wonderful literary agent Jenny Brown is a blessing, and one for which I am ever grateful. Her enthusiasm for Aldo and my writing is a continuing boon.

But most of all I must thank my wife, Alison. Without her support and encouragement this book would not exist. Thank you!

Read on for an extract from book two
in the Cesare Aldo series . . .

The Darkest Sin

BY D. V. BISHOP

Statement by Cesare Aldo,
officer of the Otto di Guardia e Balia:

I was at the visitors' parlour of Santa Maria Magdalena on a personal matter when I heard a scream from inside the convent. It was shrill, the sound of shock and horror. Another voice cried out: 'Murder! Murder!' The internal door of the parlour was opened as a nun ran past, her face stricken. 'Blood, there's so much blood—' Her words stopped, I do not know why.

I persuaded a young woman staying at the convent to let me into the main courtyard. I was familiar with the interior, having come to Santa Maria Magdalena on court business the previous day, Palm Sunday. Nuns were gathering at the north-west corner of the cloister. Several were comforting a novice who had blood on both her hands. She was trembling, her face ashen. I later learned she had made the initial discovery.

The novice directed me inside, saying what she found was on the left.

I went through the doors, passing entrances for the convent kitchen and a latrina. *The third door on the left was ajar, the smell of fresh blood strong in the air, but the floor around the entrance was clean. I pushed the door open. Inside was the scriptorium where nuns copy and illuminate holy texts. Unlit candles stood on each desk next to brushes and pots of ink. A single lantern hung from the ceiling, its light revealing the bloody mess below.*

I was not surprised that the novice had screamed.

A body was sprawled across the stones, naked and bathed in blood. More blood spread out from the corpse, pooling across the floor. I cannot recall having ever seen so much around a single body. There were numerous stab wounds, at least a dozen to the chest and torso, but it was the face that had suffered most. This had been a frenzied attack, a work of hatred.

One more thing about the naked corpse discovered inside the convent caught the eye.

It was male.

Chapter One

Sunday, March 25th 1537

*L*iving in a *bordello* spared Cesare Aldo from religion most Sundays. While most of Florence went to church, Signora Tessa Robustelli and her women stayed in bed recovering from the night before. Once Mass was concluded, men would soon return to the humble building at Piazza della Passera, south of the Arno. But this was Palm Sunday, the first day of Holy Week. Special Masses were taking place across the city to celebrate one of the most important times in the Church year, with many parishes holding processions to mark the day Jesus entered Jerusalem. If there was one thing Robustelli could not resist, it was a procession.

'Clodia! Elena! Matilde!' she shouted as Aldo came downstairs. 'We haven't got all morning!' The buxom *matrona* was wearing her finest brocade gown, a blue shawl draped across her bosom in a rare show of modesty. 'I'd like to see the procession this year!'

'Coming, signora!' playful voices chorused above, between giggles.

Robustelli eyed Aldo's plain tunic and hose. 'I take it you're not joining us.' She pointed to the stiletto tucked in his left boot, its hilt visible beside his calf. 'Father Anselmo doesn't approve of his flock bringing blades to church.'

'Father Anselmo approves of very little,' Aldo replied, 'but I doubt anyone will bring a blade to Mass.' Carrying weapons had been banned in Florence since Cosimo de' Medici replaced his murdered cousin Alessandro as the city's leader in January. Cosimo had not yet seen eighteen summers, but he was no fool. He remained vulnerable until his election as leader was confirmed by the Holy Roman Emperor, Charles V. An edict restricting weapons within the city certainly lessened the likelihood of an armed uprising by those eager to see Florence return to being a republic. Only those enforcing the law, Cosimo's own guard and the city militia were allowed to carry weapons. Being an officer of the Otto di Guardia e Balia, the most feared criminal court in Florence, meant Aldo could retain his trusty stiletto. He was grateful for that. The blade had saved his life more than once.

'Are you coming or not?' Robustelli asked.

'Not today. I'm due at the Podestà.'

The *matrona* nodded, her attention shifting to a young woman bouncing down the stairs. 'No, Clodia, that won't do. Go and cover yourself properly.'

'Why?' Clodia pouted. Her nipples pressed against the thin lace of her flimsy top, demanding attention. 'I'm proud of my body. Why do I have to hide it?'

'Because we're going to church,' Robustelli replied, 'not an orgy.'

Leaving them to argue, Aldo stepped out of the *bordello*. It was not yet mid-morning, but the sun was already touching the stones of Piazza della Passera. The days were getting longer, and warmer too. Aldo breathed in, savouring the aroma of bread baking in some nearby oven. It had been a hard winter, but spring had come early this year, bringing fresh life to the city. It was a pleasure to be alive.

Aldo strode away, heading east. Warmer days meant less pain from his unreliable left knee, so it had no need of remedies or salves. But he still cut north into via dei Giudei, the narrow street where most of Florence's small Jewish community lived. A door stood open among the houses on the left, beckoning him into the home of Doctor Saul Orvieto. How easy it would be to go inside. Aldo missed Saul, his warm hazel eyes, the ease of their friendship. But they had parted on bad terms, sundered by duty and bloodshed.

Better to keep walking. Safer for both of them.

At the end of via dei Giudei Aldo turned east again, striding towards Ponte Vecchio. This approach to the bridge was usually crowded with the stalls selling fish, vegetables and fruit. After a long, barren winter the produce was inviting again, no more frost-bitten brassica or wizened citrus. But this was Sunday, the Lord's Day, when most shops and stalls were shut. Palm Sunday processions elsewhere helped to make Aldo's progress brisk.

Aldo marched up the steady rise of Ponte Vecchio, pausing at the bridge's highest point where a gap between buildings allowed a view of the river. The water was mottled with *merda*, dyes and other liquids that drained into it from workshops. Florentines threw almost anything into the Arno. Even corpses went in the water sometimes, victims consigned to the river by those eager to banish the proof of their crimes. If a killer was lucky, or the current strong enough, a body could float miles downriver before eventually washing ashore. But most got caught on the weirs between bridges, giving river rats a chance to feast on the rotting flesh until the remains were pulled out. Aldo turned away from the Arno with a shiver.

After leaving the bridge he cut a ragged path north-east, careful to avoid larger piazze where processions were gathering before Mass. He reached the Palazzo del Podestà early, the forbidding brick fortress looming ahead of him, its stone bell-tower pointing at the sky. In a city full of beautiful buildings, the Podestà was an ugly brute, all sharp edges and glowering menace. That outward appearance matched its inner workings as home to the Otto. Little of beauty occurred within these walls. The few windows facing out were too high to offer any respite in the bleak stone. The fortress had stood for hundreds of years, and doubtless would remain for hundreds more. From here laws were enforced and those found guilty of breaking them faced judgement from the Otto's magistrates.

Inside the Podestà was an imposing courtyard, a wide stone staircase running up one wall to the *loggia* that led to the court's administrative area. A cold breeze chilled Aldo even as he paused next to the one wall touched by the sun. It was always cold inside the Podestà, regardless of the month. But Aldo's unease stemmed from the men he saw at the top of the stairs: Bindi and Ruggerio. No good ever came of them sharing words.

Massimo Bindi was *segretario* to the Otto. In theory that made him simply the court's administrator, a bureaucratic functionary whose sole purpose was to assist the magistrates. But the Florentine practice of replacing the entire bench every few months meant the *segretario* was the court's most powerful constant, able to wield considerable influence over rulings. Magistrates came and went but the bloated Bindi remained. Every day Aldo had to report to Bindi, and every day it darkened his mood.

The *segretario* was a self-serving creature who clutched his power in a clammy fist, but the man opposite him was far more dangerous. Girolamo Ruggerio was a silk merchant, among the leaders of that powerful guild, and a leading figure within the Company of Santa Maria, a confraternity with considerable influence in the Church. More than that, Ruggerio was a cunning creature capable of having anyone he deemed a threat destroyed. A few months before,

Ruggerio learned a young lover had written of their trysts in a diary. The youth was beaten to death on Ruggerio's orders. When an investigation by the Otto came close to identifying Ruggerio, he made the men who had killed for him confess. They did so without hesitation, yet kept his secret safe. Such was the power Ruggerio wielded. Blood never touched his hands – he was too clever for that.

Aldo watched the *segretario* bow low, not easy with a belly so rotund. Ruggerio had no direct authority at the Otto, yet Bindi could not help giving way. It was sickening, but not a surprise. Ruggerio swept down the wide stone stairs, the morning sun glinting off his smooth and hairless scalp. Satisfaction twisted his thin lips into a smirk, while silk robes billowed around him, the rich blue fabric adorned with fine golden embroidery. Aldo gave a small nod as Ruggerio approached. 'Signor.'

The merchant paused two steps from the bottom to look down on Aldo. 'Have we met?' Ruggerio asked. They had, but still the merchant forced Aldo to introduce himself. Everything was a joust with Ruggerio, a *stratagemma*.

'In January, when I helped find those responsible for the murder of a youth called Corsini. Two of your guards confessed to killing him,' Aldo said.

Ruggerio nodded, as if it were a distant memory, long forgotten. 'Ahh, yes. One died soon after in a prison brawl, while the other was left with the mind of an *idiota*.'

Aldo had been part of that brawl, the only one to escape with his life and wits still intact. No doubt Ruggerio knew that too. 'Le Stinche is a dangerous place. Full of criminals.'

'Quite.' The merchant studied Aldo a moment longer before descending the final two steps. 'I believe the *segretario* had a matter for your attention. I hope you will pursue it with the same vigour and fortitude as you do other matters.' Ruggerio strolled away, leaving Aldo to ponder the threat behind that farewell. A shout from above demanded his attention.

'Come to my *officio*,' Bindi called, gesturing him up the stairs.

Aldo grimaced. How little it took to sour a beautiful spring day.

Ponte a Signa had been Carlo Strocchi's whole world when he was a boy. It didn't matter that a much bigger town was just across the Arno, over the same bridge that gave Ponte a Signa its name. And he didn't care about the boats coming downriver from Florence, taking cargo west towards Pisa. Strocchi hadn't been interested in either city then, not when everyone he cared for was in the small village nestling by a bend in the river.

True, Ponte a Signa was little more than a huddle of simple houses and dirt roads, but that was enough. There were several large palazzi up in the hills, owned by merchants who only came in the scorching summer months to escape the city. The rest of the year their grand houses stood empty, villagers trudging up the hill to clean empty rooms or tend the unappreciated gardens. To Strocchi, the palazzi seemed to sneer at those below, judging them. His friends often claimed it was possible to see all the way to Florence from the palazzi – Strocchi hadn't cared. Ponte a Signa was enough for him.

That changed the week his papa died, collapsing in the garden behind their humble home. Father Coluccio gave Papa the last rites, and he slipped away that night. Strocchi had seen only seventeen summers; now he was the man of the house. But he had no talent for farming, and no siblings to help tend their rented field. Three years of hard work brought only diminishing returns. The land couldn't support Mama and him, not the way it had when Papa was alive. Strocchi admitted defeat after a spring flood took their meagre crop. Reluctantly, he left home, walking to Florence in search of work, promising to send coin whenever he could.

That was a year ago. Now Strocchi was coming home for his first visit. But as the constable got close, he almost didn't recognize Ponte a Signa. It looked so small. A few drab buildings clustered beside the Arno, the houses crumbling and neglected, dirt roads overgrown by weeds. This was where he'd had so many adventures as a boy. It had been a happy place for the most part, a community of friendly folk who smiled when they met.

Now the village looked wizened, broken. Desolate. Not at all how Strocchi had described it to his travelling companion. They had ridden from Florence on a hired horse, before entrusting the animal to the local ostler and walking into the village.

People in doorways glared at the new arrivals. Was that due to suspicion, or envy? Strocchi looked down at his clothes, at the new tunic he had bought before leaving Florence, eager to show he'd made a success of himself. The sin of pride coloured his cheeks. *Sancto Spirito*, what kind of welcome should he expect from Mama? He had been a good son, sending home all the coin he could spare, along with letters he struggled to write. Hopefully, Mama had taken those to Father Coluccio to read for her. Hopefully.

Strocchi rounded a corner and his mood lifted. The early spring flowers Mama grew every year were blossoming outside the house, their colours a joy to soften the hardest heart. The front door stood open, welcoming all. He could hear Mama humming inside, no doubt making a hearty Sunday stew, brought to life with torn shreds of basil and a generous splash of olive oil. Yes, there was the familiar smell, making his mouth water.

He was home.

'It's just like you described,' his travelling companion said.

Strocchi nodded, the smile returning to his face. 'Yes, it is.' They strolled on side by side, until Strocchi stopped a few paces short of the door. 'Would you mind if I went in first? I haven't seen Mama for so long, and—'

'Of course. I'll wait out here. Call me when you're ready.'

'Thank you.' Strocchi took a deep breath and ventured in. He paused at the doorway, letting his eyes adjust to the darker interior. Should he knock? No, that was foolish. This was still his home, even if he'd been away for a year. 'Mama? Mama, it's me – Carlo.'

'Carlo?' The sound of her voice was so warm, so welcoming. Strocchi hadn't realized how much he had missed her. It was an urgent tug at his chest, a pull so strong his eyes were brimming and his chin trembling a little.

'Yes, Mama,' was all he could say.

She appeared from the kitchen, wiping both hands on her apron, those sharp blue eyes staring at him. Then she flung out her arms and they were hugging and sobbing and laughing, all at the same time. Mama took his face in her hands and kissed him, tears of joy spilling down her rosy cheeks. 'My *bambino* is home! My boy, my boy, come back at last! Oh, how I've missed you, Carlo. Things haven't been the same since you left. Why didn't you send word you were coming? I would've made your favourite, if I had known.'

She stepped back, looking him up and down. 'Don't they feed you in the city? You're nothing but bones, *bambino*. What have you been eating?' Mama reached forward, rubbing the material of his new tunic between thumb and fingers. 'Spending all your coin on clothes. Since when did you become fond of such finery?'

Carlo laughed. He had been gone a year, was now a constable for a powerful court in Florence, and yet nothing had changed. He still couldn't get a word in.

'What's so funny?' she demanded, a playful twinkle in her eyes. 'I suppose you think your old mama is not good enough for you now?'

'No, Mama.'

'Quite right,' she said, grabbing hold of his hands. 'Come into the kitchen and tell me all about the city. Now that you're back, I want to hear everything—'

'Mama, wait.' Strocchi stopped her before she could go any further. 'I sent coin, and letters by messenger. They swore on the Bible each one reached you. Didn't you get them?'

She nodded. 'Yes, yes. I put the coin in a pot, up on the high shelf in the kitchen, you know the one. It's waiting there for you, all of it.'

'No, the coin was for you, Mama. To help you.'

She frowned. 'Why would I need help? I have all I need, now my *bambino* is home.'

'Well, did you take my letters to Father Coluccio?'

'The first few, yes. But I didn't like to bother him.'

More likely she was embarrassed at having to ask the parish priest to read them for her. As if Father Coluccio didn't do that for other villagers already. Strocchi had feared she wouldn't ask for the priest's help. It meant she hadn't heard what was in the latest letter. Strocchi guided her to a chair. 'Mama, please, sit. There's something important I need to tell you.'

'I don't need to sit—'

'Please, Mama.'

She huffed and puffed, but did as he asked. Strocchi gathered his courage. 'I've come back to visit for a day or two, but I'm not staying. I'll be going back to Florence soon.'

'Oh.' Mama's face fell. She had no time for guile or falsehood, never had, so she made no attempt to hide her disappointment. 'Well, at least you're here now. That's something.'

'Yes. And there's something else.'

Mama's gaze slipped past Strocchi to the doorway. Someone was standing there, framed in the bright morning sunshine. 'Can we help you?'

Strocchi went to the doorway, taking the visitor's hand, guiding them inside. 'Mama, I want you to meet someone. This is Tomasia.'

The young woman bowed her head a little, showing the proper respect. 'Signora Strocchi, it is an honour to be in your home. Carlo has told me so much about you.'

'Has he? I'm sorry, my dear, but I know nothing about you.'

Strocchi gave Tomasia's hand a squeeze. 'She hasn't heard about our news.'

'Oh.'

Mama folded her arms. 'Carlo, who is this stranger?'

He hesitated before replying, struggling to find the right words. 'Tomasia is . . . my wife.'

Mama Strocchi fainted dead away.